The HUNT

The HUNT

MONICA JAMES

Cover Design: Perfect Pear Creative Covers
Cover Model: Mark Robinson
Photographer: Michelle Lancaster
Formatting: E.M. Tippetts Book Designs

Follow me on:
authormonicajames.com

OTHER BOOKS BY
MONICA JAMES

THE I SURRENDER SERIES
I Surrender
Surrender to Me
Surrendered
White

SOMETHING LIKE NORMAL SERIES
Something like Normal
Something like Redemption
Something like Love

A HARD LOVE ROMANCE
Dirty Dix
Wicked Dix
The Hunt

MEMORIES FROM YESTERDAY DUET
Forgetting You, Forgetting Me
Forgetting You, Remembering Me

SINS OF THE HEART DUET
Absinthe of the Heart
Defiance of the Heart

ALL THE PRETTY THINGS TRILOGY

Bad Saint

Fallen Saint

Forever My Saint

The Devil's Crown-Part One (Spin-Off)

The Devil's Crown-Part Two (Spin-Off)

THE MONSTERS WITHIN DUET

Bullseye

Blowback

DELIVER US FROM EVIL TRILOGY

Thy Kingdom Come

Into Temptation

Deliver Us From Evil

IN LOVE AND WAR

North of the Stars

Fall of the Stars

STANDALONE

Mr. Write

Chase the Butterflies

Beyond the Roses

Someone Else's Shadow

Author's Note

THE HUNT is a spin-off to my A HARD LOVE ROMANCE SERIES. It can be read as a standalone.

Don't fall too hard for the main character. He most definitely will break your heart. Oh, and he has no mouth filter. Like none. You've been warned.

Enjoy.

One

"**F**ils de Pute!"

Smash.

Vacationing in France over many summers has allowed me to acquaint myself with the fundamental phrases such as "Bonjour," "Whiskey, s'il vous plait," and "Oh, merde!"

This right here is an 'Oh, merde!' moment.

"You said you loved me!"

"I did?"

"Yes! Menteur! Connard!"

Smash.

"That doesn't sound like something I'd say," I calmly reply, sidestepping the broken wine glass which just bounced off the wall. I'm thankful I wasn't standing two inches to the left.

"You said if you had a star for every time I brightened your day, you'd have a galaxy in your hand."

Pausing from buttoning up my pants, I shrug offhandedly.

1

"Well…now that sounds like something I'd say."

"Ugh!" screeches the wailing banshee, blindly reaching for anything she can use as a flying projectile against my insolence as I quickly continue dressing.

I've become well acquainted with this standard practice of fucking and fleeing, but I tend to forget that others haven't. I should feel bad, downright ashamed, but I don't. I don't make empty promises. I never have. I'm not looking to be saved, or to find that special someone to live happily ever after with. I lay my cards out on the table. They all know where they stand—and that's a one-night stand.

"Putain de cochon! I cheated on my husband because of you," she cries while I dance around the room, trying to find my damn tie. "Are you listening to me?"

"Yes, how can I not?" I mumble under my breath.

"Do you even care about me?" I faintly hear as I drop to one knee, still on the hunt for my favorite CK tie.

"Yes!" I exclaim, elated when I see it discarded under the bed.

Hastily reaching for it, I can't get away from this cataclysmic disaster fast enough, and her desperate voice has me internally groaning, hating how complicated uncomplicated sex can be.

"You do?"

"Do what?" I ask with a sigh, lifting myself up and coming eye level with the sniffling redhead at the end of the bed. Her flaming red mane stirs a longing in my loins, but she's just verified she can't scratch the constant itch I have. No one can, well…that's debatable.

"Care about me," she clarifies, her hazel eyes widening in hope.

Standing to my full six-foot-four height, I place a hand on her bare arm. "Look, April, you're a great girl, you really are." I mean every word, but that doesn't mean I'm going to stay and snuggle. "But I thought you understood that what happened between us, it was just…fun," I explain with a pause, hoping my honesty doesn't backfire.

When she remains quiet, her small, quickened breaths the only sound filling the room, I know she's either bought my bullshit, or I'm five seconds away from getting something else thrown at my face.

As the silence draws out, I lightly state, "So, let's just remember the good times, because I know there were multiple good times on your end," I add with a wink, hoping to lighten the mood. It doesn't.

Thwack!

"Je m'appelle June!" she yells as I raise a palm to my stinging cheek.

Oh, merde.

Well, that's my cue to leave.

Looping my tie around my neck, I reach for my suit jacket and make a mad dash for the exit. June is following in hot pursuit as I quicken my step, not interested in being a piñata.

"How can you do this to me?" she sobs, her bare feet pounding on the plush carpet behind me.

"Mon petit, I did everything you begged of me," I reply, bored by her melodramatics as I open the front door.

"Hunter!" she cries, but I cut her off.

Turning around, I witness the look I've seen countless times before—hope. They're all hopeful that I can provide the missing piece to the puzzle. In June's case, the missing piece is filling the void in her loveless marriage. She used me just as much as I used her.

"Just stop." I gesture with my palm. "Go back to your husband. He's the good guy in this story."

"And what are you?" June queries, her naked body shaking with betrayal.

"Me?" I ask, and she nods, wiping away her tears.

That's a good question. I thought I was a good guy, but the bleeding hearts of New York and its surrounding boroughs may beg to differ.

"I'm no one you want to know," I candidly reply before slamming the door shut behind me.

Taking a breather, I scrub my hand down my face, that fucking blanket of shame draping over me once again. I know why it's there and it's all her fault. She's the reason I've had sex with…I hold up my hand, needing the digits to count… five… no, I hold up both hands… six women this week, and I am still no closer to fucking this redhaired devil from my life. I thought abstaining from sex may have helped, but all it did was leave me with a serious case of blue balls, and no closer to figuring out what the hell to do.

Groaning, I trudge down the hallway, cursing the day the infernal vixen, Mary Mitts, came into my world. I was fine. Cruising along, chasing tail, happy to do my bid for the lonely hearts of NYC, and not look back once the deed was done… time and time again.

My life was perfect—a fucking Hallmark card for the bachelors of this world, then my best friend, the once upon a time infamous, Dr. Booty Call M.D. aka Dr. Dixon Mathews, had to go and fall in love.

How could he do this to me? The inconsiderate jerk.

Not once did he consider my feelings or my balls when the woman of his dreams, Madison Roberts, had a plus one who annihilated the face of every woman I've ever slept with. Some infuriating part inside of me, that needs to book an appointment with the good doctor, decided to shut up shop and want her more than I have ever wanted anything or anyone.

This makes no sense—zero—considering we both hate one another more than Liam hates Noel, and would take great pleasure in seeing the other being dropped into a tank full of piranhas and eaten alive. But I can't stop thinking about her— like right now. What is she doing? Is her nose doing that cute crinkling thing when she…whoa.

I just said the word cute. I never use that word. Ever. If someone asked me what Mickey Mouse was, I'd say he was a chump, never cute, whose balls were locked in Minnie's purse. Never would I use the word cute to describe anything, but it appears Mary Mitts has the ability to ruin my vocabulary now. Fucking perfect.

Jabbing at the elevator button, my patience is about to snap. There is only one person to blame and that's none other than Dr. Do-Little because he's doing exactly that—doing little to help me get over whatever insanity this is. He's actually finding this funny, fucking hysterical. Said this is my karma for being an insensitive prick. What does he know anyway? He's gone and done something stupid. He's basically cut off his balls and given them to Cherry Pie to wear as earrings.

He's asked her to m…m…mar…marry him. I can't even say the word without a stutter, and she obviously needs her head read because she said yes. To make matters worse, they're getting married in three months' time and expect me to be the best man. I should be the better man and tell Dix to say goodbye to his freedom and sex life, but they are so disgustingly happy and in love, and they so fucking deserve it. If anyone ought to have hearts and roses and re-runs of Friends, then it's Dix. I'm happy for him. My little boy is all grown up.

Fuck me. I need a drink. The elevator finally reaches my floor.

Once inside, I reach into my back pocket and grab my cell. My finger wavers over my contacts, the letter M a noose around my neck because I want to call her. I want to rile her up because I take great pleasure in seeing her squirm. It's like a drug to me, and honestly, I've become addicted to the taste.

From the first moment we met, I knew she was something special. She didn't drop her panties the moment I turned on the charm. I must be a masochistic bastard because I liked it. I liked that she made me work for it because I've forgotten what it felt like to be consumed with the overpowering need to crave something more than you need air to breathe.

She was my oxygen, but in the same token, she took my breath away.

She saw through all the bullshit because you can't bullshit a bullshitter. This hard exterior of hers is just a front because I know once upon a time, she let down her guard, and like so many, she got her heart broken. That is the reason why I have an urge to cover my balls whenever she's near.

Her long, fiery red hair is like an out of control inferno, which matches her personality to a tee. She is sharp tongued and crass, she makes no excuses for her filthy mouth, and that fact leaves me with a permanent semi.

Her pink lips are full, the type of lips that bring men to their knees. That, combined with a rocking body and spectacular curves, has me fantasizing about her in ways I have never done so before. I have a confession to make…I have fucked plenty of women, but love—I'm a virgin when it comes to the big L.

I don't have a sob story like Dix. No one broke my heart because I never gave it to anyone to break. It has remained under lock and key for thirty-three carefree years. Sure, I've had a couple of girlfriends, and I use the term lightly, but none really did it for me. After a while, we both lost interest, and I don't know if it was me, or them, or maybe we were just filling in time for something better to come along. For me, it was always a steady pace, not even breaking a sweat.

I didn't want to be saved, or tamed, because I wasn't interested in settling down. The thought of sharing my bed with one woman and one woman only was like a black hole sucking the flair from my loins. Some called me a commitment-phobe, while most called me a manwhore. But the simple fact was that I was happy to live my life a bachelor, Hugh Hefner-style, accepting this as my fate.

But Mary, or better known as Lamb, has completely ruined my dreams of being surrounded by endless bouncy blondes because all I want is one…maddening…libido-sucking redhead. And I don't know why. It's not like she's nice to me, or even likes me.

So that's my story in a nutshell. I have never been in love because I just didn't see the point. Dixon, regardless of what an utter pussy he can be, is the best person I know, and that cuntasaurus, Lily, tore out his heart and used it to wipe her ass. He told me that she was the love of his life, and that she was "the one." Yeah, she was the one who turned him into a raging hard-on, nailing anything within a hundred-mile radius. Even though I commended him on his sexual prowess, and applauded him on the skill to not dehydrate from all the loads he was blowing, I saw how fucking miserable he was when she broke his heart. Not only did she break it, she fucking set it on fire and destroyed him.

If that's what love does, then love can blow me.

Cherry Pie is the exception. She is an anomaly, a glitch in the system. I can't help but wonder what her best friend is. At the moment, she's a thorn in my side and a complete cooch blocker because I can't fuck anyone without picturing her soft lips, her vivacious green eyes, but most of all, I can't help but wonder what it would feel like to possess her and never let go.

Holy motherfucking donkey dicks. I need to get a grip.

With my cell still in hand, I decide to call the one person who owes me. Big time.

"Excuse me, sir, do you have a moment to discuss our good Lord and Savior, Jesus Christ?"

"There aren't enough Hail Marys to save my soul."

I can't help but laugh because we're riding the highway to hell together. "Amen! What are you doing?"

Dixon's gravelly chuckles alert me to the fact that he's probably snuggled with his honey, watching some chick flick and about to call it a night.

"Madison and I are binge watching a TV series on Netflix."

"Oh, yeah, what's that? Gossip Girl?" I snicker at my own joke while Dixon scoffs.

"Gossip Girl? What the fuck is that? An autobiography on your life?" I can hear Madison's muted chuckles in the background.

"Whatever. Meet me for a drink?" The elevator doors ping open, notifying Dixon that I'm not home.

"Where are you?" Nothing slips past him.

"Nowhere special," which is codeword for I don't exactly know.

It's a Friday night, and back in the good ol' days, Dixon and I would be on the hunt, while Finch would be the adult of the group, pleading we stop thinking with the wrong head. Goes without saying, I've been flying solo for quite some time. What, with Dixon denouncing his manwhore ways, and Finch mastering Daddy Day Care, our threesome soon became a one man show.

I'm over the moon for my friends. They've got their shit together, but the wave of nostalgia always seems to hit around ten thirty on a Friday night, which is why, most Friday nights, I'm buried between the legs of some faceless woman, who seems more than happy to forget her woes also.

"One drink, or is it past your curfew?"

A rocking brunette, who is talking to the front desk attendant, does a double take when I saunter past. Her red stained lips almost smack in delight, inflating my ego and pants. I know I'm not ugly, and have been told on numerous occasions I look like the lovechild of Chris Hemsworth and David Beckham.

I don't look like all the tools I work with on Wall Street. But they can eat me. I refuse to look the part of corporate asshole, because no one wants to fuck a stick in the mud.

I'm a stockbroker, and am a kingpin to the men of my trade because lucky is my middle name. I have illustrious connections and my portfolio would give the Wolf of Wall Street serious wood. My clients trust me because no one can say no to this face. NYSE is my bitch, and I ride that bell like a cowboy breaking in a mustang.

I'm good at what I do because I don't like to lose, and that confidence, combined with my, and I quote, "GQ" looks, never leaves me short of female attention, like right now. It's a crime that it's this easy, but when I think about the one woman who is anything but easy, I pay the lady in red a wink.

Her blushing cheeks rival the color of her skin-tight dress, which has my inner caveman pounding his chest and priming for a sure thing, but some foreign, gushy part, which I've dubbed D2, highlights the similarities that it also resembles the color of an infuriating vixen's hair.

That thought is a swift kick to the balls and I gripe aloud because this woman is ruining my life.

"Do you want your dick to fall off?" Dix says, transporting me back in time, however, this time, the shoe, or the cock, is on me.

Rolling my eyes, I humor him. "Yes, it's my dream to grow a vagina. If you have a point, get to it already. You're wasting precious whiskey time." The brunette overhears me and mutes a giggle behind her hand.

"This will get old fast, trust me. You need to stop with these random hook-ups, grow a pair, and tell a certain redhead how you feel. If she tells you hell to the fuck no, then at least you've tried."

My back instantly arcs up. "I may not have told her in so many words, but she knows how I fe—" I leave the sentence hanging, my mouth suddenly heavy with weepy babble.

Dixon ignores my emotional clam up. "No, she doesn't. At the moment, she probably thinks you're some perverted creep who has limited vocabulary."

"And what the fuck does that mean?" I stop walking and take a seat in the small lounge in the foyer, needing to pay my undivided attention to Dr. Phil's words of wisdom.

"It means you've hardly had a civil conversation with her. Underneath the fuck yous, and go eat a dicks, and I don't give a flying fucks, is a pretty awesome dude. All Mary has seen is the obnoxious cuntwaffle you can be when put into a situation you're uncomfortable with."

Crossing my ankle over my knee, I lean back in my seat, offended, even though he does have a point. "I have so spoken to her."

"No, I'm pretty sure the last time you saw her you stared at her for twenty minutes, where I had to wipe the drool from your chin. Literally."

I chuckle, remembering the incident he speaks of with fondness.

Good times.

It was last weekend. I know Dix was holding out on telling me who the maid of honor was, but it didn't take a rocket scientist to figure out who.

We had drinks at a bar down in Brooklyn, and when Mary entered, decked out in tight yoga pants and a tiny tank which showed off her sensational midriff, I had to reach down and rearrange myself because holy fuck, those tight clothes were a striptease to my libido.

Her eyes narrowed the moment she saw me sitting in the booth. "Howdy, partner," I mocked, tipping the peak of my invisible hat.

It took her all of three seconds to figure out what was going on. "There is no fucking way I'm standing within a fifty-mile radius of him."

Maddy sighed, while Dixon showed us what a strapping, strong brute he is. "He's promised to be on his best behavior. Isn't that right, Hunt?" He glared at me from across the table, prepared to castrate me if I deviated from his version of events.

"But of course."

Mary didn't buy into my bullshit, but she finally nodded. "You're lucky I love you, Maddy." The fire behind her eyes excited me, and that's when I think the drooling incident may have occurred.

I shuffled over, offering her ample room to sit by me, but I should have known nothing is ever easy with Mary. When she placed one knee onto the leather seat and leaned forward, completely disregarding my personal space, I actually pulled back, anticipating what would happen next.

Her long, coppery waves framed her perfect face, highlighting what a natural beauty she is. I was envious of every freckle that kissed her milky skin, especially the cluster which skated down the column of her long neck and across to her magnificent chest.

My bad—my eyes lingered longer than they should have, but the top she was wearing made it impossible to look away. I was lost in visions of being buried between her perfects breasts and quite frankly, I possibly could have voiced my approval, because when I came to, Mary's face was inches from mine. A strangled gasp escaped me, but she filled in the blanks.

"Let's get this straight, if I so much as think you're

fantasizing about me naked, or I catch you looking down my dress, or touching me…or yourself"—her bright emerald eyes flicked downward, while my cock hit the deck and gave her twenty—"you'll be singing soprano. Got it?"

"Sweet cheeks, if you want to get down my pants so desperately, all you have to do is ask." A pained grunt left my lungs when Dix kicked me under the table. Hands raised in surrender, I conceded. "That's a long list of demands, but fine."

Mary arrogantly smirked, which crushed me, because if I ever saw a more beautiful sight, then I don't remember what it was. She left me a slobbering fool when she helped herself to my beer, her slender throat suckling and swallowing, conjuring up images which I would revisit late that evening, and early the next morning.

It was out before I could stop myself. "I've got just the thing to quench that thirst…" My sentence remained unfinished because the fire in my pants was doused, literally, when the leftover contents of my Budweiser was poured into my lap.

She left me with a mouth full of nothing, and a cock wanting the whole enchilada.

Snapping from the memory, I refocus on the task at hand. "How about you detail all my issues over a bottle of whiskey." I know he's considering the offer, so I make the decision easy on him. "Otherwise, I can come there and we can replace whiskey with hot cocoa and cuddle under the blanket together. All three of us. You can be in the middle," I impishly add. "I'll even let you be the big spoon."

This is in the bag. I know because you learn to read someone better than yourself when you've known them for more than half your life.

"In no way, shape, or form will you be spooning me, now or ever. I'll meet you in twenty." He doesn't have to specify where.

Hanging up, I spring from my seat, elated to be having a drink with my best friend. I know that makes me sound like a needy, clingy girlfriend, but after tonight, well, after this week, I could do with some Dix time.

As I pocket my cell and am about to exit, someone gently taps me on the shoulder. Spinning, I see that it's the pretty brunette I totally forgot about. "Here." She slips a small piece of paper into my pants pocket. "If ever you feel like having that drink, call me." Her hand is still wedged in my pocket, not so discreetly fondling my dick. With a coiled smirk, she adds, "I have some top shelf whiskey…downstairs."

I've heard some decent one liners, but I give credit to the lady in red, because using an alcoholic analogy to a whiskey fiend to refer to her pussy is just plain genius. Gazing down at my Rolex, I see that I've got something else in the bag.

"What's your name?"

She bites her red, plump lip. "Mary-Ann."

Raising my eyes to the heavens, I don't know if this is an omen or a curse. Either way, maybe Mary-Ann has the cure I've been searching for. "Well, Mary-Ann, I have ten minutes to spare."

With one hand stroking my cock, she uses the other to yank on the lapel of my blazer, drawing us eye to eye. "I only need nine."

Whether it was the hint of red, or the mere mention of liquor, I'll never know, but what I do know is when life gives you lemons…make whiskey sours.

Bottoms up.

Two

Hunter

Mary-Ann was a woman of her word, and I was freshly fucked after seven minutes in hell. Although, she lied. Her whiskey was not top shelf. It was watered down, flat booze. There was no epiphany, no light at the end of the tunnel, and no weight lifted from my loins. After she power-bunnied on my lap and left without a goodbye, I was once again cloaked in that blanket of disgrace, one which seems to rain on my fun parade every chance it gets.

I was a complete two-pump chump because the moment I thought of Lamb in all of her glory, I came so hard I went blind for a few splendid seconds. Mary-Ann popped her cork straight after, as she was primed and ready to go way before she shoved me into the stairwell and climbed me like a sex-starved monkey.

As I thrust my hands into my pocket, the slip of paper with her number on it sears my fingers. I shiver when remembering her lips attempting to latch onto my face and suck the air from my lungs. Regardless of how many women I fuck, I hold onto some small scrap of dignity and will never, ever break my no kissing rule.

It sounds completely ridiculous, considering I have no misgivings when it comes to the women I sleep with, but kissing, it's just so…personal. The moment their lips veer within three feet , I hammer on the brakes, finish the job, and then hit the road.

Fishing the number from my pocket, I slam dunk it into the trash can just outside the bar, which holds so many memories. Taking a moment, I stand in front of the small neon sign and remember the countless hours spent inside. She may not be the prettiest of the bunch, or even the biggest, but this place will always be home…and cue the violins.

I know without looking Dixon is inside because that sappy part of me, D2, which was named after the man in question, always seems to emerge whenever he's near. His pussiness has obviously rubbed off on me.

Pulling back my shoulders, I run a hand through my hair, as I know he'll be able to sniff the depravity off of me. When I enter, "Witchy Woman" by The Eagles plays over the speakers, just another nail in the proverbial coffin. Arm raised high, I flip off the ceiling, eyes focused on Dixon, who sits in a booth, not at all surprised by my insane behavior.

When I get closer, I stop dead in my tracks, unable to tear my gaze from Dixon's groin. "What the fuck is that?" I cry, horrified, pointing to the sex killers he's currently donning.

He rolls his eyes and sips his brown colored drink, which better have some kind of alcohol in it. "They're called pants, not that you'd know, seeing as you've spent more time out of them, than in," he smugly replies, while I shake my head and wag my finger.

"Those are sweat pants. Since when do you wear sweat pants?"

"Hey, don't knock the pants." He slaps my finger away. "They're incredibly comfortable and I'm in free balling heaven." He points to the seat across from him. "Sit."

"Whatever, Grandpa, and only because you asked so nicely," I quip, reaching across the table to steal his drink. I toss it back, only to spit it back out seconds later. Wiping my mouth, I cringe. "Where's the scotch?"

Dixon smirks, turning over his shoulder to grab the attention of Tanya, the bar maid who's been serving us for years. She's wiping down table nine, but he doesn't have to bother because she's had her eyes glued to him since I entered. She's over by our booth in record time. "Hi boys," she purrs, batting her eyelashes at Dixon, while I suddenly feel like chopped liver.

"Hello," he replies, completely shooting her down. "I'll have a scotch, and Hunt? Whiskey?" I blanch the moment he looks at me, waiting for corroboration. I'll never be able to stomach that drink without thinking of my walk of shame.

"Budweiser for me," I amend, while Dix raises an eyebrow, seeing through my façade. Nothing slips past him.

"Sure," Tanya replies, her attention riveted on Dixon. "I haven't seen you in here for ages. I thought you were cheating on me." Her attempts to flirt with Dix go up in a flaming pile of dog shit. I sit back and yawn, accustomed to what the next thirty seconds entails.

"I've been busy with work, teaching, and I'm getting

married to the love of my life in three months, so, no rest for the wicked." Her mouth falls open and I almost feel sorry for her. She hasn't heard.

I'm pretty sure when word spread that Dixon Mathews was no longer a bachelor, all of the women in NYC went into mourning. Some may even have joined the nunnery. With those baby blues and a reputation that proceeded him, he broke the hearts of every woman who wanted to domesticate him, who wanted to lay claim to the title of taming Manhattan's most notorious man-slut.

They couldn't understand what Maddy had that they didn't, but that's the reason why she lured ol' Dix in. She never wanted to tame or own Dixon. She wanted him, flaws and all, and he had many flaws, like screwing her diabolical sister. But in the end, she saw past all of that because that's what people who are into one another do. Or, so I've heard.

"Oh." She clears her throat. "Well, congratulations. I'll be right back with your drinks." She hightails it toward the bar, yanking on the arm of Sara, her colleague, and whispers into her ear. I can see the exact moment her heart shatters into smithereens.

Dixon is either oblivious, or he just doesn't care. "What's the damage?"

He doesn't need to explain. "Why, jealous?"

He smirks and leans back casually. "Jealous of what? Catching chlamydia?"

A laugh erupts from me. "Touché, fuckwad. I need something to occupy my time now that you've gone and fallen in lo..." I pause the moment that infernal word is about to slip past my lips. I don't know why, I just can't say it without wanting to check my balls are still intact.

"Love?" Dix fills in the blanks while I groan.

"Ugh, enough with this heartfelt crap. I can feel my testosterone levels diminishing as we speak. How's Cherry Pie?" I wiggle my eyebrows, because even though she's a complete fox, I don't look at her like I do other women. If I had a sister, then that's how I view Maddy. But Dix doesn't have to know that because I love seeing him riled up.

"She's fine," he replies blankly.

"Oh, I know she's fine, but how's she doing?"

This derailment is supposed to get Dix off my case, but he stands his ground. The stubborn motherfucker. "How many women this week, Hunt?"

"Wouldn't you like to know," I counter quickly, attempting to throw him off the trail.

"You do realize you gave me the exact same speech, in this bar, a lifetime ago?"

I humor him because I know he won't let go otherwise. "What speech, oh wise one?"

He doesn't see the funny side, however. "The 'you look like shit we're worried about you,' speech."

"I appreciate your helicopter parenting, Dix, but there is no need. Really. I'm fine. Everything is great. Life couldn't be better." I sit taller, wondering where the hell my drink is.

"You can't keep screwing around, man."

"Watch me," I challenge, suddenly getting pissed. "I'm stoked you've got your shit together, but your holier-than-thou speech can blow me. Don't be a fucking hypocrite 'cause no one likes a know it all."

It's meant to be a warning to tell him to back off, but it

seems to have done the complete opposite. "I understand I'm the last person to be giving you this advice, but I'm only doing so because I care about you, you asshole. You obviously like Mary"—when I scoff and fold my arms, Dixon lays off with the Mary talk—"but I think the bigger issue here is you."

"Excuse me?" I question, lost in translation. "Me? There is nothing wrong with me."

"Why are you sleeping with anything that moves?"

"Because I can."

"I get that, but why the sudden increase?"

Where the fuck is Tanya with my drink? Wiping a hand down my face, I suddenly smell Mary-Ann's rancid perfume on my fingers, fingers that were playing her like a fiddle twenty minutes ago. "I didn't realize my sex life was so interesting to you, Dix."

"Just answer the question," he states, his resolute gaze never wavering.

"Why not? I'm single and I like sex. I don't see why there has to be a better reason. Now that you're off the scene, I have an array of women to choose from." Which is true. The men of today are little boys who like to play grown up.

Dixon weighs up my answer before slipping on his glasses. I can see the reason why women love this bastard. He's one handsome son of a gun. "How's the sex?"

I can't help but smile. "Dirty Dix. But I suppose I could share the details, considering you've been dining on the one flavor for so long."

"That's by choice," he rebukes, shaking his head. "I want to know how you feel after you've had sex with these random women. Let's use tonight's proceedings as an example."

I knew he'd smell the pussy on me. "Five pounds lighter." Peering around, I wonder if it's getting hot in here. "I feel fucking fantastic. I've gotten blown and fucked until I can't see straight, what is there to complain about?"

"So, you're having no problems…" He leaves the sentence hanging, using his hand as a gesturing tool to move his point along, but I have no idea what he's talking about.

"No problems what?" I finally ask. He shrugs his shoulders like I'm supposed to understand what the fuck this tangent means.

"No problems…ejaculating."

My eyes pop open and I burst into laughter. "Did you seriously ask me if I can drop a load okay? I don't need Viagra, if that's what you're implying. And ejaculate…? When did this turn so business like…" I pause, the wheels in my head churning over the past five minutes.

It takes me a second, but when I come to, I recoil backward and cover my chest, violated. "Oh my fucking god. Holy donkey's balls! You're psychoanalyzing me, aren't you?" He doesn't need to respond. "Quit it with your psychobabble bullshit, and stay the fuck out of my head. Are you trying to hypnotize me or something?" I peer at him suspiciously, grabbing my dick to make sure he hasn't compelled me into hating the big fella.

Dixon rubs the bridge of his nose, his plan foiled. No wonder he put on his glasses. That sneaky cockface. Leaning forward, I poke my finger into his chest. "I don't need your help. I'm fine. Everything is A-fucking-okay, so fuck you. Fuck you very much."

He slaps my hand away. "I understand, but if you ever did…"

"Pssh, stop that." I wave, gesturing this conversation is done. "I don't want you near my head. Ever."

"Well, I don't particularly want to be in it," he opposes, his jaw firm. "But I know you, man. I know what you're doing."

"Having the best time of my life? Living it up and choosing what flavor I feel like? Blonde? Brunette? Red…" I actually choke on the word and have to thump on my chest to dislodge it.

Dixon sighs because I'm a fucking lace bra—see-through. "No pussy holds some miracle cure. That remedy is within you. You just have to know where to look. You once told me your whoring tendencies were a cry for help."

I scoff. "Please. I'll be doing just that if we don't stop with this D and M soon. And besides, I never said that. You're probably getting me mixed up with Finch. He's the pussy in this relationship." But Dixon is right. I did say that to him. It was the night we met the twins, Mandy and Marisa.

Dix bowed out, while I thought I was on top of the world. That was before Mary, and before I became D2. Life was so simple back then, now it's just one giant episode of Days of Our Lives.

"Dude, just know I'm here for you, because you did the same for me. You're my brother. And besides, when the going got tough, the tough allowed some silver-haired fox named Pearl to live out her fantasy of seducing a younger man. I'll never forget you taking one for the team."

"We agreed to not speak of that ever again." I shiver when remembering the incident he speaks of. It was on the way to rescuing Maddy from what we thought was the biggest mistake of her life. Turns out we were wrong, but hey, in the end, the good guy won and the hero of this story can live happily ever after.

Tanya saunters over with drinks in hand. She barely looks at Dixon as she slides his scotch toward him, while I get the whole hog as she practically serves me my beer between her tits. "Here you go, Hunter."

"Thanks, sweet cheeks." I reach for the Budweiser, which she holds close to her sizeable chest, ensuring I don't cop a feel in the process. I make a rule that I don't shit where I eat, as I have zero interest in Tanya, so fucking her, or leading her on will just end in her spitting in my drink and forcing me to find a new place to hang out.

Dixon smirks, knowing me all too well. I may be a bastard, but I'm not a fucking bastard. Once Tanya gets the hint, she trudges off, probably wondering if Dixon is marrying me, because I've obviously renounced my manhood by playing off her advances.

"So, there's this thing tomorrow night."

I pause mid-sip, cocking a brow. "What thing? Jesus Christ, for someone who rivals the IQ of Stephen Hawking, you sure as shit act like an invasive dumbass most times."

Dixon grins, while I gesture for him to continue. "A dinner at Madison's parents' house."

"That's a lovely story, but why are you telling me this?"

"Because you're invited, you Neanderthal," he replies, reaching for his scotch.

I can't contain my excitement and fist pimp. "Fucking yes! About time I was invited to these soirees." But I reel in my enthusiasm. Something is rotten in Denmark. "Why didn't you tell me sooner? What if I've got plans?"

"I'm sure you can lay off the hunt for one night," he counters, knowing all too well what a standard Saturday night for me entails.

But I'm not buying it. Pointing my bottle his way, I bark, "Stick to your day job, Dix, cause your poker face blows ass. Spit it out."

He sighs, running a hand through his mussed hair. "Well, Madison's parents thought it would be nice for everyone to get together and talk…wedding stuff."

My ears prick up, while my inner caveman beats his chest and howls to the full moon. "Wedding stuff. So, Mary will be there?" I ask, leaning forward, my smirk resembling the Joker's.

"Yes. Finch and Heidi, too."

Tapping my fingers against the edge of the table, I wonder why he wouldn't tell me this sooner. "You're ashamed of me, aren't you?" I half tease.

Dixon shakes his head. "No, man, as much as you're an obnoxious asshole, you're my obnoxious asshole. I held off telling you because I didn't know how you'd…feel"

"Feel? And there's that word again. You need to stop talking in riddles and just grow a pair. What the fuck is going on?"

Something shifts and I can see Dixon wrestling with the truth. He doesn't want to tell me something because he thinks it'll hurt my feelings. D2 licks his wounds, while I tell that pansy ass to take a backseat. "Your significant others have bigger cojones than you two. What's the deal?"

"We didn't know if you'd want to attend because…"

"Because what?" I coax, fed up with this beating around the bush.

"Because Mary has a plus one, and she's bringing him. I

didn't know if that'd make you feel weird or not."

"A plus one? Like as in a boyfriend plus one?" I ask, my brain short-circuiting. Dixon nods, while I suddenly have the urge to slam my fist into the table. "When did this happen?"

"Just recently. She's seeing some guy she works with."

"What's his name?" I ask, fist clenched to my thigh. This is so insignificant in the greater scheme of things, but I need to know my opponent's name so I can holler it in delight when I neuter him.

"His name?" Dixon questions, confused.

"Yes." It takes all my willpower not to turn into the Marshmallow Man and destroy New York, seeking out this cockface who is Mary's plus one.

"I really don't know. It doesn't matter, dude. Just come, have a good time. Maddy's dad is a great cook."

But food is the last thing on my mind because all I want to roast is Mary's little boyfriend's nuts. "Why did you encourage me to tell Lamb how I feel if she's seeing this asshat?" I bite, confused.

"Because I doubt it's serious," he explains, which makes perfect sense, but the rational side of me is suddenly in hiatus.

"Of course, it's not serious. She's been seeing him for five seconds." But regardless, she's chosen someone else to take to this dinner. She's chosen someone else to call her plus one.

Some small part of me had hoped Mary was playing hard to get, and after she made me work hard for it, she'd finally put me out of my misery and meet me halfway. But it seems she's a sadistic witch who likes to see me grovel. Well, fuck that. Hunter O'Shea does not beg or grovel for anyone.

"Whatever, man, it's cool. Good luck to her, and good luck

to him. I'll send him a condolence card in the mail." I pull back my shoulders, refusing to let this dampen the mood.

I'm happy for Dix and Maddy, and tomorrow, I'll fucking eat cake and smile. I won't give in to the impulse to rip off this jerk-off's arms and beat him like a piñata at a ten-year old's birthday. If she wants to play, then so can I.

"Seeing as everyone seems to be bringing their nearest and dearest, you wouldn't mind if I brought someone along?"

"Who?" Dix questions. He has every right to be suspicious, but I can't stomach being the only lame ass with no plus one.

"You don't know her."

"Do you?" he poses quickly, his doctor mask slipping into full swing.

I've had enough of being dissected under the microscope for one night. Standing, I finish my beer and wipe my mouth with the back of my hand. "I'm asking to be polite, but even if you said no, screw you."

Dix raises his hands in surrender. "Fine, bring her. But Hunt..." I wait for him to continue. "No hookers." He knows me oh so well.

I fake horror. "I should be offended, but I'm not. Sayonara. Text me the details." Hunting through my jacket, I pull out my wallet, but Dixon waves me off.

"My shout. Next one is on you." I know there is a double meaning behind his words—that smart, hypnotizing warlock. I don't bother with long goodbyes because I have work to do. I need to find a date.

The chilly March breeze has me pulling the lapels of my blazer across my chest, wondering if I should hail a cab, or walk the ten blocks to my apartment on the upper east side.

While in thought, a destitute man bumps into me, apologizing profusely. His garbage bag filled with cans drops with a racket to the pavement.

Without a second thought, I drop to a squat and help him collect his loot. Whether it's Divine intervention, or the work of the devil, I'll never know, but when the paper I heedlessly threw in the trash is stuck to the side of a Pepsi can, I know this is a sign.

The man notices me staring at the number, and kindly peels the paper from the metal. "Here, sir."

I accept with a smile. "Thank you." We both stand while I pass the man the last of his cans.

I have no idea what possess me, but I decide to confide in this stranger because most times, strangers don't spare your feelings because they don't have to. "This number, it was given to me by a lady I fucked after knowing for roughly thirty seconds. My best friend, that handsome devil in there…" I point to Dix, who is on the phone, no doubt detailing to Maddy what a fucking disaster tonight was. The man nods when he looks at Dixon, appreciating his charisma. "He's getting married to the love of his life, and tomorrow, he's asked I attend a dinner. That all sounds like an episode of The Brady Bunch, right? But the problem is his fiancée has a best friend who drives me crazy, and I mean that in every literal sense of the word."

I exhale loudly, wishing this underlying need to see her would hit the high road and fuck right off. "She's bringing a plus one. Some jerk-off who wouldn't know how to handle her even if he had eight hands. I want her, and I thought that maybe she wanted me too. But now it appears she's moved on to greener pastures, so maybe it's my turn to do the same."

The man nods quietly, allowing me to purge.

"So, my question is, do I move on too, even though I don't want to? Or do I fight for her? Listen to what Dixon said and tell her how I fe…feel? I've fucked seven or eight women this week—I've lost count—and as much as I hate to admit it, Dix is right. I'm kind of lonely and maybe this is a cry for help."

Gazing down at the soiled number in my hand, I wonder if perhaps my problem is that I'm not giving other women a chance because I'm hung up on the unattainable. I've put Mary on a pedestal because that's her rightful place. Let's face facts. She belongs with someone nice, a good guy who will call her beautiful and not follow with the words ass or tits. I can't give her that because I'm not the Prince Charming type.

I tried to fool myself into thinking that she'll see something that no other woman has before, but there isn't anything there to see. All my cards are laid on the table, and it appears no one likes my playing hand. Mary isn't different because I'm no different. I'm no one special and I was living in a Walt Disney world if I thought otherwise.

"Good talk. You're a real good listener," I say, lightly slapping the man on the arm.

"So, what have you decided?" he asks, appearing genuinely curious. As Dix stands, I know it's time to hit the road.

Reaching into my pocket, I pull out my wallet and offer the man a Benjamin. He waves it off, but I press it into his palm. "Take it, you're cheap compared to how much that fucker would charge me." I gesture with my chin to Dixon. "And what I've decided is that this bachelor is back in the game."

I leave my new favorite shrink standing on the sidewalk, confused, while for me, the Mary haze has finally lifted. I was blinded by the fantasy of living my own, real life fairy tale because it appears that the world no longer needs heroes…it needs monsters for the good guys to slay.

Three

Hunter

've hit the gym, gone for a run, and showered, and it's only 9 a.m. After my revelation, I came home and pulled out my trusty black book. I have the names and numbers of many women who as ashamed as I am to admit it, I don't really remember who most of them are.

After my song and dance last night, I'll be damned if I rock up to this dinner without a date on my arm. I know this is completely petty, not to mention childish, but if I'm to get over whatever this Mary spell is, then I need to move on.

I'm sitting in my office on the 47th floor, staring out the glass window, wondering who the fuck I can call. My black book sits in my lap as I restlessly rock backward and forward in my leather seat. The names may as well be random numbers in a phone book.

There was this one girl, Siobhan, who I saw on and off for three months. She was a real stunner and smart, too. It was probably around nine months ago that we "broke" it off. It was amicable, which is why I spin around and pick up the phone. I call from my office private line, just in case this turns a little pear-shaped.

We ended things pleasantly, or at least I think we did, because when I turn the page, I see another Siobhan, but with the initial L scribbled after her name. This was obviously done to distinguish between the two. Too bad I have no idea which Siobhan is the one I want. I have no clue what either girl's surnames are.

It's too late to hang up because a bubbly voice sounds over the receiver. "Hello."

Wading through all the voices in my head, I attempt to match a face to the name. Shit. I've drawn a blank. This serves me right for not paying closer attention.

"Hello? Is anybody there?" Her high-pitched voice suddenly punches me in the solar plexus and I remember her screeching out my name as I ate her out in this exact chair. Bingo.

"Hello, Siobhan. It's Hunter."

Silence.

I don't know if that silence is due to the fact she's in shock, about to hang up on me, or if she has no idea who I am. I decide to clarify. "Hunter O'Shea. We met at Starbucks on Broadway." More silence. "We both wanted the last lemon tart," I add. As far as reunions go, this is veering toward a crash and burn.

"Holy shit," she finally says, the surprise clear in her tone.

"Holy shit indeed. How are you?" Even I cringe at the stupidity of that question.

"Me? I'm good, thanks. How about you?"

"Fine."

And it appears the third wheel to our conversation has joined us once again—silence.

Clearing my throat, I man up and pull out the big guns. "I'm calling because I was wondering if you wanted to grab a drink with me. Tonight."

"Tonight?"

Rocking back in my seat and peering up at the ceiling, I shoot myself with an imaginary gun. But I persevere. "Yes, tonight. I have this thing…and thought it'd be nice to catch up." I mouth a 'what the fuck' and roll my eyes. This is more than a little pear-shaped, it's a fucking debacle.

"I…um, Hunter, I'm really surprised you called me."

Here's hoping that surprise is of the good kind. "I know, sweet cheeks, but I've been thinking about you. Have you been thinking about me?" I drop my voice purposely low, turning on the charm. I could make this woman come in one minute flat when I knelt at her altar. Sex was a little harder, she made me work for it, but I knew the buttons to push to turn her on.

"Honestly…" Her pause and shallow breathing has me fist pumping, but it's premature. "No."

I pull the receiver from my ear and bang the ear piece on the corner of my desk. There must be something wrong with the phone. However, when I press it back to my ear, I will happily give Satan my soul if he erases the past thirty seconds of my life.

Her brutal honesty is accentuated when the unmistakable sound of a baby wailing pierces my ear over the line. From the sounds of it, the infant is young. My stomach drops and I assume the worst. "You have a baby?"

"Ah…yes, I do." Her pause also adds to the assumption. One plus one equals fuck me.

I catalogue over everything I can remember. We broke it off because she wanted a family and I didn't. We went our separate ways after she fucked the living shit out of me. I thought she wanted to go out with a bang, but now I think that bang was a wham bam thank you ma'am for putting a bun in the oven.

I suddenly feel so violated. "Oh." How do you ask someone in a roundabout way if they were sleeping around and got knocked up by somebody other than you? There really isn't a nice way, it all amounts to holy fuck balls.

My silence speaks volumes, and Siobhan suddenly bursts into laughter. I have no idea how Dix went through this and stayed sane. "I'm sorry, Hunter," she finally says around a mouthful of giggles. "Don't worry, I know what you're thinking. The baby isn't yours."

"Thank fuck for that!" I express a little louder than intended.

"But I do have you to thank for little Fiona coming into this world." God dammit! If I've counted my chickens before they've hatched, I'm going to be fucking pissed.

I have no idea what she's talking about, so I allow her to explain. "After we ended things, I met someone. Believe it or not, this person knows you too. Small world, right?"

This can't be good, but I humor her anyway. "Crazy."

"I was talking to this person about you, and well, anyway, it appears we both dated you."

My mouth moves in wordless animation because one, I never thought we were officially dating, and two, if this person helped bring Fiona into this world, then I'm assuming that person is a man, and I sure as shit know I have never dated a dude.

Focusing on the task at hand, I swallow and suck it up, now

looking at that phrasing in an entirely different light. "I'm really happy for you, but I'm not gay. Not that there's anything wrong with that. My best friend is one sexy asshole, and I'd be all over him like a rash. But I like the ladies…"

"So do I," Siobhan says, which has me screeching to a sudden stop.

"What?"

"The person I met was Molly." When I remain silent, she shows me mercy and sheds light on what the hell is going on. "Molly was the girl who served us at Starbucks. She was the one who gave you the last lemon tart.

"I went back to the Starbucks, call me a romantic fool, and we bonded over the fact we both knew you."

"You're gay?" I need her to draw me a diagram because I'm so fucking confused.

"Yes, Molly is my partner, and as you know, I was desperate for a family. So was she, so we got a donor, and nine months later, our little Fiona was born. So we have you to thank."

I don't even know what to say. "You're welcome…I guess. I'm happy for you two. Congratulations."

This is a new kind of awesome. "I was a beard then? For two chicks! That's kind of cool."

When that stagnant quiet falls over us once again, I know I need a fucking handbook, 'cause I'm in a state of constant confusion it appears. "Well, not really, when we were with you…we weren't gay."

"I…what now? I beg your pardon?" I blink once, shaking my head, because now I'm surely hearing things.

"Sorry, Hunter, but…"

"But what? I turned you gay?" I tease, but eat my words

soon after.

"Well…I suppose so."

Oh my fucking lord. I need a minute to think. "I love women, and I love women who love women, but really, you're off men because of me?"

"Yes," she bluntly replies, not sugar-coating a thing. "I guess your demoralizing and appalling treatment of women have turned us into big ole' lesbians!" Her comment is completely laced with sarcasm, and again, I'm so confused.

I know I'm no Shakespeare, but I didn't think my mouth was that offensive. It appears I was wrong. It was enough to turn Siobhan into a lesbian, apparently.

"Don't pretend this was something it wasn't. We both know you were a stand-in before the real deal. And I was the same thing for you. Please don't call me again." Well, if that wasn't a blunt fuck you, then I don't know what it was.

The line goes dead and I hang up, scratching my head and wondering what the hell just happened. I was a stand-in. Like a substitute to serve in someone else's place? Is that what the kids are calling it nowadays?

Well, that entire conversation did nothing for my ego and has me questioning my manhood. Groaning, I thump my head on my desk, in hopes of rendering myself unconscious. "Mr. O'Shea?"

"Unless you have scotch, beat it," I mumble, my cheek pressed to the woodgrain. I have no idea who is outside my door, but they have three seconds to scram before I throw my Yankees paperweight at their head.

"I can run down to the store and get you some liquor?"

Now that I've wrapped my brain around the fact I've

turned two women gay, am a stand-in, and can't seem to find a willing woman to take to tonight's celebrations, I lift my head to uncover who this soft voice belongs to.

The sun streaming in from the window illuminates a young woman standing in my doorway. Her hair is long, golden, and her glossy lips full. A pair of large, black rimmed glasses sit prettily on her small face. She's in a tight black skirt and white silk blouse, which doesn't leave much to the imagination. She is the perfect stereotype of geeky, but kinky secretary.

I have no idea who she is and believe me, I'd remember a face and body like that. "Hello, do I know you?" Not the smoothest of lines, but I'm done with the small talk.

Her pale cheeks turn a rose pink. Everything below the belt is electrocuted. "I'm Keira Celly. I'm Mr. Gail's assistant. I just started a week ago."

"Well hello, Keira Celly. I'm Hunter O'Shea, but you seem to know that already."

Fuck me, her blush swoops down the column of her slender neck. "Yes, I know who you are. Your reputation is notorious."

I don't like to brag, but she's right. However, I suddenly don't know which she speaks of—business or personal. At this stage, I'll take anything she wants to give. "So, what did you do in your past life to get stuck working for that asshole, Aaron Gail?"

Leaning back in my seat, I gesture she's to enter.

She does.

There is no love lost between Aaron and I. His efforts will always pale in comparison to mine because he can only wish to be me. I earned this glass office fair and square, and it gives me great pleasure knowing Aaron is stuck in a corner, windowless office, one day hoping to play with the big boys.

He's tried on numerous occasions to sabotage me, steal my clients, and pawn off my work as his own. Luckily, I can smell a rat, because if undetected, Gail would fly under the radar and steal what is rightfully mine.

Smiling, Keira very ladylike, holds down her skirt and sits. "Well, you weren't hiring," she offers, while I almost choke. "So I thought I'd try second best."

"Second?" I scoff, intertwining my hands behind my nape. "He's so far out of my league, I'm pretty sure he's sitting in a parking lot in Detroit sucking his thumb."

She bursts into laughter before slapping a hand guiltily over her plump, pink mouth. Sadly, she's an employee and completely off limits. I learned the hard way from Dixon—don't mix business with pleasure, regardless of the fact if I lean a little to the left, I can see the innocent, white triangle of treasure between her legs.

"That was really inappropriate. Please don't tell him." She interlaces her hands, on the cusp of begging. "I really need this job."

As much as I want to slip in a lewd remark, I bite my tongue. "Don't worry, I don't talk to the nimrod, so your secret is safe with me."

Her relief is clear. "If I can make it up to you, off the record, please let me know."

The delicate flutter at the side of her neck betrays her nerves, and for some reason, the sight has my mouth watering and wanting to cherish this sweet, innocent dove. I can't remember the last time I encountered such innocence, and it stirs something in me. Insanity maybe, because what I do next can only be classified as that.

Sitting upright, I steeple my fingers in front of me. "Well, there is this thing tonight."

"What thing?" she asks, eagerly shuffling forward to sit on the edge of her seat.

"I have this dinner and I need a plus one. I don't suppose you're free?" When she hesitates, chewing on her bottom lip, I know I've probably just overstepped a line. "I promise I'm not some creep, and you'd be doing me a real solid. It's purely platonic, but I completely understand if it's weird or…"

"What time is it?" she says, cutting me off.

I don't hide my surprise. "You want to come?"

"Sure. I owe you."

"You don't owe me anything." I wave her off because I don't want her thinking that. "If you wanted to come, of your own free will, then I'll pick you up at six-thirty."

Her pretty lips curve, and although I said I wasn't a creep, I can't stop staring at them. A blush creeps over her once again, as I'm not exactly being subtle. "Six-thirty it is then."

Whoever this woman is, I'm completely hooked. She is gorgeous and I don't get a bunny boiler vibe from her. Win, win. With a slow, measured pace, I reach for a business card and pass it to her between two fingers. She looks at it, then back at me, as if weighing the wrongdoings of the situation.

Her deep blue eyes hold me captive, and I actually am worried she might change her mind. But she shyly leans forward and accepts my offering. "Text me your address." She nods, brushing a piece of long golden hair behind her ear.

Flicking the edge of my business card with her pointer as if in thought, she has me guessing what she's thinking. "See you tonight, Mr. O'Shea."

There is a certain time and place to be called Mr., and tonight isn't one of them. Although, I have depraved images of bending her over this desk and spanking her as she calls me Sir. "Please, call me Hunter."

She looks as if she just won the lottery, because she nods quickly, holding back her grin. "Okay, Hunter." She squeaks when trying it on for size, but quickly composes herself a moment later. The action has me smiling.

Breaking eye contact, she smooths out the wrinkles in her skirt and brushes over invisible lint on her top as she stands. Sadly, the movement highlights the fact I can see her budding nipples very clearly through her white blouse.

I have no idea how old she is. At a guess, I'd say twenty-two. Way too young for the likes of me, and I suddenly feel like a perverted old man. But holy shit, her tits, curvy body, her angelic face, they are leaving me with serious wood.

Crossing my legs, I roll the chair forward to hide my looming hard on. "See you tonight." I know it sounds like a brush off, but it's either that, or she sees me pitch a tent, which really goes against my whole purely platonic speech.

She nods, tugging at a silver locket around her neck. "See you then."

I pretend to busy myself, reaching for a pen and notebook from my desk drawer. She gets the hint and turns to leave, rewarding me with a spectacular view of her ass. I'm now busying myself with attempting not to drool as I ogle her lush derriere. I can't look away, her heart shaped behind hypnotizing me with each step she takes.

The looming hard on becomes full wood, straining against

my fly. When she turns over her shoulder, I bite back my internal pain. "What should I wear?"

The mere mention of clothes has me daydreaming about stripping off every shred of her current attire…with my teeth. But I stay composed. "I'm sure you'll look hot in whatever you wear." Or not.

Shit.

It's too late to backtrack. All I can do is apologize for my crude behavior. She'll have to excuse me because all the blood has drained to my dick, but I can't exactly tell her that now, can I?

"Keira…"

But she surprises me when she purses her lips. "I better make sure I don't disappoint, then."

I choke on air, very uncoolly wheezing like an emphysemic old man. She doesn't give me a chance to reply. She instead flutters her long, golden lashes, before leaving me with a view that will be stored in my spank bank and revisited more than once today.

It's 6:25 p.m., and I'm pacing the sidewalk outside of Keira's apartment complex in Brooklyn. I'm early because I'm talking myself out of going through with this.

This is wrong on all counts. I was vulnerable—she caught me questioning whether I deserved a dick or not. There is no better time to enforce my rule of not shitting where you eat. I have no intention of things advancing with Keira, not because

I don't find her attractive, but because I know what will happen soon enough.

The sex will be mind-blowing and things will start out great. She won't have an issue with my wanting to play things cool, and I won't mind if she stays over a day or two. But then as days turns into weeks, my detachment will piss her off and she'll demand more.

More time.

More sex.

More me.

More. More. More.

I will back off, her need for more scaring the living bejesus out of me because I've seen what happens when this stage hits. Women get crazy. They get suspicious and think you're screwing around. Chances are I probably am, because we never agreed to be exclusive and she was fine with us playing it cool. But when an attachment forms, it's all downhill from here on in.

It's scientifically proven that a key hormone is released during sex—oxytocin, also known as the cuddle hormone. It's fundamental to bonding, and women produce more of this hormone, meaning they are more likely to let their guard down and dum dee dum…fall in love with a man after sex. Men, on the other hand, instead of getting a surge of the bonding hormone, we're smacked in the cock with the pleasure hormone, dopamine, which means…all we want to do is fuck.

So, my dilemma here is, once Keira's oxytocin wants to strangle me to death, I will have to see her every…single…day. There will be no escaping her, and before I know it, she's shit in my coffee and glued my balls to the chair.

Office romances can be dangerous. Note to self: abort!

Just as I turn on my heel, making a beeline for my Jeep, I hear my name being called. The oxytocins of the world are flipping me off and high fiving their sisters in crime.

Closing my eyes, I curse the day I found out what my dick could do, because lately, all it seems to do is get me into trouble. "Hey, Keira. Look…" I spin back around, prepared to give her a speech worthy of an Oscar, but I hardly remember my name when I see her standing feet away.

She is a fucking vision. Her long blonde hair is curled around her slender face. Her incredibly blue eyes are emphasized beneath her large glasses. Her lips are stained a plush peach. I can't help but stare, but the first thing I notice in that tight black dress are her supple tits. The neckline plunges so low, it stops inches from her belly button. I have no idea how she'll move without flashing the room.

If that isn't bad enough, the dress is short, stopping mid-thigh, and although she's wearing stockings, if she bends over, Holy Mother of God…my dick stirs once again—the gluttonous bastard. I've jerked off twice already, but clearly, that's not enough.

"It's too much?" she says, tugging at the hemline and shuffling her stiletto-clad feet.

It's not enough, I internally groan because I have no idea how I'm going to keep it in my pants. Pulling it together, I smile. "You look great."

I can see her disappointment, but visions of being cuddled to death spur me on. "Shall we?"

She toys with the strap of her handbag, possibly having second thoughts, before nodding. I'm thankful she has a coat draped over her arm, because I'll turn up the AC if I have to, anything to put me out of my misery.

Walking to the door, I open it for her, because the sooner we get this over with, the faster I can jerk her out of my system. I have no idea what I was thinking. When she brushes past me, her floral perfume engulfing my senses, I know the answer is I wasn't thinking at all.

She turns over her shoulder so we're inches apart. "Thanks."

I nod with a stiff upper lip smile. I know she's flirting with me and I'm a stupid motherfucker because I like it.

Once she's inside, I close the door, running a hand over my scruff because tonight can only lead to trouble. As I round the hood, I can feel her watching me. I hate that I'm already so in tune with her actions, because it means I'm interested, and that interest will soon turn into wanting to fuck her senseless, consequences be damned.

D2 is rocking in a corner, sucking his thumb, reminding me that in roughly half an hour, I'll be seeing the woman who sparked this sudden psychosis. But instead of manning up and telling her how I feel, I've instead gone and dug myself an even bigger hole.

And the award for biggest dumbass goes to…

Once I kickstart the engine, Keira looks over at me with a sparkle in her eye. She's excited. "Thanks again for asking me out tonight. I can't wait to meet your friends," says the future cuddler. I'm doomed.

Nodding, I pull into traffic, wishing tonight was one of those nights where a meteor hit, or aliens invaded the planet. But the closer we get to Westchester County, I know luck isn't on my side. All I can do is turn up the radio and set the AC to high.

Four

"**W**ow!"

Even though this is Keira's third 'wow,' I don't blame her. The white mansion in front of us is what you'd see broadcasted on an episode of MTV's Cribs. But inside are two very humble, very non-pretentious people.

I've met Sebastian and Rachel, Maddy's parents, twice, and I can see where Cherry Pie gets her good nature from. They're incredible people; they don't deserve the two other sacks of shit they sadly call their children.

Juliet, aka rancid vagina, is Maddy's stepsister who deserves bad things, very bad things to happen to her. She makes evil look like a fluffy puppy wearing a pink bow. She not only made Cherry Pie's life hell, but she took Dixon for a ride and almost ruined him. If that isn't enough of an excuse to hang her out to dry, then she blackmailed him and made him believe the baby she was carrying was his.

Maddy's fuckwad of a brother, Dylan, who Dixon will maim and kill if he ever sets foot in NYC again, just added to the shit pile. All in all, these are two diabolical people who deserve to rot in their own misery. From what I've heard, Juliet is flying under the radar, using her baby as an excuse to wedge her way back into the family. But as far as Dixon's concerned, if she so much as looks at Madison, he will pluck out her eyeballs and feed them to her dog.

Needing an exorcism after thinking about those scum of the earth, I kill the engine and put on my big girl panties. I don't need a crystal ball to be aware of how tonight's proceedings will unfold. On the drive over here, Keira was sharing her life story with me—she's from the Midwest, her dad left her when she was seven, but her family are good, Christian people who do charity work like it's second nature.

She also helped out at the local church doing food drives, selling lemonade, baking cookies, you name it—anything charitable, she was involved in with both hands. Me, I can't remember the last time I did anything charitable. The most charitable thing I've done of late was tipping the drycleaners a twenty.

A blind person in Antarctica could see that Keira Celly is way too innocent and pure for the likes of me. I even felt vile when I dropped a standard 'fuck you, dickhole' when someone cut me off on the highway. I could be a real asshole and ignore her, but why does that feel like clubbing a baby seal to death?

When I peer over at her and she looks at me with those big, blue eyes, I know that's probably the reason why. "Shall we?" The sooner we get this over with, the sooner I can drown my sorrows in a bottle of whiskey, scrap that, scotch. She looks nervous, but nods with a small smile.

We exit, it's surprisingly warmer out here than in my icebox of a car. As we ascend the smooth driveway, I notice Dixon's BMW and Finch's baby wagon parked out front. I don't see any others, which has me assuming Mary isn't here yet. Not that that matters, because when she does arrive, she'll have her plus one hanging off of her like a dead skunk. My lip curls of its own accord.

We climb the marbled stairs, the two glass doors sheltered beneath a large alcove reveal a well-lit foyer and beyond. As I ring the doorbell, Keira decides it'll be a good time to take off her coat. I do a double take, forgetting how stunning she is.

"Since when do you ring?" Dixon's light voice carries on the breeze as he opens the door, but I can hear the exact moment his good mood sours. "Hello." His attention dances between Keira and me, but essentially lands on me.

I know what he's thinking: Is Keira a Ukrainian mail order I smuggled into the land of the free. "Hello, Dixon. Thanks for having us over." It's a rare sight to see Dixon Mathews lost for words, so I can't help but gloat and primp my imaginary collar. "This is Keira. We work together." See, I managed to get through a sentence without cursing. Maybe I am a changed man.

Dix's mouth is still agape when she leans forward, stands on tippy toes because he's a fucking titan, and kisses his cheek. He clears his throat, not appearing to appreciate her friendliness. He needs to lighten up. But when she smiles and says, "It's so great to meet you," I can't help but think he's taken an instant dislike toward her.

Regardless, he's the hospitable host and opens the door to

welcome us in. Keira enters first while I lag behind, arching a cocky brow. Before he has a chance to chastise me, I flick him in the nuts. He closes the door with a wheeze.

Keira stares above, admiring the high ceilings and crystal chandelier. "This place is so beautiful," she gushes, while Dixon stands against the door, arms folded, eyeballing the fuck out of me.

What the hell is his problem?

"What?" I mouth, while Dix shakes his head, pointing to an oblivious Keira.

"How much?" I fake horror, although, it's not too far off the mark to assume Keira is a working girl, because in most circumstances, I'd have to pay someone with her looks and good manners to go on a date with me.

His question is never answered because the room suddenly spins brighter when Maddy strolls in. Dixon's sourpuss mood soon lifts and it's like Lord Jesus himself just waltzed through the door.

There is something about Madison Roberts which makes you want to be a better man. She radiates a kind of innocence, but you would never mistake her for being a pushover because she's a survivor, and she's also a fucking saint for putting up with the likes of Dixon.

"Debbie!" she says with a smile, making a beeline for me and giving me a big hug. I can't help but annoy my best friend as I squeeze her a little too tightly while pulling a pre-orgasmic face over her shoulder. Dixon pushes off the door, ready to strangle me.

He's such a strong, handsome brute.

"Cherry Pie, how are you? You look and smell delicious." I

pull out of the embrace, fearing for my life when Dixon marches over.

"I'm fantastic, and thanks. You don't look too bad yourself." She winks while Dixon rolls his eyes. This playful banter is not unusual for us. Not only is she beautiful, she's funny too, which, thank fuck for that, seeing as Dixon's humor has taken a flying leap. I have no idea what crawled up his cakehole and died. Maybe he needs a hug.

"How rude of me, I'm Madison," Maddy says, addressing Keira, who is politely standing off to the side, waiting her turn.

Keira smiles and shakes her hand. "I'm Keira. Thanks for having me over."

Maddy seems impressed by Keira and her manners, unlike Dixon, who is looking at Keira like he is strategizing ways to perform an exorcism before appetizers are served.

"Dude, come take a walk with me. I need to…show you something." As curious as I am, I shake my head because I can feel a lecture and some more psychobabble nonsense brewing.

"I'm flattered, Dix, but I'm not going to blow you." Maddy bursts into laughter, while Keira's eyes widen. Shit, I've forgotten her no swearing rule.

"I only have to follow the trail of profanities and I know where to find you." Finch, the third member of our bro-threesome, comes into the foyer, beer in hand.

This dude has been our voice of reason since we were kids and saved both Dixon and I over the years with his sappy, yet very beneficial, advice. Beneath all that hair on his face and head, lies a very sensible man. But I'll never tell him that.

"And I only have to follow the trail of pubes to find you. What's with the 70s porno bush?" I ask, rubbing under his chin.

He swats my hand away.

"Heidi likes it," he explains. Just as I'm about to drop a lewd comment, he adds, "And it keeps me warm."

Shrugging, I steal his beer. He doesn't bother stealing it back. "Where is the sexy mama?" I ask, looking over his shoulder.

"She couldn't come. Simone has a cold."

Finch is the ultimate babymaker. With three rug rats under his belt, he's in line for daddy of the year. He could handle those little ankle biters with his eyes closed. Both my friends are in the game, acting all grown up and shit, while me, I still have my training wheels on.

Which reminds me. "Finch, this is Keira."

Finch has the worst poker face. Ever. God help him if he ever had to lie to save his life. He'd be toast. "Oh, hello, hi," he says with way too many salutations. He goes to shake her hand, but she leans forward and kisses him politely on the cheek.

With greetings out of the way, we all stand around, dick in hand, waiting for someone to talk. I don't need to be a mind reader to know what they're all thinking. Why would someone like Keira voluntarily be seen in public with me?

Maddy peers up at Dixon, his stiff upper lip a sure sign he's grumpier than a bear with pink eye.

"Hunter, and hello Hunter's friend. Thanks for coming," says Rachel, Maddy's mom, as she joins the party. I can see where Maddy gets her looks from. Good DNA in that family gene pool.

"Hello, Rachel. Thanks for having me. My friend is Keira," I explain, while Rachel nods happily.

"C'mon, then. Won't you come in?" She gestures with her

hand that we're to enter instead of standing around like chumps. She walks into the living room, implying we're to follow.

There is no way I'm standing anywhere near Dixon, who looks all huffy, so I cock my arm, signaling Keira to loop hers through mine. She merrily complies and we saunter past Dix, me grinning like a pig in shit as we bypass him. His lecture can come after I've had pie.

"What would everyone like to drink?" Rachel asks, happily peering around the room.

I raise my stolen beer, while Finch shakes his head. "All good, thanks. Keira?"

She has been awfully quiet, and I realize she probably feels a little intimidated, seeing as she doesn't know anyone, including me. Even though I have no intention of seeing her outside office hours after tonight, she's here now as my date, so I'll attempt to be a gentleman. Or at the very least, less offensive.

"Could I trouble you for a sparkling mineral water?"

A cackle erupts from me, but when I'm greeted with silence, I see that she's serious. If this woman told me she was next in line to be the Blessed Virgin Mary, 2.0., I'd believe her. A shudder passes over me when even thinking that name, and those thoughts then lead to images of fiery red hair and a devil's tongue.

Rachel takes everyone's drink order, before dashing into the kitchen. On most days, I know Dixon would forever be the gentleman and offer to help, but not today. Maddy gently tugs on his arm, leading him over to the leather sofa. We all follow suit, sitting as well. I'm opposite Dix and Maddy, while Finch is on the outer, playing visual ping-pong between Dixon and me, lost in translation. Join the club. I have no idea what Dix's problem is. He is analyzing Keira closely, like he's half expecting her face to peel off and turn into a giant praying mantis.

Maddy clears her throat, as the tension can be hacked into with a fucking chainsaw.

"So…you said you work together?" asks Dixon as he leans back in his seat, crossing an ankle over his knee. His question is directed at Keira, as if wanting her to validate my claims.

She nods nervously. "Yes, I just started, actually."

Something clicks in Dixon's head and I can literally see his shoulders depress, but he still appears to be sucking on a lemon. "Do you work together, together? Or just in the same office?"

"What sort of a stupid question is that?" I toss back my beer, wondering if maybe he's finally lost the plot.

"I'm just making conversation," he counters lightly, but we both know there is no such thing with a fancy smancy shrink like Dr. Dix.

Keira shuffles in her seat, smoothing out her dress with both hands. She's nervous. I don't blame her. These questions put The Heretic's Fork to shame. "We work in the same office. Mr. Gail is my boss. Hunter's office is just down the hall from mine," she explains as Dix continues to grill her.

He nods, processing over everything she just revealed. "And how often have you seen him? Like out of ten."

Right, this is just plain ridiculous. "You're higher than a giraffe's snatch," I bark, unable to hold my tongue. "This isn't a math class. Now can it and let's talk important stuff."

"Like…" he baits me, while I accept the challenge.

"Your bachelor party," I expose, rubbing my hands together. Before he has time to object, I shush him. "Don't even bother arguing, it's happening, and you're going to have fun, god damn you." When he opens his mouth, to no doubt rain on my fun parade, I hold up my finger—the middle finger, that is. "Don't make me throw you over my shoulder, because you know I will." Keira giggles, the sound high-fiving my ego. "Just 'cause you're getting married, that doesn't give you an excuse to be a massive pussy. Don't take this rite of passage away from me, you selfish cock…a-doodle-doo," I add at the last minute when Rachel enters.

Both Finch and Dixon shake their heads, while Maddy laughs behind her hand.

"What are you talking about?" she asks, handing Keira her glass of boring bubbles.

"We were discussing Dixon's bachelor party, Rachel," I reply, smiling sweetly at her. Butter wouldn't melt in my mouth right now. "The ol' stick in the mud is opposed to having fun, it appears. Are you sure you want to marry Grandpa, Maddy?" I lock eyes with her as she looks up at him, biting back a smile. "FYI, he was wearing sweatpants the other night. Enough said." I shiver, while Maddy is unable to contain her laughter any longer.

"Oh, Dixon, I think it's lovely Hunter wants to throw you a bachelor party."

"Yeah, Dix, lovely is my middle name," I counter sweetly, fluttering my eyelashes melodramatically. "Don't hurt my feelings." Rachel offers Finch a beer, while Dixon almost lunges for the scotch she's holding. I will never tire of annoying him.

"Oh, we wouldn't want that, and besides," Rachel says, completely oblivious to my sarcasm, "I have no doubt Mary will be holding quite the bachelorette party for Madison."

Two things happen at once. I get winded, and that wind ends

up in my dick, which inflates bigger than Pamela Anderson's boobs in Baywatch.

"Yes, Rachel, but the difference is…is that my party won't involve Maddy getting arrested, or needing a rabies shot once the night ends." All heads turn toward the doorway because in strolls the woman who has me hankering for a taste of whatever she's bringing to the table.

Before me stands the triple threat, Miss Mary Mitts. I honestly have no idea how she does it, but each time I see her, I get this bubble of…something brewing inside. At first, I thought it was one too many frozen burritos, so I switched to Hot Pockets instead. When the queasiness continued however, I knew it wasn't the food making me sick. It was her. She was toxic, lethal to my system, but I have never wanted to drink the Kool-Aid more than I do right now.

Her long copper curls tumble over her slender shoulders, accentuating her elegant neck. She's in a peacock green dress, the color highlighting her creamy skin and vibrant emerald eyes. Her plump lips are glistening a rose pink, and images of fisting that long red mane and owning that fucking mouth crash into me. I can't remember the last time I've felt this way, because I would happily break my solemn vow for just one… simple…taste.

She snaps her fingers, which draws attention to the fact I'm staring at her like a creepy pervert once again. "Amateurs get caught, sweetheart. I'm a pro," I smugly reply, deadpanning her.

It was meant to intimidate her, but all it does is leave me open to her smart mouth. "You should know all about pros." Her gaze flicks to the left of me and I wonder why. When the cushions beneath me shift, I'm reminded that I'm not here alone.

Keira clears her throat and pushes her huge glasses up the bridge of her small nose. It seems she's throwing off the hooker vibe to everyone, which is funny, 'cause they're so off the mark with that assumption. She's sweet, innocent, and nice. The perfect catch—so why did I have a lapse in memory five seconds ago where no one existed but her?

"Lamb," Maddy says, standing, the forever peacekeeper between me and her BFF. "You look beautiful."

She does, she looks fucking amazing, but I'll be damned if she knows that. Rolling my eyes, I casually lean back, spreading my arm out along the back of the sofa. In turn, I half embrace Keira, but she doesn't seem to mind and shuffles an inch closer.

It takes all my willpower not to fist pump and launch off this couch like fucking Apollo 4. It may have been small, but I saw it. Mary did a double take, staring a little longer at Keira with a cocked brow. She returned her attention back to Maddy a split second later, but I've planted a seed and now…it's time to watch it grow.

"How's your sparkling water?" I ask, purposely leaning in close to whisper into Keira's ear.

She wets her lips before she speaks. "Good. It's…bubbly."

A genuine throaty chuckle escapes me, not expecting her response. "Thanks for coming. I know it's all a little weird. P.S., Dixon isn't always such a killjoy. Maybe he's running low on his favorite styling gel."

Keira bursts into a light giggle, before muting it behind her palm. She's picked up on the unforgiving vibe Dixon is throwing out, so she probably doesn't want to piss him off anymore by laughing at his perfectly styled locks.

"It's fine," she whispers. "I get the sense you're a tightknit group. Your friends are protective of you. Maybe they're afraid I'll corrupt you." She accents her sentence with a wink.

I almost give myself whiplash as I recoil, her comment throwing me on my ass. For once, I'm speechless. Mark it in your diaries, ladies and gentlemen, and Dix. Who would have thought? Maybe little innocent Keira isn't so innocent after all.

This is a gamechanger, because who doesn't like a closet bad girl? But when I hear that candid giggle, it slays me. I don't want this bad girl, and I know I'm going against all I vowed to do, and I sound like an utter weakling…but there is only one Mary Mitts, and I want her. But I can't have her because someone else does.

Which reminds me…

I pay closer attention to Mary and Maddy chatting a few feet away, because I notice it is a duo, not a threesome. What happened to jerk-off?

Could I be so lucky, and visualizing him being trampled to death by a stampede of angry donkeys has become truth?

Sweet baby Jesus.

Still slouched casually, I sip my beer before asking, "So… you're here alone?" Yes, I just dropped the world's worst pickup, but it's the best I can muster, because if she says yes, I'm going to throw her over my shoulder and make her scream uncle.

Today's little revelation can blow me. I was stupid to think I could move on because I don't even know what I'm moving on from. It's not like we've had this long-winded affair, or that we've shared more than five words, but regardless, I need to know where I stand before I give up on something that hasn't even had a chance to grow.

We never break eye contact, and fuck me, the thrill I feel from being pinned by that feral gaze leaves me tempted to drop to my knees and hand her my balls on a silver platter.

Just as she opens that mouth I'm utterly obsessed with, a voice sounds, and it's akin to flaying flesh from my bones. "Sorry, love, I must have left my cell at home."

It takes my brain a second to process that the voice is coming from a man, or quite possibly, he could be Adonis himself who just sauntered into the room. I hope to god he's talking to Finch. But when Mary averts her eyes, I know this man beast is jerk-off. Her date.

"It's okay," she says, her cheeks turning a soft pink as he kisses her lightly on the mouth.

The room is suddenly filled with a grinding, and I have no idea what it is until Keira places her hand on my thigh. "Are you all right?" I nod, unable to tear my gaze away from Mary and her date, who will lose a finger if he doesn't remove his hand from her fucking waist. "You might want to unclench your jaw then before you grind down your teeth."

I'm about to ask what she means, but that just calls attention to the fact I'm gnashing my teeth like a cornered, rabid dog. Every cell in my body has gone into overdrive, and I chew the inside of my cheek, certain I've drawn blood. Nothing else matters but fighting for Mary, gladiator style, until the death. Tough luck for cockhead…because I don't like to lose.

I spring up, fists clenched, armed and ready for combat, but Dixon is quicker and reaches me faster than a kid chasing an ice cream truck. "Chill, man. It's okay," he says for our ears only as he presses his palm to my chest, holding me back. I wrestle with the urge to shrug him off, but I calm the hell down before

I implode.

No one seems to notice the near miss because assmonkey has the balls to walk over to me of his own free will and offer me his hand. I look down at it like it's a diseased limb. "G'day, mate…" More words follow, but I haven't the faintest what they are, because I'm pretty certain he's drunk or maybe high. Quite possibly both.

I blink once before looking at Dixon for a little help. What the fuck did he just say? Is he speaking Swahili? His hand is still tented between us, and I'm so leaving him hanging because I'm not shaking when I have no fucking clue what he just said.

"Dinner is served."

Ring ding a ding!

I have never been happier to eat than I am right now.

Rachel gestures that we're to follow her. I will happily follow her to hell if it meant I'd get away from this person speaking gibberish.

Keira stands and follows Rachel without waiting for me to escort her, not that I can blame her. I'm surprised she hasn't made an excuse to use the bathroom, only to escape out the window and hail a cab out of the land of the crazy.

Cocksmoke lowers his hand, finally getting the hint. He may be pretty, but he's dumb as dog shit. I can't help but smile. Mary and her dumbass date also follow Rachel's lead, him whispering something into her ear. When his hand slips a little too low on her waist and skims the top of her ass, I lunge forward, ready to finish this once and for all.

Dixon is my voice of reason and stops me once again. "Angelo, we'll be there in a minute." Maddy nods, chewing on her lower lip.

I hate that I've put that look of worry on her face, but I can't help it. Every time he touches her, it's like I become possessed by the devil, who wants me to string him up by his hairy balls and make him my own personal piñata.

I'll make it up to her later, but for now, I need to take a chill pill.

Once she leaves, Dixon sighs. "Dude, you need to calm the fuck down."

"And you need to stop touching me," I retort, slapping his hand.

Finch is beside us, his face reflective of Maddy's. "What's going on?"

Finch knows I've had a "thing" for Mary, but the past two minutes was more than just a "thing"—it almost turned into a bloodbath. "What's going on is that guy"— I jab my finger in the direction he went —"is the Dark Lord, and I'm pretty certain he just said he's going to eat my soul. Or maybe he wanted me to dig a hole? I don't know, it's not important. What is important is that I'm not breaking bread with him. The only thing I'll be breaking is my plate over his fucking head." And there I go again, all Hulk-like. I swipe my palm out in front of me to ensure I'm not green.

Dixon runs a hand over his scruff. "Hunt, I know this is hard, but please, for the love of god, just try to be civil. Just ignore him. Better yet, pretend he doesn't exist." That would be easy, but the thought of him sitting near Mary leaves me stabby.

"Guys, I really feel like the third wheel here. What have I missed?" Finch is looking between us, desperate someone shed light on the situation.

Placing my hands on his shoulders, I state, "It's fine, Finch.

Do you think orange is my color?" which just adds to the confusion.

Finch looks at Dixon for help, but he just shrugs. "If not for me, do it for Madison. Please." His plea snaps some sense into me and my anger begins to subside.

I'm being a fucking drama queen. "Fine, you win." Dixon looks more than relieved, but it's short-lived. "But if he looks at me sideways, I will stab him with my fork."

"Stab who?" Finch screeches, noise control non-existent just like always when he gets worked up.

"Fuck me, man. Does baby brain affect men too, because holy fuck balls, do I need to draw you a diagram?" He scratches over his beard, as if contemplating my offering. "Jesus Christ, I was talking metaphorically."

Dixon laughs, breaking the stalemate. "Life was so much simpler when I was the messed up one."

I pull back, faking offense. "And what's that supposed to mean?"

"It means we're not having this conversation again. You know what you have to do. Grow a pair, or get the fuck over it before you end up someone's bitch in prison."

He does have a point. "Fine, you win, sensei."

Dixon's lips twitch and I'm glad the air has cleared, because I don't want to ruin Maddy's night. "Good, now remember, if he talks to you, just pretend you didn't hear him." His pause has me anticipating what his train of thoughts are. "That shouldn't be hard because I have no fucking clue what he said."

"Thank you!" I cry out, arms out wide while Dixon scratches his temple, confused.

"I'm pretty sure he's Australian," Finch says, raining on my fun parade.

Feeling like the old me again, now that Satan reincarnate has gone, I snicker, "Well, the land down under can grow a giant dick and eat me."

Dixon slaps me on the back. "Attaboy."

Finch huffs, while both Dix and I burst out laughing. It takes him a minute, but he finally catches up. "Oh…oh…you've got a thing for Mary and you're jealous?"

I scoff, shaking my head and crossing my arms in defiance, but Dix sets things straight. "There you go. See, you didn't need Hunter's diagram after all. Probably best that you didn't 'cause it would consist of stick figures with massive erections." Dix throws his arm around Finch and gives him a hug while Finch blanches.

And just like that, I'm me again thanks to these fuckers. "Let's go before jerk-off eats the entire table. Although, did you see the size of him? I doubt he eats anything but eggwhite steroid omelettes." The thought has me grinning from ear to ear.

"What now?" Finch asks, still playing catch up.

"His dick would be the size of a fucking prawn!" I roar in laughter. "I hope Mary brought her magnifying glass. What a needle dick!"

Finch pales, while Dixon shakes his head, doing a poor job hiding his smile.

As we make our way toward the dining room, Dix elbows me in the ribs. I grunt on impact. "You're not off the hook. We still have to talk about your date. But that can wait until after I've had a bottle of scotch or two."

I raise my shoulders in carefree manner. "Don't be hating

on my date. At least she speaks English."

Dixon smirks, while Finch nods regretfully. "Touché, motherfucker."

What would I do without these foul-mouthed bastards? Lucky for me, I'll never have to find out.

Five

Hunter

"And…er…blah…blah…kangaroo…hyagirf."

I'm pretty certain I'm rivaling Scooby Doo, as its story time with Trent, aka jerk-off. He's been chewing our ears off for the past twenty minutes about…I have no fucking clue what.

I've been on my best behavior, because I can't believe this shitstain is who I'm up against. It's fairly obvious Mary has gone insane and she needs to get her head back in the game. I almost feel sorry for him…almost—when he wraps his arm around her and draws her into his side, that remorse turns to rage. This gigantic shithead is going down.

Sure, it doesn't help he looks like he's carved from granite and that his perfectly symmetrical head is enough to make a grown man cry, but looks aren't everything, and besides, what do Mary and him talk about? He may be pretty, but he sure as hell sounds like he's chewing dog shit.

Finch is nodding, engaging in conversation, while Dixon looks as confused as me. He peers at me from across the table, raising his scotch in salute. The big fella is proud of me for keeping my cool. In response, I blow him a kiss.

Because I have been busy strategizing a takedown, I have completely ignored my date, who is sitting quietly beside me, picking at her roast like a sparrow. As far as dating companions go, I blow ass, and this is the reason why I don't date.

Mary is sitting opposite Keira. It's like looking at complete polar opposites. The polite, innocent blonde, versus the uncouth, impious redhead.

"How's your course coming along, Mary? Aren't you almost done?" asks Rachel as she cuts into her lamb.

Dixon wasn't lying when he said Sebastian was a mean cook. He has prepared a feast fit for a king. There is everything one could ever want spread before us, but too bad my appetite is for shit, because the thought of eating turns my stomach.

Mary nods, her red waves bouncing. "Yes, thank god. I just have a couple more projects to complete and then I'm done."

Mary is in her final year of interior design. From what Cherry Pie has shared, she's a fucking genius, not that that surprises me. Look at her canvas—complete perfection. She catches me staring and narrows her eyes, her warning of catching me fantasizing about her being naked ringing loudly in my ears. On instinct, I cover my nuts. Her gaze flicks downward, and a hint of a smile plays at her pink lips. It's gone before I can break out into a touchdown dance.

"What does that entail?" Sebastian sits at head of the table, seeing his guests are well fed. It's still hard to believe one of his swimmers is to blame for bringing the she-devil into this world.

"My final assessment is transforming two spaces. Before and after, that kind of thing. The problem is finding someone who will be happy for me to gut their home and office and be in their face 24/7 for the next two months.

Maybe if Dr. Genius over here didn't rent out his office and he worked full time, I could have used him as my lab rat, but I have a feeling it'll take a miracle to revamp that place."

Dixon pauses from cutting into his potatoes, looking over at Maddy for clarification. She raises her hands with a slanted smile, wanting no part of this conversation.

When Mary reads his confusion, she has no qualms setting him straight. Using her fork as a gesturing tool, she blankly states, "C'mon, Dix, that place screams old man cave."

Dixon places his silverware on the edge of his plate and finishes chewing. "Old man cave? If by that you mean professional, with a touch of modernism, then yes, I completely agree."

Reaching for my beer, I get comfy, because this is going to be fun.

"Old man cave is exactly that…an old's man cave," Mary explains without sparing his feelings. Dixon exhales in a long-winded affair, while Maddy turns into him and giggles.

"Oh, you agree with her then?" he teases, looking down at her as she attempts to conceal her uncontrollable laughter.

"Of course, she does. She has to spare your feelings, that's what people in love have to do, but me, I call 'em as I see 'em. Speaking of, I see a few extra pounds beneath that shirt, Dr. Dix. When was the last time you hit the gym?" Mary sits taller in her seat, pretending to look down her nose and scrutinize Dixon's non-existent extra pounds.

I can't contain my laughter and burst into a gruff chuckle. "Well, he is in love, so I suppose it's only fitting he gets love handles," I counter, while fuck me dead, Mary giggles. When she realizes she just laughed at a joke I cracked, she bites her top lip.

But she did it, and it was the most glorious sound I've ever heard.

"All right, enough with the old man talk. You'll offend Sebastian," Dixon says, which has the table bursting into hysterics.

The mood, thanks to Mary's wisecrack, is light, even Keira seems to be having a semi decent time. All in all, tonight hasn't been a complete disaster. Or, so I thought. As I'm cutting into my dinner, I'm certain I've just been shot in the leg.

Grunting on impact, I lift the tablecloth to see what the hell just happened. And what just happened was Dixon kicking me under the table, because he does it again.

"What in the holy hell, you cocksmoking fucker?" I mouth, impressed Dixon can lip read so well, because he smirks.

He cocks his head to the right, eyes wide. I scrunch up my brow. Is he having an anaphylactic reaction to something? When he does it again, but with more jarring and jerking, I'm certain he's about to have a stroke.

He raises his eyes to the ceiling before reaching for his napkin and using it as a subtle shield to mime, "Offer your soul."

It's official—Dixon Mathews has lost his marbles.

"My soul?" I scratch my head, so fucking confused, my brain starts to hurt.

"Moan."

"Moan?"

"Bone."

"Bone?" I almost choke in excitement. Whoever he wants me to offer a bone to, I'm in.

An exasperated sigh leaves Dixon before he drops the napkin onto the table and turns to Mary. "Hunter could offer you his home. And office, in fact."

It takes about three seconds before I catch up to speed, and when I do, I open my mouth in understanding. Oh… home. Maybe if his facial charades didn't suck donkey dicks, I'd understand he was hinting I was to offer my home to Mary to redecorate. This plan is genius, and I'm surprised I didn't think of it first.

"Isn't that right, Hunt?" Dixon says, encouraging me to get my foot out of my mouth and speak. He pointedly looks at me, hinting I'm a dumbass for not offering myself. It's not my fault I don't speak idiot.

Returning the favor, I kick his shin before turning to Mary with an innocent smile. "Sure. Mi casa es su casa," I say, attempting to act causal.

"You're joking, right?" She doesn't hide her distaste. "There is no way I'm going anywhere near your home."

I shrug, masking my hurt. "Your loss. I hear McDonald's is hiring." When she glares at me, I cock my head to the side. "No? Taco Bell then?"

"Lamb, you should consider it. You're running out of options. No offense, Hunter," Maddy sweetly says, leaning forward to look at me.

"None taken." I wave her off.

Mary looks jacked off because she knows Maddy is right, but doing this means she'll owe me, and let's face facts, I may quite possibly ask for repayment in the form of her dancing naked to the theme of Jeopardy.

"Well, I mean offense, because there isn't enough bleach to decontaminate your walls. I'd have to be baptized first before I even considered stepping foot inside. No offense," she sarcastically says, addressing Keira for the first time all night.

Keira shifts beside me, clearly uncomfortable with Mary's jab that my home is on unholy ground. Thinking back to some of the things I've done in there over the years, she isn't too far off the mark. But regardless, Keira is just an innocent bystander. However, what she says next has me almost falling off my chair. "Lucky for me, I'm already baptized then."

If I wasn't in a state of complete shock, I would high five Keira for thinking on her feet so quickly, but all I can do is grin a shit-eating grin.

Mary appears taken aback also, as her mouth parts, but then I see something damn frightening breed before my eyes—Keira has just bumped me from the top spot off Mary's shit list. Mary has just been upstaged, making Keira public enemy number one.

I fear for Keira's life when Mary snickers before leaning forward, ready to rip Keira a new one. Instinctually, I pull her into my side, helping her avoid any shrapnel, because I have no doubt Mary is seconds away from imploding.

The gesture was supposed to help Keira, but all it seems to do is piss Mary off further. She focuses on where my arm is wrapped loosely around her, staring at our union like it just told her to fuck off. I have no idea what it means, as I've never seen that look before reflected on a woman's face when in relation to me.

"I'm going out for a smoke," Dixon quickly says, intervening because he too can sense World War Three is moments away from erupting. He gestures with his head that Finch and I are to follow. Looking at Keira, still fearful that when I return, she'll be missing a limb, she smiles and nods, giving me the green light.

I risk a glance at Mary, who appears to be challenging me with that unreadable look still slathered on her pretty face. Jerk-off chooses this moment to console her, whispering something into her ear.

When the apple of her cheeks turns a dusty pink, I have images of partaking in my own acts of violence, starting with cutting off his balls with the steak knife to his left.

"C'mon, dude." Dixon slaps me on the back, hinting I'm to get up before this meal turns into a roast. With jaw clenched, I stand slowly, making a point to stare this koala hugging dickhole down. He doesn't even seem to notice or care. But Mary does, and fuck me dead, I think…I think she likes it. But that makes no sense, right? Zero.

I don't have time to think about this further because Dixon all but drags me out of the dining room and through the balcony doors by my collar. The cool breeze is exactly what I need to extinguish the fire burning under my ass.

Neither of us speak. Finch and I follow Dixon like two naughty kids caught with their hands in the cookie jar. Finch is guilty by association. Poor bastard.

When we're far enough away from the house, out of range from prying ears, he stops and turns, shaking his head at me. I recognize that judgy look right off the bat.

"What?" I ask, a glutton for punishment.

Searching through his pockets, he finds his Marlboros, obviously needing a fix of nicotine before addressing my question.

As he takes a hit, I can't help but quip, "Those things will kill you."

He snickers, blowing out a ring of smoke into the air. "You'll most likely get there first." I could counter, but he's probably right. He's mulling over what to say, but he should know by now I only like sugar-coated donuts.

"For fuck's sake, spit it out."

He accepts the challenge. "How well do you know Keira?"

"Well enough. She completely owned Mary back there." I hook my thumb toward the house, unable to get the moment out of my head.

Dixon, however, doesn't seem to see the humor. "I'm sorry, man, but I smell a rat."

I pull back, confused. "A rat? What the fuck? She's a fucking saint."

"Exactly." Finch is no help, as he clearly agrees with Dixon, because he's nodding like a bobble head. "Someone who looks and acts like her…" He leaves the sentence hanging, leaving me to join the dots.

It doesn't take me long, and when I do, the picture I draw is one of my best friends stabbing me in the back. "You smell a rat because if a nice girl wants to date me, there must be something wrong with her? Is that it?"

"Yes," Dixon replies without pause. I know I said I didn't want him sugar-coating anything, but he could at least apply a little lube before he fucks me in the ass.

"Gee, fuck you too. That's the reason you were eyeballing

her earlier. You think she's up to no good? Going to steal my billions? Try to fuck me into submission?" I offer, as he better pick one answer and explain what the fuck is going on.

He takes another drag of his cigarette before saying, "I'm sorry, but there's something about her I can't quite put my finger on."

"That's because your finger has been on and in one woman for far too long, and you've apparently lost your balls."

"I agree with Dix. Sorry, Hunter." Finch decides now is the time to pipe up and be in cahoots with Dix.

"No offense, but fuck you both." I cross my arms in defiance, ready to shove that ember where the sun don't shine.

But it doesn't deter Dixon in the slightest. "I'm sorry, dude"—what he wants to say next clearly pains him, but he perseveres—"I'm sorry, but she just reminds me of…" He seals his lips, shaking his head like he's about to hurl.

But fuck him. He started this, so he can finish it. "Reminds you of what?"

Swallowing down his revulsion, he simplifies, "It's not a what, but rather a who."

"Who? Who the fuck who?" I bark. He has three seconds to explain what the holy hell is going on before I…

That threat is never delivered because my brain finally plays catch up, and when it does, it goes into meltdown mode. "Don't you dare jinx me. You take it back," I demand, scolding him with my finger.

When both Finch and Dixon remain quiet, I know neither has any intention of revoking their claims, because both believe that the innocent, sweet, wouldn't hurt a fly, Keira is the spitting image of the antichrist in heels—Juliet Harte.

"Dixon has a point."

"No, Finch, Dixon has clearly gone insane because Keira is nothing, nothing like that queen cunt from Cuntsville. You will give her a perpetual state of bad luck now. I hope you're happy."

Finch blanches when I use his most favorite word, but desperate times call for desperate measures. And besides, if he's still offended by the word cunt, then it's probably best we're no longer friends.

I can't believe Dixon would even suggest this. Sure, she's blonde and has a killer ass too, but c'mon, this is blasphemy.

Dixon flicks his cigarette, butting it out with his boot. "Just be careful. I got sucked in by baby blues and killer curves—I'd hate for you to suffer the same fate, because believe you me, it is not fun."

"If it makes you feel any better, we just met, like literally. I've known her for less than twenty-four hours, so I'm sure once she sees the real me, she won't be coming to anymore dinners, so stop worrying that pretty little head of yours," I bark with a little bite, because deep down, I know he's right.

If Keira knew the real me, she'd be requesting a transfer to the other side of the world. Nice girls like Keira Celly just don't end up with manwhores like me. It was nice to pretend, but Dixon is right—again. But her comment earlier to Mary, maybe she too is hiding the real her.

"What is going on with Mary?" Finch asks, in tune with my thoughts.

The mere mention of her name has my cock tingling. "She's got it going on," I reply, needing to lighten the mood.

"I thought she hated you?" Finch states, which has me wondering where he's going with this.

"She does," I affirm, but Finch shakes his head.

"For someone who's a massive know it all, sometimes, you know jackshit." I choke on air, because whenever Finch uses profanity, I know I'm in trouble.

Dix nods, giving Finch the floor. "As frightening as this is, I think Mary is the female version of you."

"What are you smoking, Finchy, because I want some, pronto."

He ignores my wisecrack. "I can't help but think she's hiding something."

"Yeah, an ice-pick under her bed."

"Joke all you want, but you're both hiding behind punchlines, too afraid to face the real world because you're scared of getting hurt," he concludes. Dixon smiles proudly.

"Last I checked, you were supposed to be my friends. I think it's time I found new amigos," I state with a smirk, because Finch's theory, although slightly confusing, does give me hope that maybe I saw what I thought I saw earlier.

I could have sworn Mary was happy I was ready to beat jerk-off into a bloody pulp for touching her. At the time, I thought it was wishful thinking, but if there is any truth to what Finch says, then this is a game changer.

"You'd be the poster child for VD if not for us," Dixon candidly says. I don't argue. "Just be careful with Keira, and as for Mary…" I wait on tenterhooks. "I agree with Confucius."

"You what?" I choke for the second time in the span of a minute.

"She was ready to claw out Keira's eyes and use the empty sockets as a toilet."

All my birthdays come at once. "I love it when you talk

dirty," I wheeze, attempting to catch my breath. "So what am I supposed to do about it?"

Dixon smirks, running a hand through his hair. Fuck him. He's so enjoying this. "Let nature take its course. C'mon, let's get back." Is he fucking serious? When he treks up the hill, I know the answer is yes.

I amble behind, my mind going a million miles a minute. They've just dropped this bombshell and now I'm supposed to sit around the table and have scones and tea. How am I going to look at Mary and not walk through the door with a raging hard on? Now that I know there might be a slight chance she doesn't hate me as much as I thought she did, I don't know how to act. My palms begin to sweat and I wipe them onto my pants.

Dixon turns over his shoulder and bursts into a gruff laugh. "Welcome to my world, Hunter."

I'm in the midst of flipping him off when an angel comes into view. As much as I know things between Keira and I can never eventuate, I can't help but admire her because that's what any hot-blooded American male would do.

Finch has other ideas and nudges me in the ribs. "If it looks like a duck…"

"Walks like a duck…" Dixon adds, drawing attention to Keira's swagger.

"Then it's one fucking…hot…duck," I conclude. Their analogy can suck a dick.

Dixon doesn't bother stopping to engage in small talk and instead gives her a stiff upper lip smile. Finch being Finch is more accommodating, and asks if she'd like his jacket. She politely declines. The boys head toward the house, while I stop, wondering if everything is okay.

"I've had a really nice night but…" And here it is—the inevitable 'but you're a creep' speech. "But I have to go. I…"

I cut her off however, because she doesn't owe me an explanation. "It's cool, Keira. I get it. No need for messy goodbyes." She purses her lips, clearly mulling over what I just said.

Brushing a strand of hair behind her ear, she toys over her pulse timidly. "I was going to say I have to go because Mr. Gail asked me to grab a file off his desk and drop it in his mailbox, but I'd love a raincheck, and maybe get to know you better over dinner, just you and me."

Well, holy fuck me, Jiminy Cricket. I was not expecting that at all.

"But we're clearly not on the same page. I'm sorry for jumping to conclusions." When she sniffs, I swear an angel somewhere dies.

Suddenly, I feel like the world's biggest asshole, which is ironic, considering I was giving her a get out of jail for free card. "I just thought after tonight, you'd want to…"

"Want to what?" she coaxes, stepping forward and surrounding me with her floral perfume.

"Want to exercise the first amendment," I reply, her magnetism luring me as I gaze into her blue eyes.

"My freedom of speech?" she questions, her button nose crinkling.

I nod, falling deeper under her spell. "Yes. The freedom of telling me what you really thought of me, before flipping me off and hitting the highway. I wouldn't blame you if you did."

"Why would I do that?" Even her questions are laced with innocence.

"Because…" I lick my lips, stepping forward. "Because I haven't exactly been a stellar date. And my friends haven't really welcomed you with open arms."

She is so incredibly small. Pocket-sized. But when she grins a slow, sultry smirk, I know she's a pocket rocket ready to explode. "I'm not here for your friends." Hot tamale. My cock twitches, but I'm saved by the flaming redhead about to cut off my balls.

"Sorry to interrupt this cozy reunion…" Both Keira and I turn, looking at Mary who is feet away, her hand cocked to her hip. She is so not sorry. "But if you want dessert, break it up. We're all waiting."

I take a step back, suddenly feeling guilty, which is asinine. But regardless, I put as much distance between Keira and I. I'm waiting to see a change in Mary's face. Maybe happiness for showing where my loyalties lie, but all I get is a curled lip and a blanket of boredom in response.

Keira isn't silly and can clearly see the change in body language. "I'm not staying." I know she wants me to say something, anything, but I don't. She may not know it, but I'm doing her a favor. She'll thank me one day.

With one final heartbreaking look, she sighs, and nods her goodbyes. She bypasses Mary, which is perhaps a good idea, because I have no doubt Mary would push her into the dirt, face first.

Once Keira is gone, I stand still, knowing that I should move, but I don't. This is the first time Mary and I have been alone together. She calls to the full moon because it comes out of hiding, illuminating her like the goddess that she is.

Finch's speech plays over and over in my head. Do I really

have a chance with her? I thought the chances were slim to none.

Her feet shuffle as I make no secret that I'm checking her out, and on most days, she'd flip me off before storming off. But tonight, she does neither. She does something that she's never done before. She initiates conversation. "Your date finally came to her senses."

She did just insult me in a roundabout way, but like a dog begging for scraps, I'll take whatever she wants to give. "Too bad your date hasn't done the same." She remains unaffected, watching me as closely as I'm watching her. "FYI, I'm pretty sure your date was speaking in tongues."

Something amazing suddenly happens— she smiles. Strike me dead. She smiled because of something I said. Why do I feel like the luckiest man alive?

"He's Australian," she explains, her lips still twitching.

Pulling it together, I casually raise my shoulders. "Still, I'd burn some sage just to be sure." And this would be the moment she tells me to go fuck myself before storming off and announcing to the world what an utter dick I am.

But she doesn't.

She continues standing and staring and waiting…waiting for what, exactly?

We've never been alone with one another for this long, so I don't know what the proper protocol is. Does she want me to make conversation? Or maybe my fly is undone and she's waiting for me to notice so she can ridicule me. I check just to make sure. All clear.

D2 comes out of hiding and whispers, "Talk to her." That's great, you pussy, but talk about what?

Thinking about what D1 suggested, I decide to go with that. "I meant what I said earlier."

My words seem to snap whatever haze Mary is in and she shakes her long red mane. "You said a lot of things, most of which I tuned out for."

My dick punches a hole straight through my pants because her smart mouth is like a drug to me. "About my home," I reply, acting cool. "My door, bedroom and others, is always open."

The breeze picks up speed, delivering a shot of strawberries and cream straight to my guts. There is no mistaking this delicious scent is coming off of Mary's flesh—flesh I want to worship from head to toe.

She folds her slender arms across her body, hugging her torso as she weighs up my offer. Holy shit, could this really work? No wonder they call Dr. Dixon New York's finest shrink. I owe him a bottle of scotch or two.

Just as I'm about to give Mary my address, she smirks, but the sight has me kicking myself for ever listening to that prissy ass pussy. "I would rather flunk than owe you a favor, because I know it'll come back to bite me in the ass."

"No strings." It's out before I can stop myself, and what's more surprising is that I actually mean it, and I didn't comment about her fine, apricot shaped behind.

She laughs sarcastically. "There's no such thing with you. If I thought I could enter your home without being visually molested, then I would maybe contemplate it. But I don't want to dangle a carrot in front of a very horny, sex-starved donkey. That would be mean," she adds smartly.

"Excuse me?" I need her to draw me a diagram because I can't move on from the words carrot, dangle, and sex.

She radiates complete confidence as she accurately declares, "You want what you can't have."

My mouth pops open for so many reasons, but at the forefront is the fact she thinks I'm some desperado, peeping into her window at night, desperate for her to throw me a freaking bone. I'll have her know I'm not short of female attention. Yes, they may not be who I want, but I'm not sitting at home, knitting a fucking scarf for my cock.

And what's with this wanting what I can't have? That's a little presumptuous, no matter how true it may be.

She obviously thinks I can't control myself when it comes to her, which is a safe assumption to make given my track record, but regardless, she's just taken a giant Cleveland Steamer on my ego. My survival instinct kicks in and my pride gets jacked up to testosterone overload. "Don't flatter yourself, sweetheart."

"It's true, isn't it?"

The more she speaks, the more incensed I become, because although she's right, no one likes their faces rubbed in their failures, and that's what Mary Mitts is—my failure. I don't know how to impress her because I've never wanted to impress a girl before. But with Mary, I want the whole hog.

But as she stares at me with that cocky smile plastered on her supple lips, my bruised ego takes charge and decides to give Miss Mitts a taste of what she's missing.

Strolling toward her with no real hurry to my step, I watch as she stands her ground, refusing to be intimidated. Her confidence drives me on. I stop a hair's breadth away.

No words are spoken, but our silence speaks volumes. I make no secret of the fact that I'm combing over every inch of her flesh, admiring what I see. I linger on her swelling chest, which rises and falls with every raspy breath she takes.

If I were a sentimental fool, I could talk myself into believing that she is affected by me as I am by her, but I'm a realist. Finch and Dixon's theory is as wrong as wrong can be and it was nice living in a fantasyland for a while, but now it's time to put this puppy to bed.

Completely ignoring her personal space, I lower my face to hers, her strawberry scented breath bathing my cheeks with its sweetness. I want a taste, but I can't. She's made her feelings perfectly clear, and now it's time for me to do the same.

With a coiled smirk, I very plainly state, "It may be true, but we both know…you couldn't handle me. I would make you beg until your throat was raw, and the only reprieve would be you on hands and knees, sucking my cock to soothe your burn."

Her eyes widen before the tip of her pink tongue shoots out to lick her sudden dry lips. "I don't beg. Ever," she states with conviction, but it's a challenge.

Game on.

Smirking, I never break eye contact, pinning her beneath my unforgiving stare. "That's because all the little boys you've fucked in the past wouldn't know how to handle a livewire like you. All this delicious, milky flesh"—I risk losing a finger as I run my pointer along the slope of her soft neck—"is ripe for the picking. It's such a damn shame you don't beg, because Shortcake, you'd enjoy it as much as me."

And just like that, a nickname is born.

"Shortcake?" she asks, her bravado dimming. I can't stop myself and circle over her pulse. It's strong, flighty, and quickened.

"Yes." Seeing as I didn't lose a finger, I decide to test my luck and lean in close, inhaling deeply. She smells unlike anything I've ever inhaled before. She's an untapped fragrance and I'd do anything to lose myself in her perfume. My tastebuds salivate, desperate for one taste. "You smell like strawberries and cream."

Her intake of breath leaves me with more than a little wood, but I quash down the urge to stake my claim. "Is this the mo-moment I'm supposed drop to my knees and beg you to f-fuck me into tomorrow?" Her falter highlights my win because she can deny it all she wants, but she's turned on.

Lifting my chin, I almost come in my pants, because my lips are mere inches from Mary's. Her full mouth parts and it takes every shred of self-control not to dive inside and drown. "My schedule is booked solid until next week, but I can let you know if a vacancy opens up."

"Cocky much?" she retaliates, but it's weak. Her cheeks blush a dusty pink and the sight is akin to a sucker punch straight through my chest.

"Wouldn't you like to know?" I counter with a wink.

I can see her big, bold bravado slip into place because Mary doesn't like to be undermined. "Save your breath for when you have to blow up your girlfriend tonight."

Points for creativity, but it leaves me with an even bigger hard on. "Bye, Shortcake. As always, the pleasure is all mine." Yes, that's a complete double-edged sword, and if she wasn't such a hardass, she could be on my sword, but it appears she much prefers to march to the motto: glass, or sex life half full.

I walk past her, ignoring the stabbing of betrayal, because regardless of how that conversation ended a little pear-shaped, it was a conversation nonetheless. It was progress. I have no idea what happens now, but I can ponder life mysteries over a glass of scotch.

On my hunt for some booze, I charge straight into Keira, who is clearly anxious to leave this train wreck behind. "Sorry, I was just leaving." She won't look at me, not that I can blame her.

"How are you getting back?" I ask, my hand still attached to her bicep.

"I called a cab." When she finally makes eye contact, I feel like I clubbed a baby seal to death. It's not her fault I'm the world's shittiest date.

Whether it's my very vivid imagination, or wishful thinking that Mary is currently eyeballing the bejesus out of me I'll never know, but I decide to give her a teaser to how most of my nights start and finish.

"Don't be silly. I'll drive you."

When she bites her lip, peering over my shoulder, I can't help but smile. "Okay."

Winning has never felt this good.

Six

Hunter

The car ride back to the office wasn't as uncomfortable as I'd thought it would be. Keira reiterated how much fun she had, which had me wondering if she was just being polite, or maybe she needs to get out more.

Her asshole boss texted her like five hundred times, barking orders at her because he obviously thinks she has nothing better to do on a Saturday night than be at his beck and call. I was going to wait in the car, but decided to head up with her so I can stalk some overseas stocks.

I'm sitting at my desk, wondering where a damn pen is because I can't even remember the last time I saw the surface. Come to think of it, I can't even remember what color it is. My office is not anal retentive like Dixon's because I like a little disorder.

It has all the essentials— a bathroom, a computer, and a bottle of whiskey. It's all I need.

My thoughts drift back to Mary and how I happily offered up my home and office for her to redecorate without a second thought. I usually don't like anyone in my space and avoid taking women back to my apartment like the plague. But with Mary, I wanted her here.

The thought of her making my things hers has me rubbing my chest, as I'm hit with a bout of indigestion. This woman is hazardous to my health.

My cell chiming is a welcomed distraction. Tossing handfuls of paperwork over my shoulder, I find it buried beneath last Tuesday's New York Times.

You better be dropping the chameleon home. Dixon really isn't one for small talk when it comes to Keira. I refuse to entertain the notion that she is anything like the she-devil.

I was thinking of taking her out for hot cocoa first. I can't help myself.

Home.

Jesus H. Christ. I can hear his panties twisting in a knot from here.

Okay, Dad. Wanna tuck me in, too? Leaning back in my seat, I await his reply, because this can go all night.

Stop fucking around. And I mean that LITERALLY.

A gruff laugh escapes me. *You're so sexy when you get all riled up.*

I get the middle finger icon in response.

Dixon has nothing to worry about. I have no intention of fucking around with Keira. She's a nice girl, but I can't shake Mary's heightened response from my brain. Her rose-kissed cheeks, the flutter of her pulse, the hypnotic sway of her rising chest as she tried to keep her cool assaults my senses—I have no idea how I'm supposed to rid this woman from my system. Images of Crocodile Dundee showing her his 'shrimp on the barbie' has me snapping a pencil in half.

I don't have a choice because regardless of what I want, she's made her feelings perfectly clear time and time again. I don't know what tonight was, but there's no point crying over spilled milk. I sigh at the analogy because there's just too many innuendos which will make me feel worse.

"Sorry that took so long."

Keira's sweet voice has me quickly turning my phone off, afraid Dixon will be able to smell her in my office otherwise. When I glance upward, I'm surprised to see two crystal tumblers with an amber liquid inside.

Raising both glasses, she smirks. "Macallan 55." She knows good whiskey. The thought of drinking Gail's $12,500 bottle of scotch is too good to pass up, so I welcome her into my office.

She saunters in, placing the tumbler onto my mountain of paperwork. The smooth liquor mixes with her unique fragrance, a surprisingly delectable flavor. "I think I'm done," she says, flopping into the leather seat opposite me. "He wanted notes on Redleaf Holdings."

Reaching for my scotch, I scoff, unimpressed. "China's biggest real estate firm wants nothing to do with that asshole. I know that for a fact."

Gail has had a hard on for this company for months. He's of the belief that they're his meal ticket and he's gonna close a deal with them at any moment. Too bad, nimrod, 'cause little does he know, they only play with the big boys like me.

Keira crosses her supple legs, leaning back as she sips her drink. "He's pretty certain he's in. These notes are his pitch to Mr. Yeong, who he's having a phone conference with next week."

"He can pitch all he wants, he has no chance." I take a winner's sip from my scotch, the burn even more victorious now.

"Why not?" she asks, her bouncing high heel a hypnotizing pendulum.

Why not is the fact I know something no one else knows. Mr. Yeong is a massive Yankees fan, go figure. We made a deal over pork dumplings and a bottle of Baijiu the last time he was in town. If I could deliver him Babe Ruth's 1923 World Series Pocket Watch, then he would sell me his soul.

This was as good as a done deal, or so I thought. At the time, I didn't know this was ranked as one of the top ten most expensive pieces of Yankees memorabilia. It sold at auction for a measly 700,000 big ones, and although he doesn't expect me to buy it, he does expect me to find and bribe the owner, so they'll deliver me the goods.

I've searched high and low, but this anonymous buyer sure as shit likes to remain incognito. But giving up is for pussies. Dixon is on the case, and so is my P.I. This is in the bag, but until then, no one can find out about it.

Kiera is waiting for an answer, but I won't let a pretty face get the better of me. Tapping my pointer against the crystal and peering at her over the rim, I smirk. "I'd tell you…but then I'd have to kill you."

She purses her lips, drawing attention to the fact she's applied a fresh coat of lipstick. The color is red. The air suddenly changes and a palpable hum whips around me. Oh, brother.

"Are you sure you don't need an assistant?" Just as I'm about to tell her I work alone, she purrs something out of left field. "I'm sure you could teach me a thing…or two."

I take a moment to process what she just said because I'm sure sweet, innocent Keira did not mean that in a sexual manner. It's just my sex-starved mind up to no good again after my encounter with Shortcake.

"Me and people"—I make a pained face, bringing both pointers together—"we don't usually go well together." Which is true. I made my last assistant cry because for her birthday, I took her out to my most favorite restaurant in Manhattan—Pablo's Steakhouse. At the time, I thought I was winning at this whole boss business, but when she broke down and chanted 'meat is murder' at the top of her lungs because I failed to remember that she was a vegan, I knew I was better off a lone wolf.

My bad, considering she worked for me for eight months. That solved the question to why my lunches tasted like birdseed.

For the next month, I received such considerate gifts in the mail— brains, innards, even a suit…made of meat. For someone who claimed to be a vegan, she sure as shit knew her cuts of meat.

So, I learned my lesson because people…are crazy.

Keira sips her drink, leaving a fire engine red lipstick stain on her glass. I know this because she slinks forward, placing the tumbler on the edge of my desk.

Pinning me with the eyes of the devil, she smirks. "I'm good at taking orders."

Okay, back up. What in the holy hell does that mean?

I scold my cock, which is bathing in a vat of Artisan, my go-to fragrance because this cologne is known by another name, and that name is sure fuck.

Down boy.

No, this can't be right. I'm reading into this, way into this because when she rises slowly and rounds my desk, there is no way her nipples are so hard that they are bursting against her dress and could cut through glass. It's an optical illusion and I'm clearly seeing things.

And there is no doubt I'm hallucinating when she comes to rest by my seat, clutching the high back and spinning me forcefully around to face her. But the fact she almost gave me whiplash confirms that this isn't a hallucination. This is really happening, and she is really reaching behind her neck to unfasten the button and…oh, dios mío!

I blink. Then I blink again, hoping that maybe this is it, I've really lost it this time. But when I scrub at my eyeballs and the image of Keira standing before me, very topless, is clearer than the massive boner I'm sporting, I know things are about to turn nasty.

She confirms my suspicions when she begins touching herself, fondling those perky, more than a handful breasts. She tugs at her pink nipples, circling her areola while I almost pass out from lack of O2. What is happening? Have I skipped a chapter?

Biting her lip, she lets out a low sated moan while I will myself to look away, but god damn, the force is strong with this one. I am Obi-Wan Kenobi, a Jedi Master, and will not give in to temptation…says no one ever.

This is wrong and I need to stop this before it gets out of hand…oh, sweet Jesus, her hand is now working its way to her mouth as her lips part like the Red Sea and she sucks on her finger. Make that two. It's like a disappearing act. Now you see it, now it's gone…down her throat as she sucks on them like a popsicle made of crack.

I'm pretty certain I resemble a deer in the headlights because I can't stop looking a Keira's headlights.

"Wh-what are you doing?" I stupidly ask just in case Keira's heritage is Norwegian and this is how they say hello.

She removes her wet fingers from her mouth with a pop. "What does it look like I'm doing?" She returns to rubbing over her tits in a circular motion, eyeing me as I eye fuck the hell out of her. Her rosy nipples pucker further from the wetness slathered on her fingertips.

"Checking for loose change?" I offer, completely under her spell.

Her lips curve into a sultry smile before she places her monster pumps between my splayed legs. I should be downright ashamed. I could poke out her eye with what's currently protruding from my pants, but my pride checked out about two minutes ago.

"I've dreamt of this…" she reveals, inching the tip of her stiletto closer to my groin. I shrink away, but it's useless. Where am I going to go? She's a woman on a mission and she makes her mission clear when she makes contact with my hard on.

It's like a slap to my balls and I jump up, almost knocking her to the floor. "Keira, stop this, you're drunk." Lame as lame comes, considering she was drinking water all night, but I need her to see reason.

When she lunges for me, I use the chair as a barricade, my only saving grace from going back on an oath which is slowly looking like a dog's breakfast. It doesn't deter her in the slightest however. If anything, her eyes ignite in challenge.

"I've dreamt of you bending me over this desk and eating me out…with a spoon."

Spoiler alert! Here lies Hunter O'Shea. He lived a simple life. He died of complications…like underestimating a blue-eyed devil with a wicked tongue.

The leather creaks beneath my fingers as I clutch the top of the seat, holding on for dear life before I'm tempted to hold onto something else. I need to propel this chair forward and knock her out cold. I need to run from this room and scream for Tom Cruise to save me.

"Keira, I'm…" Ready when you are? But go with, "Flattered that you'd want to…dine with me, but this can't happen. Office romances can get messy. We'd have to see one another every day, and well, I'd never be able to look at my desk or a spoon the same way."

"Who said I want romance?"

My jaw drops because…I can't even single it down to one reason. I'm being awfully presumptuous. Women can live it up just as much as us men do, and if Keira wants to do, then do she will.

"Don't look so surprised." Her voice drops an octave.

"You're not the only one with a dirty mouth."

This is too much. It's what every perverted man's dreams are made of, but Dixon's words of warning decide to reproach me— a complete mood killer. "It's not a what, but rather a who."

But looking at Keira, I refuse to believe that he's right. Why can't this hot, sweet—scrap that—sexy woman, want me, no strings attached?

I know this is wrong, and I know I better stock up on sunblock 'cause I'm riding the bus straight to hell, but I suddenly don't care. We're both consenting adults. Actually, I better make sure.

"How old are you?" I manage to push out between clenched teeth.

"Twenty-one," she replies, her peppy tits bouncing in corroboration. "Stop overthinking it. I want you." She lasers in on my wood. "You clearly want me. What's the problem? Is it the redhead?"

And this is the time my good sense should tap me on the shoulder and call it a night. It was fun while it lasted, but now it's time to be the grown up before Kiera does something she's sure to regret.

But the mere mention of Mary and her rejection, and her plus one who gargles balls for brunch has my inner caveman punching me in the solar plexus and scolding me for turning into Finch. Mary doesn't want me, but Keira does. Even though she's not who I want, she's not a poor substitute either.

She said she doesn't want romance and this is what I do best—sex without strings. Dixon, your words of wisdom can board the Disney Cruise Line and sail the fuck away.

"What do you want?" I ask, ensuring we're on the same

page.

"Whatever you want to give," she hoarsely replies. The top half of her dress is bunched up around her waist, so her pussy is out of sight, which is probably a good thing.

Her tits are fucking glorious, and all I want to do is bury my face between them and go to town. Keira reads my train of thought because she sidesteps the chair, walking toward me as she would a rabid dog. "You want to touch them?" she poses, cupping both and squeezing lightly. I grunt in response. "You want to fuck them? Put that big cock between them and come all over me?"

I'm getting too old for this shit, because her clichéd dirty talk does nothing for me. "Sweetheart…" I finally release the chair and push it off to the side. Nothing separates us and she's in so much fucking trouble. "That's for amateurs. All the little boys you've been with wouldn't know their dick from the end of their nose. This is your final warning to back out now, because once we start, there's no getting off this ride."

Her chest rises and falls. "Show me what you got."

Challenge accepted.

Closing the distance between us, I stop when she's almost pressed to my chest. I know what she's expecting. She thinks I'm going to swoop in and kiss her like some hero out of a Mills and Boon novel. But it's been well established that I don't kiss, nor am I a hero.

As expected, even with her heels, she doesn't reach my lips, so she stands on tippy toes to invade my personal space. My hand shoots out, a knee jerk reaction, and I fist the back of her hair. She gasps, my forcefulness catching her off guard. "I don't kiss on the lips," I very matter-of-factly state.

Her hair feels like silk beneath my fingers and I have the urge to tug on it harder because I know she can handle it. When I do, she groans and arches her neck backward, the slender, creamy column all mine to devour.

Unable to help myself, I lower my chin and run my nose along the length of her neckline. She smells sweet, but my appetite raises a limp shoulder because it craves strawberries and cream. Frustrated with my constant need to compare everything to her, I dive forward and bite over her galloping pulse. I'm not gentle, but I warned her, and besides, we're way past formalities.

With my hand still threaded through her tresses, I suckle at her flesh, determined to lose myself just this once. Her moans express her enjoyment, but my dick, even though interested, knows this will be a repeat of the past few performances with no encore to follow.

Her nipples are pert, pointing up toward the heavens, surrendering to a night of empty promises. She cups one breast, while with the other hand, she works her way under her short hemline. Even though she's wearing stockings, it's fairly obvious that makes no difference as she commences to get herself off.

Such an impatient little thing. This should be fun.

When I tongue my way upward and kiss over the sensitive spot just behind the ear, she screams. Works every time. "Do you kiss on the lips…?"

"I told you, I don't kiss on…"

But she cuts me off. "Not those lips."

I'm beginning to like Keira's dirty mouth all the more. "I don't kiss…I fucking own and devour." She writhes in my grip, her breathing mounting until she's a hot, heaving mess.

Finally giving in to her not so subtle demands, I fondle her breast, flicking my pointer against her nipple. Her skin breaks out into goose bumps and her red lips part in ecstasy. "Be gentle with me, Hunter…I'm a virgin." I slam on the brakes, needing a minute, or maybe two, to process what she just shared.

Yes, she is sweet, innocent, and virginal, but I didn't think she was an actual virgin.

Slap me in a red suit and call me Saint Nick because all my Christmases have just come at once. The way she was talking, I would not have guessed that, but I suppose tonight has been a night of the unexpected. As much as I'd love to be the first man to plant my flag on her moon, I wouldn't do that to her. She deserves a nice guy and that guy ain't me.

Releasing my hold in her hair, she hums in relief, but quickly goes to work on my belt buckle. I still her fumbling fingers. "How about you learn how to walk before you run."

"How about you let nature take its course and fuck me," she counters, slapping my hand away so she can finish the job. Her vulgarity strokes my inner barbarian, but I suddenly don't want to fuck 'cause the thought of punching in her V-card at work kind of ruins the mood.

My dick is furious at me, demanding to be emancipated, and to find someone worthy of his time.

"Keira…" I tsk, gripping her chin between my thumb and pointer. "I plan to fuck you…just not with my cock." It's the perfect derailment. Win-win.

A gasp leaves her before I grip her bicep, spin her around, and push her onto my desk, tits first. I've caught her off guard, so when I yank up the hem of her dress and palm her firm ass, I know she's seconds away from melting into a puddle of the good stuff.

As I rip off her stockings, the same fate destined for her thong, I wonder if maybe it'll be different this time. I suppose I won't know if I don't try.

Rubbing my hard on over her ass, I lean forward and whisper, "So…you got that spoon?"

Seven

Hunter

The next morning I wake, primed on burning down my apartment and the ringing cell which sits on my bedside dresser.

My dick hums in satisfaction, not bothered in the slightest. After receiving a hummer sent from the blow job gods, he would happily roast in hell. And that's where I'll end up after what happened last night.

Groaning, I reach for the spare pillow and crush it over my face. I wonder if anyone has managed to suffocate themselves to death. I'll happily volunteer to try because it'll erase the images of me eating Keira out before she came all over my face.

I thought we were done, but then she dropped to her knees, ripped off my pants, and sucked on my dick until I cried mercy and saw stars. For a virgin, she sure as shit knows her way around. But I don't judge. Glass houses and all that jazz…

Once I stopped weeping for my mom to save me from the

jaws of life, I zipped up my pants and took Keira home. She chatted in the car like five minutes prior, we weren't all up in each other's business. Maybe this casual sex thing can be done.

So why was that aching void still lingering around like a bad smell?

I came home, showered, and crawled into bed. And here I was planning on staying for a long time to come if not for the infernal ringing of my fucking phone, which is sounding once again.

Throwing the pillow against the wall, I sit upright, brushing the snarled hair from my face. Whoever this caller is, I'm going to find them, rip off their hands, and wear them as a hat. The moment I reach for my cell, it stops ringing. So fucking typical.

My screen is lit up with fifteen missed calls and a bunch of nonsensical texts from Dixon.

```
Wake the fuck up!
Are you wearing pants?
For the love of god, please put on pants.
```

This is the general gist of what kind of crazy talk I'm dealing with.

When the phone rings once again, I have the urge to throw it out the window, but don't. "No, I'm not wearing pants, for your information. And if this is your attempt at phone sex, don't give up your day job."

"Shut the hell up and listen." He's so cranky in the morning.

"Hello to you, too." I yawn, in desperate need of an Irish coffee, preferably just the Irish portion. "No, I didn't sleep with her, if that's why you're calling at"—I look down at my imaginary watch—"stupid o'clock. And by the way, you do realize it's Sunday morning, as in a day of rest, as in fuck the fuck off."

"Hunter…"

He doesn't get to finish whatever spiel I was in for as it appears everyone is on crazy pills because someone is at my door. "Oh, for the love of camel piss, who the hell is that?" I remove the phone from my ear to ensure I'm not hearing things.

When the bell sounds once again, this time however in a long, continuous drone, I kick off the blankets ready to murder whoever won't remove their finger from my buzzer. "Dixon, if this is you at my door, I swear to god I'm going to burn you alive."

"Would you stop talking already and put on pants…"

Mid-stride to my bedroom door, I realize I am butt naked, and had no qualms answering the door this way, considering whoever is at my door is not staying. But I suppose the big man is right. Wouldn't want my ninety-five-year-old neighbor to keel over and call it a day if she's the one at my door.

Hunting through my drawers, I slip into a pair of CK boxer briefs and that's it. Charging through my apartment with Dixon still on the line, I bark, "Where's the fire? I know you love me and miss me terribly, but these stalker phone calls couldn't wait until after breakfast?"

"I'm calling to warn you that…"

"That you're the world's most annoying friend who has nothing better to do on a Sunday morning?" I offer as I stampede through my living room, three steps away from committing murder. "You better cherish that motherfucking finger, asshole, because I'm about to rip it off and shove it so far up your ass your—" The moment I yank open the door, my words die in a tangled heap and I forget how to speak.

If I knew sign language, I would be signing holy fucking shit a brick fuck me dead and call me Elvis because Mary is standing at my door. Not the Virgin Mary, as that's a lot more plausible than Mary Mitts, but it's her. She's here, on my doorstep, with her finger pressed to my doorbell.

"I'm calling to warn you that Mary is on her way over," Dixon concludes, his tone laced with complete hilarity.

"This is information that would have been helpful five seconds ago, genius," I wheeze, thankful my speech has returned.

The doorbell dies in a strangled cough when Mary's finger slips from the button. Her usual rosy complexion is suddenly set alight when she scans me from head to toe. Oh, for fuck's sake, the indigestion returns. I rub a circle over my chest, and am surprised when Mary follows the movement, her glossy lips parted. Is she unwell?

"Are you going to stand around like a primate? Invite her in," a voice which sounds an awful lot like Dixon demands. That's when I realize it is Dix and that I'm standing at my front door, in my underwear, with my cell pressed to my ear as I visually consume the hottest woman on earth.

I go against Dixon's suggestion because I've seen Buffy, I know what happens when you invite the pretty ones into your home. "What are you doing?"

"Smooth, Hunt, real smooth." Dixon's running commentary can go eat a dick.

Licking her lips, she appears to remember that she's here voluntarily and clears her throat once. "You invited me, remember? Or did you suffer short term memory loss overnight?"

Scratching my head, I wonder if maybe Keira's pussy was a black hole and she sucked me straight into the twilight zone. "I do remember, but I also remember you telling me you'd rather poke a grizzly bear in the ass with a short stick than come anywhere near my home."

Dixon exhales loudly.

"Well, I'm desperate," she states, which opens up a whole different can of worms. She closes her eyes for a split second, realizing her poor choice of words.

Every part of my body inflates, so ready for the challenge. "Shortcake, I'm flattered…"

"Oh my god, just forget it." She goes to turn, which is like a swift karate chop to my throat.

Both Dixon and I yell, "Stop!" at the same time. I should hang up, but he's here for moral support, and god knows I need it, because I'm wading in shark-infested waters. I thank the angels above when she doesn't punch me in the nuts and stays rooted to the spot.

Her emerald eyes hold me prisoner as she waits for me to make the first move. "Please, come in." I stand back, sweeping my hand toward my home.

She narrows her eyes, waiting for a punchline, or catch, but none follow. I'm too tongue-tied to even remember my own name. After a slight pause, she nods and walks past me. The polite thing to do would be to move out of the doorway so she can enter, but polite and me have never really seen eye to eye.

She doesn't allow my hulking frame to intimidate her and strolls past me, her arm brushing my bare chest. Sweet Jesus and all that's holy. I have seen the light and her name is Mary Shortcake Mitts. From a single touch, my body goes into overdrive and my cock is poised and raring to go. She smells fucking delicious. My mouth actually waters and I quickly dab at my chin to ensure I'm not salivating.

She's wearing skinny jeans, Chucks, and a baby pink knitted sweater which has her fiery red waves coming to life. Her ass is absolute perfection, bound compactly in the tight denim. When she turns back around from inspecting my living room, I flick my gaze upward, pretending I was not checking her out.

"Nice home."

"Thanks." I refrain from saying nice ass. See, I'm learning.

When she clears her throat again and tugs at the diamond stud in her ear, I realize she's finding this as uncomfortable as I am. "I really could use your help, and as much as I hate admitting that, I need you. Your home," she quickly corrects as I'm on the cusp of doing a victory dance around my coffee table.

"Sure, no problem. What do I have to do?" I ask, the phone hanging limply by my side. Dixon is probably stuffing his face full of popcorn, eagerly awaiting to see how this unfolds.

"Nothing really. Just allow me to take over your home and office for the next two months. You won't even know I'm here." She attempts to grin, but it fades as she swallows hard.

That's very fucking unlikely, but I nod. "Okay, sounds easy enough." She rubs her hands together as if she's suddenly nervous that I agreed.

Cocking my head to the side, I notice she's a lot more twitchy and fidgety than I've ever seen her. She's usually as cool as a cucumber, but her flushed cheeks are rosier than usual.

What is up with that?

"Awesome, so, um, did you want to get dressed or something while I get started?" She's pinning me with those drop dead gorgeous eyes, but when she averts her attention downward and then back up again, I actually get winded.

Is she checking me out? No, that's not possible. She'd rather dig out her eyeballs with an ice cream scoop than look at me of her own accord.

Running a hand back and forth over my scalp, mussing up my hair, I nod. Her interest floats to my arm, or more specifically, my bicep. I tilt my chin, peering up at my bowed arm, with my hand still resting atop my head.

When she becomes aware of me attempting to decode what the hell is the matter with her, she literally takes a step backward and fumbles with her backpack straps as she removes it from her shoulders. "I haven't got all day. Go get dressed before I throw up my bagel."

Ah, there she is. The Mary we all know and lov…okay, now this is just getting weird.

What I once thought, or hoped was desire, I now know was repulsion because Mary will always look at me like the Hunchback of Notre Dame. It doesn't matter that I'm in peak shape, run five miles a day, and am not a bad looking dude, I just don't get her whistle wet.

Not interested in being a sideshow freak any longer, I leave her to comb through her things and ransack my home while I shower and sing "Beautiful" by Christina Aguilera to my reflection.

I close my bedroom, pressing the phone to my ear. "Well, I would say she's not a morning person, but that was her being friendly."

"You really are an idiot," Dixon says with a laugh. "What was with all the long pauses?"

He heard, or rather didn't hear it too? Interesting.

Opening my drawers, I pull out a clean t-shirt and some socks. "I don't know. She was looking at me funny."

"Were you standing at full salute?"

I pause from rummaging through my underwear drawer. "I should be offended, but I'm not. And the answer to your question is no. I don't think," I add as a sidenote.

"Regardless, this is your opportunity to show her what a great guy you are."

"You realize you're talking to me and not Finch, right?" I close the drawer and search for a pair of jeans.

"Hunt…just talk to her."

"What am I supposed to say?" I ask in all seriousness, because if there is a handbook, I need to do some serious cramming.

"I don't fucking know. Ask her about her course. Or if she likes Schnauzers or not."

I scrunch up my face. "She likes Schnauzers?"

Dixon groans. "I don't know. The question was rhetorical."

"Oh right. Shit. I need you to feed me lines through an earpiece. I'm going to crumble." Rubbing the perspiration beads from my brow, I know this is a taste of what's to come.

"You'll be fine. You're already a changed man." When I wait for him to elaborate, he explains like I'm Tweedledee. "You didn't sleep with Keira."

And he's Tweedledum. "Well…" I rub the back of my neck.

"For fuck's sake. You're going to give me an ulcer."

I bite back my smirk. "I didn't fuck her."

"Oh, thank the lord."

"…with my cock," I reveal before he gets too excited and nominates me for a Nobel Peace Prize. "I'm a giver, Dixon. You know this."

"No, you're an asshole. How did this happen?"

"Don't tell me it's been that long you need me to draw you a diagram," I reply, thoroughly amused.

"I don't know why I bother." He sighs.

Needing to cut this conversation short because Mary is just outside my door, I enlighten him. "I tried to fight her off, I know you don't believe me, but it's true. Then she made reference to her pussy and me eating it out with a spoon, and then one thing led to another and I was bending her over my desk. She wanted me to fuck her, but she's a virgin, a fucking virgin, and I may be a bastard, but I'm not a fucking bastard. So I blew her, she blew me. All in all, a pretty low key Saturday night." Only then do I take a breath.

"She's a virgin?" Dixon questions suspiciously. "But yet she was fine with you feasting on her kitty like a fucking key lime pie before she dropped to her knees and sucked you off like it was no biggie?"

"Language," I playfully scold. "But yes, that's about it in a nutshell. Speaking of nuts…holy shit."

Dixon isn't interested is me relaying a step-by-step account of my sexscapades. "Dude, something isn't right. Remember what happened when someone was bent over my desk?" I can hear him reaching for a sick bag from over here.

"Yeah, she double clicked her own mouse. So what?"

"I just don't like this."

Rolling my eyes, I make my way into my en-suite. "I made it perfectly clear I wasn't interested in an office romance. And neither is she."

"That logic is one of a dumbass, especially if she really is a virgin."

"Now you're doubting her virginity. You have serious trust issues. Go hug a teddy bear."

"It's your funeral," Dixon says, the fight fading for now.

Stripping down to my birthday suit, I smirk. "You'll have to speak up, I'm naked."

"And on that note, I have to go find my fiancée to burn that image from my mind. Don't forget your pants." The line goes dead.

Tossing my cell onto the basin, I turn on the shower and wait for it to warm up. Dixon has no idea what he's talking about. Yes, Keira surprised me last night with her unexpected sexual aggression, but everything is kosher. There wasn't an ounce of embarrassment in the air once the deed was done, and she didn't even drop a 'see you at work on Monday.'

As I step into my glass shower and stand under the spray, I begin to wonder if maybe there is a problem with this picture. Was I not memorable enough for her?

Groaning, I reach for the shampoo and quash such soppy bullshit from my mind. This is just Dixon's touchy feely crap messing with my head, that's all. We had casual sex—well, oral sex. Just because she's not banging down my door and getting a tattoo to commemorate our union doesn't mean something is askew. Whatever happens tomorrow, I'll deal.

Washing the shampoo from my hair, I condition and then reach for the soap. My body is already heightened thanks to

Mary being feet away, so when I wash over my semi, there's no guessing what happens next.

The girl who has been my go to for months is in the next room. That thought has my cock straining and I grunt at the force. This would be the time I rub one out, but I suddenly feel like a vile pervert for even considering it.

My dick twitches, a silent demand I stop procrastinating and get the job done, but I just…can't. It feels wrong for some reason and I don't know why. There is no doubt I'm turned on by her, so why can't I get this show on the road?

Slamming my fist to the wall, I lean my forehead to the tile, allowing the water to cascade down the back of my neck. I'm frustrated, not just sexually, but inside as well. I've had no qualms jerking off to her before, so why the sudden change of heart?

The stupid whimsical center in question does some sort of flip flop in my chest. I put an end to such nonsense by thumping over it once, kickstarting some sense into it. This hard on isn't going anywhere, so I switch the faucet to cold and think about The Golden Girls.

Five minutes later, and suffering a mild case of hypothermia, I dry off and dress. I don't bother styling my hair, but instead run my fingers through it. Splashing on some cologne, I'm ready to face the storm.

Mary has been left unsupervised for far too long and I won't lie, I'm a little scared, as I have no idea what I'm walking into. My bare feet pad across the carpet as I amble down the hallway and take a right to enter the living room.

When I round the corner, I stop dead in my tracks, because what I'm greeted with requires my undivided attention. Mary is stooped over, measuring tape in hand, as she looks from left to right, as if attempting to calculate the measurement in her head. What is heart stopping, however, is the fact she's bent over, ass in the air.

I can't help myself and lean against the doorjamb, admiring the view. Her apricot-shaped behind is just too much. I've always been an ass man, but this takes my obsession to a whole different level. Arms and ankles crossed, I angle my head to the side, needing to view this marvel from every viewpoint there is.

Her long hair is flipped forward, all wild and ruffled, just how I'm feeling right now. If this is what I'm in for, for the next two months, I just may die one happy man. She mumbles something under her breath. It sure sounds a lot like she's giving someone an earful, but there is no one in the room other than me.

Maybe she's gathering ammo, because god knows the next two months are going to be interesting. No time like the present, I suppose. "You really should bend your knees. Unless it's your intention to look like Quasimodo."

She springs upward like a pogo stick on the juice. Turning over her shoulder, she glares at me, while I don't bother moving from my perch. I'm most comfortable seeing her jacked off. "It's my intention to get in and out as soon as possible. Where's your bedroom?"

If only those words were spoken in an entirely different manner, but never mind, it's still an open door. "If this is your plan to seduce me, let me tell you…it's working. I don't need hearts and roses. Good ol' fashioned dirty talk works wonders." She rolls those beautiful eyes and turns around.

With hands on hips, she scans me from head to toe. She's

probably thankful I'm clothed. She lingers on my hair, which has me wondering if maybe a bird has perched in it from the time I left the bathroom. It needs a cut. I self-consciously run my fingers through it and wonder what's come over her when her cheeks turn a brighter pink. Maybe she smoked some crack before coming here. It would explain her erratic behavior.

"Follow me," I say, pushing off the doorway.

Her soft footsteps behind me reveal she's following, so I lead the way, not making a big deal over the fact Mary is stepping foot inside my bedroom of her own volition. If I knew she'd want to scope out my whole apartment, I'd have tidied up a bit, but too late now. She can see this untamed beast in his natural habitat.

I enter my room, the cologne still lingering in the air. At least it smells good, because it sure as shit looks like a bomb has exploded inside. I'm not neat by nature. Clean yes, but I just don't have time to iron and roll my socks into bunny ears.

I step off to the side, allowing Mary to pass me and do her thing. What I hear however, is the unmistakable sound of a rubber glove snapping into place. She smirks when I resemble Scooby-Doo. "If this is a prostate exam…don't be afraid to use two fingers." Mary coughs back a laugh, but soon recovers.

She studies the room, slipping on the other blue latex glove. When her gaze lands on my king size bed, she curls her lip in aversion. "Mind if I take a look around?" I'm surprised she asked.

Sweeping my hand outward, I bow gallantly. As she walks to the far wall and unsnaps her measuring tape, I can't help but ask, "What are the gloves for?"

She scoffs. "Are you serious? I don't know what I'll find in here and where it's been." On cue, she lifts a red lacy thong from the corner of my room with the end of her tape. She flings it at me, disgusted.

I dodge the flying projectile, wondering who they belong to. "Hey, don't judge. I look good in red."

"Whatever happens in your private life is none of my business. If you choose to date insecure airheads with daddy issues, then kudos to you."

I fake horror. "I'll have you know, I don't date. Get your facts right." She ignores my quip and instead goes to work measuring my room.

I stand out of the way, not wanting to bother a genius at work, because that's what she is. I'm utterly entranced by her attention to detail and how she uses her small hands as a viewfinder. I don't know what she's seeing through her linked fingers, but when she stands in the middle of the room, spinning from left to right, it's like she's looking into the future.

Sighing in thought, she walks over to my window and splits the curtains in half. The bright sunlight streams in. While I'm convinced I'm melting, Mary kicks off her sneakers and jumps onto my bed. Now I'm certain she smoked crack.

"Do you want to have a pillow fight?" I ask, hooking my thumb toward the door. "If you do, there's a hot blonde just down the hall…" Images of Mary and my neighbor dancing around in their underwear flood my brain. Mary thrusts out her palm, warning me to stop.

"I'll admit, you've surprised me."

"Oh, I know. I'm just full of surprises." I polish my fingernails on my t-shirt.

"You're full of something," she mumbles. "I wasn't expecting well, this." Sweeping her hand toward my room, she nods, impressed.

"What were you expecting? Lava lamps, foosball, and pictures of naked ladies taped to the walls?" When she doesn't reply, I can't help but laugh.

"This entire space has so much potential. The artwork in your living room, local artist?"

She's referring to the two charcoal sketches I bought from a gallery downtown. "Yes, they caught my eye the moment I walked past the window. I backtracked because I needed them hanging on my walls." The first is of a woman, back turned as she sits in a chair, tying up her hair. A burst of light comes in from the top corner, bringing the sketch to life. "The slope of the woman's neck and the definition to her slender arms has mesmerized me for countless hours. I've sat in my La-Z-Boy, staring at the image, wondering just who this woman was. There is an underlying sadness to her which is absurd, considering I can only see her back, but I get the sense she carries the weight of the world on her shoulders. No matter how shitty my day, I always look at that picture and realize everyone has their own crosses to bear." Mary's mouth parts as she listens intently. "And the second one is pretty self-explanatory. The all-seeing eye. I like to call her Mom."

The mood instantly lightens and Mary laughs. "They are both really beautiful. I think they complement this place and I would love to continue the theme throughout your home."

Tapping my chin, I pose, "You're not going to turn my apartment into some weirdo abstract art cavern, are you, where my kitchen stools will be bicycle seats and I'll have to use a kitty litter tray to go to the bathroom?"

Mary, still standing in the middle of my bed, keeps a straight face as she explains, "No, I'm going to give your home a touch of class, and the first thing that needs to go is this disease-infested bed." She turns over her shoulder to look at the cavities in the slatted wooden headboard to cement her point. "I don't even want to know how they got there."

No, she doesn't. It involved a Russian beauty, a pair of handcuffs, and a bottle of extra virgin olive oil. "Okay, point taken. So you'll use this room?"

She bites her lip while looking around the space. "Yes. I can smell the puta ingrained in the walls."

"You're multi-lingual? Is there anything you can't do?" I tease, while she smirks.

"You have no idea."

Touché.

She examines all corners of the room, her gaze fleeting back over to an old fashioned wooden chest you'd expect to see on the set of Vikings. "That, however, can stay. What's in the box?"

"Wouldn't you like to know," I reply, loving this cat and mouse game we're playing.

Talking to Mary is easy. There are no pretences because we're both straight shooters. This is the first conversation I've had with a woman where I know no matter what I say, or no matter how hard I turn on the charm, it won't make a lick of difference because Mary is different. She sees through all my one liners because she's got a comeback for every one. And if that doesn't make me harder than a ten-foot snowman's cock, then slap a red nose on me and call me Bozo the Clown.

She purses her lips in defiance and I know what she's about to do even before she jumps off the edge of my bed and makes a beeline for the chest. Just as she's two feet away, I frankly state, "I'm glad you're wearing gloves, 'cause I'm not going to lie, it's porn. And a lot of it."

She freezes mid-step, her face pulling into an adorable scowl. "What is it with men and porn?"

"Do you really need me to explain?"

I'm expecting her to kick me in the nuts and tell me to go to hell, but I should know by now that Mary Mitts will always keep me guessing. "Sure, I've got nothing better to do." My eyes bulge from my head when she continues her trek to my porn hub and places her perfect ass onto the chest. She crosses her legs and folds her arms 'cause it's apparently story time with Big Ted.

I don't even know how to give a 101 on porn because quite frankly, I think I'll offend her. Rubbing the back of my neck, I try and think back to the speech my dad gave me when I was ten. "Son, it's perfectly normal to masturbate. It's all part of growing up." God bless the son of a gun. When I told him my hand was practically glued to my dick 'cause I broke into his porn stash when I was eight, he handed over the reins to my mom, while he invested in a better lock.

Mary's dimpled smile exposes her utter delight at seeing me squirm. "Ah, c'mon now, cat got your tongue?"

She's baiting me and it's totally working. Wetting my lips, I hope I can get through this without showing her exactly the reason why we need porn. I start with the basics. "It all comes down to evolution. Our brains"—I knock on my skull—"we're hard-wired to be walking wood. We're very visual individuals and respond to images, especially of the naked kind, much more quickly than women do. Evolution proves that a dude's sole purpose is to copulate and spread his little guys whenever, wherever he can.

"When the opportunity knocks, we are more than happy to lay down our arms and fuck." Her cheeks blister a bright red, but there's no going back now. "Porn is like being in a candy store and the flavors are; the not so innocent cheerleader jelly beans, the desperate housewife gummy bears, and the naughty, naughty schoolteacher lollipops. It wets whatever appetite, fantasy we have and it's like ice-cream—we eat it up 'cause it's there and we can."

Mary's chest begins to rise and fall, which is so not helping the inevitable predicament, which will happen in approximately two minutes. I saunter toward her, needing to witness her rosy flesh up close. "Isn't it cheating if they're married? Or in a relationship? Or what if they're just some porn fiend who likes whacking off ten times a day? Doesn't having so much variety at their disposable only feed the addiction?"

I need a moment to catch my breath cause the word 'whacking off' has never sounded so innocently filthy. Focusing on her question and not the persistent pirouetting in my pants, I shake my head. "Studies on lab rats show that a male rat will only be into the same female for so long."

Mary scoffs, her arms constricting around her. "Gee, not so different to the entire male species then."

I arch a brow as I sense an undertone of hurt. Whoever hurt this goddess will pay dearly with his knotted balls dangling from a powerline. "No matter what Mrs. Rat does to entice him, the male just doesn't want to play. However"—I raise my pointer when Mary is no doubt about to tell me to blow this speech up my ass—"when a new female is introduced, the male rat can't help himself and he's all over Mrs. Rat like a kid eating free cake."

"Is that true?" she questions with a grin.

"Absolutely." Taking a step closer so my knees almost touch hers, I relish in her accelerated breath.

She weighs over what I just said and I can suddenly see the struggle behind her delicate eyes. "But what if porn gives Mr. Rat an itch Mrs. Rat can't scratch and he goes out and cheats with a field mouse who can suck a golf ball through a garden hose?"

I burst into laughter because that visual was quite colorful indeed. "That's nothing to do with porn, that's got to do with the person, or in this instance, Mr. Rat and his lack of balls and morals. He can't blame porn for being the reason he cheated. He's the reason. Jenna Jameson the Mouse didn't tell him to stick his dick in some five-dollar hooker. He did."

Mary nods slowly, gnawing on her bottom lip. The sight hurts. I suddenly want to wrap my arms around her and protect her from all the rat bastards out there.

"So you see…" I place my hands in my pockets before I do something stupid. "Porn isn't cheating. If anything, it gives us ideas to perform on our lucky spouses. If you have one, that is."

When her eyes flick up to meet mine, I almost hit the deck. "And if you don't?"

I have been a fucking saint hitherto, but a man has his limits and Shortcake has just proved she's my limit—my hard limit. Bending ever so slowly, I come to a stop when we're face to face. Her sweet breath fans my cheeks and I'm hit with that mouth-watering strawberry and cream fragrance. This is wrong, but I can't let her think I've gone soft, I'm quite the opposite in fact. "Then good luck to the woman we find and fuck senseless until she forgets her own name."

An actual whimper slips past Mary's lips, but I don't mistake this for more than it is. Just 'cause we're talking about sex in a roundabout way doesn't mean she'll lower her guard and let me throw her over the chest and eat her out until next week.

Jesus Christ, the image is too much.

This is the time I call it a night, but fuck me sideways, I don't think I'll survive this look she's giving me. I can't determine whether she wants to tell me to fuck off…or fuck me. Either option suits me just fine, 'cause whatever Mary wants to give, I'll take…on my knees.

Unable to stop myself, I give in to temptation and brush a stray curl from her cheek. A strand of hair should not get me hard, but it does. Her creamy flesh beneath my finger shoots a current of a gazillion volts straight through me.

I need to talk because the need to kiss her, oh my fucking god, yes KISS her, is real. "So moral of the story is a dude's porn stash…is basically the equivalent to your vibrator."

Something is happening and I have no idea what. Mary's eyes drop to my lips before she uneasily licks hers. Her flushed cheeks, dilated pupils, and heavy breathing all point to one thing—but that's not possible. This woman hates me, all delicious, lithe five-foot-four of her wants me dead.

So why is she not slapping my cheeks and calling me a dirty manwhore when I inch closer to her lips? And why am I not slamming on the brakes because I don't kiss—ever, but that rule seems to be obsolete when the supplest pair of lips are a hairs breadth away?

I'm fucking rolling in her perfume. Slathering it all over my body and inhaling it like a new drug. She is all goddess, and if I don't touch her, I'm going to explode.

Placing my palm to her cheek, we both moan at the contact, and when she parts those lips, I'm as good as gone. "Hunter, wh-what are you doing?"

My name has never sounded sweeter. "Shortcake, I don't know…you tell me." The ball is in her court. I'm liquefying and my brain turned to mush about fifteen minutes ago, so I'm in no state to be the one calling the shots.

"I…I…" she fumbles, never breaking eye contact.

"You what?" I ask, tugging at the lobe of her ear, before tracing my pointer down her throat. Her pulse is hammering, a sure sign she's about to either surrender, or flee.

"I…oh god," she whimpers, biting her lip when I work my finger back up and paint over her jawline in a slow sweep.

"You have three seconds…three seconds to stop me before I part those fucking lips with my tongue, and I won't be gentle about it."

Holy fucking shit. When I hear the distinctive sound of her rubbing her legs together, a tell-tale that she's as worked up as I am, I can deal with the consequences later. And besides, her three seconds are up. I dive forward, so ready to be a eunuch by morning, but all I connect with is air.

"I have to go. I'm sorry." Mary ducks under my arm and makes a mad dash for the door. I sway unsteadily because she not only threw me off center physically, every part of my body is kicking and screaming, throwing a full-blown tantrum. "Don't go. I'm the one who's sorry. I just got caught up in…" In your eyes, your smell, the need to throw you over my shoulder caveman style and fuck you eternally, I silently add. "In Mr. and Mrs. Rat's happily ever after," I settle on.

But she doesn't stop. She's a blur as she runs down the hallway and straight into the…

"That's the kitchen!" I shout out, hot on her tail.

"Fuck!" she curses, running back out and taking a left toward the living room and front door.

"Shortcake, please stop."

"Hunter, no, just leave me alone." She bumps into the corner of the couch and yelps, but continues hobbling toward the door.

"Okay, I'll leave you alone," I plead, afraid she'll take out her eye otherwise. "Just stop running and let me drive you home." Just when I think she's seen reason 'cause she's stopped and turned around, I realize she's grabbing her bag and hitting the road faster than a marshmallow roasts in hell.

I know if I corner her, she's likely to rip off my head and use it as a bowling ball, so I stop chasing her, even though every part of me is screaming that I move. "Please talk to me."

She yanks open the door, her hand braced on the handle. Her shoulders rise and fall steadily, her breaths leaving her in winded pants. "Okay fine, I'll talk to you…" With back turned, she wraps up something that could have flourished into something epic. "This was a big mistake. I'll see you in three months." She slams the door shut while I groan, fisting at my hair and leaving my hands atop my head as I stare at the door.

Three months is Dixon and Madison's wedding. She's made clear she has no intention in seeing me before then. How could this happen? So fucking stupid to make a move. Story of my life. Sighing, I make my way to the kitchen, needing to drown my sorrow in scotch.

D2 decides now is a good time to remind me…I should have just asked her if she fucking likes schnauzers.

Eight

Mary

'm fucking crazy.

Throw away the key to my padded cell because this insanity appears to be incurable. I have no idea why I'm here, but the thought of being anywhere else leaves me with a throbbing ache in my chest.

Anyone would think that after last night, I'd have learned my lesson, but no, here I am, ready to make a fool of myself once again. I left Hunter's apartment, promising myself that this was the last time…the last time I wanted to throw good sense to the wind and climb him faster than a rocket filled with spider monkeys.

I'm sick, that's the only explanation.

I don't even like him, well, I don't think I do. Yes, he's ridiculously hot with his sea green eyes, a jaw line that goes on for days, and a body that rivals Captain America, but he's also obnoxious, foul mouthed, and not to mention the list of women he's been with could fill Noah's Ark…twice. But I can't stop thinking about him, and when I'm near him, I can't stop thinking about him touching me…everywhere.

I can't believe I've fallen for his bullshit. I'm no better than all the other hoochies who are lining up, waiting for a turn. I hate him, I remind myself, but a small, bothersome voice whispers I hate him for making me want him because this wasn't supposed to happen…I was never meant to fall for Hunter O'Shea.

The moment I met him, I knew I was in trouble. He oozed confidence, sex appeal, and that mouth…I should detest that mouth, but I don't. I want it all over me. I pretended to hate him because he makes me feel things I haven't felt in a very long time. Maybe ever. I thought he'd give up by now, but he hasn't, and his perseverance makes me crave him all the more.

But I can't tell him. I can't tell anyone. Not even Maddy knows. As far as she's concerned, I'd bake a cake at his wake, but that's so far from the truth.

When my high school sweetheart, Corey, ended things because I wasn't "exciting" enough for him, he not only broke my heart…he broke me. To the outside world, I was having the time of my life, being single and carefree in the greatest city in the world. But I was hurting. I couldn't understand how the man I gave my virginity to could cheat with some random barfly and lie about it for six months.

If the man I trusted more than life itself could lie and cheat on me, then what hope was there for the rest of the male population? Men are dicks, and they think with their dicks, and I was happy to live alone with my fifty cats, but then my best friend had to go and fall in love.

Madison and Dixon are living proof that true love does

exist. She's yin to his yang and regardless of the fact that he used to be New York's biggest player, he gave all of that up for her. He changed because he wanted to change. But Dixon is the exception to the rule. He's like a four-leaf clover. People talk about them, but no one has been able to unearth one, no one, bar Maddy, which seems fitting, considering he's been her lucky charm. He would fight for her until the bitter end, and that's the reason, not that I'd ever tell him, that I respect and like him so much.

But there was no way another Dixon could exist. I mean, at first, I was having a hard time believing he was the real deal, so to even fathom another knight in shining armor was out there was just plain stupid.

But enter his best friend, Hunter O'Shea.

Make no mistake however, Hunter is no Prince Charming, and honestly, if he were the one to deliver the all saving kiss to wake Sleeping Beauty from her slumber, I think she'd prefer to remain a comatose virgin. But I like that he makes no apologies for who he is. I like that he speaks his mind, no matter how crude, or who he offends. I know where I stand with him. There is no bullshit. And after the bullshit Corey put me through, he's like a breath of amazingly smelling fresh air.

He stirs a longing inside of me, not only physically, but emotionally as well. And after last night, after our near miss, I'm fucking scared. And that's my dilemma.

The problem I'm faced with is I can't give him my heart because I know he will not just break it, he will set it on fire and blow the fragments to the wind. Corey left me with this insecure, raw wound and I'm afraid of what will happen if I try to mend it. I'd grown accustomed to the reality of being alone, but then Hunter walked into a room, and it was like my heart kickstarted back to life.

I may talk big, but deep down, I know I will never be able to keep up with the likes of Hunter. When Corey said, I wasn't "exciting" enough for him, he wasn't talking about the fact I wouldn't go sky-diving with him, he was talking about my performance in the bedroom.

I thought I was an okay lover, but he made it sound like I was a dying starfish, and I should have been grateful that he didn't cheat on me sooner.

I'm afraid if I give into temptation, Hunter will laugh at my inexperience and stop wanting me as much as I want him. Sometimes, fantasy is so much better than reality and my measly list of bedroom partners will only prove this fact and send Hunter running to the nearest corner to get lovin' from someone who knows how.

Someone like Hunter O'Shea doesn't settle down. Thanks to Dixon renouncing his place in whoredom, Hunter has taken the place of New York's biggest player and he doesn't want some inexperienced, fumbling, born again virgin anywhere near his heart, because that's what I want.

So, all in all, I need to forget about him and this unhealthy obsession because it will only end in ugly tears and a weeklong binge of watching Hallmark movies of a love life I can never have.

But I can't forget about him. How do you forget someone like Hunter O'Shea?

And that's the reason why I'm on the verge of hyperventilating as I'm riding this elevator to his office floor.

See, refer to my previous. Fucking crazy.

Once the doors part, I wipe my sweaty palms on my dress and tell myself to woman the hell up. I have no idea what I'm doing, but I'm not going to overthink it, because if I do, I'll need a wastebasket to throw up my blueberry bagel.

Thanks to some subtle snooping, I know where his office is. I can pretend that this is a business call, but deep down there's no denying the need to see him overrides any rational thinking, because rationality was lost the moment we locked eyes.

It's all hustle and bustle, men in sharp suits, and women in designer threads rushing around with phones pressed to their ears. No doubt they're all on the line with potential investors, which make this firm the biggest and most successful in NYC.

Nervously, I brush a strand of hair behind my ear. I don't exactly blend in, and quite frankly, I stick out like dog balls, but everyone is too busy to care. I had no idea what the dress code was, so I decided to dress like a fellow redhead who owned the office she worked at. Miranda from Sex and the City may not have been as glamorous as her other three counterparts, but she had style.

I'm in a dark navy dress with white belt and matching shoes. Because it's a typical cold morning in the Big Apple, I have on my long red coat, which just seems to bring out the copper in my waves, but it was either this, or ripped jeans. Makeup is minimal, but I have on a pink gloss and mascara—a girl can never have enough of either.

I peer down the long hallway, wondering if maybe I should ask someone if I'm going in the right direction, but when I look to my left and see two girls with love hearts basically pulsating from their eyeballs, I know I don't have far to go.

The pretty brunette is sitting at her desk, fanning herself

with a small notebook, while her friend, a stunning blonde, is leaning against the partition as if needing the support before she crumbles into a heaving mess. "Mr. O'Shea is so hot."

"So hot," the blonde repeats, nodding eagerly, while I slow down and pretend I've got something stuck under my shoe.

"He was in line for coffee and oh my god…he smelled like he rolled in a barrel of heaven."

"He looks fucking edible in that pinstripe suit. Did you see that ass? Dear god, I just want to take a bite." Both girls giggle, while I contemplate taking off my heel and stabbing them repeatedly in the eyeballs.

"I wonder if he has a girlfriend." Yes, I wonder that too. Just who was Goldilocks he was with the other night? I cringe, wishing I'd used another reference because all I can think about is if his bed was "just right."

"Rumor has it he has lots of them. Not that anyone can blame them. Timothy, the new intern, he told me he saw…" She pauses for dramatic flair, before she continues. "His you know what when they were in the bathroom, and he said it was huge. Like porn star big."

More giggles and gushing, while I need to find this Timothy and ask for details.

"He said he was jealous because it was one…beautiful… cock."

And that's my downfall—literally.

I fall sideways into the wall, scaring the living shit out of the two girls and myself. They yelp, while I steady myself from giving myself third degree carpet burns. When I come to, I come eye-level with my informants, who so know I was eavesdropping.

The blonde crosses her arms with a scowl. "Can I help you?"

I refrain from saying yes, show me where Timothy sits because the longer I stand, staring like a rabbit caught in the headlights, the more attention I draw to myself. Thinking on my feet, I nod with a smile. "Da liegt der Hund begraben."

Both girls look at one another, completely confused, while I wave goodbye and quickly hightail it out of there, thankful I remembered the only German I learned in college. It loses its meaning because when translated it literally means that's where the dog is buried, but they don't know that as they wave back, thinking I'm a client.

My nervousness is quickly forgotten because I need to find Hunter before I blow it and make a bigger scene when ACC escorts me from the building, asking whose dog I just buried. I turn down a small corridor, and not looking where I'm going, run straight into a solid brick wall.

It knocks the wind from my lungs and clearly the sense from my brain because I have a sudden urge to dry hump this wall while I lick it…naked. My heart starts an unhealthy beating and I'm certain I'm on the verge of having a stroke. Not understanding what's going on, I peer upward, and upward again and choke on air.

"Shortcake?"

I curse whatever god is looking down at me and laughing at my expense because this is a big office, huge in fact, so why, oh why did I have to bump into him?

"I have a name," I bark, shrugging out of his hold because even though he's touching me over my coat, I'm currently on fire.

He raises his hands in surrender with a lopsided smirk.

Fuck him. Does this man ever look unattractive? And would it kill him to have a bad hair day? Speaking of. His dirty blond strands are raked back messily, like he used his fingers as a styling tool to tame the disorder.

His sea green eyes are examining me closely, always so expressive, because in his case, they truly are the window to his soul. His chiseled jawline is covered in a dark scruff, highlighting how delicious his curved lips are.

The blonde's comment comes to mind, and now that he's here, up close and personal, I can completely see what she means. The dark gray pinstripe suit hugs his hulking frame, showcasing every bump and hardened plane along the way. The way it sits snugly over what he's packing in those pants should make this garment illegal in every country in the world. The crisp white shirt is brought to life by a silk burgundy tie, but in true Hunter fashion, the top button is undone and the tie is loosely knotted.

He looks like he belongs on a runway in Milan, showcasing attire for bad boys because that's what he is. It's not possible that someone is this good looking, but standing before me is living proof that perfection exists. But regardless of the fact that I'm staring at what could quite possibly be Chris Hemsworth's doppelgänger, I pull back my shoulders and quash down the need to lick his face.

"Not that I'm unhappy, but given the fact I'm still cleaning the skid marks you left in your haste to flee my apartment, what are you doing here?" His voice is deep, hoarse, like he just woke up, leaving me with obscene images which make my girly parts sing.

This needs to stop. Now. "Gee, a touch dramatic, don't you

think? I left because I had better things to do, like right now, so stop wasting my time and show me where your office is." A ghost of a smile plays at Hunter's lips.

I wish I could attempt to be civil, but I'm afraid if I do, it'll be an avalanche of words and feelings and I won't be able to stop.

"You're here because you still want to use me as your lab rat?" His innocent wording has me remembering his analogy from last night of Mr. and Mrs. Rat, and I suddenly feel faint.

Refusing to give in to my hormones, I roll my eyes. "Careful, if you open your mind too much, your brain just might fall out." His gruff laugh doesn't help the predicament in my underwear.

"Follow me."

He turns, leaving me with a glorious view of his ass that has me licking my lips. I wonder if he'd notice if I took a sneaky pic on my phone. Getting my head in the game, I stop being such a pervert, and focus on school. Regardless of the fact I want to devour every square inch of his skin, I do need his office and home to finish my course.

I follow in silence, unable to tear my gaze from his strapping body. He has an air of arrogance about him and emits a raw animal magnetism which has girls and boys alike wanting to get all up in that tall, dark, and handsome.

As I'm admiring the dirty blond strands in his hair, we take a right and I walk into what can only be described as the lair of a closet hoarder. "This is not your office." I forget all about my pent-up sexual frustrations, and focus on the clutter which has my eye twitching.

"Why, what's wrong with it?" he asks, stepping inside, expecting me to follow.

I, however, stand at the threshold, peering around the doorjamb, afraid what will come out and bite me if I enter. "What's right with it?" Holy shit, this place looks like a graveyard where office stationary goes to die.

His desk has mountains of paperwork and books heaped on top of it, having me questioning when the last time he saw the polished surface was. A laptop sits on top of a pile of old newspapers, with a crystal tumbler sitting just within reach.

An outdated leather couch sits along the far wall, which in the 80s would have been a cool feature wall, but now the offensive orange is an eyesore. The wooden bookshelves are the only saving grace, but the countless number of books shoved haphazardly along the shelves has me itching to bring order to the anarchy.

The view is spectacular, allowing one to get lost in the city that never sleeps, but that's exactly what I'm faced with, because this place is a train wreck.

Finally gathering the nerve to enter, I test that the faded gray carpet won't pull me into a giant sinkhole. When I think it's safe, I take a step inside and turn in a slow circle. I may have bitten off more than I can chew, but I'm not a quitter, and besides, this just means I'll have to utilize every second of the next two months.

My entire body cartwheels at the thought because it means I have no other choice but to see Hunter every…single…day.

Tapping my chin, I take a deep breath before gathering the nerve to talk to him. "I thought it'd be bigger." Yes, complete innuendo, but I can't help it because when I turn around to face him, I almost choke on my own tongue.

He's leaned up against the front of his desk, arms and ankles crossed as he watches me with those eyes. A strand of hair has slipped forward, shaping his sharp cheekbones and adding to the rebellious vibe. "It's not the size that matters, but rather how you use it, and Shortcake, I know how to use it."

Deadpanning him, I can't help myself. "A big dick doesn't mean anything if it's attached to a bigger dick, so you may as well have a three-inch crooked vibrator."

Hunter bursts into uncontrollable laughter, while I high-five my foul mouth. I can give as good as I get, and I'm addicted to the way his mouth twitches and how he consumes me with a fire when I don't hold back.

Most guys can't keep up with my dry humor, hence another reason why I'm still single, but it seems to have the opposite effect on Hunter, who looks seconds away from tackling me to the floor. "All this vibrator talk is making me hungry, have you had lunch?"

Ignoring him, I hunt through my bag with shaky fingers and pull out my cell. "Mind if I take some pictures?" He nods, allowing me free rein to take over his office and home.

I go to work, snapping pictures, as I'll use them for my before and after presentation. As I'm working with the light to capture the best photographs, I decide to take a panorama to remember the entire space I need to revamp. I start from one end and then slowly pan across. The moment Hunter appears on my screen, still resting against the edge of his desk without a care in the world, my mouth goes dry and my earlier reflection of him being a runway model doesn't seem too far off the mark. The camera loves him.

He doesn't mask the fact he's staring directly at me, which excites and confuses me all in the same breath. "Haven't you got work to do?" I ask, the camera still on him.

I watch him through my screen as he shrugs. "Yes."

I'm expecting him to elaborate, but he doesn't. He continues his vigil, rubbing his thumb over his lip while watching me closely. My cheeks heat and I know I'm turning a bright pink—the joys of being a redhead with pale skin.

Just as I'm about to retort with a smartassed response, a voice which sounds like angels singing to the tune of Ave Maria floats through the air. "Oh, sorry, Hunter, I didn't realize you had company."

I would know that voice anywhere because I was subjected to its sickly sweetness Saturday night. Turning so quickly I almost give myself whiplash, I see none other than Goldilocks standing in Hunter's doorway, two coffees in hand.

The first thing I notice is how incredibly gorgeous she is. Like not just pretty, but so beautiful it makes grown men cry. She's wearing a simple white summer dress, but nothing can look simple on her. Maybe she and Hunter can star together on the cover of Vogue, summer edition.

My fingers curl into fists, but I ignore the urge to kill and destroy, and rip out her long golden hair, strand by strand.

"Hi. Mary, right?"

She knows my fucking name. Don't act coy. But I nod with a stiff upper lip smile. "Yes, and you're Karen, right?" Childish and completely immature, but I can't acknowledge her because that will mean she's here, in Hunter's office, liable to drop to her knees and suck him off.

"It's Keira," she corrects with a small smile. The minor details don't count. What does count is why is she here?

I know she was his "date," but I didn't think they were

actually a thing. I think the better phrasing here however would be I had hoped they weren't. I feel like a complete loser for coming here, expecting what exactly, I don't know, but I most definitely was not expecting to be the third wheel, and that's what I am.

She has two coffees—one for him and one for her, because that's what people in relationships do. They bring their partner coffee.

Trent has never brought me coffee, which is sad on all counts, considering we work together, waiting tables. But we're not in a relationship, hence the no caffeine at work, or any place. I brought him to dinner because I knew Hunter wouldn't be alone. I couldn't sit there and watch him fawn over some bimbo while I fantasized about writhing beneath him as I screamed out his name.

We kissed once, and I blame that on the excessive tequila shots I did. Trent is a nice person, but he's just that—nice. The most noncommittal word in the English language. When he touches me, I may as well be holding onto a dead fish. There are no fireworks, no stars flashing before my eyes. All I feel is… boredom.

I know Hunter thinks we're more than friends who shared more than a drunk, non-earth-shattering kiss, because at dinner, whenever Trent touched me, I pretended it was Hunter. Each kiss, sweet whisper, I imagined it was him, and when I said to him he wants what he can't have, it was wishful thinking, hoping he'd corroborate my claims and when he did, I almost believed him. Almost.

The person standing in the doorway holding two cups of coffee is the reason why Hunter and I can never be. He won't settle for just one flavor—he wants them all. And Keira appears to be the flavor of the month—the flavor who can keep up with his sexual prowess because he admitted my fears—I'll never be able to keep up with the likes of Hunter O'Shea.

"Okay, I'm done here," I say, hating that relates to more than just my time here.

"You're leaving already?"

Turning over my shoulder, I can't hide my surprise. "Yes, I wouldn't want to interrupt your coffee date."

Hunter pushes off the desk, walking toward me, while I take two steps back. "Date? Keira asked if I wanted a coffee as she was getting one for her boss."

"She works here?" I ask, my pitch a little flightier than usual.

"Yes." He nods firmly.

Well, I don't know if this a good or bad thing. But when she pipes up, "Actually, are you free tonight? I wanted to show you something," I know it's a bad thing, a very bad thing because no guessing what she wants to show him. It rhymes with MY VAGINA.

I've never been good with competition because quite frankly, I don't like to lose. Curse this jealousy and my wicked tongue. "Oh, I need to swing past tonight. I didn't have a chance to finish what I started last night." BOOM! I mean that in every possible way there is.

Choo choo. Can you hear that? It's the express train, ready to take my soul to hell.

I can see the exact moment Little Miss Sunshine turns into Xena Warrior Princess. I never bought her innocent act for one minute and am convinced she's going to clothesline me right here in Hunter's office. Her eyes narrow and I'm certain her fingernails sharpen into claws. In response, I smile sweetly.

Hunter's gaze flicks between Keira and I as he rubs the back of his neck, clearly attempting to decipher what's going on. If he denies me, I'm going to knee him in the balls. "Well, in that case, it'll have to wait. Sorry, Keira. You can always email me if it's important." I'm sure she'll take him up on that offer as she probably has snapshots of her cha-cha on file.

"No problem, but remember, Friday, you're all mine."

Check and mate.

Her red lips twist into a cunning smirk, while I envision what she'd look like bald. On cue, the sunlight bounces off the metal handle of a pair of scissors sitting atop the mess on Hunter's desk.

Hunter clears his throat, looking at me like I'm to show him mercy. Not on his life. "I better make tonight worth my while then." Hunter grunts in the back of his throat, while my ego does a backflip in victory.

It appears we're all speaking in innuendos because there is no polite way to say BACK THE FUCK OFF.

Keira will clearly fight dirty, but who can blame her? I'm not naïve. I have no doubt they've already slept together, or at the very least, he's seen her parade about naked. I'm sniffing around her bone, and although I should back down, all I want to do is lift my leg and mark Hunter as mine.

This is the reason why I need to stay away from him, because if I lower my guard and let him in, I won't share. I will claw out any bitch's eyes if she looks at him sideways. But there is something about Kiera I can't quite put my finger on.

I don't buy her girl next door smile. It's all an act and I need to know why. Deciding to go home and do some recon, I lock eyes with Hunter, who seems more than just a little confused. "See you tonight."

This is the moment I leave and snoop the internet for any dirt there may be on Goldilocks, but my feet are rooted to the floor. Hunter and I are caught in a deadlock because I know he feels this ever-present pull between us. My body is pulling in one direction, but my heart is slamming on the brakes.

"See you tonight," he repeats, snapping me from my daze. I nod, too afraid to speak.

Keira makes no attempt to move out of the way, but she can bite me. Shoving past her, I relish in the contact when she almost goes hurtling into the bookcase. "Oh, sweetie, be careful. There's a bookshelf there." I don't wait for her to reply because the evil scowl is all the response I need.

I have no idea what a can of worms I've just opened, but if Keira wants a war, then she's got one.

Let the games begin.

Nine

Mary

I have no idea what I'm doing. I passed the point of no return about two hours ago when I called up Hunter's office, pretending that I was UPS and had a parcel for Keira, but her surname was unknown. I was hoping the clueless receptionist would confirm that a Keira…worked there.

She did.

Keira Celly. The name of my new arch nemesis. I have no idea, apart from the obvious, what my beef with this woman is, I just know I want her to take a slow walk through fast traffic.

As I'm trying on outfit number six, my phone rings. It's hidden under my pillow because Trent has called me about ten times. I know I really should talk to him, but I don't know what to say. After Saturday night, I've been giving him the cold shoulder and not returning any of his messages.

Once I get tonight over with, I'll tell him that I'm not interested. It's better I end things before they get out of hand.

When it sounds once again, I decide to switch it off because I don't want any distractions as I'm jumpy enough. I lift my pillow, but instead of seeing Trent as the caller, it's Maddy.

I quickly answer. "Hey!" I say with a little too much enthusiasm, as I'm worried she'll see what a shitty friend I am for not telling her about my current lapse in mental state.

"Hey yourself. Why are you so chipper?"

Breathe, Mary. "Can't I be happy to talk to my best friend?"

Maddy laughs. "Aw, I've missed you too. How you been?"

Oh, you know, just the standard—losing my mind. "I've been good. Just trying to organize my last assessment."

I wait for it because I know what she's going to say. "Oh my god, you haven't?" Even though she was the one who gave me Hunter's address, I'm certain she believed I wouldn't go through with it.

Walking back over to the mirror, I wonder if my outfit is too much. I have on a royal blue, high waisted flared mini skirt and a light gray tank which ties at the front. I'm probably showing way too much cleavage. "Yes, I have. Like you said, I'm running out of options. I really don't have a choice." Which is half true.

I can hear Maddy walking into another room as the TV in the background slowly fades to silence. "Are you sure this is a good idea? I mean...you hate Hunter."

If only that were the truth.

Reaching for my black and gray spotted scarf, I wrap it around my neck to tone down the desperate and dateless vibe. "Yes, the man is an utter primate. His apartment just confirms this."

"So you ended up going over Sunday?"

Maddy was in the shower when I called her and Dixon

picked up. I told him if I could be bothered, I would drop in to see Hunter and asked if he knew if he was home. Dixon isn't stupid. He knew I was going and he probably didn't tell Maddy because it wasn't his story to tell. Nothing slips past him.

"Yes, I did. I did what I had to and then left. I could only handle being alone with him for like two minutes." Not an outright lie, but just not the way she thinks.

"I'm surprised I didn't get a call from NYPD," she says with a chuckle.

Her comment has me thinking about little miss goody two shoes. "What's the deal with the blonde?"

"Which one?"

A stab to the heart almost renders me unconscious, but I continue. "His date." I can't keep the bite from my tone, but quickly recover. "I saw her today. At his work," I explain, not needing to go into detail, as Maddy knows home and office is all part of the deal.

"What about her? She seems nice."

Pull it together, I instruct my mirror image as I sweep down my body with a few pumps of my favorite perfume. "She seems like a complete phony. She's definitely hiding something."

"Not you too. Dixon also seems to think she's hiding some deep, dark secret." From Maddy's tone, it's quite evident she doesn't agree.

My ears prick up. Interesting. "Well, Dixon does know best."

She bursts into laughter, the light sound instantly calming my nerves. "Since when?"

"Since I agree with him," I reply, curling a limp lock of hair around my finger to give it oomph.

"If I didn't know any better, I'd say you were both jealous."

The cell slips from my ear and I quickly scramble to pick it back up. "Please, jealous of what? Being another notch on his bedpost? I don't think so."

"I don't think he's met the right girl, that's all. I know you'll disagree, but I think Hunter would make a great boyfriend. There really isn't anything not to like. He's a good guy once you get to know him."

I pause, lip gloss wand en route to my mouth. "Maddy, have you gone insane? He can't keep it in his pants for more than five seconds. Not to mention, since your fiancé left him his big manwhore shoes to fill, he's been screwing anything that walks. I'm not saying he's a slut, but let's just say his penis volunteers a lot. And when someone says he's a good guy once you get to know him, what they really mean is he's an asshole, but you'll get used to it."

Rant over.

Maddy is cackling in uncontrollable laughter while I huff, annoyed that he isn't even here and he's able to get under my skin. I need a drink. "I think you two would make a great couple."

"Yes, like Sid and Nancy. Bonnie and Clyde. Milo and Otis."

"Milo and Otis?" Maddy asks, confused.

"Yup, 'cause we'd fight like cats and dogs." I have no doubt this is true, but it doesn't stop me from daydreaming about her comment. Maybe in another lifetime. "Speaking of Satan himself, I have to go. I was due at his apartment like an hour ago."

"You're going back?"

Throwing everything I need into my handbag, I sigh. "Yes,

desperate, remember?" I mean that in every literal way there is.

"Do you want us to come over? Offer some moral support?"

Bless her, but hell no. How high-strung I am, she'll see right through me and I have no doubt she'll make me talk to Dixon about feelings and all that other sentimental crap. "No, it's okay. I won't be staying long."

"All right. Good luck," she singsongs, not making me feel an iota better.

"Thanks. I need it. If you don't hear from me, it's because I've crossed the Mexican border and changed my name to Juana."

"Okay. Your secret is safe with me. Have fun."

Once I hang up, I feel like the world's shittiest friend. I want to tell her, but I don't even know what I'm feeling, so how can I put it into words? It'll all come out in a rush of gibberish, leaving me flustered and tongue tied.

Grabbing my red coat, I lock up my apartment in Brooklyn and walk to the subway. No one bar pretentious assholes drives in New York. The subway is all one needs to get around. And besides, the forty-minute train ride gives me the guts to rearrange my lady balls and attempt to act semi-normal as I prepare for what the night will bring.

Yes, it's true, I need to take pictures, but once that's done, what happens then?

Oh my fucking god. What is the matter with me? I sound like a schoolgirl with a crush. 'In and out,' I chant to myself as I enter his apartment complex and push the elevator call button. This place is rather posh and I'm surprised they haven't thrown Hunter out for offending the tenants with his foul mouth.

The concierge, a younger guy, doesn't hide his curiosity at

what I'm doing here, as I don't exactly fit in. I'm too dressed to be a hooker, but not in lavish riches to be a resident. He tips his black hat when he sees me eyeing him. "Going to see Hunter?"

"What?" I bark, my temper simmering. What the fuck is that supposed to mean?

He can clearly see me seething and quickly backtracks. "I was just wondering because all the pretty girls go up to see him."

Peering down at his nametag, I have just added Marvin to my shit list. "You really need to stop talking."

He pales and waves both hands in front of him. "I just meant…" But he soon zips his lips when I envision him doused in fuel while I strike a match.

Lucky for Marvin, the elevator arrives because I'm seconds away from shoving that bell so far up his ass he'll be speaking with a chimed lisp. "Please feel free to vacate the room whenever you see me next." He nods, knowing better than to argue with a fired-up redhead.

I storm into the elevator, stabbing at the button which will take me to Hunter's bordello. My nerves are soon replaced with anger because what the fuck do I look like—one of Hunter's groupies? I'm offended, not to mention pissed off that whenever an attractive woman enters the building, it's assumed she's here to see the manwhore.

Anger is good, I can work with anger. It's all the other stuff that is confusing me and clouding my vision. Maybe if I live in a perpetual state of rage, this obsession will eventually fuck off.

The moment the doors part, I march down the hallway, intent on being here for no longer than five minutes. I do need his apartment, but that doesn't mean I need to look or speak to him. From now on, it's purely professional, and if an unprofessional thought crosses my mind, I'm going to punch myself in the boob.

Standing tall, I bang on Hunter's door. I could ring the doorbell, but I figure I'll pound on his door, rather than his face because that's sure to happen when he opens this door. I impatiently tap my foot against the carpet—what's taking so long? My scarf is cutting off my air supply, so I rip it off and stuff it into my bag.

With hand poised, I'm about to knock once again but almost fall flat on my face when the door opens and my underwear disintegrates into thin air. Fuck him and the hot horse he rode in on. He's standing before me in blue jeans with a hole ripped in both knees, a white V-neck t-shirt and bare feet, which also happen to be sexy. I can't help but take note of how big they are. You know what they say about big feet...big...shoes! I internally yell, primed and ready to sucker punch myself if I don't push such inappropriate thoughts from my mind.

"Always so impatient," Hunter says with a smirk, his bulky bicep flexing as he rests his arm against the doorjamb.

"It's 'cause I want this over and done with as soon as possible." Hooray for me, but when I push him out of the way, that celebration is short-lived. He feels amazing, and he smells even better. What is he wearing? LadyKiller—getting men laid since 1981. But he has no problems achieving that on his own.

When the door closes behind me, I put as much distance between us and make a mad dash to his bedroom. Extremely rude, but I don't fancy a bruised nipple. The moment I enter, I can't help but notice how much tidier it is. When I was here last, I did just turn up announced, but now it's plain to see he's put away his clothes and made the bed.

Why does that touch me in ways it shouldn't?

Just as I curl my hand into a loose fist, Hunter enters and looks at me like I've gone completely mad. He's not too far off the mark. Ignoring my need for violence, I hunt through my bag and do what I came here for.

I don't even care that the lighting totally blows, because if I don't leave this room in thirty seconds, I'm going to explode. A push pull effect is tearing me right down the middle because every emotion I feel is quickly counterbalanced with an opposing thought. I hate him. I want him. He is hot. He makes me sick. I want to lick him. I want to punch him in the nuts. I want to touch his nuts. I need help.

Not even bothering to look over the photographs I just took, I shove my cell into my jacket pocket and turn on my heel. I'm panting, and the harder I clamp my lips shut, the louder my desperation bounces off these bedroom walls.

I need to leave, because I can't pretend anymore.

Charging down the hallway, I remember to turn left instead of right and hope to god I don't trip over my feet in the process. Although, a concussion might be preferable, because when he calls out my name, I know all my convictions are long gone.

"Mary! Wait! Where are you going?"

"Home," I spit, keeping my eyes focused on the doorknob and nothing else.

When he runs past me and uses his colossal body as a barricade however, I know this is going to take some muscle, because he's not moving without a fight. "What's up with you? Did your favorite book boyfriend die or something? Why are you so angry…well, angrier than usual?"

When I try and shove past him, he latches onto my upper

arm, stopping me from moving an inch. I try and break free, but it's useless. "I'm not angry," I snap, still fighting with him to let me go.

"You could have fooled me. What's wrong?"

It's like I'm attempting to brush a bee off of me as I wiggle out of his hold. "Nothing, I just don't want to take up any of your precious time, because god forbid I deny the lonely hearts of New York your cock!"

Okay, well, that just spiraled rather quickly.

Hunter releases me, his mouth slightly tilted in humor and surprise. "Are you angry at me because I'm irresistible? That's not my fault. Blame my parents."

I know he's trying to make light of my insanity, but Marvin's comment just cements what an utter idiot I am. I'm not special. Hunter only shows interest in me because I'm probably the first woman who's told him no. He wants what he can't have, but if he gets it, I'll be last week's news, and I'm done being disposable. I'm no one's understudy.

"I'm angry at you because I don't like being seen as some harlot in your harem!"

Hunter purses his lips, completely lost in translation. "Shortcake, did you smoke crack before coming here?"

Annoyed, I throw my hands in the air and attempt to push past him. But he stands his ground. He's as stubborn as he is infuriately hot. "Hunter, just move." In response, he folds his arms and leans back against the door, eyefucking me. "I'm sure you have better things to do...do being the operative word in that sentence."

I can't believe how worked up I am, but I'm at my breaking point. Since I met this man, he's pushed every button and I've pushed back, but now I've run out of fight. I surrender, and that just makes me a faceless number in a long line of many.

"You're not going anywhere until you tell me what the hell is wrong." He makes no attempts at moving, which leaves me with no other choice. Without a second thought, I raise my knee and connect with his balls.

A pained grunt leaves him as he topples over, clutching his nuts. I may play dirty, but desperate times call for desperate measures and I don't remember being more desperate than I am right now. I attempt to wedge past him, but his hand shoots out and closes around my forearm. Add bionic man to his impressive resumè.

"Holy shit," he wheezes, clutching onto his junk with one hand while trapping me with the other. "I think you broke me."

"Good," I shout, wriggling like a worm on a hook.

"I should…make you kiss it…better," he breathlessly teases, peering up at me as he's still keeled over.

"I'm sorry, small objects are a choking hazard."

He bursts into a pained bout of laughter, before forcing himself to push past the agony and slowly coming to stand. I know I'm in trouble. I can feel it. It should frighten me, but it doesn't…it excites me.

"Now… are you going to tell me what the fuck is wrong, or am I going to have to force it out of you…with my tongue?"

I blink once. "You wouldn't dare," I challenge, standing on tippy toes, fuming.

"Oh, I would dare. I double dare," he counters, nostrils flared, hair wild.

He is a fierce beast, a ferocity consuming him as he devours every inch of my body with a fire behind those eyes. My body instantly slackens because I'm no match, I can't fight him. Not because I'm weak, but rather, the pull is too strong.

Poking him in the chest, I know this will come back to bite me in the ass. In a way, I'm hoping it does. "What are you going to do about it?" Poke. "You talk big"—poke—"but that's all you do, talk"—poke—"fucking ta…" The last word dies in a strangled heap because Hunter launches at me, catching me completely off guard.

At first, I think he's going to kiss me, but instead he places his palm over my mouth, lowering his face to mine. He scours every inch of my face, as if committing to memory every feature, because what he's about to do will change everything.

"What I'm going to do…what I'm going to do is," he repeats, his voice dangerously low, "they say you are what you eat…and right now, Shortcake…I'm going to eat you."

I have no time to react because he's on me, kissing down my neck and sucking violently at my throat. I arch my head back, desperate for more because it's not enough. He chuckles against my skin, the warmth from his breath spreading goose bumps all the way to my toes.

With frantic fingers, he pushes the coat from my arms, almost ripping it from my body when it catches on my watch. I need to feel more, so much more, and blindly reach for the hem of his t-shirt, craving to feel flesh upon flesh.

But Hunter smacks my hands away because he is about to make good on his promise. Tearing his mouth away, he silently asks permission, beseeching me with those magnetic eyes, and god strike me down, I nod. It's all he needs as he lifts me roughly and carries me through the room.

My heart is going a million miles a minute, but I'd die

happy, because when he tosses me onto the couch and looks at me like I'm his new favorite dessert, I know these next few minutes are going to be the best of my life.

I shuffle up the cushions, expecting him to cover my body with his, but he doesn't. He stands at the foot of the couch, watching me like a lion hunts his prey. "Wh-what are you doing?" I'm suddenly nervous he's had second thoughts.

"What did you mean about being a harlot and all that?" he asks, tilting his head to the side as he's clearly looking up my skirt which sits indecently high.

He's got to be joking. "You seriously want to talk about this now?"

He nods, rubbing his thumb backward and forward across his bottom lip. "Yes," he replies matter-of-factly, while I groan and throw my head back in frustration. It snaps back up just as quickly though when he declares, "I need to know what I did to piss you off, because if this is the end result…then I'll piss you off every day from now on."

Swoon.

I know he won't give in until I do, so my modesty takes a backseat. "Your asshole friend downstairs assumed I was one of your playboy bunnies."

He arches a brow. "What friend?"

"Marvin the shithead." It takes a moment for what I said to sink in, but when it does, Hunter bursts into inappropriate laughter. "Keep that up, and you'll not only piss me off, you'll incite World War Three." I push down my skirt and sit upright in defiance.

"Oh, Shortcake, you have no idea how fucking wrong you are." He doesn't just speak, he fucks each word, each letter, and leaves me a hot, wet mess. "Marvin knows who you are."

"Are you sure you're not the one who smoked crack?" I counter, unmoved.

Hunter tongues his cheek, looking to the left as he composes himself. "He knows who you are because I've spoken to him about you. Many times, actually."

I lick my suddenly dry lips. "And you what? Had a picture of me on hand? How does he know what I look like?"

The room suddenly gets smaller, or maybe Hunter grows to godlike proportions. "No, Shortcake, I told him that you were the only woman who can bring a man to his knees by a look alone. With all that fiery red hair, a pink pout which promises nothing but trouble, and a mouth which leaves me hard for days, he only had to take one look at you and know who you were."

I gulp. "I thought it was because you had a legion of women knocking down your door."

Hunter smirks, the sight too much for words. Placing one knee on the arm of the couch, he commences a slow crawl toward me. I instantly fall downward, unable to stay upright even if I tried. "Why did you tell Marvin about me?"

My chest is rising and falling so quickly, my words are punctuated with breathless tremors. Hunter places both hands either side of my head, keeping his full weight off of me as he scans down my body in one long, slow sweep.

I open my legs to accommodate his massive frame, and he slides between them like he was meant to be there all along. "Because…I have never met anyone quite like you before, Miss Mary Mitts."

I'm waiting for him to elaborate, but he doesn't. He searches my eyes, delving so deep I'm afraid of what he'll find. I want to ask him what that means, but talk time is over when he lowers those sinful lips and kisses over my cheeks, my chin, then down my neck.

He suckles at my racing pulse, the sting shooting all the way to my center. Tossing my head back, I squeeze my eyes shut and get lost in the feel of his luscious lips and the bouquet of his woody cologne. He fists a hand in my hair, tugging sharply as he works his way lower, tonguing over the tops of my rising breasts.

As he's nestled between my legs, I can feel him lengthening against me. The consciousness sends my body into sensory overload and I can't stop panting like a cat in heat. He releases me and I almost sag in relief because his grip, his kisses, they aren't gentle, or testing the waters—Hunter takes and consumes me, hungry to savor every last piece of me. And I like it.

Powerless to stop, I thread both hands through his hair, the soft strands easy to hold on to. I envision using them as reins as he makes good on his promise. The mere thought of what he's about to do has me whimpering.

He tongues the pillows of my breasts, before reaching between us and hurriedly unlacing the ties on my tank. He splits it apart, allowing him greater access to my breasts. He buries his face between the junction and hums in complete satisfaction.

"How is it even possible that your smell gets me hard?" To accentuate his point, he bucks upward in case I can't feel him nudging closer to where I'm desperate for him to be. Knowing I elicit this response from him is an aphrodisiac within itself. I feel downright desirable.

Unable to speak, I roll beneath him, loving the feel of his

firm body pressed to mine. I'm impatient however, and want him everywhere all at once. Reading my needs, he slips a hand into my tank and cups my left breast. I'm ashamed to admit that I almost come because he feels so good.

"These are fucking magnificent," he hums, rolling his thumb over my pearled nipple.

There isn't much room for him to move around in my top, and the restriction just adds to the heightened state I'm already in. "Please…" I hate how needy I sound, especially since I made a point of stressing that I don't beg—ever—but it looks like Hunter wins.

"Please what?" he questions, his huskiness sending my hormones into overdrive.

"Please…more."

"More? That sounded like begging, but that's impossible, right? You don't beg. Ever."

Groaning, I clench my teeth together with my eyes still squeezed shut. The flames of hell are licking at my pussy and if he doesn't extinguish them soon, I will do so myself. I slide my arm between us, so ready to get this show on the road. But Hunter slaps my hand away and tsks me.

"Don't you dare take that rite of passage away from me. You've made me wait long enough."

I finally open my eyes, the room spinning as I attempt to gather my bearings and not pass out. Hunter is hovering over me, his hand still inside my top. He is almost too gorgeous to look at. His tousled hair flicks forward, framing his jagged face. His eyes are consumed with a blackness, the sea green depths eaten up by wanton desire.

"What do you want?"

"Everything," I reply without pause.

His pink lips slant into a wicked promise, and I suddenly am thankful for being a greedy little girl. "I'm not planning on being gentle."

A jolt of electricity zaps my pussy in anticipation. "Good. I can handle anything you give."

"Don't be so sure."

I have no time to ask what exactly that means, because he rips his hand from my top before seeking solace beneath my skirt. The moment he rubs two fingers over my underwear, a low growl rumbles from his chest. "I could say all the clichéd things, like you're so wet, your pussy feels like heaven, but I'd rather be blunt and tell you I'm going to eat you out and we're both going to fucking love it."

Fisting my underwear in his grip, he tugs and they rip like they're made of paper. I only thought that happens in the movies, but I'm living proof that panty ripping is a real-life thing. Hunter tosses them over his shoulder, smirking when a flush overtakes me.

"Do you blush all over?"

"Only one way to find out."

He groans, his gaze dropping to my heaving chest, betraying how turned on I am.

Sitting back on his heels, he reveals just how turned on he is because the bulge lurking from his jeans is near frightening. I gulp.

Leaning forward, he runs both hands up my thighs, eyes pinned to mine as he hikes up my skirt with the sweeping movement. When it slips higher and higher until it sits bunched up around my waist, the reality of me being butt naked hits home, and I instantly attempt to shut my legs.

"Uh-uh. Spread your legs," he instructs, his fingers pressed lightly into my inner thigh. I know I don't have a choice, so I comply. He takes a moment to thoroughly explore me, his eyes riveted to my naked center. "Strawberries and cream has never been more fitting."

On cue, I redden, and Hunter growls.

Finally, his eyes flick to mine and I sink into the cushions, afraid he's about to make good on his word and eat me whole. He swoops down and nestles between my legs, pushing my right one out further. I'm completely exposed to him.

He hums before lowering his mouth to the junction of my thighs and licking my entrance in one long, wet, painfully slow lick. I instantly rocket off the couch. It's been so long since I've been intimate with someone this way, as Corey was never a fan of oral sex—giving, that is. Receiving was a whole different story.

Pushing him from my mind, I focus on the way Hunter guides his lips and tongue around my heated flesh, lapping at me with a languid rhythm. There is no hurry to his actions because he knows in about three seconds, I'm going to beg he put me out of my misery.

His fingers squeeze my inner thigh, working alongside the cadence of his mouth. His scruff abrades my sensitive skin, almost to the point of it being painful, but the pleasure overrides the sting. He brushes his lips backward and forward, as if he's attempting to bury himself inside of me, slathering my arousal all over him.

My body tingles, but it's not enough. "More," I shamelessly demand, peering down to watch where we are joined. I'm utterly captivated by the way he moves, knowing his way around like those lips were crafted especially for me.

"I'm trying to be a gentleman." His breath is a wicked torment, adding to the fire burning within.

"Be one tomorrow. Now, I just want, no need you to get me off." No point beating around the bush—no pun intended. He chuckles against my needy pussy.

My hips soar off the couch, but Hunter fixes a hand around my waist and gives me what I want. He drives his tongue into me before biting my clit gently. A primitive growl escapes me because I'm certain I'm about to die.

My near death doesn't deter him however, because he continues licking, biting, suckling until I'm wriggling to flee this sinful bliss. It's almost too much. The way he works my body, knowing when I'm close, before he slows down and skates around where I want him to be.

If this wasn't torturous enough, he lifts my leg over his shoulder, opening me wider and using his entire tongue to lap me up. I scream and a string of expletives leave me. He's everywhere all at once and does something which has me seeing stars. He lifts the hood of my clit and tongues me until I'm squirming and bucking wildly on his face.

A knot begins to form, and each time his tongue and lips move over me, it begins to unravel dangerously fast. He senses my need for a release and starts to lick faster, harder, inserting a finger while his lips are still attached. I'm so full I'm certain I'm going to burst, but I drive my hips forward, taking everything he wants to give.

He wasn't joking when he said he was going to eat me, because that's exactly how I feel. He's consuming me from the inside out, and as he tongues over my inflamed center, I know it won't be long until I'm eaten alive.

I thrust my hips violently, fucking his face as he fucks me with his tongue. I'm hot, sticky, but I can't stop. My release is so close I can taste it. Hunter is like a starved animal, and when he pulls his lips away and inserts two fingers into me, pumping them in and out while watching me watching him, I can't control the scream that rips from my chest.

His lips are red, swollen from eating me out with such ferocity, and it drives me wild seeing my arousal smeared on his face. Our eyes our locked, just how his fingers are inside of me, and I've never felt more wanted than I do right now.

"Your cunt is my new favorite cheat meal," he hums, licking his lips, savoring my taste. I moan, his dirty words only adding to the pinnacle I'm about to reach.

I can't take it any longer and arch my back, opening myself up as wide as I can go. I need him to finish this, finish me. "Please," I croak, closing my eyes. "Please, Hunter…I need to come." There, he got what he wanted—me begging, it's now time he gives me what I want.

"Oh, Shortcake, I should just torture you a little more, because you sure as fuck have tortured me." He twists his fingers, stretching me so wide, my muscles screaming in blissful agony. "But I just can't help myself."

He pulls out his fingers and lunges forward, sealing his mouth over me and tonguing me so fierce, my body goes lax and I see stars. Pride is no longer part of my vocabulary as I ride his face, reaching down and clutching his hair in both hands. I hold him prisoner, chasing my release, because when he sucks over my clit, writes his name with his tongue over it, and inserts two fingers, I let go and I'm not exactly quiet about it.

I scream like a banshee, writhe uncontrollably, and cry happy tears, because something amazing happens, and Hunter feels it too. He continues milking me until I'm dry, dry humping the couch beneath him.

I'm too far gone to realize what is happening until he groans and it's fairly obvious he's followed suit in his pants. He is mumbling under his breath, a jumble of holy fucks and oh my god, she's a unicorn. Good to see I'm not the only one who's lost their mind.

My body is trembling and my heart is running an imaginary race. As I look down at Hunter, I see those sweltering eyes staring at me like I'm an alien. I have no idea what is going on until he wipes a hand down his saturated face.

A blush overtakes me because holy shit, that orgasm was the most intense one I've had—ever. It was like something exploded inside of me.

Hunter works his way up my body, licking his lips and humming. "I should be so ashamed I came in my pants like a prepubescent teen, but holy fuck, that was so hot." I chew the corner of my lip, attempting to conceal my smile. But he tugs it free. "Own that shit, Shortcake because you just inflated not only my cock, but my ego too."

When I arch a brow, totally lost, Hunter chuckles. "Oh, god, that's even hotter because I know I was the first guy to make you come so hard you…"

He leaves the sentence hanging, appearing to want to beat his chest in pride. "I what?" I ask, as I know this was different. I felt like I was on the cusp of dying.

He shakes his head, that look of bewilderment assailing

him once more. "Mary Mitts…you're a squirter. I'm coated in your flavor and I want more. So much more."

"A what?"

Question time is over, because when Hunter slides down my body and opens my legs once more, I know this lesson is one better shown.

Ten

Hunter

Three days later

Just call me Judas, because I must have killed Jesus Christ in my past life. That's the only explanation to why this current clusterfuck is happening to me.

Three days ago, something amazing happened, probably the best fucking thing that's happened in my entire life. Mary came over, intent on ripping me a new one. I had no clue that me fearing for my life would result in me coming in my pants like a tween, but I'd happily renounce my manhood if it meant Mary squirted all over my face again and again.

Yes, she's a squirter, and she showered me with her musk, which I want to bottle and place on my pillow like a little mint. She is like a unicorn amongst hopeful, horny men, longing for that one day they'll catch a glimpse of this magical creature. But I didn't just take a peek, no, I was riding that unicorn, or rather, she was riding me.

I was like a starved beast, feasting on her until we both fell into a satisfied slumber, and we didn't even have sex. She didn't even touch my cock, and I felt like I'd been screwed six ways to Sunday. I slept like a baby, so ready to have morning sex with this anomaly, but when I woke, she was gone.

Poof! Gone into thin air.

Maybe I'd dreamt it, but her scent still lingered on my tongue, so I knew it really happened, but where was she? I waited, thinking maybe she'd gone out to get coffee. But an hour later, it was fairly obvious that unless she was getting coffee in Jamaica, she wasn't coming back.

Not wanting to crowd her, I showered and got ready for work. I half expected her to be at the office, tearing up my carpet while I teared at hers. But she wasn't. When AM became PM and I was looking at my phone like the antichrist, I knew Mary had done a me—she fucked and flew.

I felt so…dirty, yeah, I see the irony, but that soon turned into detachment. Whatever, we had a good time. I don't know what I expected to happen. With that as my marching tune, I forgot about Mary and her magical vagina and focused on not focusing on her.

Day two I was fucking jacked up and jacked off. The least she could do was call. What if I'd suffered a concussion from her riding my face like a bull? But the radio silence was a swift kick to the balls, because I knew she wasn't calling.

Mid-afternoon, I wondered if maybe I should call the hospitals. Maybe she was hurt? Maybe she was running with scissors? Or maybe she was dehydrated from all the water loss? I don't know how many times I picked up my phone, the blank screen staring at me, a blatant reminder of what a pussy I was being.

I asked Keira to hide my phone in a place I'd never look, which she did. Twenty minutes later, I was begging she give it back. Of course, there was a price to pay. She made me promise to take her out for dinner. At that stage, I would have agreed to sell her my soul. When she retrieved the cell from my jacket pocket, I knew it was time to fuck the day off with a bottle of whiskey and porn.

I was ready to wank Mary from my system, focusing on the busty blonde bouncing on my screen, but my dick went into hiding. I literally had to make sure it was still there. Maybe it was the porn. But after twenty-five different DVDs, one thing became apparent—my cock only comes out to play for Mary.

Done with the spectacle, I gave in and I called her. This was a first. When it went to voicemail, her message did what twenty-five pornos couldn't—I got hard.

Hi, you've called Mary. Sorry I missed your call, but if you leave a message, I'll get back to you as soon as I can. Oh, but if you're a blond-haired asshole, whose named starts with Hunt and ends in screw you, lose this number. Beep.

I had to dial again in case I was hearing things, but nope, it was clear as day. I had managed to piss Mary off once again, but this time, it appeared she wasn't giving me a second chance to show her just how sorry I was.

I racked my brain, attempting to figure out what the fuck I did to offend her. We passed out well spent on the sofa, so unless I offended her somehow in my sleep, she's gone completely crazy. And what better person to talk about this insanity to than the one and only Dr. Dix.

"Hello, Susanna, you look positively ravishing. Is that a

new sweater?" I say, waltzing into Dixon's office. His loyal receptionist and forever bodyguard peers up at me from behind her desk. There is no sweet talking her, however.

"Dr. Mathews is currently with a patient, Mr. O'Shea. Can I take a message?" She peers at me over the top of her glasses, ready to chase me from the building if she sniffs a hint of corruption.

"I'll wait," I reply, placing my forearms along the counter and smiling sweetly. She purses her lips, but continues typing.

Looking at my watch, I see that it's almost 12 p.m. Surely, he's almost done. Wondering who is listening to the pearls of wisdom, I stand taller and strain my neck to look at Susanna's computer. Not even making eye contact, she's onto me and clears her throat.

If I wasn't desperate, I wouldn't be here, but I need someone to tell me what the fuck to do. Drumming my fingers on the counter, I whistle the tune to Mission Impossible while questioning if it's too early for scotch.

I called in sick today because I literally feel like my stomach is eating itself and I can't spend another day in limbo. "How long…"

Susanna holds up her finger, a silent warning that she'll have no problems mounting my head as a trophy to these walls.

Dixon's voice booms through the foyer. "I'll see you next week, Ms. Tully."

"Thank you so much, Dr. Mathews. I feel so much better."

When I see just who Ms. Tully is, I know I got into the wrong business. Ms. Tully looks like Miss Universe. When she locks eyes with me, she rewards me with a wink. My shattered ego could do with the boost, so I lean on my cupped palm and give her a killer smile.

Dixon is behind her, slashing at his neck, but he can shove it. "Hello." Ms. Tully batts her eyelashes.

My cock barely rises from its perpetual slumber. But even if it decided to stop wearing black and emerge from this state of mourning, Dixon, as usual, is the forever cockblocker. "Mr. O'Shea, it's so wonderful you could make it." It is? "The itchiness gone then? What about the rash?" The world has fucking lost its mind. "I told you chlamydia doesn't have to be a crippling illness. The gonorrhoea however…" and he makes a pained face, while Susanna covers her mouth to stifle her laugh.

Ms. Tully's smirk transforms to a disgusted frown as she makes a beeline for the door, leaving a trail of smoke in her wake.

"Nice, asshole," I say, while Dixon grins.

"What are you doing here? Why aren't you at work?" As he takes a closer look at me, he rubs over his chin before sighing. Am I that obvious? "Ms. Vale, cancel lunch." It appears so.

He doesn't wait for me to speak, but instead turns on his heel and walks into his office. I follow. Once I step foot inside, I can't help but laugh. Mary was so right. Such an old man's cave. The thought of her leaves me breathless and I idly rub over my aching chest.

"What the fuck happened now?" he asks, sitting on the edge of his desk, folding his arms.

"Jesus Christ. I hope that's not your lead in, 'cause if it is, I have no idea how you're still in business."

Dix rolls his eyes while I slump onto the leather sofa. "Hunt, whatever you want to say, just say it. You honestly cannot shock me anymore."

Time to test that theory.

Casually crossing an ankle over my knee, I lean back and place my arm along the top of the sofa. "So, I have this friend…" Dixon pinches the bridge of his nose and shakes his head. I ignore him. "Let's call him…Hugh. Well, he had the most amazing thing happen to him a few nights ago. A woman named…Shortcake, she and Hugh have recently put their differences aside and played nice…but that's the problem… they played too nice…" I wonder just how much I should share.

Fuck it. He's getting the uncut version.

"Played?" Dixon asks, cocking a brow.

I nod. "Yes. Hugh wore Shortcake out, and before he knew it, Shortcake wanted to…bake a cake, because she was ravenous. Hugh hand-picked Shortcake's…strawberries. Actually, they were more like melons." I lick my lips when remembering those pillows of perfection, but I need to focus. "But anyway, Shortcake begged Hugh to whip her cream and he did, twice, and before Hugh knew it, Shortcake was squirting cream all over his face. Hugh then whipped his own cream, which he spilled in his pants." Dixon looks stupefied, but I continue. "They both fell asleep after their hunger was quenched, but when Hugh woke, Shortcake was gone. He didn't think much of it, but it's now three days later, and Hugh is wondering what happened, because he's become addicted to Shortcake's cream cake and is pretty certain he will slip into a hypoglycemic state if he doesn't have another taste."

Smirking, I breezed through that. Dixon has no idea this is me.

He blinks once, before opening his mouth and saluting his finger, but changes his mind at the last minute and seals his lips.

I wonder if the hypoglycemic line was too much.

He peers up at the ceiling and takes three deep breaths. "You…" He raises his pointer, needing a minute. "You fucked Mary?" he gasps after a long pause.

"What?" I fake innocence, sitting forward, mouth agape. "Me? This is about my friend, Hugh."

But Dixon doesn't buy it and scratches over his brow. "You don't even have a friend named Hugh! And whenever you use a food-inspired analogy, I get hives, especially when they are about fucking my fiancée's best friend!"

I raise my eyes upward. "Calm down, you drama queen. I didn't fuck anybody. Neither did Hugh. And Mary? I'm pretty sure I said her name was Shortcake. Were you even listening to me?"

"Then what the fuck happened? Hugh"—he uses air quotations to humor me—"just what? Whipped Shortcake's batter and now she's done a runner?"

I flick the side of my nose, before pointing my finger. "Now you're catching up. Yes, that's exactly what happened. Why?"

"Why what?"

"Why has Shortcake gone underground?" I ask without missing a beat.

"Because Shortcake probably realized what an utter idiot Hugh is and wishes she skipped dessert!" Dixon replies, pushing off his desk, dumbfounded.

My stomach sinks and I rub my chin. "Hugh doesn't, and that makes him crazy, right?" The mood settles as Dixon can read my sincere confusion.

He walks over to where I sit and sighs. "Hugh needs to tell Shortcake how he feels. Just because they ate cake together doesn't mean everything is going to be sweet."

He's right. The ache returns. "She makes Hugh physically ill. He wants to vomit whenever she's three feet away."

Dixon smirks. He's so enjoying this. "That's called love, my friend."

I gag on air and thump on my chest to dislodge the obstruction. "No, it's called losing one's mind. The fighting Hugh can handle. He can't handle the…" I pause, probing for the right word. "The constant sea sickness he feels."

"They're called butterflies," Dixon says, filling in the blanks, while I wonder if maybe he needs a nap.

I recoil, twisting my lips. "What the fuck is that? Hugh is pretty sure it's indigestion."

He bursts out laughing, wiping the corner of his eyes. "Hugh is a fucking moron."

Yes, yes he is.

No closer to figuring this out, I ask, "So, Shortcake is MIA because…" I gesture with my hands that Dix is to elaborate.

"Because maybe she got scared. Maybe she needs time to clear her head."

I was hoping he'd say that, but her voice message—what a clear fuck you. "What should he do?"

Dixon sits down on the couch and drops his linked fingers between his splayed legs. "He should call her." Just as I'm about to rebuke, he persists. "If he already has and she's made it clear she's angry at him and he has no idea why, then he needs to grow a pair and talk to her face to face."

I cringe. That sounds like an awful idea. "What if he's scared she'll rearrange his face with a cheese grater?"

"Then he needs to get over it, man the fuck up, and fight for what he wants. The fact she allowed him anywhere near her… cake"—I grin. This analogy is fucking genius—"in the first place means she feels something for him too."

My heart kicks against my ribcage. "Really?"

Dixon nodding is like witnessing a blind man regaining his sight. "Yes, really. From what I know about Shortcake, she doesn't take too lightly to having dessert with just anyone. He just needs to talk to her. Over coffee, that's it. Sex tends to complicate things because it's not what most people have difficulties with. It's the talking about one's feelings which leave us tongue-tied."

Mulling over his sermon, I realize that he's right. Hugh and Shortcake had no problem getting down and dirty, but Mary and Hunter…Hunter and Mary, could we really have a civil conversation about what happened?

I suppose there is only one way to find out. "Gee, you sure know a lot."

Dixon smiles, before slapping the back of my head. I grunt on impact. So much for the heart to heart. "It's my job. Now go. Hugh needs to sort out his shit." He's right. No wonder people pay a small fortune to spend an hour with this guru of love.

Standing, I have a new lease on life. I will find Mary and demand she talk to me, because we need to get to the bottom of this once and for all. "Hugh is indebted to you. He will make sure you don't get your balls covered in honey, and tied to a pole naked, in Tijuana, at your bachelor party."

Dix stands with a smirk, pointing to the door. "And I will make sure Shortcake's best friend doesn't find out about this until Hugh finds his balls."

"Hugh thanks you." I bow in gratitude.

My pants vibrate, and I wonder if my cock has finally stopped being a wimp. But when the vibration continues, I know it's my phone. Yanking it from my jeans pocket, I answer without seeing who the caller is.

"Hello?" I'm breathless in anticipation, while Dixon looks at me like I've lost my marbles.

"Hi, Hunter." My body deflates. Dix's eyes widen, but I shake my head.

"Oh, hey Keira." His hopeful mask is replaced with war paint and he walks over to his desk, uninterested.

"Sorry to call you, I know you're sick…" I can hear her sincerity, so I wonder what's wrong.

"It's fine. What's up?"

A heavy sigh leaves her. This can't be good. "I think you need to come into the office."

"Why?"

"Um, because Mary is here," she whispers, appearing to fear for her life.

"Mary?" I bellow, a little louder than intended. Dixon's interest is now totally piqued and he sprints over, gesturing that I'm to put Keira on speaker. I do.

"Yes, she arrived about ten minutes ago. She's…I just think you need to come here. And soon."

Dixon runs a hand through his hair, his cheeks inflated. He looks about as happy as a penguin in a microwave. "Go," he mouths, while I wonder if he secretly hates me and wishes me dead. Whatever Mary is doing can't be good.

"Okay, I'll be there in fifteen." I have no idea what's going on, but the fact Mary is at my work is good, right?

I look at Dixon for any last words. The ones he gives me

pretty much sum up my life. "Sometimes, bad things happen to good people, but in your case…it's karma."

I've prepared myself for every possible scenario.

I have no idea what I'm walking into, but from Keira's terrified tone, I'm not too sure if I'll end this day with all my limbs attached. The elevator doors part and I pop my head out, afraid Mary is waiting in the wings, ready to throat punch me and kick me in the balls.

The coast is clear, so I step out and make my way to my office. It feels like I'm walking a death march, but that end result seems like an easy way out, because when I turn the corner and see Keira outside my door, biting her nails, I know this will end in tears.

"Keira?" I whisper, not wanting to alert Mary that I'm here.

She turns swiftly, her eyes wide and filled with terror. "Oh, thank god. I tried to keep her out, but she threatened to cut off my hair." On instinct, she draws her blonde locks over her shoulder and twirls the strands into her fist.

"You did the right thing." Something shatters against the wall, followed by a string of profanity. "Go back to your office. This isn't going to be pretty." When she hesitates, I press. "Believe me, Keira, you being here will just make things worse."

She finally nods. "If you need me, you know where I am." I appreciate the gesture, but if I go anywhere near her, I have a sneaking suspicion Mary will castrate me and make good on her promise to scalp Keira. She brushes my upper arm before leaving me alone with Huffy the Dragon.

I take a deep breath, say a prayer, and open my office door. The moment I do, a book almost connects with my head. A few inches to the left, and I'd be blind in my right eye. "What in the actual living hell is the matter with you?" I roar, using the door as a shield when Mary reaches for a paperweight off my semi-cleared desk.

One good thing about her tirade is that my desk has finally seen daylight, and who would have thought, it's black. I could have sworn it was brown.

With crystal paperweight in hand, she narrows her eyes into mere slits. "I ask myself that daily, but I still have no fucking idea why I thought messing around with you would be a good idea!"

"You need to calm down!" Probably not the smartest thing to say, seeing as she's armed and ready to take off my head.

"You need to not tell me what to do!" she rebukes, her fiery red hair appearing to set alight as she storms to where I stand.

Quickly darting from the firing line, I slam the door shut and dance around the room. Mary follows in hot pursuit, threatening to render me unconscious with the brick she still holds. "I'm sorry if you're having post-coital tristesse." She curls her lip, not at all amused at my attempts to lighten the mood. "Post-orgasmic blues." When she continues looking at me like I'm speaking Chinese to a Zimbabwean, I realize I'm going to have to be blunt. "You're missing my cock."

"Ugh!" she screams, raising her pitching arm, prepared to throw a strike. I duck and weave, hopeful a moving target will be harder for her to get a clean shot. "This is exactly the reason why I need my head read. I can't believe I let you touch me."

I raise my finger, still running circles around the room. "Yes, you did. In many places, and with many of my body parts," I reason, hoping she remembers the two amazing orgasms I gave her so she stops this rampage. "And you liked it," I add, in case she's had a lapse in memory.

When there is a hole the size of my head in the wall, thanks to the flying missile Mary just hurled, I begin to think that theory may not be too far off the mark. "Shortcake, please, for the love of my balls, please stop and tell me what's wrong."

The desk is the barricade which I use to prevent Mary from strangling me, and it allows me to catch my breath. When she lunges right, I lunge left. If I didn't know any better, I'd say her behavior is that of a scorned, jealous lover, but that can't be right, because that doesn't apply to us.

She grips the edge of the desk, springing forward, while I stand my ground. I'm a fucking sick bastard, because her anger is turning me on. "I saw the text message from Little Bo Peep."

"Who?" I pull back, completely confused.

"Don't play dumb, although, in your case, I do question your mindset if you think the blonde down the hall is suitable screwing material." When she hooks her thumb over her shoulder, I know she's talking about Keira.

"What are you talking about? The last time I saw you, you were completely sated, and I was completely slathered in your come, what the fuck has Keira got to do with this?" I ask, shaking my head, baffled.

Mary takes a deep breath, her reddened cheeks reminding me of her pink flesh as I devoured her like she was my last meal. "I woke up to get a drink of water, and I wasn't snooping, but I saw your cell and the message that polluted your screen, highlighted what a fucking idiot I am."

"What message?" I scream, hands spread out wide.

"Oh, don't give me that baloney. I saw it, Hunter!"

"Well, I'm glad you did, because I sure as shit haven't." There is only one way to end this. Thrusting my hand into my pocket, I yank out my cell and scroll through my messages. Mary is obviously high because there are no…oh, shit.

Can't wait for you to bend me over that desk of yours again on Friday night.

In my defense, I didn't even know she sent it. I was too preoccupied with eye fucking Mary's name in my contacts list to even notice Keira had sent me this incriminating text. But even so, why does Mary care?

I can't help the grin which plays at my lips. I know it'll infuriate Mary further, but I've come to accept that in times of crisis, I like to add fuel to an out-of-control fire. "Are you"—I tongue my cheek, buying time—"jealous?"

Mary scoffs, folding her arms, but fuck me dead, she is. This has got to be the best day of my life. "Oh, Shortcake, there's no need to be jealous. There's enough of me to go around." To emphasize my point, I grab my crotch and wink.

It's all said tongue in cheek, so when Mary's scowl twists into a smirk, I thank the good lord that she's seen reason. "Thank you so much for sharing. You really know how to work that inch," she says in a sickly-sweet voice, interlacing her fingers over her heart as she batts her eyelashes. The sight is supposed to fake innocent and gratitude, but I have a feeling I'll be walking with a limp in point two seconds.

"An inch? I'd say it was more nine." I hold out both hands lengthwise, hoping to display my size.

She giggles, and I swear to god, if Satan had a doorbell, this would be it. "You're so big," she coos, reaching into her handbag. "My pussy was on fire. It's never been eaten out like that before." I don't like to brag, but a shit-eating grin takes over my entire face. "Oh, Hunter, take me now. My loins are so juicy for your little popsicle."

Hold up. Little? I slam on the brakes. Is she making fun of me? "Okay, now you're just being mean," I retort, as I watch with interest when she bares a lighter. "I didn't know you smoked."

Mary gushes dramatically, all doe-eyed and ready to use my innards as a washing board. "My panties are currently smoking being in your manly presence."

"All right, enough, how about you…" The words go into hiding when Mary reveals what else she's hiding in her bag of tricks.

The shine from the bottle of lighter fluid she's holding sparkles brightly, bringing to light what Mary intends to do. Flipping off the top, she titters. "I only think it's fair I now set your world on fire, considering you were kind enough to slot me into your busy manwhore schedule!"

She wouldn't. But when she douses my desk with the fluid and flips open the Zippo, I know that she would. She will.

"You're fucking crazy!" I bellow, my dick almost punching a hole in my pants because this look of jealousy suits her.

I don't care she's seconds away from burning down the building, because this rage was brought on due to the fact she's so fucking green-eyed, she would burn this desk, my entire office, as it'll eradicate the memories of me fucking around with someone other than her.

As the flame flickers brightly, I'm left with no other choice but to pounce forward, cup the back of Mary's neck, and drag her toward me. A whoosh of sweet air coats my face as it leaves her lungs as I wasn't exactly gentle about drawing her face to mine.

I examine every last inch of her, wanting nothing more than to smash my lips to hers, but if I do, I won't be able to stop, and I'm a fucking coward, because that thought scares me more than I care to admit. This woman has the ability to annihilate me and throw caution to the wind. Until I know what she wants, I have to keep an ace up my sleeve.

But now, now I'm going to fuck her senseless in every corner of the room.

"Drop it," I demand, my eyes flicking to the open flame she still holds.

"Do you really think that's a good idea, considering your desk is covered in an accelerant which will ignite before you can salvage your precious black book?" she smartly replies. Shit, looks like she just found another reason to hate me. In response, I snare her hair in my fist and pull her head backward.

Her pupils dilate and a moan leaves those plump, pink lips. "If I didn't know any better, I'd say you like to play rough. It was pretty evident three nights ago when you fucked my face and begged me to eat that needy pussy out."

Her body grows limp, unlike my cock. "I was horny. I haven't had sex for over a year. You caught me in a weak moment," she spits, eyeing me furiously.

Sweet victory to my ears, because I plan on breaking her

drought until she's walking with a permanent limp. "And what about now?"

This fucking desk is all that separates me from ripping off Mary's little dress and doing unspeakable nasties to her body for hours. "Another weak moment," she confesses, flipping the lid back onto the Zippo, the flame extinguishing, but the fire within me explodes.

I let her go, but that's because when I fuck her, nothing will stand in my way. Storming the desk, I latch onto her wrist when she makes a break for the door. Spinning her around, her lithe form slams into my chest, where I hold her prisoner. She attempts to wriggle free, but it's weak. She wants this as much as me.

"It's a damn shame you ruined that desk, because I've pictured fucking your cute little ass over it time and time again."

"I'm not interested in being one of your whores," she snarls, standing on tippy toes to eyeball me. She doesn't even reach my chin.

"FYI"—I place my hands low on her hips and pull her in to me so she can feel my erect cock—"I never fucked Keira. Yes, I ate her out until she was crying out my name, but the entire time, all I wanted…all I ever seem to want…is you."

"And that's supposed to make me feel better?" she spits, her anger fueling. "I don't share my toys."

"Is that all I am to you?" I ask, rubbing between her legs deliriously slow. "A walking dildo?"

She catches her lower lip, her eyes drooping to half-mast. "If you can't beat 'em, join 'em, right?"

"And that's what you want? Friends with benefits?" A small part of me hopes she says no, but who am I kidding. This is what I know.

"We're not friends," she counters, gasping when I walk my fingers down her delicious ass and squeeze hard. "But the benefits part…bring it. I want it all."

Those words are what every commitment-phobe wants to hear, so why do I feel so empty inside? Because you want more, D2 pipes up, but Mary has made it clear what she wants and where we stand. She can't deny our attraction, but she isn't stupid to play this off as being something more.

Getting my head in the game, I quell down the urge to fight her and focus on playing my part, because I will surrender to this woman beyond a shadow of a doubt. "Okay then, now that that's settled, you said something about beating." Mary's body twists into a pliable mass when I lower my lips and bite over her chin. "Well, Shortcake, rest assured, there will be a lot of that, because you're moments away from beating me off with those pretty lips."

"Just shut up and fuck me already," she pants.

Her words get me harder than Ron Jeremy's hedgehog. "Yes, ma'am." I wish I could savor her, devour every last inch and take my time, but if I don't get inside of her, like right now, I just may go blind.

Unleashing her, I eye fuck the living hell out of her before gripping the hem of her blue dress and tearing it from her body. She's standing before me in nothing but a black bra, underwear, and heels. "Take those off." I gesture to her lace, boy shorts, needing her naked pronto.

She doesn't argue and lowers them down her supple hips and milky thighs. When she kicks them off to the side and goes to slip off her heels, I tsk her. "Those stay. Now show me those fucking beautiful tits."

The moment she reaches behind her, I unbutton my jeans and take hold of my shaft. I always go commando, as underwear is such a waste of time. When she unclasps the bra, but holds the cups to her chest, I almost come in my pants, because Mary Mitts may talk big, but deep down, she's sweetly shy.

"Don't make me come over there and rip that off your body. It looks expensive," I warn, rubbing my hand up and down my cock. A honeyed flush takes over her entire body when she watches with wide eyes as I jerk myself off.

"I'll show you mine if you show me yours," she dares, but I'm already two steps ahead as I thrust my jeans down, cock on full display.

Her first reaction has me rethinking my decision, because when she averts her eyes and gasps, I suddenly feel like an animal. "Look at me, Mary," I order, because if she can't bear to look me, she sure as shit won't be able to handle me fucking her until I'm paralyzed from the waist down.

It takes her a few moments, but she finally meets my eyes before they drop lower and lower, finally coming to rest at my dick. I don't stop fisting my cock and celebrate when her chest begins to rise and fall quickly. She watches me closely, rubbing her thighs together when I quicken my strokes.

Her nectar is so sweet, and I want it all over me. I want her. "Holy fuck," she gasps, her eyes glued to my cock.

I know my dick is impressive, but I've never felt nobler than I do right now. I need to bury myself in this woman. "I won't ask you again."

My demand seems to snap her from her coma, and she finally puts me out of my misery and bares herself to me.

My hand pauses because I can't multitask. I need to pay my undivided attention to the sight before me.

I knew she was beautiful, but this takes beauty to a whole different level.

Her copper waves contrast her milky flesh, highlighting every single sun-kissed freckle, which I want to trace with my tongue. Her breasts are full, perky, but not in a Hollywood, fake tits kind of way. They're natural, and my god, I want to motorboat the fuck out of them. A heart-shaped freckle on the curve of her right areola has my mouth watering as I want to take that pearled nipple into my mouth.

Her hips are curvy and I like it. I like that she's real. But when I take in her bare pussy, I want to drop to my knees. I've seen my fair share of pussies over the years, but Mary's... she's utterly delicious. I have no idea how I'm going to last because I'm on the cusp of coming on looks alone. Her pussy is ripe, and all I want to do is take a bite.

She steps forward, swallowing, before lowering her hand. She settles her grip over mine, moving up and down my cock. Even though it's not her palm jerking me off, the sight of her tiny hand over mine, over my dick, has me grunting and pumping my hips.

"Do you have any protection?" she asks, licking her lips, gliding her hand with mine. I nod, eyes locked with hers.

She releases her hand, only to grip the hem of my t-shirt, indicating she wants it off. Whatever Mary wants she will get, so I loosen my hold, reach behind me, and yank off my shirt by the collar. I toss it and my jeans over my shoulder, standing proud in my birthday suit.

Mary studies me closely, whimpering. The sound is my

undoing and I lift her up. She wraps her legs around me and concedes defeat. I round the desk, wishing it wasn't doused, because all I can think about is bending her over it and watching my cock enter her over and over again.

She sinks her teeth into my neck, sucking and groaning over my pulse, which has me seeing stars. Without a second to waste, I slam her onto her feet and spin her around. "Hold onto the chair," I command, and she does, turning it so the back faces us.

The high-backed leather seat looked good in the store. Now it's going to look even better when I fuck Mary over it. Reaching for my discarded jeans, I pull a condom from my wallet and almost tear the wrapper in half with eager fingers.

Mary's bouncy ass is posed in the air as she turns over her shoulder to watch me wrap myself up. I have done this countless times before, but it feels like I'm a fumbling virgin as I try and roll it down my shaft.

The moment it's on, I advance forward, so ready to lose myself in this woman and never be found. She's braced her hands either side of the headrest, giving me my new favorite view. Running the heel of my palm down the middle of her back, I lick my lips when I come to the pleat in her ass. She shifts her hips, but there is no way she's denying me this luxury. I continue tracing downward, groaning when I come in contact with her puckered plum, but that will have to wait for another day.

Scooping my fingers, I hook my way into her sex, humming when I feel how fucking ready she is. She spreads her legs, opening herself up to me, giving me permission to take and give. I begin pumping two fingers inside of her, wanting her to be primed and ready, because when I fuck her, it's going to be rough.

She bounces against me, bucking backward, her head dropping forward as she moans. My fingers are suckled by her needy flesh, and I can't wait to be encased in her warmth. With the other hand, I reach for her swaying breasts and tug at her pebbled nipple. She screams and fucks my fingers, chasing her release.

She's more than ready, and prolonging the evitable would just be cruel to the both of us. So withdrawing my fingers, I place a hand to her hip and lead my cock to her entrance. She arches her back, spreads her legs wider, and grips the top of the chair. She's offering me the most treasured delicacy when she presents her ass, hinting what we both want and need.

With cock still in hand, I edge into her slickened lips, a gasp leaving her when she feasts on my throbbing head. I'm not even a quarter of the way in, and I already feel like I'm going to come. "More," she demands, bowing her hips to accommodate my size.

Gritting my teeth, I slide in deeper, my cock slithering inside of her, never wanting to emerge ever again. She hisses, a small cry for help as her fingers clasp the top of the chair. "Oh… god." Her words vibrate all the way to the tip of my dick.

She's breathing in slowly, as I know I've stretched her wide. "You okay?" I ask, as I can feel every part of her shifting to lodge this delicious intrusion.

She nods and rocks slowly, testing the feel of me rooted deep inside. Warming her up, I pull out sluggishly, sliding against her g-spot, before nudging my way back in. She groans and begins to milk me impatiently, her hungry sex clenching so tightly, I think I'm going to cry. I'm trying to be slow, gentle, knowing Mary hasn't been intimate with someone for quite some time, but when she bucks her hips, I lose all control and sink all the way in.

We both groan before I pause, needing to savor this moment, because we're at long last locked as one. Looking downward, the sight of me sheathed inside of her is almost too much, and I can't stop myself. I begin to move, plunging in and out, mesmerized by the way my dick and her pussy meet. It's a perfect fit.

"Hunter…" she mewls, thrusting her hips and meeting me stroke for stroke.

The sensation of being inside of Mary has every nerve ending in my body firing. I can feel and taste her as our bodies move in sync perfectly. She grinds on my cock, moaning and bowing low, deepening the angle.

I sink into her over and over, pulling all the way out, before plunging all the way back in. I ensure she can feel every hard inch of me because she's the reason I'm this worked up. The room is filled with our impassioned moans, most likely drifting down the hall, alerting my fellow colleagues that this is the best day of my life.

I increase the tempo, because I know she wants more and so do I. I drive into her like a wild animal, throwing my head back as I clutch onto her waist with both hands. "Oh, fuck." No one has ever felt this good.

I know I'm being incredibly rough, but she can handle it. She thrusts onto my cock, impaling herself faster and harder, screaming and writhing when I hit all the way home. "I've never felt this…" she pants, her sentence unfinished.

Just hearing her voice is a sucker punch to my cock, and I slam so hard into her, she propels forward, growing lax. I know she's close. "You okay, Shortcake?" I breathlessly ask, never breaking rhythm. She nods, whimpering when I reach down and play with her swollen clit. She instantly lets out an ear-splitting scream and sags.

The chair is whining under the pressure and I know it won't be long until Mary buckles too. I'm still not done, not even by half, so I kick the chair out from under her, clasping her waist and scooping a hand under her quivering stomach.

My cock is her anchor and I continue driving into her so fiercely; she collapses onto the desk, front first. There is a small patch she didn't saturate, and she holds onto that section like it's her safety net. She spreads her arms out wide, clutching onto the edge, needing something to hold onto as I fuck her without remorse.

"Oh my god!" she cries, her body flailing around like a rag doll, as she's gone limp.

"Do you want me to stop?" If she says yes, I just may die, but I need to know she's enjoying this as much as me.

"No. More," she commands, slamming onto me, a second lease of life taking over.

She is wild, untamed, stroking the beast in me. I cup both hands under her belly, pivoting her hips so I can deepen the angle. Her warm, silky sex drains my cock. "Fuck!" I roar, my balls hitting her pussy as I penetrate her cavernous heat.

The sight is too much as my dick entering her is like a masterpiece sent from above. I grind down on her clit, eliciting a raw scream. Her ass is poised high and I can't help myself as I smack her cheek—hard.

"You fucker!" she shrieks, crashing down on me and clenching my dick so hard, I wail in delight.

"You like me smacking your ass?" I groan, palming her reddening behind.

"I like it when you don't talk and fuck me," she breathlessly retorts, turning her cheek, her pink lips parted in pure ecstasy.

Her sassiness spurs me on. "Good, 'cause I plan on fucking you every"—thrust— "single"—thrust—"day. And when you can't take it anymore, you're going to fuck me with those pretty lips. Or maybe… I'll fuck you someplace else." To parade my depraved thoughts, I smack her ass again, harder this time. She thrashes about, screaming in utter decadence. "Would you like that?"

Beads of perspiration collect on her pinkening skin and I want to lick every single one. "I asked you a question," I hum, rolling my hips and decelerating the momentum, which is not what Mary wants. I can do this all day because prolonging her orgasm means I get to stay this way forever.

Her eyes and lips are sealed shut, but I know how to make her talk. Reaching down, I circle my pointer against her clit, which has her undulating beneath me. Her bud is so swollen. She's seconds away from coming. But until she answers me, that orgasm will remain a hair's breadth away.

"Fuck me…" she cries, attempting to kickstart my cock, but the sight of her pussy gasping for me has me stopping altogether, still rooted deep within. "Hunter! Please!"

When she attempts to rise, I press my chest to her back, trapping her. Stretching my arms over hers, I interlace our fingers. She smells like strawberries and cream and sex, and I want to fucking eat her whole. "I'll fuck you when you answer me. Do you like it?" I whisper into her ear, suckling the shell.

She moans. "Yes, I love it. Own me."

Music to my ears. "How does my cock feel inside of you?" I roll my hips, ensuring she can feel every single inch of me.

"It feels so…good," she pants, surrendering. "And if you stop, I think I'm going to die."

"What a way to go," I reply, increasing my tempo. She hums in relief. Still encasing her body with mine, I give her what she wants and fuck her mercilessly.

"Never stop," she pants, racing toward the finish line. "Please. I want you everywhere."

"Everywhere?" I question, gritting my teeth, my balls squeezing tight.

"Yes. All those places you said…I want it…I want you."

Those three magical words are my destruction and I pump into her so vigorously, the desk shifts forward with the force, but I don't stop. I shoot upward, clutching her waist, and pistioning my hips so quickly, gasps of air push from my lungs.

Mary screams, collapsing, which is my cue to reach down and flick over her clit. It's her kryptonite, because she shudders and comes with a thunderous cry. The sound is my downfall, and with two quick pumps, I follow, howling when her pussy drains me and a gush floods around me.

Oh god, I'm swimming in Mary's honey once again and I've become addicted.

Aftershocks rock her body, and I stay embedded inside of her, the gravity of having the best sex of my life forbidding me from pulling out anytime soon. Tiny whimpers leave her parted lips as she gulps in mouthfuls of air.

"Are you all right?" I ask when she begins quivering.

"Yes. That was just so…intense," she replies once her breathing settles.

Leaning down, I kiss where her neck meets her shoulder, savoring the fragrance. "That was only the beginning."

She turns to look up at me, eyes wide, but they're soon consumed with a newfound hunger. Her flushed cheeks, wild hair, and pink, swollen lips has a longing rousing in me once again. She gasps.

"Ready for round two?" I don't wait for her to reply. I withdraw, only to flip her onto her back with a smirk.

Her nipples pebble the moment her astounded gaze lands on my cock. "Is that even possible?"

Pulling off the condom, my stare is rooted to her pink, glistening pussy. "Anything is possible when you're involved."

I reach for another condom, slipping it on with a lot more poise this time. Mary watches, a shockwave rocking her body. I want to beat my chest in pride. Standing between her spread legs, I hook my wrists behind her knees, and drag her toward me. She yelps, but that soon turns to a low moan when I suck two fingers and slip them inside of her. "It's okay, Shortcake. Just hold on and enjoy the ride."

Eleven

Hunter

"So, I think if we move this here…then it'll give you more blah blah blah…" I really wish I could concentrate on what Mary is saying, but with her delicious derriere waving in the wind, all I can deliberate over is whether it's too early to go down on her again.

It's Friday, and my week has been filled with fucking Mary anywhere, anytime. You'd think I'd have my fill by now, but each time I taste her, I'm left with a hankering for more. I'm man enough to admit that I'm addicted to her. She's all I think about, and when I'm inside of her, nothing else matters.

I've never felt this before.

Whenever she's around, I feel sick to my stomach and I have an endless supply of Tums on hand. I really wish I could talk to Dixon and Finch, but it's an unspoken rule between Mary and I that whatever we're doing remains solely between us.

I wouldn't even know where to start anyway, because how

do you explain something which makes zero sense?

"Are you even listening to me?" she asks, standing to full height and ruining my view. She was bent over, ass high in the air as she explained the feng shui principles to my office.

The leather chair, which holds such fond memories, squeaks as I rise. Mary soon bites her lip, knowing she's in trouble. The notebook she holds trembles in her hands before she presses it to her chest. Like that can save her. "Can you stop looking at me like that?"

"Like what?" I question, stalking toward her, hands dug deep in my pockets.

Her cheeks turn a rose pink as she backs up. "Like you want to eat me."

Her retreat just stokes the inner competitor and I continue hunting her until she bumps into the wall. "You didn't mind me eating you this morning. Or yesterday afternoon," I counter smartly, running my thumb along her bottom lip, happily reliving the memory.

A flush creeps up the slope of her creamy neck and my mouth instantly waters. I want to follow the current with my tongue. "I have work I have to do."

"So do I," I reply, stopping only when we're pressed front to front. A choppy exhale leaves her, the sound betraying her nerves.

I take a moment to appreciate every single inch of her, because I'm insatiable when it comes to her. Her copper waves are tied back in a low bun, but thanks to our early morning activities, wisps have slipped free. Her tight t-shirt hints at the blue silk bra she's wearing, but I know firsthand, considering I ripped it from her body about an hour ago.

I instantly get hard.

"Hunter!" she gasps, eyes wide as she feels how happy I am to see her.

"Yes," I innocently retort, leaning forward and nuzzling the side of her neck. I hum as I bask in her familiar bouquet.

"You can't be serious," she says breathlessly, instantly growing slack against me.

"I'm pretty sure the hard on I'm sporting is confirmation of just how serious I am."

"I don't know why I bother getting dressed."

"I couldn't agree more," I concur, kissing over her galloping pulse. Just as I walk my fingers into her jeans, a knock sounds loudly against my door. "Go away!" I yell, but the persistent knocking continues.

"Hunter? It's me, Keira."

I literally can feel Mary's body freeze up and grow colder than a snowman's dick. She latches her fingers over my wrist to stop me from reaching the goods. Groaning, I know this is a losing battle, so I remove my hand and sigh.

"Make sure you include a lock on your list of things," I say, pointing to the fallen notebook by her feet. She cracks a hint of a smile.

I rearrange myself because I don't want Keira getting the wrong idea. When I open the door, she stands before it in a white dress, which may as well be made out of plastic wrap. On any other day, I would be wiping the drool from my chin, but now, I just wish she'd go away.

When I stand in front of the doorway, my arm extended high against the doorjamb, prohibiting entry, she nervously tugs at her pearl earring. "Can I come in?" She makes a point to look at my barricade.

"I'm busy. Can it wait?" Subtlety has never been my strong suit, especially now.

I wish I could erase the night I gave in to temptation with this woman. My life would be so much easier, because every time I look at her, I'm reminded of what a fucking bastard I am.

"I won't be a minute. It's about tonight."

"Tonight?" I question, scrunching my brow.

"Yes, but judging by the look on your face, it's safe to assume you forgot we made plans to go out to dinner."

"We did?"

She nods.

Shit, I need to start writing this stuff down.

"It's fine. I was coming here to tell you I can't make it, anyway." I exhale prematurely. "Mr. Gail insisted I accompany him to have drinks with some potential clients."

I scoff, shaking my head in disgust. "That guy needs to give up. People can smell his desperation a mile away."

"I wouldn't be too sure," she ambiguously counters. "He's meeting up with Mr. Yeong's people. The phone conference he had with Mr. Yeong this week went really well."

"What?" I bark, almost falling from my perch.

She nods, confirming my worst fears. "Mr. Yeong can't get to New York until next month, so he's sending his colleagues to talk shop."

"That double crossing motherfucker," I mumble, running a hand through my hair.

This cannot be happening. I thought Mr. Yeong and I were good, but apparently patience isn't a strong point. If I can't deliver what he wants, then Gail may have a shot.

Examining Keira closely, I tilt my head to the side. "You do realize by telling me this you could get fired."

"I know," she confidently replies. Closing the distance between us, she runs her fingers up and down the length of my tie. "But I thought you should know. You're not worried, are you? I mean, you were pretty confident this was in the bag, thanks to the little secret you're guarding." I pull back, impressed.

Keira isn't as naïve as she plays herself to be. She knows I've got something over Mr. Yeong, but now that something means jackshit if I don't find that fucking pocket watch. "Sweetness, I'm not worried. I was just fantasizing about Gail living in a carboard box under the Brooklyn Bridge when I seal this deal before he has a chance to say ni hao to Mr. Yeong's people."

She purses her red lips. "I guess I'll see you tonight then?"

"Abso-fucking-lutely."

"I'll text you the details," she counters, her fingers still stroking my tie very suggestively.

She just did me a solid, so I don't make a fuss. "Thank you. I owe you a drink."

A low hum escapes her as she draws me toward her with my tie. "You owe me a lot more than that."

She's right, but when I hear a bang and a jumble of curses blast from behind me, I know it's time to say goodbye. Gently retrieving my tie, I smile. "Put it on my tab." I don't wait for her to reply, but instead back up into my office and close the door in her unimpressed face.

Taking a moment, I press my forehead to the woodgrain and groan.

"What's the matter? Sad she didn't offer to give you a

blowjob as well?" Mary doesn't hide her contempt.

"If things go south tonight, the only blowjobs being given will be by me. I'm screwed." I sound like a complete drama queen, but if Gail snags this deal out from under me, then I may as well set up a craigslist profile now.

"What's wrong?"

Turning my cheek, I see that Mary stands beside me, arching a brow. Could it be she's worried about me? Wishful thinking can eat a dick. "What's wrong is that Mr. Yeong is my client, and he all but promised me his allegiance, but there's a catch." She waits for me to elaborate, and without a second thought, I do. "If I can find Babe Ruth's 1923 World Series Pocket Watch, then we have a deal. The problem is, this watch is rarer than a unicorn shitting bricks."

"Surely it can't be that hard to find?"

Pushing off the door, I interlace my hands behind my neck and begin pacing the room. "I have my P.I. and Dix on the case. So far, nada. I thought Mr. Yeong was a good guy, but obviously I was wrong. Isn't there any loyalty left these days?" I think aloud, still pacing.

"Goldilocks seems to know the first thing about loyalty to you. Too bad she just threw her boss under the bus," Mary retorts.

"Oh, screw Gail. He's only here because his mom was feeling generous and didn't swallow. Keira just saved my ass."

Those words, no matter how true they may be, have Mary's hands furling into tight fists. "Well, that's probably because you fucked her ass."

"I didn't fuck anyone's ass," I coolly reply, coming to a standstill. "Keira is a virgin."

Mary's eyes widen to the size of disbelieving saucers. "I highly doubt that. If she sat on a barstool, she'd slide down it."

She's so adorable when riled up. "Call it what you will, but she didn't have to tell me. Now the question is, what am I supposed to do about it?" On cue, my cell chirps.

It's sitting on top of my filing cabinet, seeing as I no longer have a desk because Mary did eventually use it as firewood. She reaches for it and curls her lip. "She must have you on speed dial. Seven p.m. The Pink Box. How appropriate." She rolls her eyes and tosses me the phone.

"Where are you going?" I ask as she begins stuffing her notepad and measuring tape into her backpack.

"I need to get ready. I'm going out tonight."

"Oh?" I wait for her to throw me a fucking bone, but all she does is leave me with more questions than answers.

"Good luck, but I'm sure superhero, The Untouched Virgin, will swoop on in and save the day."

"Mary, wait!" I lunge for her as she brushes past me, intent on leaving me without an explanation why. She peers down at where we connect, but doesn't shrug me off.

"Maybe if you finish early enough, you could swing by?" I know how desperate that sounds, but I think I already miss her, and I'm not even horny.

She seems surprised I would ask her, and I guess I am too, considering she made it clear she was only interested in a no strings attached deal. "I, um, maybe." She shakes her head, quickly backtracking. "I don't think so, though. Besides, three's a crowd."

I know she's referring to Keira, but she doesn't even come into this equation. If I had my way, I'd be spending the night with Mary, devouring every single inch of her, but looks like we're not on the same page. I then have another thought. Maybe her plus one and me make three. "Okay, cool. Have fun then."

She appears hurt I didn't fight harder, but I don't want to come across as a pushy jerk. "You too." With utter regret, I let her go and turn my back, because if I look at her a second longer, I just might shed a tear.

She's lingering, and just when I think she's changed her mind, the door shuts, cementing the fact that tonight can eat a giant dick and blow me.

I'm on my third scotch and I've only been here for fifteen minutes. "Leave the bottle." The bartender doesn't argue, as I've just given her the night off.

Skimming my finger around the rim of my glass, I can't shake this heavy feeling in the pit of my stomach. I could pretend it's got to do with Gail—the slimy grease ball, but I know it has nothing to do with him and everything to do with Mary.

I can't help but wonder what she's doing and who she's doing it with. She didn't specify where exactly she was going, and my mind is conjuring up god-awful scenarios of her being wined and dined by the Australian dickhead.

She's failed to mention Trent, which has me hoping her lapse in sanity has passed. Mary doesn't look like the cheating type, but she apparently is the friends with benefits type. Am I the only friend? Or does she have a few? The thought has me unscrewing the lid of my scotch and filling my glass full.

"You're starting early." Keira sits down beside me. In my head, I thumb my nose at Mary when she doesn't slide down it.

"Yeah, I need to get wasted to deal with your asshole boss. His brown-nosing skills are actually better than his job skills." I turn my head to the left, almost gagging when I see him re-enacting some ridiculous story of what looks like him pole vaulting over an elephant's scrotum.

Mr. Yeong has sent his two righthand men. I thought they were on my team, but them being here proves their loyalties lie with no one. Gail is being his usual asswipe self, which works in my favor as Ming and Jie look as amused as me.

"Why don't you put everyone out of their misery then and tell me how I can help? Two heads are better than one," she sweetly purrs.

"Why do you think I hold some miracle cure?" I question, genuinely curious.

Reaching for my glass, she throws back the entire contents before wiping her glossy lips with the back of her hand. "Because I know you, and you'd have Mr. Yeong as a client by now if you could. Something is stopping you."

She waits for me to corroborate her claims, but I smirk in response. It's going to take a lot more than a pretty face and a night filled with empty promises to make me spill—although I had no qualms telling Mary.

Glancing down at my watch, I see that it's been a minute and thirty-seven seconds since I thought of her. Go me. "Nothing is stopping me. Unlike him"—I point my finger at the jockstrap who is now laughing at his own joke—"I take what I want, when I want. I'm just biding my time."

Keira doesn't look convinced, but seems to forget what

we're talking about when she crawls her fingernails up my thigh. "I should be offended then." I jolt when she shamelessly grabs my cock. "You've yet to take me. Is that because you don't want me?"

"Just biding my time," I repeat, latching onto her wrist to stop her from manhandling me. Her touch is not what I crave and her hands feel so wrong.

"It's the redhead, isn't it? I never took you for the settling down type, especially since you play the field so much."

"Pardon me?" Her admission is like a punch to my kidneys.

Keira thankfully releases me from her vise-like grip and turns so her back is pressed up against the bar. "I heard her on the phone as she left your office. Whoever she was speaking to is certainly in for a good time tonight."

I taste blood. "What are you talking about?"

Keira crosses her legs casually. "She asked if they were ready to be fucked like an animal." I resist the urge to cover my ears and sing Taylor Swift at the top of my lungs.

There must be some mistake. There is no way Mary was offering the goods to someone other than me. I've become infatuated with her, and in my eyes, she's mine. But that's the problem…she's not. Mary has laid all her cards out on the table, like I did with all the women I slept with, but now that the shoes on the other foot, I want a redraw. If this is karma, then karma can fuck right off.

The thought of someone else touching Mary has me wanting to maim every man in the USA and abroad. But Keira's revelation has kicked my ego, and no, all I can do is lick my wounds. "She can fuck whomever she likes. We're not exclusive. Just having fun." God, that tasted like acid.

Keira smirks. "Good to know. So I guess that means the same principle applies to you then?" Yes, in theory I suppose it does, but I don't want anyone else. I just want Mary, but it appears she doesn't feel the same way.

Straightening my spine, I pour a decent helping of the brown gold into my glass. I take my time gulping it down. Once I'm done, I lean in close, completely ignoring her personal space. But the small intake of breath reveals she doesn't mind in the slightest. "You guessed right. I'm not attached to her, or anyone, in fact. I'm a free agent and I come and go as I please."

This is, in fact, all lies, because the thought of touching another woman has me itching to cut off my hands and dick. But my bravado gets the better of me.

Keira's hands are dug deep into her blazer pockets, and if I didn't know any better, I'd say she was downright rejoicing in the news. "Good to know."

Before I have a chance to reply, a rich laugh has every part of my body perking up and demanding my utmost attention. I know who it belongs to even before I see the woman who is singlehandedly ruining my life.

Mary stands feet away, looking utterly appetizing in a simple black dress, but nothing looks unadorned on her. Her long waves are tumbling around her shoulders, and images of fisting those locks as I sink into her heat over and over again assault me, leaving me breathless.

She doesn't make eye contact with me, but I know she can feel me scouring over every inch of her body. She's talking to Ming, laughing at something he says. It's the first time I've seen him smile all night, but who can blame him?

Mary listens intently before pointing to a jade amulet which hangs from his neck. He peers downward, fingering the charm, nodding at whatever Mary is saying. She holds the interest of the entire room, and that includes Gail, who suddenly swaggers over, primping his collar and running a hand through his shitty brown hair.

If he so much as looks at her, I will kill him, and that's not an exaggeration. He stands by, chiming in on their conversation while I crack my knuckles, the need to murder overriding any other emotion.

Just as I launch up, ready to beat Gail to a bloody pulp, Mary rips out my heart and takes a shit where the whimsical center once sat. She peers up at him and turns a lovely pink. Some chicks might find him attractive, but surely Mary can see past those bulging muscles and angular chin. Sadly however, when she places her hand on his bicep and laughs at whatever the fuck he just said, it appears all she sees is another admirer in a long line of many. She can literally take her pick of the room, because Ming just looked down the low neckline of her dress.

Keira's admission of what she heard earlier today was obviously true, because Mary is dressed to the nines. My overactive imagination decides now is the time to plant images of Mary writhing under some hulking male, her lips parted in pure ecstasy as he delivers orgasm number ten.

"Hunter?" Keira's sweet voice shatters an image I want to erase from my brain with a rusted pickaxe. "Everything okay?"

"Peachy," I counter, forgetting the glass and taking a swig from the bottle of scotch.

It's like a car wreck—I know I should look away, but I just can't. I watch as Mary's gaze bounces between Gail and Ming, both appearing to outdo the other with their conversational ping-pong. When Gail bends low and whispers into her ear, I can't hold back my urge to neuter this cunt any longer.

Guzzling down more than half the bottle of scotch, I'm about to smash it against the edge of the bar and use the jagged neck to stab Gail in the jugular, but stop mid-stroke when Mary meets my eyes. My entire focus shifts and I fail to remember my need to kill when she smiles.

Who would have thought a simple smile could bring down a nation?

She averts her gaze when I very openly eye fuck the living hell out of her. I don't care who knows, because I will be making it pretty clear in three seconds when I march over, throw her over my shoulder, and fuck her until it's only my name she calls.

Just as I'm about to make good on my word, she gestures to me and then to Ming. They exchange a few words before she gestures he's to follow her—follow her as she makes her way over to me. Keira stands beside me, reminding me that she's still here.

"Hunter," Mary says, while I'm thankful she used my name, as I just forgot it. "I met your friend, Ming. You didn't tell me he was into feng shui."

"He's into what?" Now that I'm semi-coherent, I wonder if maybe Mary is drunk.

Ming laughs at my reaction. "It's true, but if you tell anyone, and by anyone, I mean Mr. Yeong, then I will deny it." Did he just make a joke? And he's into feng shui? Since when?

My mouth hinges open. "What's going on here?" If this is code for some kinky, oriental shit, then I'm going to throw down with every motherfucker in this place.

Mary explains. "I noticed Ming's necklace." I instantly

look down at it, noting the dragon carved into the jade stone. "He said in his country, it means good luck. I then went on to explain how I know a little about it because I'm currently transforming your office into a feng shui oasis."

"You did?" I question, my brain unable to catch-up fast enough.

She nods, while Ming nudges me with his elbow. "I didn't realize you had a spiritual side, Hunter."

"Neither did I," I quickly counter, while Mary closes her eyes briefly and shakes her head at my ignorance. "Oh yes, I'm all over that spiritual shit. I mean stuff." I quickly backtrack, while Ming smiles happily.

"I'm also redecorating his house," Mary swoops in, covering my slip. "Maybe when I'm done, you and Mr. Yeong could come over and see it?" This woman is a wicked temptress.

Ming looks at me and I nod eagerly.

"Mr. Yeong will be very happy to know this. He didn't think you were interested in doing business with him any longer." I look at Mary, then back at Ming. It takes me a minute, but holy fuck, she's here to save my ass.

I don't know how she knew, but she knew I'd be standing around, dick in hand, while Gail tried to schmooze his way into Mr. Yeong's inner circle. "Of course, I'm interested. I thought he was the one who turned rogue." I make a point to look at Gail, who watches us closely.

"Mr. Yeong will not go back on his word. And neither will you?" I know what he's asking, but he's clever enough not to reveal our secret.

"You can tell Mr. Yeong it's under control."

Ming nods, looking at Keira, who quietly observes. "Please

thank Mr. Gail for inviting us out, but we must leave. My sister is waiting."

"Hold up. You're not here to see Gail?" I ask, confused, as Keira made out this meeting was to talk shop.

"No. My sister is moving house. She needs the muscle." He flexes his impressive bicep with a grin.

"And you flew all the way from China to help her move?" I ask with a smirk.

Ming slaps me on the shoulder playfully. "She's my little sister. And it's a big house." I don't argue. "Mr. Yeong is waiting. Time is of the essence, Mr. O'Shea." No pun intended. I nod, his point received loud and clear.

Ming nods at Keira, who is as quiet as a mouse. I notice Mary examining her closely. I wonder what she's thinking. We watch as Ming and Jie leave, not bothering to accept Gail's business card as he waves it in the air.

Once they're gone, I turn to look at Keira. "I thought you said this was a business meeting."

She shrugs, looking as stumped as me. "That's what I thought too."

I instantly feel sorry for her. The sooner she learns Gail is a sly snake in the grass who can't be trusted, the better for her. "I told you he was a lying son of a bitch. Don't sweat it, Keira, you'll soon learn." When her lower lip trembles, I reach out to rub her upper arm.

It's meant to be a kind gesture, but I may as well have fingered her in public. "I'll leave you two lovebirds to it then."

Just as Mary turns to leave, I pounce forward and capture her forearm. "Hey. Where are you going?" I bend low, begging she look at me, but she averts her gaze while chewing on her lower lip. No, this won't do. "If you'll excuse me, Keira." I don't wait for her to reply, but instead lead Mary toward the bathrooms. I'm surprised she doesn't resist.

When we reach the Ladies, I let her go, expecting we'll speak in private out here in the hallway. But when her eyes dart from left to right and a pink flush overcomes her, I know she has other things on her mind.

Before I have a chance to ask what's going on, she fists my shirt and shoves me into the bathroom. I stumble, not expecting her forcefulness, but when she releases her hold, only to lock the door behind her, I know this is only the beginning of things to come.

We're caught in a deadlock, the air crackling around us, but this is her show. "I'm surprised she didn't blow you out there." No guessing to whom she's referring.

"You should know all about that," I counter smartly, wondering who exactly she was speaking on the phone to. "How was your evening? Have fun?"

"Yes, lots." That smart mouth will be the death of me.

"So why are you here then?" I question, as I honestly have no idea why. She owes me nothing. She works that bottom lip, buying time. The small space suddenly becomes as stifling as the sun. "I asked you a question."

"And I fucking heard you!" she bites back, marching forward. I stand my ground because her aggressiveness makes me hard.

"Well…"

Her choppy breathing just inflates my semi, and before long, I'll be able to cut through glass.

My persistence is pissing her off, which just spurs me on,

because the last time she got that crazy look in her eye, she coated my face with her sweetness. I hum when reliving the memory.

"I can't believe you're actually falling for her doe-eyed, virgin act," she spits.

"Even if it was an act, what business is it of yours?" I pose, baiting her to tell me what I want to hear.

She's the one who set these rules, who told me we're not friends. But now she's here, saving my ass, confusing me even more than I already am.

Her nostrils flare, as I've obviously pushed a button. "I told you…" she states slowly, pressing us chest to chest. Her heart beating against mine is an unexpected head rush. "I don't…" Wrapping her hand around my nape, she stands on tippy toes, leveling us. "Share my toys," she concludes.

Her scent kicks me low, and all I can focus on are her lips and how much I want to kiss them. But the problem I'm faced with is if I kiss her and she walks away from me, walks into the arms of another man, I will die. Sex is usually the most intimate part to two people uniting, but for me, nothing is more sacred than a kiss.

I don't know where I stand with Mary, and if she sees me as just a plaything, then kissing her will ultimately lead to me saying things she doesn't want to hear. It will kill me when she leaves, because that's how this is bound to end.

We never promised one another anything more than this. I'm the one who had to complicate things and go and fall in lov—I stop myself before I say something we both regret. I'm at her mercy, and that's exactly what I'll be calling when she slams her lips to mine.

I immediately feel lightheaded, as I can't remember the last time I was locked in such a tender embrace. Her mouth is warm, soft, and every part of me is begging I meet her halfway, but I just can't. "You do realize you've kissed every part of my body but my lips, right?" Her breath slides down my throat, tempting me to throw caution to the wind.

"I don't kiss," I reply, allowing myself this reprieve for just a little longer as I slide my lips against hers.

"Why not?" She groans, her body hugging into mine.

Fisting her hair to hold her in place, I sashay my mouth side to side, smearing her bright red lipstick. "'Cause I don't want you falling in love with me."

Her eyes widen, but little does she know, I've just expressed my fears out loud.

I taste strawberries. I also taste my demise, because I want nothing more than to end this torment and surrender everything I am. But what she says next just confirms what this is.

"Don't worry, that's not going to happen, because this is a no strings deal, right?" With those lips pressed to mine, I want nothing more than to argue that no, there are lots of strings, many, and they're lassoed tightly around my heart. They are siphoning off my air supply. But that's not what she wants, and for once in my life, I'm not going to be selfish.

"Absolutely."

Mary nods once. Our lips are still caught in a stalemate, hinting that Mary wants more than just a kiss.

"I'm not going to fuck you in here." Don't get me wrong, I've fucked in plenty of bathrooms, but with Mary, it just seems wrong.

"That's fine," she whispers. "You can fuck me back at your apartment. But now, I'm going to fuck you." I wonder if she's carrying a strap-on in her bag, but she makes her intentions clear when she unbuckles my belt. Her deft fingers undo my button before lowering my fly.

She knows from experience that I'm commando and that I'm hard.

She takes my cock in her hand, fisting my shaft with skill. She knows what I like because she's worked her way on and around it countless times this week. I exhale heavily, filling her lungs with air that filled mine. The visual is almost romantic, but when she increases the speed of her rhythm, all romance takes a backseat, because now I just want to come.

My pants pool around my feet, leaving me exposed and at her complete disposal. As we're still pressed front to front, there isn't much room for her to move, but I love being locked this way with her.

My jagged breathing whooshes down her throat as she bites and lays tiny kisses on my parted mouth. I greedily pump my hips, the feel of her palm sliding up and down my dick too intense for words. With the other hand, she reaches down and fondles my balls. It's a sharp sting—pleasure versus pain.

Our eyes are united, Mary watching me as I unravel in her palm. "If she touches you again, then I won't."

"If this is an ultimatum, then you'll be happy to know you win," I reply with a smirk.

"Good. Looks like we both do." When she sucks my bottom lip in one long, wet pull before sliding down my body and positioning herself on both knees, I understand what she means.

Mary has yet to go down on me, which has been completely fine. I have loved being the giver, but seeing her kneeling before me stirs a longing and my cock twitches. She peers up at me from under those long lashes before licking her lips and focusing her attention on my dick.

"You keep looking at me like that and I won't be held accountable for my actions."

A smirk tugs her curved lips. "Don't make a mess. This is a new dress." She doesn't wait for me to reply, but I don't think I could, because seeing her brush her hair to one side and lowering her mouth to my cock leaves me speechless.

Her mouth forms a small, perfect O as she slides onto the head of my dick. A thunderbolt strikes straight through me, but I refrain from moving, wanting Mary to go at her own pace. I'm unable to tear my eyes away from her sucking and licking my tip painfully slow. She tongues the underside before suckling at the head.

"Oh, sweet holy fuck!" I groan, gently caressing her cheek in gratitude.

She rests both palms against my thighs as she bobs up and down sluggishly, testing how deep she can go. The sight of her lips wrapped around my cock is forever singed into my brain, and from this day forward, it belongs to her.

She slides down further, before pulling back up—repeat, and before long, she's taken half my shaft into her mouth. Her cheeks are hollowed as she sucks me deeply, using a hand to cover what she can't swallow. In seconds, her hand and mouth work in sync, and she conducts a tempo which has me almost losing my shit.

I'm trying to be gentle, but when she pulls back, sucks my

sensitive head, and circles her tongue, all bets are off and I buck my hips forward. I slide down her throat, almost coming when she hums.

Sweeping her hair from her face, I hold onto it, using it as reins. I'm utterly mesmerized by the way she sucks me off, her tiny hand fisting me as she bobs up and down. I bow into her, making sure I don't go in too deep, too fast. "You are a fucking goddess," I growl when I hit the back of her throat. She moans around me, the sound vibrating all the way to my balls.

She lifts my shaft and draws backward, slapping my head against the flat of her tongue. I've been blown countless times before, but this…this is something else. She sinks back down and clutches onto both my thighs, dipping madly.

Her tempo speeds up, and by her impassioned moans, I know her pussy is clenching, so ready to fuck. I try and gently coax her off, wanting to return the favor, but she shrugs me off and dives in deep, almost swallowing me whole. Although she gags, she continues working my cock with fervor, milking me, making her intentions clear.

Tears leak from her eyes as she sucks, licks, and tongues me until I pump my hips, so ready to shatter. My fist is locked firmly around her tresses, guiding and controlling her tempo. With one hand still pressed to my thigh, the other dips under her dress and moves in a manner which has me wanting to weep.

"Holy shit. Do you know how hot you look right now?" I growl, not knowing where to look first, as it's a smorgasbord of visual feasts. My words spur both her mouth and hand beneath her dress on as she increases the speed of both.

My release is so close I can taste it, but when Mary moans

around my dick, the distinct sound of her fingers slipping deep into her wet pussy, it accelerates and kicks me in the balls. I pump my hips while she whimpers, never missing a beat.

The familiar sensation builds and builds, and I know what's coming, and it's going to come in waves. I gently push her cheek, enticing her to let go, but she seals her lips and slides all the way down. "Mary!" I grunt, attempting to pull out, but she won't let me go. "Oh, fuck. Shortcake, I'm going to come. Like right now."

I try and hold back, but when her body shudders and I visualize her fingers playing with her ripened clit, I lose all control. Tossing my head back, I pump my hips wildly, almost unforgiving as an orgasm is ripped from my center and I explode with a thunderous roar into Mary's mouth.

She takes everything I give, her tiny moans of her pleasuring herself while she pleasures me is the most erotic thing I have ever heard. Once the last aftershock rocks my body, I yank her up and press her back to the wall.

Her lips are swollen, her red lipstick smeared, but in this moment, she's never looked more beautiful, never looked more mine. Without a word, I drop to my knees and hike up the hem of her dress. As I bury my face into her slick pussy, I know I'm in trouble because I'll never tire of wanting her…forever.

Twelve

I am sore in places I didn't even know could be sore. But when the snoring, hulking giant besides me rolls over and spoons me, it's so worth the pain.

I'm in the one place I promised myself I would never end up—Hunter's bed. Sure, we've had sex in, on, and around it plenty of times, but to actually wake up in it the morning after is a whole different ballgame.

After he took me back to his place and had me screaming his name, I collapsed, in fear of never waking any time soon. I expected he would wake me when he wanted me to leave, but as the sunlight streams in from the curtains, I know that never happened.

Looking down at Hunter, I can't deny that I've fallen, and I've fallen in deep. I have no idea when this happened, but the more time I spend with him, the harder I fall. And that's the problem. Regardless of how I feel, he doesn't feel the same. I suggested this friends with benefits arrangement because the thought of not having him at all hurts more than eventually having to let him go.

But I'm going to revel in this madness because I'm sure he'll get sick of me soon. Last night was nothing short of amazing, but I play hardball time and time again because I'm scared he'll get bored. Sometimes I think he feels for me what I do for him, but then he proves it's just wishful thinking when he doesn't want to kiss me, or confirms this is a no-strings attached deal. Or when Keira is basically blowing him under the bar.

I went last night because I was convinced she was given her marching orders. As I left Hunter's office, I saw her crying in her sleazeball boss's office. I was certain he had fired her, discovering she had told Hunter about Mr. Yeong. So you can imagine my surprise when I saw her all but dry humping Hunter's leg.

But I went for a handful of reasons. The first being, I wanted to gloat when I told Hunter the news. But when I saw her fondling him, a possession so fierce took over, I forgot any other reason. When I saw Aaron Gail, alarm bells sounded loudly, just how they did when I first laid eyes on Keira.

He was cocky, probably accustomed to women throwing themselves at his feet, but when he flirted, I was so in, and I planned on shaking my tailfeather to uncover what exactly he's up to. There is no doubt he lied about his so-called meeting with Mr. Yeong's people, so now that that's failed, what will he try next?

Ming seemed confident that Mr. Yeong would stay loyal to Hunter, so I wonder to what lengths Gail will go to sever that allegiance.

I can't shake the feeling that Keira is looking out for herself and using Hunter for her own personal gain. She told him about the supposed meeting to knock her boss from the perch, only to replace him…with herself.

My gut tells me she wants Mr. Yeong for herself. What a way to climb the corporate ladder, by literally climbing Hunter. There is clearly no love lost between her and her boss, as he chewed her out over what exactly, I still don't know, but I'm planning on finding out, hence me flirting back with the braindead Gail.

Keira is so desperate for Hunter to share his triumphs with her because it's a man's world, and she will obviously fight dirty to get what she wants. The whole virgin act clued me onto her plans. So did the fact I spied on her once Aaron left his office and saw her take off her glasses to read a text message. She clearly doesn't need them, but she wears them because they, just like her virginal gig, are a ploy to seduce Hunter into telling her his secrets of success.

The problem is I need evidence, because right now, I sound like a jealous…girlfriend. I can't tell Hunter about my hunch, because when it comes to vagina, he's twenty shades of stupid.

I should just mind my own business, but the other reason I went last night is lying beside me. I missed Hunter. I missed him so much I couldn't even think straight. He obviously thought I was hitting the town, which I supposedly was, but after I spoke to Maddy, who informed me she and Dixon would be screwing like rabbits because she hadn't seen him all week, I knew I was flying solo.

But the thought of going out, getting grinded on, and engaging in mindless conversation made me long for the annoying jerk even more. This wasn't supposed to happen, so the question is, how do I make it stop?

"I swear to god if this is a dream, I will be fucking pissed." That husky voice should be illegal. So should those amazing green eyes, which open slowly, focusing on me. Hunter's hair is wild, tousled from sleep. He smirks up at me, not at all bothered he's using my boobs as a pillow. "Is this the time you suggest we have morning sex?" He reaches for my hand and interlaces our fingers casually.

His entire presence shouldn't affect me the way that it does, but my heart does a tiny flip flop while my lady parts somersault in delight. "Really? You literally just woke up," I reply, unable to hold back a smile.

"Well, I literally woke up with morning wood," he counters, lifting the sheet so I can see him standing tall and proud. "It's not every day I wake to a pretty woman in my bed." His admission surprises me, and the shock shows.

"That surprises you?"

"Is that a trick question?" I tease, unable to resist as I brush locks of hair from his cheeks.

"I'll have you know you're the first woman who has slept over in a very long time."

"How long?" Now that he's talking, I plan on grilling him until he clams back up. He's let slip that he hasn't dated, like ever, but he's never really gone into detail.

Nuzzling into my right breast, he lazily runs his tongue along the edge. "It's been that long, I really don't know."

I gasp, my head falling backward as he thumbs over my pebbled nipple. But I won't allow him to distract me. "Ballpark?"

"Hmm…" he says, his warm breath sending goose bumps

all down my body. "Maybe three years."

"Three?" I squeak, part in shock, the other half in ecstasy.

Leaning up on an elbow, he casually traces his pointer around my areola and nods. "Give or take. I really am not interested in complications."

His confession could be taken two ways—am I not a complication because he feels the butterflies too? Or am I not a complication because he doesn't care enough about me to make it complicated? Ugh, I'm so confused.

"I'm glad I'm not a complication then," I state, hoping he sheds some light on this before I drive myself nuts.

Sucking his thumb very suggestively, it pops from his lips. "I never said that."

"Then what"—the words catch in my throat when he thumbs over my nipple—"am I then?" I manage to conclude, holding back my moan.

He appears hypnotized by my breast, but if I didn't know better, I'd say he was weighing the best way to not put his foot in it more than he already has. "You're…easy."

My mood instantly sours, and I slap his hand away. "Gee, thanks a lot." I attempt to get up, but he doesn't let me move an inch. He rolls on top of me, our naked bodies pressed as one.

"I didn't mean it like that." His crooked smirk just pisses me off more. "I meant being with you is easy."

"Oh." But what does that exactly mean? I want to ask him, but I'm afraid. If he tells me I'm easy because there are no emotional ties and what we have is just sex, I will ugly cry and it won't be pretty. Sex is easy, but the relationship part, that's hard.

I'm left with more questions than answers once again.

Just as I grow some lady balls and open my mouth, ready to

ask him once and for all, he swoops forward and kisses the side of my neck. He works his way down, his whiskers delectably pricking my heated skin.

Once he reaches the junction of my collarbones, he traces a path down the middle with his tongue, detouring to my left breast. He laps at it coolly, in no real hurry, and knowing Hunter and his stamina, we could be here for a while.

As his mouth works me into a frenzy above the waist, below joins the party when he glides his hand between us and rubs two fingers along my entrance. It's impossible that each touch feels even better than the one before, because when does this stop?

Opening my legs, I want to forget about my insecurities, because when we're like this, nothing is clearer. What I can't vocalize, my body makes up for through touch. His fingers test the waters, but I'm always ready for him.

He draws my nipple into the warm hollow of his mouth the same moment he slips two fingers inside of me. I raise my hips, the pressure almost too much. There is something different to his touch, the sense of urgency skating under the surface, instead of dominating his every move.

The tiny pitter patter to my heart is one I've not felt before. It feels so full, like at any given moment it will explode from my chest and show the world that it beats for only one man. I am so fucking screwed.

Just as he moves over to my other breast, his cell on the bedside table sounds, and the song is funnily enough one I can relate to. "Why is Celine Dion your ringtone?" I ask with a giggle. The infamous love song from the movie Titanic fills the room.

"Just ignore it," he says from around my nipple while his fingers are still working a fever down below.

"I can't," I reply, as Hunter has done some weird shit before, but now I'm totally intrigued.

My nipple springs free, but he doesn't stop the delicious intrusion below. Reaching over, he picks up the cell and sighs. "Hi, can I call you back? I've kind of got my hands full." His wicked grin has me biting my lip to stifle my moan. He continues sinking his fingers into me, watching me closely, which has me bursting into flames. "What? You're here now?"

Not interested in an audience, I attempt to shut my legs, but he drives them back open and increases the tempo. I have no idea who he's talking to, but I do know they're standing outside his door. My hips buck into his fingers, my swollen clit so needy and sweltering, I want to cry.

"Okay, fine, fine, give me five minutes." When I cry out, arching my back, he smirks. "Actually, make that three."

He hangs up, tossing the phone over his shoulder, never missing a beat. My body twists and turns, the gravity of him stroking me so intimately and with such dominance is almost too much. I'm so fucking wet and a victorious grin breaks out on Hunter's cheeks. I know he loves it when I get this worked up.

"I really wish I could fuck you right now. But that'll take a lot longer than three minutes." He leans down, his long hair tickling my chin as he sucks over my hammering pulse.

"Oh god," I cry, opening my legs as wide as I can.

"Shortcake, you're one greedy girl. This cunt can never get enough, can it?" I moan, his dirty words perpetually elicit this response from me and he knows it.

"No," I whimper when he withdraws his fingers and frenziedly rubs over my clit.

"Good," he hums, still suckling my neck, undoubtedly leaving a hickey the size of Texas behind. "Because I will never have enough of it. Of you."

I'm too far gone to even comprehend his words and come with an ear-splitting shriek. My body thrashes beneath him, tears leaking from my eyes, the orgasm robbing me of breath. Hunter wrings every last drop from my body, until I'm lax and well-sated in his arms.

I know I've coated him with my arousal, but before him, I didn't even know my body was capable of the things it's experienced over the past few days.

When I finally stop moaning, I open my eyes, watching on in horror and desire when Hunter licks his fingers clean. "You taste as good as you feel." An inferno overtakes me, which only has my tormentor grinning smugly.

"To be continued," he whispers, biting my chin before standing and riffling through his drawers for some clothes.

Sitting upright, I hold the sheet to my chest, watching in delight as he steps into a pair of faded blue jeans. Soft tufts of dark hair paint his navel and lead all the way down to an impressive V. He leaves the top button undone as he hunts for a t-shirt. His washboard abs ripple and roll. Oh my fucking god have mercy on my pink bits.

When he slips into a fitted white tee, he notices me staring and smirks. I need to stop because he's cocky enough. "Who's at the door?"

Running his fingers through his hair, he ties it low. "My mom," he replies casually, while I almost fall out of bed.

"What? Your mom is out there?" I point to the door, in case I had a lapse in hearing. He nods, while I pale. "Hunter, you were getting me off while on the phone to your mother?"

"Yeah, I told her my hands were full," he teases, while I spring from the bed, frantically searching the room for my clothes.

"What are you doing?"

"What does it look like I'm doing?" I reply as I drop to the floor to look under the bed.

"Why?"

Blowing the bedraggled hair from my brow, I turn over my shoulder, incredulous. "Why? 'Cause I'm butt naked in your bedroom and your mom is feet away." I holler in delight when I see my dress wedged near the headboard.

"She'll understand when she sees that butt. It's a crime to keep it confined." As I'm parading my ass high in the air while reaching for my clothes, Hunter lunges forward and slaps me playfully. Yelping, I turn around to see him masking a shit-eating grin behind his palm.

Ignoring his childish, but adorable antics, I quickly slip into my dress and attempt to tame my mane, but give up and instead tie it into a high ponytail. "I'm going to the bathroom," I announce, grabbing my bag from the dresser.

"Why are you so worried about meeting my mom?" he asks, which has me slamming on the brakes.

He's right. I have no idea why I'm behaving like a crazy person. It's not like Hunter is my boyfriend or anything. A sinking feeling weighs heavily in my stomach at that awful fact. And here comes insecurity, our forever third wheel.

He's waiting for me to reply, so sucking it up, I shrug

offhandedly. "Because if we're going to keep this"—I gesture with two fingers between us—"a secret, then I better not look like I've been fucked six ways to Sunday. I'm sure she'll tell Dixon, who will tell Maddy, who will probably wring both our necks for not telling her. I don't know about you, but I'm not eager to face the firing squad about our little indiscretion. And besides, I'll have to see your mom at Dixon and Maddy's wedding, and I prefer that isn't the first time she sees me clothed."

Hunter ponders over my revelation before he nods. I turn on my heel and enter the en-suite, gently closing the door behind me. Leaning against it, I calm my raging nerves, wishing I was meeting Hunter's mom under completely different circumstances.

I need to chill the fuck out, because I knew what this was from the very beginning. I don't have a magical vagina. I never expected Hunter to change who he is for me. But the problem is, I've changed, and I didn't even know it. This is neither the time nor the place, so I quickly wash my face and use my finger as a makeshift toothbrush to make myself as presentable as I can.

Once I've washed the shame clean, I quietly walk down the hallway, hoping that it was a short visit and Hunter's mom is gone. But when I turn the corner and see a woman doting over Hunter, I know luck isn't on my side.

Her emerald eyes instantly widen, while I wish I'd tripped and rendered myself unconscious. "Hello. I'm Mary. Maddy's best friend." I don't see the point in sugar-coating anything because I see this as a Band-Aid—just rip it off and deal with the sting later.

She looks up, and Hunter, raising an eyebrow, simply slips

his hands into his pockets with a stiff upper lip smile. Such a non-committal gesture which again, makes me want to eat a gallon of ice cream and listen to Justin Bieber on repeat.

"It's so lovely to meet you, Mary. I'm Marie, Hunter's mom." She walks around Hunter, who looks like he'd rather be having a prostate exam. I extend my hand, but she bypasses it and goes in for a hug.

I hug her back half-heartedly, as I wasn't expecting her to welcome me so graciously. For all she knows, I could be some barfly her son picked up the night before. "It's nice to meet you too."

When we part, she examines me closely with a smile. There is nothing but curiosity and delight radiating from her petite frame. I really don't know what to say because I want to make a good impression, but I'm afraid if I open my mouth, it'll be verbal diarrhea and I will thank her for giving birth to such a remarkable son.

"I was going to ask my son to join me for breakfast, but I can see he's busy."

Hunter runs a hand down his face, shaking his head, while I blanch. "Oh, it's fine. You can go. I'm only here because Hunter has been kind enough to allow me to ransack his home and office. I'm studying interior design," I explain before she thinks I'm some deranged lunatic. "Almost done, actually. My last assignment is to redecorate a space and document the progress." I'm completely rambling, but I'm scared of what happens when she asks me a question and I blurt out the fact that I'm sleeping with her son.

She nods, processing over everything I just shared. "Well, god knows this place could do with a female's touch."

"Hold up," Hunter pipes up, hands raised, while I smirk. "You never said you'd be turning my home into Barbie's penthouse with glitter and doilies and shit."

Marie stifles a laugh while I roll my eyes. "I'll just pretend you didn't say that."

"Shortcake, I'm serious," he states, while his mom and I don't overlook my nickname.

"Okay, fine, you win." I mock sigh, pretending Marie isn't watching our exchange with an inquisitive eye. "No doilies. Has he always been such a pain in the ass?" I whisper loudly behind my hand as I point in Hunter's direction.

Marie bursts into laughter. Hunter smirks, a dimple hugging his whiskered cheek, which promises punishment for my smart mouth. My cheeks instantly heat.

"You must join me and my husband for dinner tonight, Mary. He'd love to meet you."

"What?" I ask, gasping for air, my playfulness subsiding and terror soon taking its place.

"I can see you're both busy now, but how about tonight?"

Marie looks at me kindly, while I look at Hunter to throw me a freaking bone. What is the proper protocol here? His cheeks puff out wide as he exhales slowly. Oh my god, I want to die. Please, floor, swallow me whole.

Just as I'm about to make up some excuse that I'm allergic to…dinner, Hunter leaves me speechless. "As long as it's Mexican, we're in."

We are?

Marie claps once, excited, while I smile like a deranged circus clown, wondering if it'll be rude if I sat down and breathed heavily into a brown paper bag. "Wonderful. I'll let you pick the place. Invite Dixon and Madison too. We can triple date." Air gets lodged in my throat and I subtly thump over my chest. Now I really need to sit. "Text me the details. It was so lovely meeting you, Mary." All I can do is grunt in response.

She gently caresses my arm before hugging Hunter affectionately. He stands rigid, but smiles when she playfully tugs at his manbun. She shoulders her bag before turning to me. "By the way, I love your dress." The cherry on top is when she winks. She so knows what's going on, because who in their right mind refurbishes a home in a little black dress? But I think it's safe to say the sane ship sailed a long time ago.

I smile in response, as I can feel word vomit rising. Hunter sees her out while I have a mini freak-out.

This is bad, so bad. Meeting Hunter's mom and liking her is not part of the plan. I was supposed to get over him by now. I thought if we finally scratched the itch, I would be cured, but all I'm left with is fucking hives. I rub at my neck, the itchiness about to consume me whole.

"Are you all right?"

I jump five feet, placing a hand to my thundering heart. "Yeah, fine. I think I'm allergic to you," I tease, needing to douse this sudden attachment with humor. "Which is why I think you, Dixon, and Maddy should just go to dinner."

"Oh?" His handsome face pales and I feel like I've just kicked a puppy. "You don't want to come?"

"I do!" I reply with a little too much gusto. Reining it in, I clear my throat, hoping to regain some composure. "I just…is it weird?"

Hunter takes a step forward, while I force my feet to stay rooted to the spot. "No, it doesn't have to be. I mean, sooner or later we will have to see Maddy and Dixon together." He advances forward slowly, pinning me with those eyes. "If we start acting differently, they'll know something is up." I gulp. "And nothing is different, well, apart from the obvious, right?" he purrs, stopping an inch away. "You still think I'm a disgusting pig. And I still think you're the most infuriating woman on this planet."

My head nods, but I can't be held accountable for my actions, because sweet baby Jesus, he is epic. He's sex on legs with whipped cream and a cherry on top.

"So you see…we will eat Mexican and I will pretend that I'm not envisioning your naked taco." I can't help but laugh, because I know what he's doing and I appreciate he can be the grown up and not make a big deal over this.

"Okay, it's a date. Deal! I meant deal." Holy fuck, if that wasn't the mother of all slip-ups, then I don't know what is.

Hunter cocks his head to the side, examining me closely. I sizzle and pop under his gaze. "If you want to call it quits, just say the word."

I almost give myself whiplash as I take a step backward. My worst fears have just been spoken aloud. I knew this day would come. I just thought it wouldn't be so soon. "No, that's not what I want." Working my lip, I ask the inevitable. "Why? Do you?" I'm certain he can hear my heart breaking and my pink bits weeping.

The silence is killing me. Just as I'm about to excuse myself and cry a river in private, his warm palm engulfs my cheek. "No." I can't help but breathe a sigh of relief. "You've made it clear what you want, and I'm happy with your demands."

'Earth to Mary—tell him!' my inner voice screams. Once

and for all.

"I…" But I quickly seal my lips shut. This is the time a non-coward would speak up and mend the error of her ways. But I'm scared, fucking terrified, in fact. What if I confess I'm beginning to have feelings for him, and in response he tells me to grow up and take a number?

It may all seem like hearts, and roses, and endless orgasms, but what happens when that fades? I'm no one special. Just Mary Mitts, the ginger-haired, average Joe Blow, from the Bronx. Hunter will grow bored and find someone else to whet his appetite. I need to remember that the next time I get carried away and picture our happily ever after.

Corey has broken me, but I'll be damned if I'm played for a fool a second time around.

"Good," I reply, but nothing about this is remotely good. What does feel good however, is his thumb caressing the back of my ear. But forcing myself to concentrate, I persevere. "Now, I'm going to go home, shower, and hit some stores so I can finally get out of your hair."

He blinks once, my words appearing to snap him to focus. "Oh, right. Can I come?" He reads my hesitation and smirks. "It is my apartment and office you're redecorating. Surely I have a say." And then he says stuff like this, which gives me a small shred of hope. I need time to clear my head.

Gently turning my cheek to sever our connection, I shake my head, while every part of me screams in protest. "I think it's better I do it alone." That holds more than one meaning.

"Okay, no worries," he replies without fuss. A small part of me wishes he did. "I'll text you the details about tonight."

"Great."

Now would be the time I turn and leave, seeing as I made a big song and dance about wanting to do it alone. But leaving him has me missing him all over again. I really need to talk to Maddy about this, but the truth is, telling her would mean I would have to admit to myself that I, Mary Mitts, have fallen deeply and irrevocably in love with…Hunter O'Shea, and there isn't a damn thing I can do about it.

Men like Hunter don't settle down, they especially don't settle down with women like me—women who want a fairy tale ending. Tears threaten to break past the floodgates, so I quickly turn my back and leave, and attempt to figure out what the hell comes next.

I have no fucking idea what I'm doing, that much is clear, because if I did, I would turn back around and forget the day I ever met Hunter. I was stupid to think I could pull this off. I never saw Hunter as just a fuck buddy. He was always something more. If only I had been honest with myself and him from the very beginning, I wouldn't be walking into Siesta's with my heart lodged in my throat.

Today, I did some soul searching and realized that there is only one way I can end this insanity—I have to tell Hunter how I feel. If he laughs in my face and forgets my name come morning, then at least I know.

Needing to give my brain the day off, I actually did what I said I was going to do and went shopping for Hunter's home and office. It probably wasn't the best idea to get my mind off of him, but it gave me the thinking time I needed.

Tonight isn't the time to air our dirty laundry, but now that I've come to a decision to finally grow a pair and tell him, or at least hint that this isn't just a booty call for me, the sooner I can stop acting like a nutjob.

If only I was honest earlier, none of this would be happening, but it is what it is and now I have to deal with fixing this mess. Yes, I'm scared, but I'm even more terrified of not giving this a chance to grow. That's my mantra as I walk into the Mexican restaurant in Hell's Kitchen, because what's the worst that can happen?

The place is packed, a sure sign the burritos are as good as the fishbowl margaritas they're infamous for. As I'm about to ask the charming hostess where my party is sitting, I see something which sanctions that I'll be drowning in those fishbowls to survive the night.

Standing a few feet away is Hunter. He looks incredible, which is nothing new, and what's also customary is the fact he's talking to some blonde bimbo who looks seconds away from offering the shot she's holding from between her fake boobs.

He laughs at something she says, and even leans in close to hear what she's saying above the traditional Mexican music, which is blaring loudly over the speakers.

To onlookers, the sight seems innocent enough, but I recognize that look echoed in those doe eyes, because it's the same one I wear whenever Hunter's in the room. She wants him, and from the shit-eating grin plastered on his stupid, smug face, I dare say she's in with half a chance. They're definitely flirting. I cover my mouth, seconds away from throwing up my lunch.

Spinning on my heel, intent on fleeing and not looking

where I'm going, I charge into some poor person who is in the firing line. Apologizing profusely, it isn't until I look up and see the gods are wagging their finger at me, hinting this isn't going to be easy.

"Mary?" Marie says with nothing but concern. "Is everything all right? You look like you've just seen a ghost."

Pulling it together as best I can, I try my best attempt at smiling without bursting into ugly tears. "Hi, Marie. Yes, I'm fine. I just remembered I left something in the car. I won't be a minute." That was supposed to be my cue to leave and never return, but when a handsome gentleman steps behind Marie with her coat, I know chivalry runs in the O'Shea family.

"Oh, you sound just like me. I left my coat in the car." She turns over her shoulder and smiles at her doting husband—Hunter's dad. "Thank you, Ralph. This is Mary. Hunter's friend." The moment we're introduced, it's obvious they both know I'm currently screwing their son.

Ralph—I can see where Hunter gets his good looks from—gives me a polite kiss on the cheek and a gentle smile. "Great to meet you, Mary. You deserve some kind of medal for putting up with my son."

I laugh, but it's strained, because this is just plain awkward.

"Ralph, would you walk Mary to her car? She left something behind."

"Oh, no, that's totally okay!" I express a little louder than normal, alerting everyone to my impending hysteria. "I'll be back in a minute."

"Where are you going?" Damn him and his deep, honeyed voice to hell.

"Mary left something in her car. I told your father to go

with her. The streets aren't safe for a nice, young lady like her to walk alone," Marie explains, because my mouth has become drier than the Sahara Dessert.

Hunter chuckles, which irritates and turns me on all in the same breath. "More like the streets aren't safe from her." It's supposed to be a joke, but I'm in no mood to laugh.

Making a point to look at the bar, where the blonde floozy was probably getting ready to rack up tequila shots and dip her naked body in salt, I eye Hunter something wicked. He's come to read me so well.

"Oh no, are you still sad about One Direction? Don't worry, Shortcake, I hear Harry is going solo and we all know he's the talented one, anyway."

I know what he's doing. This is the usual banter we'd engage in, and if everything is supposedly fine between us, then I should play along. But he's lucky I'm not kneeing him in the groin and finding the puta who was flapping her fake lashes his way.

"It doesn't surprise me you know all about their careers—your stash of women's underwear surpasses the number that's been thrown their way—ten to one." Hunter clutches over his heart dramatically, but I'm only half joking.

"Oh, you two," Marie gushes with a cheerful smirk, not at all bothered that I called her son a manwhore in a roundabout way.

Ralph couldn't look happier. "I like this one."

They ask the server where our table is while Hunter lags behind, appearing to puzzle over why I want to throat punch him. "Hi," he mouths. In response, I flip him off with a sarcastic grin. He quickly reads loud and clear that I'm not playing, and attempts to reach out, but I slap his hand away, and narrow my eyes in warning.

Marie and Ralph are oblivious to our sudden stalemate and follow the waitress to our table at the back of the room. Hunter subtly reaches out to caresses my ass, but I swat away his advances and eyeball a final warning. He raises one hand in surrender, while using the other to cup his balls.

The moment I see Maddy, tears well in my eyes. I feel like it's been years since I last saw her, not mere days. She instantly deciphers my mood and worry overcomes her. This is exactly the reason why I never should have listened to my vagina and stayed away from Hunter. If this turns pear-shaped, so many people are bound to lose.

"Lamb?" She stands and is by my side in a heartbeat. "Are you okay?"

I want to pull her aside and divulge all my secrets. Tell her that no, I'm not okay, and I need to book an appointment to see her fiancé. But I suck it up and smile. "Yeah, as good as good can be, considering I have to spend my Saturday night with this annoying jerk. No offense, Marie and Ralph."

"None taken," Ralph says, while Marie's light laughter hints they're oblivious to my meltdown. Maddy, however, isn't convinced, because she knows me better than I know myself. But she lets it slide.

We all take our seats, and I'm thankful when Hunter slides into the booth to sit near Dixon, while I slip in beside Maddy.

"Hello, I'm…"

"I'll have a strawberry margarita, please. Is that fishbowl the only size you have?" I blurt out, interrupting the waitress, whose mouth is still open, mid-introduction, before I rudely interrupted her with my desperate need to get wasted, pronto.

She quickly regains her composure and nods. "Si. That's the biggest size we have. You wanted smaller?"

"No! The bigger the better," I foolishly say, because Hunter arches a smug brow. Fuck him and the cocky horse he rode in on. "After the week I've had," I explain to the waitress, "I've come to realize that life is short…and so are some other things I've come in recent contact with." Hunter chokes on the beer he stole from Dixon, while I return a smug look of my own.

The waitress nods in understanding, a fallen victim to the same crime.

Once she takes everyone's order, the table grows quiet, no doubt everyone wondering about my sudden need to give every fishbowl patron a run for their money. "So, how did it go with the redecorating?" Marie innocently asks, unknowingly giving away my whereabouts to Dixon and Maddy.

"It went well. I was able to find most of what I was looking for."

Ralph, so like Hunter in his cool demeanor, leans back in the booth, arm laid atop the red leather back. "Lucky for you, then. I'm sure my son has made you rethink having kids."

It's supposed to be a joke, but the mere mention of kids and Hunter has my cheeks setting alight. Hunter, of course, is in tune with my response, but he stays silent, watching me closely.

"Your son has made me rethink a lot of things," I reply, but only he and I understand the true meaning behind my words.

Marie goes on to ask Maddy a few questions about the wedding, but I'm barely listening, because Hunter is currently scrutinizing me like I'm a science project. Dixon appears to be examining me also, before his attention flicks to Hunter. He so knows something is askew, but the mere notion that Hunter and I would be sleeping together is so farfetched, I don't think he would even jump to that conclusion straight off the bat.

Our waitress returns with our drinks, placing mine in front of me with a sympathetic smile. This is going to be a long night.

Thirteen

"So, suit? When are you free?" asks Dixon, but suit fitting is the last thing on my mind, because at this rate, I will be dead before the night ends.

Mary has been avoiding me all evening, and although this is stock standard behavior, I get the sense this isn't for show.

I know we agreed to act "normal," but this is something else. The moment she laid eyes on me, I instinctually wanted to protect my balls and ask her what's wrong. Earlier today I threw her a freaking bone, hoping and praying she would put me out of my misery and confirm that this is something "more."

But once again I got carried away with a HEA because she's made her feelings clear on more than one occasion. But when she met my mom, she was nervous, that much is sure, and although she claimed it was because she didn't want to let the cat out of the bag, I don't believe her.

This morning, waking up to her was a feeling unlike any

other. I expected she would bail like a thief in the night, so you can imagine my surprise when I woke to find myself clinging to her like the desperate man that I am.

All day I wanted to call her, tell her how I felt, because I'm done being a little bitch. I know Mary is happy with what we've got going, but if I don't tell her how I feel, or at least hint that this isn't just a casual fling to me, I'll fucking lose my mind.

"It's okay, Hunter, if it's easier, you can wear something you already own." Maddy's sweet voice reminds me that I'm sitting at a table with my nearest and dearest.

"No, he cannot," Dixon pipes up, nudging me with his thigh to wake me the fuck up. "He will wear that electric blue velvet suit with pride."

"What the fuck?" I recoil, curling my lip. When Maddy conceals a smile behind her hand, I know that he's thankfully joking.

"How about you, Lamb? I know you're busy with school, but think you can squeeze me in for some dress shopping?"

Mary peers up from slurping on her second fishbowl, appearing as lost in thought as me. "Sure, Maddy, anything you want." We both sound as unexcited as the other, giving off the impression that this wedding is as painful as pulling teeth.

Maddy slouches in her seat, no doubt ready to call an intervention because her two best friends are apathetic jerks. Dixon is awfully huffy, and I know the minute we're alone, he's going to drill me for information. But for the first time in my life, I can't tell him jackshit, because I don't even know what to say.

"So, how's the makeover going?" Dixon asks Mary. The question may seem innocent enough, but I know what this sly snake is doing.

"Almost done." She keeps it simple, but I can see she's nervous as her fingers tremble when clasping the straw.

"And how have you survived dealing with this big guy?" He bumps into me, while I play it cool.

Mary shrugs, finally meeting my eyes. I wish I was better at facial charades, as I would convey some sort of message to reassure her that she's doing good. But I know if I make one wrong move, Dixon will see straight through me and he won't be shy in using my innards as a brand spanking new tie.

So I reach for my beer and casually take a sip, allowing her the floor.

"I think it's fair to say once I'm done, I'll need to pay you a visit or two." But her response is weak.

"Yes, my son has the ability to drive one crazy," my mom says with a smile. I've never seen her so happy to be in the company of a woman who I clearly like, or any woman, for that matter. I may have Mary fooled, but my mom's eyes are wide open, and she likes what she sees. "But it appears that's his way to show someone he cares."

Oh, for fuck's sake. She may as well have skywritten that I'm a pussywhipped little wimp.

Dixon taps his pointer over his lip, furrowed brow lines reveal he's deep in thought. I need to rein this in, and I need to do so now. It's fairly obvious something is going on between Mary and I, and as much as I want to divulge our dirty little secret because I don't want it to be that anymore, that's not what Mary wants. I promised her I would act "normal" and our normal is to throw down and show no mercy.

God save my soul. "Have you been reading your Nicholas

Sparks books again? You know the only person I care about is yours truly." I jab my thumb into my chest. "Gets less messy that way. It also saves me from having to deal with meddlesome, bossy women. I already have one of those." I pointedly look at my mom, who pales. "Like the Polish proverb says—a bachelor and a dog can do anything."

"You don't own a dog," Dixon says, raising his eyes to the ceiling and ruining my words of wisdom.

Raising my finger in defiance, I'm about to detail my plan to adopt all the Bali street dogs, but when Mary turns a shade of green, before launching from her seat, I seal my lips shut. "If you'll excuse me."

She doesn't wait for anyone to ask if she's okay, because she's out the door faster than The Flash. Without a second thought, I too stand, frantic to see if she is all right. However, Maddy has the same thoughts as me and shoots up also.

"Let him go," Dixon calmly says, interlacing his fingers through Maddy's. The simple gesture has me realizing what a fucking idiot I've been for not telling Mary how I feel sooner. Maddy's concern is clear, but she eventually nods, trusting Dixon.

As I make a move, Dixon latches onto my wrist, stopping me. I'm about to ask what in the holy hell he's doing, but a look alone can convey a thousand words, and this look is Dixon's most infamous one. With a puckered brow, he cocks his head to the side, a silent warning that I'm to fix whatever mess I've made.

I was stupid to think I could fool him. Not only is he Dr. Phil on steroids, more importantly, he's my best friend. I nod once, promising to make things right. I owe that to everybody, especially Mary.

My mom knows what I have to do and smiles. Regardless of how many times I've fucked up in my life, she's always stood by my side, and now is no exception. I quickly dash toward the exit, hoping to god Mary hasn't caught a cab to Antarctica by now.

Shouldering open the door, I frantically search from left to right, my heart dropping when Mary isn't anywhere to be seen. There is no way she could have fled too far, so I go with my gut and bolt left. The sidewalk is bustling with happy New Yorkers obscuring my view, so I not so gently jostle them out of the way because they're wasting precious time.

I don't have a plan. My whole intent is to find Mary and then take it from there. She will probably hate what I have to say because this is going against everything we agreed on, but I can't lie to her, or myself a second longer.

When a burst of red catches my eye, I lead with my feet and heart, and take off in a dead sprint, calling out to Mary. I know she's heard me because everyone in a hundred-mile radius turns to see what the fuss is about.

I'm not an idiot. I know she won't make this easy for me, but the thrill of the chase, of finally telling her how I feel spurs me on, and I quicken the pace. I excuse myself as I elbow past people, each step becoming more frantic than the one before it.

"Mary! Stop!" But she doesn't. My voice only seems to inspire her to run faster, and before long we're both running the streets of Manhattan, but I don't plan to ever let her go. The lights turn green, but that doesn't stop Mary, who seems to pick up speed, obviously preferring to get trampled by traffic than talk to me.

The thought of her hurting herself has me racing forward, not caring who I bowl over in the process, because all that matters is her. Just as she steps out onto the road, I lunge forward and latch onto her forearm.

I'm far from gentle as I yank her back onto the sidewalk. A horn blares as a driver waves his fist in the air, eyeballing Mary as she almost ended up like a squashed bug on his windshield. The thought of her being hurt makes me crazy and that passion leads me.

"What the fuck, Shortcake? You eager to be roadkill? You could have gotten yourself killed!" She attempts to break free from my hold, but I hold on tight. "Answer me!"

She violently turns to face me, ready to answer me with her fists, but I've come to read her so well. I weave from the strike zone, which infuriates her further. "Let me go!"

"No!" I shout just as loudly as her. "What in the hell is wrong?"

She scoffs, the sound flipping me off. "What's wrong is that I'm a fucking idiot, that's what. I can't believe I—"

But she abruptly pauses, averting her eyes. Her response has me tightening my hold and forcing her to look at me. "You what?" I offer, so lost in translation. She levels me with a blazing glare, still attempting to break free.

We're standing in the middle of the sidewalk, a complete obstacle to passersby, but I'm not moving an inch until she tells me what's going on. The anger is radiating off of her in waves, and before long, I know she'll buckle and submerge us both.

When she finally looks at me, a startled gasp leaves me because she looks like she's going to cry. "I'm disgusted at myself for letting this get so far," she confesses, swallowing down her revulsion. "I thought I could do this, but at every corner, there seems to be a line of women waiting their turn. How can I compete with them when you've got half of America ready to take my place?"

"What?" I manage to choke out, because I'm certain I'm hearing things.

She shakes her head, ripping from my hold. I'm too shell-shocked to stop her. "Tonight was a perfect example of how you'll never change. The moment I turn my back, some bimbo is ready to throw morals to the wind just for one night with you! My ex-boyfriend, my high school sweetheart, he made a fool of me, but I'll be damned if I ever get treated that way again!" The pain is palpable beneath her anger. This asshole is the person who broke Mary's heart. He's the reason she can't seem to open up. But at least she has a reason.

Me...I'm just a fucking coward who never allowed anyone in, too afraid to get hurt.

Her tiny hands dig into my chest as she pushes me, her anger burning all the way to my toes. I stumble, too stunned to even move. Is she talking about the flirty blonde I met at the bar? The same one who yes, offered to blow me in the bathroom, but the one I politely thanked and escaped from because her forwardness had me missing Mary more than I thought humanly possible. And just who is this ex-boyfriend? I will find him and skin him alive.

"Shortcake..." She doesn't let me continue. Now that she's started, it seems she can't stop.

"No, fuck you, Hunter! I'm not interested in hearing about your manwhore escapades." She stands on tippy toes, trying her best to level me with her fiery eyes. All it does is leave me breathless with the need to consume her, like now.

"The thought of sharing you, of having another woman touch you…" Her words are filled with possession, and laced with warning, and they leave me harder than a fucking rock. "Has me wanting to commit unspeakable acts of violence with a smile. I don't want to share because I'm greedy and I want you. All of you. Every single, annoying inch of you. I don't even like you on most days, but on the days when I do, I like you…a lot, and I'm fucking crazy, because you don't feel the same way and I…"

My body takes over and I do the only thing I can—I smash my lips to hers, and I don't look back. I never will.

The moment my mind plays catch up, I freeze, because I've forgotten what it feels like to embrace another so closely. But this is Mary, the woman I've wanted from the very first moment we locked eyes and she stirred this longing within. Nothing has felt more natural and it feels like I've finally found my home.

Without further thought, I nudge her quivering lips open with my tongue, silently seeking permission. She allows me entry and lets me stay for a very long time. A small gasp escapes her, but when she finally opens up, it's the best fucking feeling in the world.

We kiss like starved animals, pawing at one another, uncaring that we're making out in public for all to see. Her lips taste unbelievable, and I doubt I'll be able to remove myself of my own accord any time soon. But the way she threads her fingers through my hair and tugs fiercely, I think the sentiment is more than mutual.

Tiny mewls fill my lungs as she gasps and sighs into me, her exhalations breathing life into me over and over again. I suckle her bottom lip before sealing my mouth over hers and possessing every piece of her.

Our tongues duel, a perfect union of push and pull, because the moment I surrender, she takes control. She fists my hair, angling her strawberry-coated lips for her pleasure as she seeks out every curve of my mouth with her lips and tongue.

Needing to get as close to her as I can, I unite our chests, rubbing my massive erection against her. She moans and sucks my tongue. I'm not above dragging her down an alley and fucking her senseless because I need to be inside of her while our lips continue this dance I never want to end. But this…this is way past a physical union, this is fucking epic.

Slipping a hand around her waist, I venture lower, squeezing her ass as she licks the seam of my mouth, languidly slow. Now that the urgency has simmered, we both sip and taste the other, relishing in the delicacy that has me angling my head to deepen the union.

Our tongues sluggishly battle in an erotic dance, while our bodies follow suit, and before long, I don't know where mine ends and hers starts. Her kiss is pure sex, and the thought of fucking her while locked this way almost has me coming right here and now.

She fastens both arms around my nape, her fingernails digging into my flesh. The sting only adds to the heightened sensation of what I'm feeling and I growl into her mouth before circling her tongue with mine.

I can feel her pearled nipples through the thin cotton of my t-shirt and visions of her slick pussy have me pressing my hard on deeper and harder into her.

"Oh, fuck," she whimpers into my mouth. If I don't stop

in the next five seconds, I'm going to come in my pants and it won't be pretty.

Even though I'd rather cut off a limb than detangle my body from hers, I lay tiny kisses over her mouth and suckle her bottom lip, before severing our unity. She stumbles forward, almost in a drunken state as her eyes open and she slowly focuses on where we are and what we just did.

A beautiful pink overtakes her creamy skin and I barely resist the urge to kiss over every inch of her rose-hued flesh. "Y-you kissed me," she states, blinking once.

I nod coolly, brushing the curls from her cheek. "Yes, I did."

When I offer nothing more, she runs that wicked tongue along her top lip, tempting me once again. "But why? You said you don't kiss."

I can understand her confusion. "I don't, but it was the only way I could shut you up." My words are gentle, and she smirks.

"Just disregard whatever I said," she quickly backtracks, but it's too late.

Shaking my head, I place a hand to her cheek, ensuring she looks straight at me when I deliver her my soul. "No, I won't, because I…" Her swollen, well-kissed lips part, but I silence her with my pointer. "I won't, because I like you…a lot, too."

Her lips grow slack beneath my finger. "You do?"

"Yes, I do. I wanted to kill that kangaroo hopping asshole."

"You did?" she asks, eyes wide.

Tracing the ridge of her lips with my finger, I rein in the memory of him whispering into her ear before I seek him out and send him back to the land down under missing an appendage. "Yes, Shortcake. Contrary to your beliefs, I haven't wanted another woman more than I do you. You didn't just take my breath away…you breathed new life into me." And just like that, I feel a thousand pounds lighter. Is it really that easy?

"Hunter…" she whispers, her lower lip trembling. "I don't understand. I mean, you wanted a no strings relationship."

"No, you did," I counter, deciding to lay all my cards on the table and see what happens when I do.

She sighs, brushing a piece of hair behind her ear. "I only said that because I thought that's what you wanted."

Fuck…me…dead. Can this woman be any more incredible? "That's not what I wanted. How could I want another woman when I have you, Mary?"

Tears prick her eyes. "But Keira?"

"What about her? She is no one, a mistake, one I never should have made. But I won't make any more."

She works her lip, pondering on this newfound honesty, which has D2 fist pumping in pride. "So, what happens now?"

And that's the million-dollar question.

Cupping her cheek, I kiss over her trembling lips while she mewls. "What happens is that we don't use labels. We just continue this, because this"—I sashay my mouth over hers— "feels fucking incredible. I may not be the Prince Charming type…"

Mary smiles, placing her palm over my heart. "Who said I want Prince Charming? Just smack me on the ass and tell me that ass is yours." And just like that, I fall deeply, and eternally in love with Mary Mitts.

"I love it when you talk dirty."

She laughs, her fingers curling into a loose fist.

"I have baggage…like lots," she confesses. "My ex-boyfriend, he broke me. He thought it was okay to cheat on me and then blame me for his infidelities because I wasn't exciting enough for him. I have trust issues because of it, and seeing all these women fawn over you…it just makes me feel like an insecure crazy person most of the time."

When she sniffs, the urge to find this asshole and hang him out to dry shoots to priority number one. "He's clearly an idiot who lacks balls. We all have baggage, Shortcake. Mine is…" I search for the right word. "Complicated, because well…"

"What?" she asks, searching my face for clues.

Here goes nothing. "I've never really dated. Like ever, really. It's not because I didn't have options, it's because well"—I rub the back of my neck—"I guess I just never really wanted to spend that much time with anyone and be tied to them in such a serious way. It wasn't personal, it was just me. I just wasn't wired that way. The thought of dating…it scared me, it still does." Just because we've made progress doesn't mean I'm ready for her to move in. "I have no fucking idea what dating involves and odds are, I will mess up. A lot."

"I'm scared too. Sometimes I can be kind of crazy."

I burst into a gruff laugh. "Then let us figure this…whatever this is, out together," I say, hoping my confession doesn't make me sound like Captain Needy.

"So you've never dated, and I've only ever dated one guy?" I nod. "I can't believe you've never been in a serious relationship before. I just figured someone special broke your heart, hence the need to change partners every week."

"Sorry to disappoint. I'm not Dix. And it wasn't every week," I state with a smile.

She folds her arms, full of spunk. "I've seen your black book."

Busted. I don't bother denying it. "I guess I was just waiting for the right woman…"

When a gasp escapes her and she pales, I know I've said too much. I need to hold off with the heartfelt confessions until we figure out what exactly it is we're doing. But once again, Mary leaves me breathless.

"Take me back to your apartment?"

Oh god, I am gone. She owns every piece of me and I'll wear that fact like a fucking badge of pride. "Oh, Shortcake, you're in so much trouble." My cock will soon kick itself if I don't take this woman home and gorge on her until I'm stuffed full.

"Trouble is what I do best…so is sitting on your face," she states, nonchalant, while I gag on air as the image is just too much.

Reaching for her hand, I interlace our fingers, smiling like a creep at such a simple union. She senses my happiness, and before long, we're both smiling like depraved circus clowns. "Lamb?"

That shot of reality rattles the cage, and we both turn to see Madison and Dixon standing feet away. Dixon is standing behind Maddy with his arms crossed, not at all surprised by the fact we're holding hands like we're in the second grade.

Mary's guilt is instant. She exhales. I gently squeeze her fingers, a silent promise I'll never let her go. "Maddy…" She pauses when Madison looks down at our hands like we've just given birth to the antichrist.

"What the fuck is going on?" Dixon smirks, because whenever Maddy curses, it's on like Donkey Kong.

Mary sniffs, her remorse for not telling Maddy what we were doing sooner is palpable, and my inner barbarian rises to the challenge, ready to defend my woman, because I can't stand to see her cry. "Mary and I have called a truce because, well…" Jesus, this is a lot harder than I thought. Looking into those virtuous eyes, I feel like a thief stealing her innocence. Poor Dixon. He doesn't stand a chance.

He nods, reading my thoughts loud and clear.

"Mary and I are…"

"We've been fucking," Mary blurts out, while I'm tempted to holler a hell yeah, we have!

"Ha ha. Very funny," Maddy says with a laugh. But that soon dies in a strangled heap when no one laughs with her. "Oh my god. You're serious?"

Mary nods once. "I'm sorry I didn't tell you. I just…I didn't know how."

Madison pales. Dixon places his hand on her shoulder. "Angelo, are you okay?"

She stares at Mary and I like we're body-snatchers, holding her friend's hostage. "Did you know?" she simply says.

I really hope the spare bed is comfortable, because I have a feeling that's where Dixon will be spending many lonely nights from here on in. "Yes."

Damn, that even hurt my cock.

"You told him?" Mary exclaims, tilting her chin to look up at me. There goes my hard on and the prospect of eating Mary out all night.

Just as I'm about to try this honesty shoe on for size, Dixon steps in. "No, Mary, he didn't. I figured it out myself. Hunter is all beauty and no brains."

"I'm offended. And so is Hugh," I rebuke. That plan was supposed to be foolproof, but Dixon is no fool.

"We'll talk about it later," Maddy says, while Dixon sucks it up like the true champion that he is. "So, you've been…" She uses her hands as gesturing tools, because saying it aloud will mean she'll need to accept it as truth.

Mary nods, letting my hand go and stepping toward Maddy. "Yes, but not for long. I know that doesn't excuse the fact I didn't tell you, but I didn't even know what was happening until about five minutes ago."

Madison waits for her to continue, but it's now my turn, because I should have done this weeks ago. "I like Mary. A lot. That shouldn't come as a surprise. But you can imagine my surprise when I discovered she liked me too. It's not just sex, Cherry Pie."

I want her to know that I would never treat this like some game. I know we've all got something to lose if this goes south.

Madison sighs, her compassion, which we all love about her, shining through. "Okay, good. I just…wow, this is just… wow." Her cheeks puff as she blows out a heavy breath.

"I know. This is why I was trying to find the right time to tell you, but I should have just been honest. I'm so sorry. Can you forgive me?"

Madison is Mother Teresa incarnate, and in this moment, I think we all fall in love with her. "There's nothing to forgive. We all need to deal with our demons in our own time. But if you hurt her, Debbie, I will fucking kill you."

A laugh erupts from me. It seems she's not so saintly after all. "Understood."

Dixon smiles, attempting to wrap his arms around her slender waist. But it seems her understanding nature ends with us. "Don't even think about it."

He raises his hands in surrender, unable to wipe his grin clean. "I'm at your mercy, Angelo."

"You'll be at your own mercy for the next few days," she bites back, turning over her shoulder to look at him.

I'm pretty sure I just witnessed him coming in his pants. She drives a hard bargain—hard being the operative word.

Mary throws her arms around Maddy, and it appears she'll never let her go. But that's okay, because now that our secret is no longer that, we won't have stolen moments, but rather memories which are ready to be made.

Dixon meets my gaze and nods. If I don't know better, I'd say the son of a gun was proud of me for finally stepping into the land of the adults and embracing it with both hands. "Don't fuck this up," he mouths.

And he's right. I can't, and I won't.

Crossing my heart with my middle finger, I play it off, but I mean every word, because I would rather break my own heart then break Mary's.

Celine Dion sounding from my back pocket reminds me that before I decided to join the hopeless romantics of this world, I was having dinner with my friends and parents, who are still back at the restaurant.

Dixon bursts into husky laughter when he hears my ringtone. "I still think it's you who likes that song and not your mom."

I scoff, wrapping my arm around Mary's shoulders as she nestles into my side. The gesture is so natural, but both Maddy and Dixon almost fall over their feet. Just wait until they see me take her pretty lips and indecently make out with them.

We walk back to the restaurant, couples embracing how

normal couples do because that's what Mary and I are—I think. The thought has me wanting to clarify something. "So…I know I said we weren't going to use any labels…"

Mary's head snaps up, worry reflected in her eyes. I soothe her concerns, kissing the tip of her nose. "But just so we're clear, you're my girl, and fucking anyone except me is off the table. However, fucking me on a table or wherever you please is completely acceptable."

She smirks. "I thought that was pretty self-explanatory. Why would you think otherwise?"

"Keira said she overheard you talking to someone about fucking them like an animal." My teeth clench at the memory, so I envision Mary riding a unicorn, naked.

Mary stiffens in my arms. "Why would she tell you that?"

By her rigid response, I don't want to sully something amazing with talk of Keira. Delivering the basics, I reveal, "She just said she'd overheard you. Is it true?"

When she nods, I breathe steadily, attempting to calm down. "Yes, it's true, but…"

Covering my ears, I sing Katy Perry loudly, not at all interested in the details. When she removes my hands, I wonder if she'll see me in the same light if I broke down and cried. "But I was talking to Maddy."

"What now?" I shout, unable to contain my excitement. Dixon looks over her shoulder at me, while I wiggle my eyebrows. He turns back around, not at all entertained by my enthusiasm.

She laughs, slapping my arm. "No, you pervert, I meant she was telling me she hadn't seen Dixon all week cause of work, and she was…" She pauses, leaving the rest to my very vivid imagination which has no problems filling in the blanks.

"So what Keira thought she heard was actually not true, which doesn't surprise me, because she's a gigantic liar."

There's no reason to continue this conversation because all that matters is that Mary hasn't been fucking anyone but me, and I plan on keeping it that way. "If it makes you feel any better, I can engrave your name in my underwear. Like they did in the 50s."

"You don't wear any," she giggles. She does have a point.

Leaning in close, I whisper, "I'll get your name tattooed on my cock then." I suck the shell of her ear into my mouth while she groans.

The sound is too hot for words. But when she purrs, "You'd have to ink my middle name and surname too, otherwise there will be a lot of room left to play with," I almost lose it right then and there in the street.

"Okay, deal, what's your middle name?" I'm surprised I can construct a coherent sentence right now. I lose the ability soon after however.

With a slanted grin, she replies, "Annabelle."

My cock struts his shit cause that's a whole lotta words. "That's quite a mouthful."

Subtly reaching forward, she rubs over my hard on and cups me firmly. "So are you."

Holy fucking balls.

If this is what being in a relationship entails, sign me up.

"You're in so much trouble," I repeat, humming when she continues rubbing my dick just how she knows I like it.

However, when she rears upward and bites over my racing pulse, I know I'm the one who's in trouble—deep, deep trouble.

Fourteen

One month later

"So, I think once the filing cabinets I ordered arrive, I'm pretty much done. I…" But I lose all train of thought when Hunter presses his hardened chest to my back and sucks over my racing pulse.

You'd think I'd be used to his kisses by now, but nope, each kiss, touch is something new.

The past month has been something else. No more stolen moments or kisses because now that Hunter and I have kissed, we can't seem to stop. I didn't even realize how much I loved making out like a teenager, but kissing Hunter is unlike anything I've ever experienced before.

He stuck true to his word and we haven't resorted to labeling what we have, but that's okay, because I know he's been faithful, and that's all I ever wanted. I don't need to declare to the world that he's my boyfriend, because as long as we know what we mean to each other, then screw everyone else. I also think it'll freak him out, seeing as he's never had a serious girlfriend before.

I still can't believe I'm the person to break the mold.

Considering this is his first "relationship," so far, on most days, he's taken to it like a duck to water. Sometimes he forgets to call, or I catch him looking at an attractive woman, but old habits die hard. He's learning and so am I. When I catch him, I want to pluck out his eyeballs, and push the unsuspecting woman down the stairs. But instead, I tell myself he's with me and me only, and I have to remember that. My insecurity still lingers, but it'll take time.

My mom is desperate to meet Hunter, and I will introduce him soon, but I'm still getting used to the idea of us being friends and not enemies. We're taking things slow because this is uncharted waters for us both.

"You've done a remarkable job. That desk is the perfect height for me to—"

"Okay, Casanova," I say, cutting him off as I turn. Wrapping my arms around his nape, I peer into his sea green eyes. "Do you like it?"

Hunter takes my breath away and now is no exception. He looks incredibly sexy in a navy suit, his hair groomed, and heavy scruff challenging the image of a stuffy, conservative businessman. "I don't just like it. I love it. You're most talented with your hands." He smirks and my insides go kaboom!

"I'm pleased. I just have a few more things to do in your bedroom, and then I'm done."

"I've liked having you in my bedroom. And in my bed," he mischievously adds, laying a gentle kiss over the crease of my mouth. Goose bumps lick every inch of flesh and my greedy body demands more.

We had early morning sex, which extended late in the AM, but Hunter wouldn't release me until he was satisfied I walked with a well-sated limp. But no matter how much he gives me, I always want more.

"Well, that's because I got a state of the art, posture correcting mattress and disposed of your old one with fire," I quip. Regardless of our newfound truce, our bickering will always prevail until the end of time.

"Now, now, there's no need for you to be jealous. I can handle only one nymphomaniac at a time." My mouth parts, while Hunter chuckles. "I'm not complaining. I love that you're a gluttonous sex-crazed maniac when it comes to my glorious cock."

I burst into laughter. "Please. It's either we fuck, or I have to talk to you. God forbid that happens."

That slanted grin I've grown to love tugs at his sinful lips. "Fuck that. Who wants to turn into one of those boring couples who...talk." He shudders playfully, while I rein back my excitement over the fact he just referred to us as being a couple. "Speaking of his and her t-shirt wearers, are we still on for dinner tonight with Dix and Cherry Pie?"

Who would have thought I'd be a fan of double dating?

Nodding, I press my chest to his, desperate to feel his burly body against mine. He hums low, the sound striking between my legs. "Yes. Maddy would have my head. She's so nervous about everything running smoothly, and by that, I mean she's worried you're going to dump Dixon in Mexico with nothing but a school girl's outfit and a bottle of lube."

"Moi?" He fakes horror, nestling his hands low around my waist. "Please. Give me a little more credit. I'd at least be there to film it." Arching a brow, he surrenders with a low chuckle. "Okay, fine, you win. No lube."

"You're impossible," I reply lightly, biting the inside of my cheek when he dips low and squeezes my ass.

"Speaking of lube…" My cheeks flush, which is exactly the response Hunter had hoped for. Almost every part of my body has been explored by him, all but one.

I tremble in his arms, the sensation almost too much. "In your dreams, O'Shea."

"You and your fine ass make a nightly appearance," he counters without pause.

That mouth—I love it and I love… But I stop soon after I think thoughts which are bound to get me into trouble.

Nuzzling into my neck, he suckles along the flesh, sampling and savoring like I'm his most favorite meal. My eyes roll into the back of my head as an untamed moan slips free. "You are so fucking sexy. Please tell me you forgot to wear underwear on purpose because I need to get inside of you like right now."

He drags the hem of my skirt up my legs, and lucky for us both, I most certainly ditched the offensive garment, as they just get in the way.

Just as he's inches away from exposing my ass, a light knock sounds at the door. We both groan, but I know we will have to continue this later because Hunter is waiting on his "source" to come back to him with news of the infamous watch.

We've both looked high and low, but to no avail. Although he would rather slice off his balls with a rusted butter knife than admit he's worried, I know deep down, he's concerned Gail will get to Mr. Yeong first.

It seems petty to me, but this is how someone with Mr. Yeong's standing acts. He is so accustomed to getting everything he wants, that he thinks he can throw impossible demands around like finding a needle in a haystack is an easy thing to do.

If I were Hunter, I would tell him to shove it, but it seems to be personal now that Gail is involved. And Hunter is also a man of his word. He's tenacious, determined, and driven in everything that he does. He is still certain Mr. Yeong will stay loyal to him, but if Gail found that watch before Hunter, I have no doubt loyalty between them would be long forgotten.

Luckily for Hunter, he's kept the conditions of their deal a secret, which is why I've ordered filing cabinets rivaling Fort Knox, because now he can file away his secrets under lock and key.

When the knocking strikes once again, Hunter gives my lips a quick kiss. "You'd think they pay me to come here to work, right? How fucking rude."

I giggle, quickly rearranging myself before I flash my ass to whoever is outside the door.

However, when Hunter opens the door, I wish I was still half-dressed, because I would gladly moon the skank who just entered the room.

Hunter and I agree on most things—that a red car does drive faster, lemon with Corona is for pussies, and that fries with mayonnaise are the bomb, but when it comes to this doe-eyed Pollyanna, we are universes apart. For obvious reasons, I want to throat punch her, but physical violence aside, I still don't trust her and am certain she's still scheming. The problem is, I still don't have any proof.

If I were a better actress, I could attempt to act semi-civil and dig for dirt. But every time she opens that perfect pout, I want to shut it with my fist. To know Hunter and her have been…together, erases all hopes of me uncovering the truth from her firsthand.

"Oh, sorry, did I interrupt?" she says melodiously.

She's so sweet she'd give diabetes, diabetes.

Hunter opens his mouth, but I interject. "Yes, actually you did. We were seconds away from christening this new desk." I run my fingertips along the polished wood, relishing in the fact that the old one, the one which Keira knew far too well, sits in a burned heap.

Hunter smirks proudly, which tickles me pink. He doesn't conceal the fact we're seeing one another, and when he looks at me with that feral look glistening in his eye, I'm tempted to shake imaginary pom poms and chant rah, rah, rah!

But pushing aside the green-eyed monster, I grab my bag and make a beeline for the door. I've got work to do. "Where are you going?"

"To the bathroom. I suddenly have the urge to throw up."

Hunter sighs, shaking his head, but it'll be a cold day in hell the moment I play nice with this wolf in hooker's clothing.

I can basically hear her lady parts weep in relief now that they're alone with Hunter, but I shove down my jealousy because I'm determined to try this trust thing on for size. I refuse to allow the skeletons of my past to rule whatever this is with Hunter, and it's my newfound outlook on life that leads me in the direction of Gail's office.

Whatever Keira is up to, I have no doubt Gail is up to something far worse. I know where to find him, seeing as he's training for the upcoming New York marathon. His meal times are on a meticulous roster, and as I look down at my watch, I see that he's chowing down on his bland meal of chicken and something leafy and green.

I've tried to be subtle and kept the stalking to a minimum, but regardless of my attempts to be sly, Hunter has let drop that he thinks I have the hots for the disgusting slime ball. It's all said tongue in cheek, but I know if Hunter caught Gail even looking at me sideways, he'd have no qualms ripping out his windpipe and using it to play "Greensleeves."

That thought warms my heart and stokes the constant fire burning within.

Most men are stupid, I say most because there is a small exception who although they think with their dicks, they don't lead with them all of the time. Hunter falls into this category on most days. As does Dixon, whose loyalty toward Maddy has me hoping that one day, I can be as grown up as them.

Dipping my hands into my low cut, silk blouse, I push up my boobs, impressed how this push-up bra complements the girls. Puckering my lips to ensure they're still coated with my pink gloss, I run my fingers through my hair to ensure I have a freshly fucked look.

The pièce de résistance is I hike up my skirt, making a modest hemline an indecently short lure for hormone-driven idiots like Gail. The moment I step foot into the lunchroom, I can practically see Gail's mouth hit the floor.

Whatever superfood he's eating is suspended mid-air as he openly checks me out from head to toe. I instantly feel like bathing in acid, but the thought of this creep potentially sabotaging what Hunter has worked so hard for spurs me on.

This is the first opportunity I've had to undertake Operation Burn in Hell because the deeper I dig, I just know I'll unearth whatever vile plans this bottom feeder has planned. Once I get to the bottom of his agenda, I know Keira's will soon follow.

And that's why I saunter toward the coffee machine, ensuring to wiggle my ass each step of the way.

I've used this coffee machine a thousand times before, but I stand in front of it, twirling a lock of hair around my finger while bending low. This, of course, is done with intent to ride the hem even higher than it already sits.

"Need a hand?" If Chlamydia and Ebola had a baby, then Gail's voice is what its wailing would sound like.

But for the greater good, I remember why I'm here and giggle. "There's just so many buttons. I can never remember what does what."

Turning over my shoulder, I batt my eyelashes, just how his assistant has mastered the art of flapping hers. Just when I think it's too much, he stands and adjusts his belt. "Don't worry that pretty little head of yours. Leave the hard stuff to me."

Oh my god. Do girls actually fall for this bullshit? When he ambles over like he's Mr. Universe himself, I know the answer is yes. It makes me appreciate Hunter's dirty candor all the more. He may be filthy, but at least he doesn't make me want to render myself unconscious so I forget our conversations ever took place.

Gail's heavy-handed cologne has me nigh on gagging, but I continue standing like a dim-witted moron as he reaches for a mug and places it under the nozzle. "These buttons here tell you which drink selection you can make. Can you see?" Neil Armstrong could see the buttons he's pointing to when he landed on the moon, but I lean in close, purposely grazing his arm with my boob. Brushing back my hair, I pretend to need a moment to take in everything he just said.

When ten seconds pass, I turn to him, mouth parted in staged awe. "Wow, you're like, so smart."

"I'm not just a pretty face, darlin.'" I actually throw up in my mouth a little. "But I suppose you can be forgiven because hanging around that dumbass, O'Shea, is sure to rub off on you."

Digging my fingernails into my palm to stop myself from slapping that smug smile from his cheeks, I inhale deeply and focus on why I'm here. "Hunter is just someone to have fun with. I like having fun."

And that right there is the magical word—fun. The word is what every man looking for a good time wants to hear.

He slithers closer and I can see why some women may find him attractive. He's all muscle with big baby blues, but unlike Dixon, his are icy and cold. He's also an enormous, arrogant asshole.

I decide to go in for the kill, because my quota for fucktards has been reached. "Do you like having fun?"

Gail licks his thick lips as he pushes the Long Black button on the coffee machine. "Fun is my middle name. Maybe one day I can show you what the buttons on my Aston Martin do." I've never wanted to castrate someone more than I do right now.

Revoking his right to reproduce seems just, because this world has more than enough assholes, but I smile sweetly. "Sure, I'd love that."

Gail reaches into his back pocket, retrieving his wallet. When he produces a crisp white business card and pen, I know he wants my digits. Swallowing down my aversion, I quickly scribble my cell number, and for good measure, draw a love heart near my name. "Call me," I purr, passing him the card.

"Did you seriously just ask me if Beijing is in India? Please put someone on the phone who isn't a complete moron." I'd recognize that voice anywhere. I'm overcome with an immense sense of guilt, but I remind myself why I've resorted to liaising with this jerkoff.

Gail smugly pockets my number, winking when Hunter barges into the lunchroom about to rip whoever he's speaking to a new one. However, when he sees Gail standing a little too close for comfort, his anger is redirected. "I'll call you back."

Needing to distract myself before I blow my cover, I reach for the coffee and take a small sip. Gail looks happier than a pig in shit when he turns around, no doubt locking eyes with Hunter. I need a moment to compose myself.

"Are you lost?" Gail quips, while my fingers clench around the mug.

"How about you get lost," Hunter barks without pause. "Or better yet, how about you do the world a favor and go play in traffic."

A smile tugs at my lips. Gail has no comeback, of course. I hear him collect his unfinished lunch before the door slams shut. Hunter is by my side in three long strides.

Finding my lady balls, I eventually crane my neck to look up at him. There is no mistaking his anger and curiosity, but I simply continue sipping my coffee, hoping he will let it slide.

"So… any reason why you didn't throw that scalding cup of coffee into Gail's face?" he asks, my hopes dwindling.

Shrugging, I reply, "And waste a perfectly good cup of joe

on that asshole? I think not." In and out, I tell myself, steadying my breathing, but he so knows I'm lying.

"I may not be a relationship guru, but I know when a woman is lying to me. Do you think he's prettier than me?" This is so like Hunter to make a joke when he's insecure.

"Of course not," I scoff.

The mood turns serious and Hunter reveals we're still both finding our feet. "You'd tell me if you were getting bored, right? Or I'm doing something wrong? Did I leave the toilet seat up?" He's grasping at straws, and it seems we're both learning the ropes when it comes to this relationship. "I suck at this whole dating thing."

Putting his mind at ease, I shake my head. "No, you don't."

"So I've got nothing to worry about?"

His sincerity is too much. "Cross my heart," I reply, doing exactly that. "Besides, Gail and I were just talking. Unlike Keira, who wants to do a lot more than talk whenever you're involved."

Deflection—the best way I can deal with this situation without buckling and spilling the beans.

Hunter sighs, running a hand over his scruff. "As much as you hate Keira, she's once again put her neck out to save my ass." My interest is completely piqued. Hunter continues. "I have to go to China. Gail has once again been sniffing around Mr. Yeong, and I'll be damned if that little shitstain ruins what I've worked so hard for. Keira showed me phone records and emails exchanged between them. It appears Mr. Yeong is falling for his utter bullshit, and seeing as I'm no closer to finding this fucking watch, I need to talk some sense into him, face to face."

Alarm bells sound. Who on earth has phone records on hand? Or prints out emails? A scheming, sneaky so and so, that's who. Keira's actions have just cemented what I need to do. She will obviously resort to any means to win Hunter over, and is using his hatred for Gail as a bargaining chip. I see right through her façade, and I'm certain she wants me and Gail out of the picture so she can have Hunter, and his success all to herself. Hunter is the perfect package, and she will clearly stop at nothing to get what she wants.

Well, she's got another thing coming, because that perfect package is mine. It's time to step up the ante. "When are you leaving?"

Hunter removes the cup I'm clinging to for dear life. "Tomorrow if I can get a flight." Perfect. The sooner the better. I don't have a second to spare. As I'm detailing over ways I can get Gail to talk, Hunter sneaks up on me and steals my breath away. "Fancy a trip to China?"

"What?"

His wicked lips twist into an amused grin. "You've got something against Chinese food?"

Shaking my head to hopefully knock some sense into it, I reply, "Of course I don't. I just, wow…you want me to come with you?"

He nods, looping a hand low around my waist. "Yes. I do."

My heart not only swells, it inflates to triple its normal size. But I can't go. Finding out what Keira and Gail are up to is my main objective. If my gut is right, Hunter will thank me in the long run.

Stepping into his arms, I bask in his virile fragrance, coupling the scent to home. "I wish I could, but I still have so much work to do. With you gone, I might actually have half a shot of finishing what I started." That's a complete double-edged sword, but Hunter nods, none the wiser. "You're a complete distraction."

A crooked smirk plays at his lips before he lowers his head and kisses over my racing pulse. Tipping my head back, I close my eyes and allow him free rein. "See, this is exactly what I'm talking about."

"Okay then, I'll stop."

Just as he attempts to pull away, my hand shoots out and I thread my fingers through his soft hair. Holding him in place, I hum when the warmth of his breath trounces against my needy flesh. "Let's not be rash now."

He chuckles against me.

"Thank you for asking me. On any other occasion, I would have loved to come, but maybe next time?" I phrase it as a question, hoping there will be many more invitations to travel the globe with my worldly boyfriend.

Hunter suckles at my nape, his tongue and lips working me into a frenzy. Each lash seems to strengthen my adoration for him, and before long, I know I'll reach the point of no return. I wonder if I'm already there.

"I'll take you anywhere, Shortcake." Be still my heart. "But right now, how about I take you back to my office and we also finish what we started." Be still my lady parts.

With that said, I temporarily forget my devious plan to bring down Gail and Keira and focus on the man who is sure to be the death of me…but my demise has never felt this good.

"Okay, so you'll be back in a week?" Maddy asks, frantically scribbling in her diary.

It's Friday, and like most Fridays, we're out at some bar, having drinks and discussing the week which passed. Tonight, the topic of discussion is the forthcoming wedding, and Hunter leaving for China tomorrow morning.

"Yes, a week tops. Don't worry, Cherry Pie. Besides, I'll have my cell. You can call me anytime." When he reaches for her hand and rubs it reassuringly, I can't help but fall harder for him.

"It'll be okay, Angelo. The wedding is a few weeks away. We've got this." Dixon kisses her cheek, his touch appearing to appease her worries instantly.

"I'm still here, Maddy, and if Hunter is unavailable, I'm sure his secretary can take a message," I can't help but quip.

I'm surprised Keira didn't invite herself to China. But I guess she's the perfect chameleon and doesn't want to clue Gail into her double life.

"What the hell do you need a secretary for?" Dixon asks, wrapping his arm around Maddy. "It's not like you do any work." Hunter flips him off, while I decide to vent to the only person who seems to agree with me.

"I'm talking about Keira," I clarify, reaching for my vodka—it's the perfect chaser to wash the rancid name from my mouth.

It appears Dixon needs the same medicine as me, because he blanches before downing his scotch. "Please tell me you've forgotten her name by now."

I scoff, wiping my mouth with the back of my hand. "As if. She's like a bad smell that just won't go away." Batting my lashes and trying this doe-eyed look on for size, I coo, "Can I get you another coffee, Hunter? Oh, your shoelace is undone. Here, let me get that for you. You want me to wipe your ass while I'm down here?" Dixon bursts out laughing, impressed with my Keira impersonation.

Hunter smirks as he leans back in the booth and interlaces both hands behind his neck. "My, my, that shade of green suits you."

I roll my eyes. "Jealous of her? Please. I'm not jealous. I'm just surprised at how fucking stupid you can be. She flashes her ass and you're all goo goo gaga." I'm getting riled up, but this is tame. I don't want to offend Maddy with my offensive cursing.

"I'll have you know her ass is the ugly sister compared to yours." So not helping, considering I know he has grounds for comparison. The need to strangle her amplifies tenfold.

I elbow him in the ribs before standing. "I'm going to the restroom."

"I'll come." Maddy stands too, while Hunter slips from his comfortable perch.

"Uh oh. This can only mean trouble. What do you women do in there? Strategize world peace?"

"Wouldn't you like to know," Maddy tactfully says, while I don't bother with diplomacy.

"We're going to talk about what an utter dick you are."

Hunter laughs exuberantly, while Maddy loops her arm through mine.

"I can't take you anywhere," she teases, before leading us toward the bathroom.

Once inside the cubicle, my cell chimes. Thinking it's Hunter, I unlock my phone and open the message with a smile. That soon turns to a horrified retching when I see what's on my screen.

It's a dick pic—a tiny dick, so definitely not Hunter. The caption has me soon guessing just whose needle dick this is.

Wanna have fun? Call me.

My gag reflex works overtime as I swallow down my vomit.

Gail's cock looks like a Sphynx kitten in a bright pink turtleneck. I quickly type out a reply so I can delete this image and then burn my phone.

I can't wait to have fun with that...
I'll be in touch.

I quickly obliterate the obscenity from my screen, wishing I could do the same to the image in my brain.

Needing some fresh air, I launch out of the stall, only to meet Maddy's eyes in the mirror as she reapplies her lipstick. "What are you up to?" she asks, mid-stroke.

"Nothing," I singsong, walking toward the basin.

"Uh huh. You've got that same look you had when you cut off Chloe Taylor's pigtail in third grade."

"She was asking for it," I reply, turning on the faucet and washing my hands. "Ashton asked me to go steady, not her."

Maddy smiles, the memory a fond one for both of us, as it highlights simpler times. "What's your beef with Keira?" I raise my eyebrows, pausing from pumping the soap dispenser. "Apart from the obvious."

"I don't trust her," I frankly declare. "She also has the type of face you want to greet with a brick."

Once Maddy is done applying her pink lipstick, she caps the tube with a smirk. "Someone sounds like a jealous girlfriend." *And this is exactly the reason why I need proof.*

"Me? Jealous? I don't think so."

"So, you're his girlfriend then?" *Damn, I should have seen that coming.* "Hey, no judgment. God knows it took me a while to adjust, but as long as you're happy…"

I dry my hands on a paper towel, stalling, looking at her as I ponder over her words. *Am I happy? I suppose I am.* The butterflies are definitely present when Hunter is around, and when he's not, I miss him. Like a lot.

Maddy bursts out laughing, wrapping her arm around my shoulder. "You're so screwed." *I don't bother arguing.*

We exit the bathroom, discussing shoes and jewelry and all things white, but both come to a screeching halt when we see two skanks lingering around our table, nothing but trouble following them.

The busty blonde and perky brunette are very openly flirting with our men. Dixon yawns, looking more interested in the game on the TV, but Hunter, forever the ladies' man, smirks at whatever Malibu Barbie just said.

My insecurity, which has laid semi-dormant, raises its sleepy head. Looking at the scenario, all I get in response is a half shrug and an *I told you so.* But I refuse to believe Hunter hasn't changed. There is no way he'd touch this plastic bimbo with a ten-foot pole, but when she sits near him and he doesn't stab her with his fork, I begin to doubt my certainty.

Maddy and I march over, thankfully she's holding onto me because I'm contemplating ripping out the bimbo's hair extensions one by one. "I'm pretty sure Alley Cat's is that way," I state, hooking my thumb over my shoulder toward the vicinity of the infamous strip club.

Barbie looks utterly offended. She's lucky I didn't greet her with a drink thrown in her face. "I'll call you," she has the balls to say to Hunter. Why does she have his number?

He opens his mouth to say god knows what, but I interject, because this just got personal. "Lose his number, sweetheart… if not, you'll be losing your teeth."

She narrows her eyes and rises, ready to no doubt give me a piece of her mind, but my threat isn't empty. She has three seconds to leave, because this bitch will be going down. "Just stop right there," I command, placing my hand out to stop her advances. The floor is mine and I intend to own it. "I already don't give a fuck."

Hunter's hoarse laughter fills the air, while Maddy shoulders past the brunette, who topples over in her ridiculous heels. "Oh, I'm sorry. I didn't see you there," she sarcastically says.

Dixon welcomes her into his arms, where she very possessively kisses the living shit out of him. What a way to mark her claim. The women get the hint and hobble off, both ego and ankles bruised.

Maddy and Dixon are making out like it's 1999, while I place a hand on my cocked hip, glaring at Hunter something wicked. I don't know if I want to kiss or kill him. A thought plays at the back of my mind. Did he just give her his number? Or if she already had it, how well does he know her, and by that, I mean how many times have they fucked?

The bile returns.

A million emotions run rampant, but for some stupid reason I focus on my fries, and the blob of mayonnaise sitting dead center. These weren't here before I left, so I know the waitress brought them when we were in the bathroom and Hunter took the liberty of dousing my fries. I know it's insignificant, but in a weird way, it placates my anger, because it's the simple things which mean so much.

He did this without a thought, just how he has a hundred times before because he knows I like mayonnaise with my fries. He also tolerates me sleeping with socks even though it drives him crazy. Being in a relationship is about compromise. It's also about trust— trusting that other person to not revert to his manwhore ways because you…are…enough.

And the way he's looking at me—part humor, all possession, I feel like more than enough.

"Outside."

Hunter doesn't argue. He shoots upward, never breaking eye contact with me as we leave Maddy and Dixon to their very public PDA.

I'm a livewire, ready to electrocute anyone in my path. The cool air laps at my heated skin, but it doesn't even touch the sides, because I'm currently on fire. "Shortcake…she's someone I used to…know. Years ago."

His pause infuriates me further and I continue marching down the street, unsure exactly where I'm headed. "I don't even remember her name."

So not helping.

Pushing past pedestrians, I breathe a sigh of relief when the herd thins, as I'm moments away from doing something which will surely get me arrested. I turn down a dingy alleyway, the ones your mom tells you stay away from when you're a kid, but now, I embrace the darkness.

"Would you stop and talk to me!"

His desperation matches my fury—a lethal combination.

"Mary, for fuck's sake, stop!" The second he makes contact with me, wrapping those long fingers around my wrist, a hunger overtakes me and I attack.

Spinning, I slam my chest to his, threading my fingers through the hair. Jerking his head backward, I pin him with a feral stare.

A gasp leaves his parted, pink lips—lips I want to fucking devour whole. "Now that you've got me, what are you going to do?"

It's a challenge, one I'll happily accept.

A moment of clarity is overshadowed by the fierce need to consume, demolish, and possess, and nothing else matters but this. Our lips collide, and it's a flurry of hands as we tear at one another, ready to strip flesh from bone.

I dig my fingernails into his scalp, desperate to claw my way into him and never leave. His tongue circles mine as he tastes and samples my frenzy. This isn't going to be gentle. A sense of ownership has tackled me from behind, and all I can think about is marking Hunter as mine.

"I want you inside of me," I whisper against his lips, unfastening the top button of his jeans with haste.

"Here?" When I thrust my hand into his pants and am greeted with his blistering hard on, I grunt in response.

Wrapping my fingers around his heavy shaft, I begin to stroke him, eager to feel him inside. He jerks into my palm, sealing his mouth around mine as we kiss. It's hard to believe he had a thing against kissing, because this is beyond words.

He bites my bottom lip before severing our mouths, and

before I can question what he's doing, he grips my upper arms and spins me, slamming me up against a brick wall. His strength is exactly what I need.

With desperate hands, he hikes up the hem of my dress, and without delay, rips my thong clean off. He palms my exposed cheeks, humming in utter delight. "I want to lick every part of you." He runs his pointer along the pleat of my ass. "You drive me fucking crazy, you know that?"

I wiggle my behind and he groans.

"Don't tempt me."

He presses his chest to my back, reaching around my hip to pay attention to my needy clit. When he feels how slick I am, he hums in approval. Without a second to waste, he inserts two fingers into me, stretching me wide.

"Oh god…" My eyes droop to half-mast as I focus on this and nothing else.

He pumps in and out, circling my ripe center, which has me yelping in carnal need. "You'll be the death of me." My hips undulate, welcoming this tender intrusion with complete gratification.

He pinches at my clit before removing his fingers and slipping them into my mouth. I suckle at them, tasting myself on his fingers, an unexpected head rush. "See how good you taste." His digits pop from my lips as he yanks them out, only for him to suck at them himself.

The imagery is enough to almost make me come.

He inserts his slick fingers back into me, always the gentleman to ensure I'm ready to take that monster cock inside. When he feels I'm more than ready, he rubs his scorching erection against my ass, kicking my feet out wide.

I'm seconds away from begging, when he suddenly retreats and curses. "Fuck, I don't have any protection." I almost sob. "It's okay, Shortcake, let me take care of you."

He makes his intentions clear when he tunnels his fingers in deeper, but they're a poor substitute for what I want. Without any regrets, I still his movements and say, "I don't care."

"What? It's okay to go bareback?" His surprise is clear, but we can think about the repercussions tomorrow, because now, I need him inside of me.

When I feel him hesitate, I reach behind me and grip his length. He hisses, but doesn't resist as I arch into him, showcasing my intentions. Withdrawing his fingers, he presses his chest flat to my back and cages me with his brute strength. I splay my hands against the wall, bowing my back, offering myself to him.

He groans in approval before I feel his blunt, hot head nudge against my pussy. His silken cock feels amazing and I want so much more. "This is going to get messy." I wonder if he too reads the double meaning behind his words.

"Good," I counter. "Give me everything you've got."

He runs his tongue along the length of my neck before wrapping an arm around my waist and driving me back onto his shaft. We both cry out, the feel of him, in the flesh, sliding against mine is just too holy for words. He stills, as if wanting to drag out this heightened sensation as long as he can.

Hunter has been inside of me countless times before, but there is something pure, almost seamless being fused together this way. There are no walls, no barriers between us, and a sudden heavy weight settles within my heart. "Don't break me," I whisper.

He knows of my past, of how my high school love broke me, but this is the first time I've expressed my fears aloud. This raw union has changed me forever.

"I promise," he vows, accenting his oath as he begins to move.

Everything is intensified. Each stroke has me crying out and forgetting my own name. He starts slow, cussing each time he pulls out, before sinking all the way back in. Like always, our bodies move in sync, pushing and pulling, the perfect yin to yang.

We increase the speed, the cadence a hot, heavy melody, his cock piercing into me over and over again. The alleyway is filled with grunts and the slapping of flesh, and when Hunter pinches my gorged center, I scream.

He growls into my ear, fucking me senseless.

The bricks are coarse, and when Hunter realizes he's slamming me up against them, he quickly curves his upper arm so I'm able to use the muscled surface as a makeshift pillow. I rest my cheek on his forearm, the kind gesture involuntarily bringing tears to my eyes.

"You feel fucking incredible." His breathy admission has me mewling and racing closer toward the edge. "This is unlike anything."

He's steering my hips, ensuring I take every hard inch of him, so when he drives me backward and buries himself so deeply within, I have no other choice but to chase my looming release. I ride his cock, just how I know he likes me to, bucking into him until our bodies are a frantic blur.

When he hits my g-spot, I literally see stars and come fiercely with a thunderous sob. He milks every tremor, playing with my clit until I'm thrashing about, certain I'm going to die. Once I'm spent, he pulls out with a grunt, before I feel a silky warmth coat the small of my back and ass.

His primitive growls excite me once again and I turn over my shoulder to watch him spill his seed. The sight is glorious, his long, hard cock standing tall and proud. His eyes are squeezed shut, the corded veins in his neck bursting as he cries out in utter ecstasy. Once he's done, he sags against me, kissing my neck, my ear, any place where his lips can find flesh.

We stay embraced this way, until with one final kiss against my throat, he pulls away. He holds me in place, surprising me as he rips off his t-shirt to wipe me clean. "That's not necessary," I hoarsely say. "I was prewarned. Now you've gone and ruined your t-shirt."

Once I'm clean, he tosses his now soiled shirt into the trash. "So worth it."

Turning sluggishly, my jelly legs barely hold me up when Hunter stands before me, topless, slowly rearranging himself into his pants. He leaves the top button of his jeans undone, the soft curls painting his belly button highlight his rock-hard abs and mouth-watering V.

He scratches over his ripped flank, as if deep in thought. I'm about to ask what's up, but he beats me to the chase. "I was going to give this to you before…" When he reaches into his pocket and produces a silver key, I stop breathing. "With me being away, it'll be difficult for you to finish your project, so um…here is a key to my apartment."

He extends it, and I stare at the dangling piece of metal, blinking back my tears. This is big, like really big. It's also a sign that he trusts me, just how I do him. No matter my fears of him hurting me, or him being too good to be true, I have to roll with the punches and accept this man as being nothing short of perfect.

Accepting his offering, I twirl the simple object in my hand. But it means so much.

"I want it back when I come home though," he teases, drawing me into his arms and kissing the tip of my nose.

"I think I'm going to miss you," I fearlessly declare. It feels good.

His surprise is clear, because this candidness is something new for us. We're both usually guarded, but tonight, something has changed. "What do you know?" he finally says with that lopsided smirk. "I think I'm going to miss you too."

Could it be Hunter has not only given me the key to his apartment, but to his heart as well? A girl can only hope.

Fifteen

Hunter

"I mean no disrespect, like none, but come the fuck on. Why can't you call him?"

The petite woman behind the desk shimmies her chair away from the crazy American as she most likely reaches for her hidden can of mace.

After flying thirteen-odd hours to get here, I don't want to fuck around. I want to see Mr. Yeong, talk some sense into him, have some sake, and then go back home. Mary's sweet kisses still linger as she dropped me off at the airport yesterday morning, promising to welcome me home in nothing but heels. But Mr. Yeong's secretary is being a complete mood killer, because no one seems to know when Mr. Yeong will be back in town.

I suppose this is my fault for up and leaving without a solid plan, but this guy is a workaholic. It's smart business. That's why his office is open on a Sunday. I just assumed he would be here, but apparently, he's not, which makes me all the more suspicious that something is rotten in Beijing.

"Fine then, I'll just wait here." I literally mean the spot I stand when I use the marbled counter as my La-Z-Boy.

My plans are foiled however, when a mean looking Korean Hulk Hogan saunters from out of nowhere, ready to chop suey my ass. "We will let Mr. Yeong know you visited."

"Visited? This isn't a social call. This is business. Business which Mr. Yeong and I need to discuss immediately." My pleas fall on deaf ears, however.

Sick of hearing my own voice, I reach into my suit pocket and retrieve my business card. "In case he lost my number. Thanks." The secretary accepts it as she would a diseased limb. "For nothing," I add, tempted to sprint into the elevator doors behind her. The hulking macho man reads my thoughts and stands in front of them, arms folded, daring me to make his day.

This is nothing but a waste of time, so I leave. When I eventually find where Mr. Yeong is holed up, I'll be sure to tell him his staff are complete asshats.

The streets of Manhattan have nothing on the bustle in Beijing. It's like Times Square on steroids. On most days, I would sightsee, definitely have a beer or two, but today, I just want to catch a cab back to my hotel and sleep this fucked up day away.

D2 decides now is a good time to pep up and announce his belief that my sullied mood is because I'm missing Mary. I hate to admit it, but it's true.

This past month has been fucking incredible, and that's not just because fucking Mary is incredible, it's because every minute I spend with her is equivalent to being the best minutes of my life. Oh my god, I sound like a Michael Bolton remix, but it's the truth.

Giving her a key to my apartment should have freaked me out, but it didn't. In my unromantic brain, it seemed like the logical thing to do, because I want her there in my apartment, always. I know it's a big deal to some, but to me, it felt liberating to finally rid myself of this stigma.

I like Mary. She likes me. I don't see the point in fucking around.

I know she's guarded at times because of what her asshole ex-boyfriend did to her, but I'm not like that ball-less little chump. I still feel like I need to thank her when she lets me bury myself in her.

I still don't really know the proper protocol when it comes to dating, but I'm learning. Even though we're both comfortable with the no labels, Mary is my…girlfriend? Partner? What are the kids calling it nowadays? Either way, she's my woman, and being here is taking time away from slapping that fine ass and kissing those addictive lips. What a complete moron I was for not kissing her sooner. Just think how many kisses I've missed out on.

I rub over my chest, the ache amped tenfold. I try not to think about her because this happens…I hurt, and then I feel the need to binge on sugar. Holy shit—I'm turning into Finch.

A small part of me is waiting for the other shoe to drop. There is no way my life could be this perfect, right? I haven't told anyone, too afraid Mary will run, and Dixon will laugh, but I'm fucking terrified. There's got to be a catch. Dating can't be this easy, I mean if it were, half the soppy country ballads are a lie.

People talk about the hardships, that relationships are hard work, but this is the easiest thing I've ever done. I'm scared one day I will wake up and all of this will all just turn to shit.

Focusing on getting the fuck out of here, I type out yet another text to Ming, who also seems to be MIA. I can't help but think Keira was right and this cold shoulder is thanks to that fuckwad, Gail.

What does he have that has a smart man like Mr. Yeong falling for his bullshit? And that's the million-dollar question.

Catching a cab back to my hotel, I buy a bottle of scotch, which I plan on making long, sweet love to. Kicking off my shoes, I fall face first onto the mattress, hating how empty the bed feels. I need to cut it with this soppy bullshit now.

The only cure is porn.

Deciding to check out what kinky shit I've got on my pay per view, I scroll through the selections, not even remotely interested in what's up for offer. I'm actually falling asleep, remote control in hand, when my cell pings on the bedside table.

Reaching for it, I smile like a dopey fool when I see who the message is from.

Your apartment is so quiet. I didn't realize what a loud mouth jerk you are.

I know you miss me and my loud mouth...

Maybe ;)

My dick stirs. This is fucking ridiculous. Now her text

messages have the capability to make me hard? This is a new low.

Whatcha doing?

I don't see the point in being coy. **I was about to watch porn, but the selection is rather dry...no pun intended.**

Tossing the remote onto the bed, I settle against the headboard and unscrew my bottle of scotch.

Porn? I'm disappointed. You're in Beijing!

Just as I'm about to backtrack, apologizing for my uncouth behavior, she adds something which accents the reason why I am completely smitten by her.

Surely there is a ping pong show you can catch.

My heart aches. I thump over it to stop this starry-eyed nonsense.

I'm sure there is, but I'd rather watch a different kind of show...

I take a swig of scotch, the smooth burn exactly what I need. The dancing buttons on my screen taunt me. I'm moments away from telling them to hurry the fuck up.

I suppose it'd be mean telling you I got myself off on your side of the bed about ten minutes ago.

Whatever scotch is left in my mouth dribbles down my chin as I re-read her message.

My hard on is now rock solid. **I'll have you know I'm typing this message with my cock.**

You're so multi-talented.

I so want this conversation to end in me coming in my pants. I'm such a nasty bastard. **So...what are you wearing?** An oldie but a goodie.

Nothing.

Holy guacamole. I know it's after 2 a.m. and Mary does sleep naked, but she's over there and I'm over here. The struggle is real.

I've forgotten what nothing looks like...

After two minutes of nothing, I'm wondering if I need to touch up on my sexting skills. But when my phone lights up, I'm certain the message is sent from the big man himself because this can only be described as divine.

It's a picture of Mary—naked.

I thought I catalogued every freckle, every curve of her milky soft skin, but I thought wrong. She's taken the picture from above, showcasing her entire body from head, down… down. Her rose nipples are pearled, giving life to her tear-shaped breasts. The small freckle near her areola has my mouth watering, desperate for a taste.

Memories of kissing that belly, running my tongue in and around her navel, flood my brain and fill my pants with the need to unleash this hunger for her. Unbuttoning my pants, I take my dick in hand and begin to pump.

I feast on her pussy, the sight is just too much. The flush to her skin reveals she wasn't kidding when she said she just got herself off. I've memorized her comedown. That soft pink she turns just after those soft mewls slip past her plump lips is what I fucking live for.

`Are you jerking off?`

`Holy fucking yes, I am.`

`I've showed you mine…show me yours.`

It seems only fair. Deciding to give her an action shot, I continue pumping my cock while taking a happy snap.

Quickly sending my very hard cock into cyberspace, I fist my shaft, using the naked picture of Mary as my inspiration to bring this home. It won't take long, considering I missed her touch the moment I set foot on the plane.

I zero in on her lips, lips which have changed everything I

ever believed in. Kissing them, listening to what they've had to say, watching them consume every part of me has slayed me, and I don't know what I'd do without them. Without her.

You're so beautiful...

Completely uncaring that she described my dick as she would a flower, I come in my palm, grunting loudly as I milk myself dry. Now that beats watching porn any day.

Once I reach for some tissues to clean myself up, I reply the only way I can. **So are you.**

:)Thank you. I'll add sweet talker to your list of talents. I'm going to sleep. Am so tired zzz

I take a long sip of scotch to drown my sorrows that she's hitting the hay. **Why are you so tired? What did you do last night?**

The dancing dots are no more, hinting Mary may have fallen asleep, phone in hand, but after a couple of minutes, they return. *Nothing really. Just saw Maddy.*

I don't know why, but something inside of me, some may call it intuition, screams at me that she's lying. But why would she lie? There's no reason for her to.

Just as I'm about to ask what exactly 'nothing really' means, she signs off. **Goodnight. I miss you xoxo**

XOXO has never tickled the cockles of my heart more than they do right now. **Goodnight. I miss you too. I love…**

Whoa, back the fuck up. Was I really about to write that I loved her? The word on my screen confirms that yes, I was.

Quickly backtracking, I decide to stick to the basics and not declare my undying love over a text. That would be awkward. **Goodnight. I miss you too.**

Once I've stared a hole through my screen, ensuring there are no more messages, I decide to go to sleep as well.

Nothing will ever, ever compare to Mary, but I reach for the lumpy pillow, realizing just how much I really do miss her, because it seems to fall asleep, I need to pretend this stand-in is her. Dixon and Finch would be so proud.

I've never wanted to run over my phone with a bus more than I do right now.

Not even bothering to look at the screen, I blindly reach for my cell off the bedside dresser and bark, "What the fuck do you want?"

"Good afternoon to you too, Mr. O'Shea." That smooth, confident voice can only belong to one man.

Sitting upright, I brush the hair from my brow. "Well, aren't you one hard man to track down. What did you do? Forget your wife's birthday and split town?"

Mr. Yeong laughs, always a fan of my humor. "I must apologize for my absence. Things have been rather crazy. I believe you're in Beijing."

"Yes, that's right. I was hoping for a one on one."

As always, Mr. Yeong has the floor and he will only speak when he's ready. To kill some time, I gulp down a mouthful of scotch.

"Yes, okay, that should be fine. I have forty-five minutes to spare at six." Looking at the clock on the wall, I see that it's 5:15 p.m. "Do you know where Temple Restaurant is?"

"I'll find it," I reply, springing from the bed and rummaging through my suitcase to find something presentable to wear.

"Very good." The line goes dead, but I'm unsure who hung up first.

I shower in record time and am out the door, hailing a cab. I have no idea why we're going to a restaurant. Who the hell can order and eat a meal in forty-five minutes? Although, with Mr. Yeong, I wouldn't be surprised.

Thankfully, the cab ride isn't too painful, and I'm out in front of Temple with thirty seconds to spare. I open the lavish door and am immediately greeted by three servers. "Hello, Mr. O'Shea. May we take your coat?" This would be comical if my job and pride wasn't on the line.

"No, I'm good. Thanks."

All three bow, before silently hinting I'm to follow as they scurry through the very impressive, traditional looking Chinese restaurant. This place reeks of money, but it has a gentler note with feng shui looking items like marbled yin yangs, bamboo water features, and gold statues of buddhas I've seen Mary admire, sprinkled around the place.

I could use some feng shui mojo right now, because when I see Mr. Yeong sitting in what looks like a golden alcove, I know he means business. This man doesn't want to hear excuses. He gets what he wants, when he wants, and the fact some simpleton from America can't find a humble watch is not working in my favor. I'm surprised a man with his connections can't find the watch himself, but who knows, maybe this is what he does for fun—tortures stupid Americans.

"Thank you for meeting with me, Mr. Yeong." He doesn't bother standing and points to the throne opposite him. I sit. I'm poured three different sorts of drinks before we're left alone.

Mr. Yeong is a fifty something, self-made billionaire. He struck it rich because he's a smart businessman and followed a dream of not only building houses, but selling them as well. Real estate is his game and he's damn good at it.

On most days, I admire and respect Mr. Yeong's success because nothing but hard work and determination got him there, but on days like today, when he's pissing me off because a man of his intelligence should know better, I can't help but rage.

Taking a sip of what I'm assuming is wine, I measure my words, because I know I only have a few of them. "I know you're a busy man, so I'll cut to the chase." Mr. Yeong nods, appreciating my frankness. Deciding to honor this code, I declare, "You obviously think it's okay to fuck me in the ass without any lube."

I'm not sure if he'll appreciate such directness, but time's ticking—literally.

"What do you mean?" he asks, leaning back in his seat.

"What I mean is, why are you dicking me around, Mr. Yeong? We've known one another for years. I've given you advice whenever you've asked. I thought we were solid. But now I hear you're talking to some bottom feeding brownnoser, who couldn't give two shits about you or the hard work which has seen your empire grow."

Just the thought of that scumbag has me reaching for drink number two.

"You've heard the saying, 'don't put all your eggs in one basket'?" he poses, always the enigma.

"I have. And surely you've heard the saying, 'you lie with dogs, you'll get fleas.' I just don't get it. Help me understand why you'd even consider doing business with Gail. He is not someone you want to work with. Or to represent you."

Mr. Yeong nods, appearing to consider everything I just said. And then I wait, wait for him to eat into my thirty-nine remaining minutes.

"Here, have a fortune cookie." He slides the cookie along the bright red table cloth.

If this were anyone else, I would tell them and this cookie to eat a dick, but I reach for it and unwrap the innocent looking gimmick. There better be some sort of answer inside of here, otherwise, I want a recount.

Snapping it in half, I expect to see the typical white piece of paper, spewing words of "wisdom." Instead, all I'm left with is a fistful of crushed cookie. "Looks like my fortune is working on EST time." I toss the handful onto the table, so not surprised I got left with a handful of nothing.

Mr. Yeong smirks, reaching for his cookie. Once his snaps open, it too reveals there is nothing inside. Whoever manufactures these things needs to take the fortune out of their fortune cookie spiel. "A great fortune depends on luck."

"If you ever give up your day job, you could always write for this mob."

I know there is a lesson to be learned, but I can't help comparing my empty fortune to how I'm feeling right now. "Mr. O'Shea, I admire your tenacity. The fact you're here shows strength, determination. I'm a man of my word, and now that we have an equal playing field…"

"Excuse me?" Surely I misheard him. How in the hell do we have that? Gail is in no way, shape, or form on my level. "We had a deal."

Those sharp eyes focus, a cat among the pigeons, as Mr. Yeong shatters my world forever. "Yes, you're right, we do, but now that Mr. Gail knows what I want…the players may have changed, but the game has remained the same."

"What do you mean?" The golden walls begin to close in on me and I suddenly feel like I've been kicked repeatedly in the balls.

"Mr. Gail is also looking for the watch." Holy motherfucking hell. "Things have now shifted. Let the games begin, as you Americans like to say."

"What do you mean, he's looking for the watch? You told him?" I spit, clenching my fist against my thigh. I thought Mr. Yeong was a man of his word. Now I know he's just a greedy, narcissistic asshole.

"No, I did not. He called me, promising me he could deliver on what you've failed to do."

So many thoughts are crashing around my brain right now, but at the forefront is, how the fuck does he know?

"I can see you're surprised."

"No shit," I reply, shaking my head in utter disbelief.

"He told me an office romance had led to him finding out…"

This just goes from bad to fucking apocalyptic. "Office romance? With who?" Every nerve ending in my body is firing, my fight or flight response ready to kick in and save me from the truth.

Mr. Yeong folds his hands on the tabletop, cool as cool can be. "A woman with hair the color of fire." The air hitches in my throat, because suddenly, I can't breathe. "Matches her personality, I believe. I think he said her name was…Mary."

…Time stands still and nothing else matters, because the inevitable has just joined us for dinner. "There must be some mistake," I utter more to myself than to him.

Mr. Yeong goes on talking, but I don't listen to a single word he says, because nothing matters other than the fact Mary sold me out. She was the only person I told, the only person I trusted, and in return, she crapped all over my honesty, and in the process, she broke my fucking heart. But my heart doesn't just break—my entire body does.

There must be some mistake. My self-preservation kicks in, because I'm seconds away from throwing down. But thinking back to last week, I was certain I caught Mary and Gail in the kitchen in some weird moment. At the time, I shrugged it off as my vivid imagination playing tricks on me, but processing over every small moment, I thought she was a little friendlier than usual, I now know I was right on track.

Mary has been sleeping with the enemy—the perfect fuck you. But why? None of this makes any sense. I need to call her.

She needs to tell me there's been some mistake.

I don't know how that cunt knows about the watch, but quite frankly, I don't care. All I care about is mending something which I thought was unbreakable.

Kicking back my seat, Mr. Yeong pauses from whatever bullshit story he's telling. "With all due respect…you, Gail, and your pathetic watch can go fuck yourselves. I'm out."

I should take great satisfaction in doing something which I should have done months ago, but I feel empty—a stranger in someone else's skin.

I don't bother waiting, because we're done here. I don't intend on seeing this man ever again. I thought he had honor. I was wrong.

Charging through the restaurant, my goal is to get out of here before I do something I will forever regret. The bustling sidewalk just adds to my fury, so I hustle down the road, desperate to find a quiet place to call Mary and find out what the fuck is going on.

I manage to find a small walkway, not ideal, but off the noisy street. With anxious fingers I dial Mary, but her phone is off. Refusing to jump to conclusions, I text Dixon instead.

Hey, man. Did Mary and Maddy catch up last night? Did I miss anything big? I try to keep it level, not clue Dix onto my current clusterfuck of events.

As I'm waiting for him to reply, I lean up against the brick wall, taking a moment to collect my thoughts. There's got to be a reasonable explanation why. I refuse to believe this is as black and white as it seems.

My cell buzzes in my palm. Flipping it over, I can only hope Dixon has the answers I seek. But the message isn't from Dix. It's from Keira.

I'm really sorry, but I had to tell you. I know you wouldn't believe me, so here's proof.

The lag feels like hours, but when an image flashes onto my screen, everything is slowed down because I'm certain the world stops spinning.

The proof Keira speaks of is a photograph of Gail and… Mary. There's no mistaking they're out for dinner, a candlelit one at that. Mary looks beautiful in a flaming red dress, accenting her trademark locks.

A bottle of champagne sits in the center of the table, both glasses half full.

To onlookers, this looks like a romantic dinner between two people who are clearly into each other, but to me, all I see is my stupidity for ever believing I deserved a happily ever after. People like me don't get a HEA. I'll always be a manwhore in gentleman's clothing.

Another message comes through. Again, from Keira. This one is Mary's number…on the back of Gail's business card. In case the picture message wasn't clear, the love heart near her name clears up any confusion.

I'm hypnotized by the images—it's a morbid insight into what my future holds. I still don't want to believe it, but the evidence is damning, because a picture doesn't lie. But this is impossible. I refuse to believe it. She wouldn't do this to me.

When my phone sounds once again, I contemplate smashing it against the wall. But I man up and read the message from Dix—the proverbial nail, if you will.

Nope. Mary has been MIA. Probably missing your sorry ass.

So my suspicions have been confirmed. Mary was lying. She never saw Maddy like she claimed to have done. At the time, I wondered why she lied, I now know why. She couldn't exactly divulge the fact she was having dinner with an asshole like Gail because that would lead to her confessing that her after dinner mint would be his cock! Bile rises, but I push it down.

A surge of anger comes spurting from me and the end result is me smashing my fist against the wall. I barely feel the sting because no pain can compare to the one lodging within.

I need to do something, anything, so I fucking run.

I have no idea where I'm running to. It doesn't matter, either way. I just need to free myself from this weight—the vibration of…I told you so. Was I a fool to think that this was different? That Mary felt for me what I feel for her? No. Just no.

I keep running, the world passing by me in a blur, but the chaos complements the raging war within. I don't know when I'll stop, I just know that when I do, I'll see this for what it is— for what it's always been.

Running further and further, I wish I could do the same for the thought playing a loop inside my head. No matter how desperate I was to believe that what we had was real, the truth shatters any misconceptions, setting me straight—I can't believe I was stupid enough to think that I was enough, but now that my eyes have been opened, I won't make the same mistake ever again.

Love can blow me.

Sixteen

Mary

It's Wednesday—four whole days since I last saw Hunter. As pathetic as this sounds, it feels like four years.

He's been busy, I get that, but it's been radio silence since our very hot sexting session. I really miss him. I hate not hearing from him because my suspicious nature ends up conjuring scenarios of him and thirty-five women playing naked tag.

I guess my worries are because I'm guilty of lying to Hunter, but I tell myself it's for the greater good. But having dinner with that scumbag, Gail, felt anything but good. On the plus side, I found out that he too knows about this notorious watch. The question is, how did he find out?

He wouldn't divulge just who told him, which has me questioning everything I thought I once knew. It's now survival of the fittest, I guess, because if both Hunter and Gail know, then it's who can bring game and convince Mr. Yeong they're the better prize.

There is no question to who that may be, which really has me rethinking what angle Mr. Yeong is playing. Something fishy is going on. I just can't seem to figure out what.

Keira has been her usual smug self. I peg it down to her also being in the running of delivering what Mr. Yeong wants, as I have no doubt she knows too. She is a status seeker, desperate to climb her way to the top, uncaring who she steps on to get there. Under different circumstances, I would admire her tenacity, but now, I just want her gone.

Hunter's office is now complete, and I must say, it looks incredible. From what it was to now, it reflects everything that Hunter is. Bold, sleek, and commanding. The simple, glacier white paint scheme has brightened up the place, coupled with the modern, stylish office furniture of dark mahogany wood and glass panes, has turned his office into a corporate den fit for a king.

I'm thankful everything can now be locked, his desk included, because some of the stuff I found was information you wouldn't want falling into the wrong hands, like his little black book, which can now be used as confetti.

Taking one final photograph of his office for my portfolio, I close and lock his door, and decide to grab a coffee before I hit the road.

I have no idea where Gail is, which is a good and bad thing. I'm thankful I don't have to see him, but I don't want him popping up like some jack in the box. Even though I left before appetizers were served, I still feel like a lying cheat for even agreeing to dinner with him.

As soon as Hunter returns, I'll tell him what I've been doing, because my CSI days are over. I'm not cut out for this double life. I know he'll be mad as shit, but I just hope he can understand why.

Turning the corner, I freeze in my tracks because I could swear I just heard Hunter's voice. But that's impossible. There is no way he's here. Shaking my head, I pin it down to me now hallucinating he's here to fill the void of him being gone.

My cell chimes, and I practically dig at my back pocket to retrieve it. Hoping it's a message from Hunter, I'm not looking where I'm going and blindly walk into the kitchen. It's from Maddy, asking if I'm free this afternoon to go shoe shopping.

Just as I'm punching out a reply, I hear a voice which unmistakably is Hunter's, but it can't be. Snapping my head upward, I almost topple to the floor when I see that it is, in fact, Hunter's, because he is here, in the flesh, standing mere feet away. He looks like utter shit, and his hand is bandaged up, but nonetheless, he's here.

My mouth moves in wordless animation, because what in the ever-living hell is he doing here? But more importantly, why is Keira hanging off of him? Her red fingernail is suspended mid-stroke along his collar.

My phone falls from my fingers, smashing the moment it hits the linoleum, which mirrors how I'm feeling right now. I have two options. I can run and cry, or I can advance forward and ask what the fuck is going on.

I decide to go with the latter. "You're back?" I can't keep the utter disbelief from my tone.

After three long seconds, he finally decides to pay me the respect of looking at me. But when he does, I wish that he hadn't bothered. The usual playfulness and hunger are now replaced with nothing. There is no emotion behind his eyes. All I see is emptiness.

"Yup, I'm back," he replies coolly, still not shrugging off Keira's advances.

"And you didn't think to tell me?"

He shrugs with a stiff upper lip. "It slipped my mind. I thought you'd be busy anyway."

"Busy? What the fuck?" I ask, on the verge of throwing up.

I'm waiting for him to reward me with that lopsided smirk and tell me he's joking, or at the very least, explain what's going on. But he does neither. He simply leans against the counter, looking at me like I just sacrificed his first born to the devil.

Keira nestles in closer to him, while I search the room for something pointy to gouge out her eyeballs. "You need to leave. Now." She has the gall to peer up at Hunter. And he's got an even bigger nerve to nod, giving her permission. The world is on crazy pills.

To add salt to my gaping wound, she stands on tippy toes and kisses his stubbled cheek. I wish I could mask my pain, but I can't, and tears sting my eyes. She struts past, nothing but a victorious grin following her out the door.

Now that we're alone, it's the ultimate standoff. Hunter doesn't budge, which means he has no intention of speaking. I'm surprised he didn't follow Keira out the door.

"W-what's going on?" I stumble over my words, because I'm seconds away from crying.

Folding his arms, he pins me with a cold stare. "I don't know. You tell me."

"Hunter, enough. Stop talking in riddles and tell me what's wrong? Why didn't you call me? When did you get back?"

"Yesterday," he blankly replies, while a wheeze leaves my

lungs.

"Yesterday? Why didn't you call me?"

"I thought you'd be indisposed."

"Doing what?" I yell, arms out wide.

He narrows his eyes and the space between us fills with nothing but darkness. "I guess the better question there is who."

My heart begins to race. My palms begin to sweat. I'm certain I'm seconds away from having a panic attack. "Excuse me? Are you implying you couldn't call me because I was too busy fucking half of Manhattan?"

When he shakes his head, I hope to god I'm lost in translation. "No, not half of Manhattan." I take a premature breath, because what he says next leaves me gasping for air. "Just one person."

I'm utterly offended, not to mention, so confused. "I'm done playing games. You either tell me what's wrong, or I walk. I didn't sign up for this."

Hunter has the audacity to laugh, but nothing about the sound is cheerful. He pushes off the counter, stalking coolly toward me like I'm prey. I stand my ground, refusing to budge until he tells me what's going on.

He stops a few feet away, surveying every inch of me. Normally, I would smolder under his gaze, but now, I just feel empty. "The last time we spoke, you said you saw Maddy. Was that true?"

Oh…god. He knows? But how?

"Was it true?" he presses, jaw clenched.

Everything begins to unravel. If only I had told him the truth. "No," I confess. Hunter curls his lip, recoiling backward. "I can explain!"

But I can see it's too late for explanations. "Explain what, exactly? That you're a cheater? A liar? A chameleon?"

I may be many things, but a cheater I'm not. That's a massive deal breaker for me, and to be accused of being one—I'm more than insulted. "Like you can talk!" I snap, advancing forward. "The minute I turn my back, you're offering your cock to Keira on a silver platter!"

He sniggers, shaking his head, the anger rolling off of him in waves. Caging me with his imposing form, he lowers his face inches from mine. "I didn't think you'd mind…seeing as you're fucking Gail."

I stagger backward, his ugly words ricocheting in my ears. "Dinner is a lot different than fucking," I snarl, revealing my true whereabouts the night he called.

Hunter exhales, appearing to steady his breathing. "The fact you had dinner with that motherfucker…" He pauses, swallowing. "Whether you're fucking him or not, it makes no difference. You lied to me. I can't believe a word you say."

My world starts unraveling and I have no one to blame but myself. "Let me explain!"

"No," he firmly states, pulling away and taking a piece of me with him. "I can't even look at you, because when I do, all I see is that red fucking dress!"

I attempt to decode what that means, because what in the hell…it takes me a minute, but I soon realize he's talking about the dress I wore to dinner, the dress which I now must burn. How does he know what I wore?

A lightbulb goes off and I shake my head, horrified. "You're spying on me? Did you even go to China? Or was all of this some test to see if I'd open my legs the moment you crossed international waters?" I shout.

My emotions are off tap, bouncing from anger, to sadness, to completely insulted, back to anger.

Hunter's jaw is clenched so tightly, I'm certain he's about to break teeth. He looks torn, but there's something else. There's something he's not telling me, which is the main reason behind this insanity.

"Someone who actually gives a fuck about me thought I should know."

No points for guessing just who this good Samaritan is.

No matter how hurt I am, this is my fault. I never should have lied to Hunter and told him from the get go what I was doing. But these accusations, how can he believe I would do that to him? Yes, I went to dinner with Gail, but he won't even let me explain why. Does he really think that little of me? Of us?

When we're braced in deadlock, I know the answer is yes.

"I fucked up, and I'm sorry," I confess, sniffing back my tears. "But if you'd actually listen to me and let me explain why I lied, you'd understand."

Hunter sighs, eyes vacant. He's just as torn as me.

Taking a risk and hoping stepping into the lion's den won't leave me with scars, I step forward, needing to be close to him. My heart breaks when he shifts backward.

"I have no idea what's going on. But it appears you don't, either. Whatever you think you saw, I can assure it's wrong. And Keira, who I'm assuming is the person who told you, is a lot smarter than I thought she was. I mean, it seems she's able to break apart something I thought was pretty solid. But maybe I was right after all..."

Betrayal tears slip past the floodgates and roll down my

cheeks. Hunter's face softens, but it's too late. "You really are too good to be true."

There, I said it. The monkey on my back. I knew this was bound to happen sooner or later, because some fairy tales are just a tragedy in disguise. My entire body weeps, and I need to leave before I cry ugly tears.

I turn to leave, but Hunter lunges forward, seizing my wrist. "Shortcake…"

Once upon a time, his touch was everything I craved, but now, it's a sad reminder of how one's world can come crumbling down before their eyes.

I wait for him to tell me this is all going to be okay, but when his fingers eventually slip away, I know that nothing will be okay between us ever again. Unable to stomach this sorrow, I walk from the kitchen, not naïve enough to think Hunter will follow.

This can't be happening. But I suppose I don't even know what is happening. Hunter has returned from China with a fistful of puzzle pieces, but they don't fit into this very elaborate puzzle. Tears begin to flow freely, and I know before long, I won't be able to stop.

Diving into the safety of the bathroom, I slam the door shut behind me and lean up against the woodgrain. Closing my eyes, I allow the ugly tears to fall, but they soon take a backseat when I hear I'm not alone.

"Oh, ssh, sweetie. You knew you were always going to lose." That voice…I want to silence it, and the person it belongs to. I have no control over my body when my eyes waver open and I focus on a smug Keira. This is her fault, and she is going to pay.

I charge forward, forgetting my tears, my anger spurring

me on. She reads my intent to kill her with my bare hands and yelps, running into the safety of a stall. Her spineless actions only inflame my rage, and I pound on the door, kicking and screaming that she face me like a woman.

"I swear to god, if you don't come out, I will…" but my threat is never delivered because it appears Keira is always a step ahead.

"She can fuck whomever she likes. We're not exclusive. Just having fun." I know Hunter is not in the stall with her, but the voice I just heard was definitely his. It sounds once again, in case I didn't catch the memo the first time around.

"Just in case you're wondering…that was recorded last night, right before Hunter fucked me, and he fucked me good."

No, not again.

Placing a hand over my mouth to hold back the vomit, I stagger away from the cubical door, the walls closing in on me as I attempt to breathe. "There must be some mistake…" but how can I deny what I just heard? And what I just heard was my worst nightmare come true.

That hypocrite. That motherfucking liar.

"I feel sorry for you. All this time, you thought you were special. You thought you could tame New York's biggest player, but in reality, you were just someone to have fun with. I guess I'm that person now."

Her triumph is clear, but I suppose that's because she's won.

"Makes you wonder, doesn't it? How many other people did he fuck while you two were apparently a thing? I mean, if he thinks it's okay for you to fuck whomever you like because you were never exclusive, then surely, it's okay for him too. I know it was more than okay last night."

I want to scream, kick down the door, and tell her she's wrong. But I don't, because she's right. This entire time, I was fooling myself into thinking that Hunter could remain faithful. I wanted to believe so badly that he had changed, changed for me, but this recording proves I was so wrong. I was caught up in a future I wanted to believe was real.

We were never exclusive, and Hunter is only angry I had dinner and supposed sex with Gail because he's a narcissistic asshole who can't stand I interacted with the man he hates more than anyone in this world.

His big ego is bruised because only he can play the field, it seems. Well, fuck him. Fuck Keira. Fuck it all. I storm from the bathroom, unable to be in here because I'm on the cusp of suffocating.

Everything is haywire. My good sense tells me that this is wrong. Hunter would never do this, and what we had was real. But the man I saw moments ago is not the man I thought Hunter was. I never thought I'd see him so cold, not even giving me a chance to explain.

Everything I thought I knew has been turned on its axis, and I don't know what's right and what's wrong. Tears blur my vision, and I don't realize who I've bumped into until it's too late. "Mary…"

Hunter attempts to touch me, but it's too late. The thought of his hands on me makes me physically ill. "No, leave me alone!"

"I'm sorry," he says, but the sad part is, I don't know what exactly he's sorry for. "I should have told you…" I already know! "I should have let you explain…" But we're way past explanations. I've heard all I need to hear.

When he tries to reach out once again, I do the only thing I can. I slap his cheek so hard, I'm certain I've broken my hand—but I welcome the sting. "Don't you touch me ever again! You have some nerve."

He rubs his reddening cheek, moving his jaw from side to side. "I deserve that, but—"

But nothing. "No!" I repeat. I can't stomach him making excuses for his deplorable actions. I'll never be able to forgive his betrayal. "Leave me alone. I never want to see you again."

I ignore the torture behind those eyes, because it's wishful thinking, and it's what got me into trouble in the first place. "Mary, please…I need to tell you something…"

"Why should I listen to what you have to say when you couldn't show me the same decency? Us…" I gesture with two fingers between us, tears pooling in my eyes. "We're a mistake. I'm done. We were fooling ourselves into thinking this was something it clearly wasn't."

"You don't mean that."

"Yes, I do." His words playing on a loop encourage me as I allow one single tear to fall. "I mean, once a manwhore…always a manwhore. Goodbye, Hunter."

He blinks once, his face a perfect blank sheet. "Goodbye, Mary." I refuse to believe the waver to his voice is because his heart is breaking just like mine.

White noise fills my head and I hit the ground running, too afraid of what happens when I'm forced to deal with the biggest mistake of my life.

Seventeen

Hunter

Three days later

"Dude, seriously, call me back. I'll be back from Boston tomorrow. If I don't hear from you, I will be breaking down your door." The line goes dead as Dixon hangs up for about the ten millionth time today.

The past three days, I've not left the apartment because I'm afraid of what I'll do, or what I'll say if I do. Mary has shaken up my entire world, but this time, it's not the good kind of chaos.

After I told Mr. Yeong to go fuck himself, I was on the first plane back home. My first instinct was to find Mary and demand she explain what the holy fuck was going on, but with a lot of thinking time to spare, I realized I needed time to process everything I'd uncovered.

The pictures Keira sent erased everything I thought I knew and left me with this gaping hole in my chest. It reiterated the reason why I don't date, and why I never should have given in.

I never gave my heart to anyone because I knew this was bound to happen. Some may call me a coward, but I was smart to avoid this current clusterfuck I've found myself in.

I miss Mary—I fucking need her more than I need air to breathe, but she has ruined me. She never denied lying about dinner with Gail, and that betrayal cuts me deep. How could she think I would be okay with that? And then there's the issue of love hearts near her name.

She said there's a reason why she lied, but how can I trust a word she says?

I hate that this distrust has rooted deep within because before this, I trusted Mary with my life. I gave her a key to my apartment for fucks sake. But maybe I got swept up in the romance? In the possibility of actually being happy?

You really are too good to be true.

Her words have rung loudly since she confessed something which I felt every moment I spent with her. I was constantly waiting for the other shoe to drop, but now that it has, I only realize how badly I want for things to go back to the way they were.

When I found her, tears streaming down her cheeks, running from the bathroom, I wanted to beg her to forgive me for treating her the way I did. Yes, I was angry, I still am, but I should have manned the fuck up and not been such a drama queen and listened to what she had to say.

I wanted to tell her the reason why I was so upset. It wasn't the dinner itself, or that she told Gail about the watch. It was the fact she broke my trust. This whole dating thing is foreign to me. So maybe she had cold feet because we had gone from naught to perfection in weeks. But whatever the reason, if you don't have trust, then you don't have anything at all.

But I'm torn, and this is my dilemma.

Pacing my bedroom, the room which Mary has turned into my own personal sanctuary, I groan, unbelieving what a fucking idiot I am, because regardless of everything, regardless of the fact she has torn out my heart, I want to tell her that I forgive her because I…love…her. We all make mistakes, god knows I've made my fair share, but I want to work this out because what we have is too good to quit.

I have no idea what this says about my self-respect, because if this were any other woman, I would be drowning in faceless pussy by now, forgetting my woes. But Mary isn't any other woman, she's my woman, and in spite of everything, I want her back.

I thought I could stay mad at her forever, but the moment I saw her tears, saw her vulnerability, I wanted to forget everything that had happened and start afresh. We're not saints, we're sinners, but sinning is a lesson learned. And I've learned mine. I've learned that I should have acted like an adult and asked Mary if she'd hit her head and suffered temporary insanity before I jumped the gun.

When I caught Mary crying, a self-satisfied Keira emerged moments after, smirking a cat got the cream smile. When she saw me however, her entire demeanor changed and she asked if Mary was okay. That was so out of character for her and a voice inside of me yelled that she was masking her guilt.

She was beyond flirty in the kitchen. I was seconds away from telling her to fuck the fuck off, because even though she thought she was doing me a favor by spilling the beans, all she had done was fucking ruined my life. I know the truth is supposed to set you free, but she was completely smug about catching Mary out, like this was some game and she had won. But there was never a competition.

I've laid low, needing time to lick my wounds, but I can't hide away forever.

Sighing, I brush back my snarled hair, my hand still throbbing like a bitch. Needing painkillers to dull the pain, I make my way into the kitchen and swig back two pills with a Budweiser. I'm a fucking mess, and I know the only cure is sitting inches away.

I can snatch my keys off the counter, drive my sorry ass over to Mary's apartment, and demand she talk to me. She can call me names, because most of them are true, but she can't deny me when I profess my love for her, and ask that we work past this, because what we have is too valuable to lose.

Mid-sip, my cell chimes. I know it'll be Dix or Finch, as both have been blowing up my phone.

Contemplating changing my number, I reach for it in a huff, but pause when I see the text message on my screen. It's a game changer. And it's exactly what I need.

One clever asshole once told me… nothing is impossible. In case you're wondering, that asshole is you.

I remember that occasion well. It was when Dix and I were on a mission to stop Maddy's imaginary wedding. Times were simpler back then because I wasn't the one losing my mind.

Rubbing over my chest, I can't shake this feeling and I know I will never be able to unless I stop this pity party for one. Look at everything Dix was able to achieve by just being honest. No matter what happens, I can't give up until I try.

Tossing back my beer, I slam the empty bottle onto the counter and fist my keys. I don't bother changing my rumpled clothes, because all that matters is finding Mary and doing what I should have done days ago—listened.

Now that my decision is made, my feet can't keep up with the urgency and I all but run toward the front door. Sadly, the door has the same idea as me and runs toward my face as it swings open with a force so great, I stagger backward once it smacks me in the nose.

Cradling it, I ignore the blood streaming from it because standing before me is my assailant…Mary.

Her chest is rising and falling frenetically. She looks ready for battle. But when she sees me, standing in the middle of my living room, blood coating my fingers and staining my white shirt, her eyes widen in horror.

"Oh my God! Are you okay?"

The fact she didn't sucker punch me and asked about my wellbeing is a good sign, but my brain decides to flip me off and remind me of the picture and the fact she's fucking my arch nemesis for fun.

"Oh yeah, totally fine," I mutter around my hand. "Just bleeding out half my body weight. No biggie." Now is not the time for sarcasm, but it's the only way I can deal with this mess.

Sprinting for the bathroom with my head tilted back, I search blindly for a towel. Only when I manage to drop my toothbrush and toothpaste onto the floor and shatter my favorite cologne do I find a handtowel.

"Here, let me help you." That sweet voice is one I've missed more than I thought humanly possible, and even though I'm so conflicted, I allow her to tend to my wounds.

She guides me to sit on the toilet seat as she gently removes my hand so she can press the towel to my nose. "Keep your head back," she instructs when I attempt to look at her.

I do as she asks.

The next few minutes are filled with silence, which isn't a bad thing, as it allows me to accept that Mary is in fact here, nursing me back to health, instead of speeding up my demise. She looks tired, the bags beneath her eyes hinting she's had as little sleep as me.

Her hair is pulled back into a loose bun, and every freckle is exposed because her face is free of any makeup. Her usual creamy skin, buttered with pink-hued cheeks, now looks pale, translucent. It pains me beyond belief to see her this way.

"How's it look, Doc?" I tease, needing to lighten the mood before I break down and sob like a baby.

"You'll live," she replies, ensuring to not meet my eyes. I'm done playing. She's here for a reason, and I intend to find out what that is.

With a cautious touch, I gently place my hand over hers, but as expected, she recoils and jumps so far backward, I'm surprised she didn't end up outside. The bloodied towel falls into my lap, but nosebleed or not, it's time to get to the bottom of this.

Tossing the soiled towel into the basin, I stand, looking at the damage in the mirror. My face is caked in blood and my nose is double the size. With my sprained hand, and now swollen nose, I feel as battered externally as I do on the inside.

With nothing left to lose, I stand tall and very directly stare at her, waiting for her to meet my eyes. When she finally gathers the courage, it's on, and I know this won't end pretty. "Why are you here?"

She scoffs, folding her arms tightly. "For a number of reasons. First and foremost is to return this." With frantic fingers, she reaches into her pocket and produces a key. No guessing what it opens.

"What are the other reasons?" I ask, standing my ground.

My unwavering stance doesn't intimidate her in the slightest, but I never expected it to. "I need to take pictures of your bedroom…" Her pause incites World War Three. "But I can come back if I interrupted your gangbang!"

When she attempts to turn, I pounce, latching onto her bicep. She shakes me off so violently, I almost lose my balance. "You have some fucking nerve. I'm not the one who thought having dinner with a complete cockhead was acceptable behavior. Nor was I the one who thought fucking someone else would be okay!"

She snarls, ripping her arm from my grip. Her tiny hands beat against my chest. "For your information, I had dinner with Gail to try and save your ass!"

"Oh, that's rich." I snicker, shaking my head as I seize her wrists. "I've heard some bullshit stories in my time, most of which I've been the author of, but that takes the cake!"

This is spiraling rather quickly, but there is no sugar-coating what's been done.

"It's not bullshit. I didn't even get to appetizers. I had half a drink and bolted out the door," she spits, still fighting to free herself.

"Why, Mary, would you agree to go out with him in the

first place? Please, explain, because I am so fucking confused!" I level her with my fury, which only seems to ignite hers.

"Because maybe if you weren't so fucking blind when it came to Keira, you'd see that she and Gail are up to something. All I needed was proof, because accusations are just that if you don't have evidence!"

"So you thought offering your pussy would somehow present all the proof you needed?" My jaw clenches, and the need to kill Gail reaches astronomical levels.

"I never offered him anything, you idiot! I'm not like you. I can actually stay faithful!" she screams, finally breaking free. She tugs at her hair, tears stinging her eyes.

"I have no idea why you think that. I have been faithful."

"Enough! I've heard the evidence."

I won't stand by and accuse her of something I haven't done.

She said she went to dinner with that asshole because she needed proof…well, I have all the proof I need.

Taking a deep breath, I reveal what I should have days ago. "A picture speaks a thousand words, and these two pictures have spoken about ten thousand words. They've spoken to me nonstop since I first saw them!" Yanking the cell from my pocket, I turn the screen so she can see her betrayal and how she's fucking broken my heart.

Her chest falls intermittently, but when she sees the picture of her and Gail, and when I scroll across so she can see her digits, I'm afraid she's stopped breathing all together.

"So, you see, you speak of proof…how much more proof do I need?" I wave the screen in her face, wishing that maybe, just maybe, there is some colossal mistake and she will make all of this go away.

"W-where did you ge-get that?" she stutters, her eyes as wide as saucers.

"Why does it matter? You needed your proof…well, here is mine. It's fairly obvious this dinner was to celebrate the fact you fooled me, and fooled me real good." When she cocks a brow, I'm done with her lying. "You can imagine my surprise when Mr. Yeong told me that it's now an equal playing field because that bastard, Gail, knows all about the watch."

This is the moment I'm expecting to see Mary crumble, because her ultimate betrayal has been revealed. But she doesn't, and the wind gets knocked from my sails when she calmly nods. "I know, he told me."

I recoil, curling my lip. "What do you mean, he told you? He told you because you told him."

It's like we're speaking in tongues, because she shakes her head. "I did not. He already knew about it when we had dinner. That was the reason why I agreed to have dinner in the first place. I knew he was up to something, so yes, I may have flirted a little to get him to think I was interested, but I did it because I wanted to uncover what he was up to. I wanted to protect you."

I close my eyes, my utter stupidity kicking me in the dick.

"I thought I was so clever, trying to get information, but he was two steps ahead because he knew about the watch and made it clear that he wasn't telling me how he knew. So everything was for nothing and blew up in my face."

"That's not possible." I stagger backward, winded.

"It's the truth, Hunter. I have no idea why you'd think I'd tell him. Or why the hell I would fuck him…when I was fucking you."

It should be music to my ears, but it highlights what I've

done, what I've ruined because I was too scared of being happy. "Mr. Yeong told me that Gail said you'd told him about the watch, and that you and him were…together." I almost gag on the admission.

Mary shakes her head slowly, not a hint of guilt showing. "Well, someone's lying, and no guessing who that is."

"But if you didn't tell him, then who did?" I ask, so lost in translation, my brain is about to close shop.

The mood shifts from anger, to hurt, to confusion. Why would Gail tell Mr. Yeong what he did? And how did he know about the watch if Mary didn't tell him?

She appears as baffled as me. There is still a small bubble of doubt that she's lying to save her ass, and I hate that I can't trust her completely. But this is so fucked up, like a script of some bad daytime TV show.

"Follow me."

The urgency to her step has me following without question, because if she can explain what the hell is going on, then I'm in. I watch as she hunts through her bag, producing her cell. "Who are you…"

"Shut up," Mary demands, cutting me off. "If only you had listened, none of this would have happened."

"What are you talking about?" I bark, offended.

"I have a hunch," she reveals, frantically pushing buttons on her phone. "I can't believe I didn't think of this sooner. I wanted proof…and it literally was in the palm of my hand this entire time. Rookie move," she mumbles to herself.

I watch silently as she sets down her phone onto the kitchen counter, tapping at the screen and desperately scrolling through what looks like video footage. My interest is completely piqued and I stand beside her, thankful she doesn't knee me in the balls.

It takes me a second, but when I recognize the backdrop, I cock my head to the side. "Is that my office?"

"Yes," she blankly replies, rewinding through a blur of imagery. "There is a camera in there." When my mouth hangs open, she adds, "Don't worry. It's hidden."

"Oh, that makes me feel a whole lot better. Why are you spying on me?" I'm now insulted. The shit I do in there is not pretty.

"Please, don't flatter yourself. Everyone has one. There are creeps out there. This is solid evidence in a court of law. And besides…" She stops her manic searching, meeting my eyes. "I thought it would give us something fun to watch when we finally christened that desk."

A longing hits me low at the possibility of never living out that dream.

Our attention returns to the screen and when a blob comes into view, Mary pauses the image. The footage may be grainy, but there is no mistaking the blob has a face, and that face is Keira's.

"I knew it," she spits, quickly backtracking, until she disappears from view. Mary continues searching and stops when Keira enters my office. The date in the top corner reveals it was taken a week ago.

"What the fu…"

"Ssh…" Mary shushes me, increasing the volume on her phone.

We both watch, completely absorbed as Keira makes her way into my office. She closes the door, looking from left to right like a thief, scoping out her surroundings. When the coast is clear, she saunters forward, running her finger along my desk.

She's stalling, and I wonder why. She reveals her true motives a moment later when she rounds my desk and opens the drawer. "What the fuck is she doing?"

Mary's heightened breathing matches the galloping of my heart. I suddenly feel so violated when she taps her chin after her snooping came up with nothing. But that pales in comparison to when those eyes, eyes which I once thought were nothing but innocent and kind, focus on my unlocked filing cabinets—the very same ones Mary goaded me about.

She smirks, running over to them, before dropping to her knees and hunting through them madly. It takes her a while, because there is no method to my madness, but I know when she finds what she's looking for because she mutters, "What a fucking moron," making me feel even stupider than I already do.

This would be the time Mary delivers a well-deserved I told you so, but when the door opens, we're both lost for words. In strolls Gail. My skin crawls, knowing he's been inside my office. I'm expecting Keira to quickly stow away what she's found, but I should know by now, nothing is what it seems.

Gail's cocky saunter has Keira smirking, using my favorite chair as a barrier as he hunts her like prey. "Did you find it?"

Keira holds up the file proudly.

Edging closer to the screen to see what she is in fact holding, I groan, scolding my stupidity. She's sporting Mr. Yeong's file, the file which has a two-page report detailing my progress on finding the fucking watch. I can regret my foolishness later because something nasty, and I don't mean that in a good way, is about to take place.

"Yes. So now that I have it, what are you going to give me in return?"

"Don't be a bad girl, Keira, otherwise, I'll be forced to punish you." Gail prowls closer and closer to her, and when he unfastens his tie and begins to unbutton his shirt, I actually throw up in my mouth.

The moment he's topless, I've seen more than enough, but Mary nudges me in the ribs, demanding I see this through.

"I've been a very bad girl, Mr. Gail." Keira twirls a lock of hair around her finger, while Gail snarls like a dog.

I just can't. It hurts my eyeballs.

"You know what happens to bad girls, don't you?"

Move over, Ron Jeremy, we have a new hedgehog in town.

It happens before I can turn away or render myself unconscious, but Gail pounces on Keira, kisses the living shit out of her, before bending her over my desk, where he fucks her like an epileptic slug. "Oh, god, no." My face twists in sheer horror. "Sweet baby Jesus, why?" I'll never look at my index roller the same way. No surprise that he's a two-pump chump, but I've forever been scarred when he comes with a high-pitched squeal.

This is the ultimate fuck you—literally.

Mary mercifully turns off the video as I'm moments away from rocking in a corner. "Well…" She clears her throat. "I thought she was in this for herself, but apparently, I was wrong."

I have no idea what that means, because that video is a clear indication that they've been fucking for a while. I can only hope that was the first time they used my office as a bordello.

As I'm contemplating calling a priest to exorcise my office, Mary exhales. This was an ordeal for the both of us, and I wouldn't be surprised if she suggested counseling, but what she says next just proves that when it rains, it fucking pours down a shitstorm.

"That must be hard to watch."

"You have no idea," I confirm, shuddering. "It pains me to say, but I now have to burn down all your hard work because there is no fucking way I can go inside that office without a bubble suit and a gallon of bleach."

It was meant to be a joke…well, sort of, because I do plan on ripping up the office, floor to ceiling, but Mary doesn't look amused. "That girl certainly gets around. It's a wonder she can get any work done. Between fucking her boss and blowing you, she sure does have her hands full. Although, I can see why she favors your cock."

The brakes are slammed on and I jerk my head so quickly, I'm certain I've given myself whiplash. "What now? Who's blowing me?"

Mary narrows her eyes, ready to kill. "There's no need to lie. The cat's out of the bag." She cringes. "I really wish I used another phrase."

I'm now the one who is far from amused. "You think Keira is blowing me?"

"I know for a fact she's doing a lot more than that," she counters quickly.

I'm so lost right now, I don't think a GPS could even steer me in the right direction. Siri, help! "You're mistaken. She was fucking me over, yes, but I never touched her." When she rolls her eyes and pushes off the counter, I press, "It's the god honest truth."

"Just stop. I heard the recording."

My brain short circuits, unable to take yet another surprise. "What recording?"

"The tape where you say…" She holds up her finger, licking her lips. "She can fuck whomever she likes. We're not exclusive. Just having fun." Her low voice I'm guessing is supposed to mimic mine, but why is she reciting something that was said a lifetime ago?

When I continue staring at her like she has two heads, she flies into a rage. "You can't deny it, Hunter. I heard you. Keira played me the recording in the bathroom. She then detailed how you fucked her into a well-sated heap!"

This explains her tears and the slap which rattled my teeth.

"I'm not denying it," I say, intruding on her need to kill. She steps forward, no doubt ready to slap me again, but I grab her wrist. "I did say that, but it was weeks ago. The night when you met Ming, Keira rounded me up and told me she'd heard you speaking to someone I now know was Maddy. She made it sound like you were ready to screw anything with a pulse. I didn't know it was Maddy, so I assumed the worst. What you heard was me licking my wounds."

Her mouth parts and her need to kill lessens.

"My huge ego had control of my mouth for a split second, but it appears that second was exactly what Keira needed as collateral. I didn't even know she was recording our conversation, because no one except crazy people do that shit. I didn't mean a word of it. I was just…hurt." God, I sound like such a pussy.

"B-but she said you had slept together."

"Well, she's a fucking liar, but there's no surprise there." I loosen my hold, believing Mary will need time to process everything that's just happened. I sure as shit do.

I take a moment to digest everything without giving myself indigestion.

So, it appears Keira is the root of all evil as she and Gail were in cahoots this entire time. I know without a doubt our first encounter was not accidental. She set a trap, and like a stupid rabbit, I got caught.

Her job was to get close to me, as Gail hoped I'd fall for her sweet, virginal act, which I did. But what he never anticipated was me falling in love with the woman of my dreams, foiling their plans on overthrowing my empire.

When her constant attempts to seduce me failed, they decided to up the ante and not only destroy my career, but my personal life as well. The funny thing is, they saw what I was too blind to see. They knew if they destroyed my relationship with Mary, nothing else would matter, because winning isn't worth the effort if you don't have anyone to share your triumphs with.

Keira was never on my side. All the times I thought she was looking out for me, both she and Gail were actually setting this plan into motion because they planted a seed…and sat back and watched it grow. We played right into their hands, but the sad part is, they didn't destroy us…we did.

They were hoping their plan was foolproof, and for a second there, it was. How fucking stupid could I have been?

It appears Mary has done some investigating of her own. "I knew Keira was evil, but this takes it to a whole different level. When I saw her crying in Gail's office, I thought he was reprimanding her for spilling his coffee, or not booking his favorite restaurant, but I bet he was chastising her for not trying harder. You were supposed to be easy, but then…" She seals her lips shut, averting her eyes.

I'm so tired of pretending, because this is the first time I've felt like I can breathe in days. Risking a finger, I slowly brush the back of my pointer down her cheek. The moment I make contact, her skin breaks out in a shiver. "But then you came along and changed my world forever," I confess, unable to stop even if I wanted to.

"This entire thing was about power, control, and greed," I reveal. "With my past, Gail thought it was a done deal. He was certain I'd succumb to her advances, confessing my secrets mid-orgasm. But what he never realized was that Keira was the fluffer, but you…you were the real deal."

She lifts those eyes, the eyes which have me denouncing all I believe in and love because she is my goddess, my deity I bow to and worship. "I was?" she whispers, leaning into my touch.

"Yes, Shortcake. You were." I hate speaking in past tense, but we both have a lot of soul-searching to do.

I have no idea where this leaves us, because until I speak to Keira and beat the truth from Gail, we're given half the story, and to move forward, I need all the pieces to see where we went wrong.

"So you believe me?" she asks, her lower lip trembling, the sight breaking my heart all over again.

"Yes, I believe you. I never should have doubted you in the first place."

Her shoulders sag and she looks ten pounds lighter. Now, it's make or break. "Do you believe me?"

She has every right not to. I'm far from an angel, and given my track record, she had every right to think I meant what I said on that recording. In the past I may have, but that was before I met and fell head over heels in love with her.

I skim my fingertip over her trembling lips, unable to stop myself because I've craved her touch. Whatever her response, I will deal, just as long as she lets me touch her. She does, but there is something missing.

She opens her mouth, but I know what she's going to say even before she says it. "Yes, I do, but…" One simple word can hold the weight of the world, and now is no exception.

"But what?" I gently ask, brushing my thumb over the apple of her cheek.

"Keira and Gail…they played at both our insecurities, and it worked. It's ridiculous to think I believed Keira, but that's the problem…I believed her. What does that say for our future? If we don't trust one another, then we don't have anything. This entire situation could have been avoided if only we were honest."

Every part of me mourns because what she says is true. I don't want it to be, but it is. It is ludicrous to think I ever believed Mary would do all that I thought she did, but the important thing is, that I did. I would rather believe a lie, than accept the truth because the truth of spending forever with one person is fucking daunting, and to a former manwhore, a self-confessed commitment-phobe, Mary is someone who scares the living shit out of me.

"I should have been honest from the very beginning. I'm so sorry."

But she shakes her head, placing her palm over mine. "The same thing could be said about me. If I had just told you of my suspicions, we could have worked this out together. But that's our problem." Her lower lip trembles. "I think we've been single for so long, we don't know how to co-exist without hurting each other. We're still learning, and we're bound to make mistakes along the way, but this is just…" She sniffs, her eyes peeled to her sneakers.

Cradling both her cheeks, I coax her to look at me because I know what comes next. "Too much?" I offer, and after a moment, she nods. I tell myself to man up. The waterworks can start later.

"I know most people would be able to get over this and move on, but I don't think I can. You've got the power to ruin me, and I'm scared. Every time I'm with you, I can't help but question…am I enough?"

"You're more than enough, Shortcake," I affirm, leveling her with my sincerity.

She smiles, but it's so bittersweet. "Thank you, but I have to believe it. I just…I don't think I'm ready." Tears sting her eyes while I watch on, not believing that our future is ready to crash and burn. "I'm sorry for calling you a manwhore."

"It's okay. It's the truth." I sigh, wishing I could erase all the women I've ever slept with, because none of them matter. My past has finally come back to bite me in the ass. I lower my hands, suddenly feeling unworthy of touching her.

She surprises me when she interlaces our hands. It's the simplest of gestures. "It may have been, but not anymore. I hope when looking back on what we had, you can say you learned as much from me as I have from you."

"So that's it? We're done?" I swallow past the lump in my throat. She sniffs, but eventually she nods. "…Fuck me."

This is so final, and although I hate it, it's the only way for us to move on. We would be stupid to sweep this under the carpet and not learn from our mistakes. I suppose most people could move on together, but we're not most people.

I can say with confidence that Mary is the first person that broke my heart, because I've finally learned how to love. Love sets you free…and I have to do the same for Mary if she doesn't want me. Fight for her! my inner caveman screams, but I no longer want to be someone's stand-in.

"I know it sounds petty, but I need to be in a relationship with myself before I can even contemplate being in one with somebody else. And you, Hunter"— she draws me toward her —"are something else. You take my breath away, and I'm afraid I'll forget how to breathe on my own."

So, it appears we're breaking up because this all-consuming love has the ability to overthrow us both, and we're not ready for that type of commitment because what we have…it has the possibility to be epic—a true life fairy-tale. But if we can't trust one another, if Mary can't look at me the same way my parents, Dix, and Maddy look at one another, then I don't want to settle.

A small part of me feels like it's dying, but knowing Mary will look back on what we have with nothing but fond memories makes me feel like the luckiest man alive. She gave me a chance and taught me self-sacrifice, because I would gladly lay down my happiness if it meant she lived her life with a confident smile.

This has got to be the most anti-climactic breakup—ever. I was expecting tears, maybe even a broken leg, but it appears our story isn't filled with angst or ugly tears. Don't get me wrong, I'm hurting, and when she walks out that door, I don't plan on leaving the apartment for a month.

"So, what happens now?" she asks, working her luscious

bottom lip.

I need to stop focusing on shit like this because if we're going to move on, then first and foremost, we have to learn how to be friends. "We went from enemies to lovers. I think we missed a step," I reveal, extending my hand and throwing my manhood to the wind.

Mary peers down at it, her brow arched. "You want to be friends?"

I nod. "Yes. I still want you in my life, because before things got complicated, you were my most favorite person to annoy." She bursts out laughing, the sound music to my ears.

"Maybe we could work from there and see what happens? Friends it is, then." She slips her delicate hand in mine, shaking with vigor and a smile. Sadly, the moment we touch, my dick is far from impressed with this truce, highlighting that although my intentions are good, I still want her more than ever, and I doubt that'll ever change.

She reads my heightened response, and her reply is that her nipples blossom under the thin cotton of her white t-shirt. I fight with my depravity, trying to look anywhere but at her chest, but I just can't help it. I've come to realize I'm an all right guy, but I never claimed to be a fucking saint.

"You better go…" I manage to push out between clenched teeth.

"Yes, I better go," she confirms, but her hand is still locked in mine.

"Shortcake…" I warn, wrestling with my morals, because we literally agreed to being friends thirty seconds ago, and all I want to do is kiss the living shit out of her.

"Hunter, just stop talking." She pounces on me, smashing

her lips to mine and sucker punching me with her strawberry kisses. I don't stand a chance, because this quite possibly may be the last time we lock this way, and if that is in fact true, then I'm going to enjoy every minute. Fuck the confusion and mixed signals, I can deal with that tomorrow.

She laces her hands behind my nape, standing on tippy toes to gain full access to every part of me. Our tongues duel, battling to conquer the other, but when she rubs herself against my hard on, it's evident that we're both winners.

I want to be gentle, tell her that I love her, because I do, I fucking do, but she doesn't want to hear it, and besides, words escape us both as we're fueled by our untamed passion to consume one another whole. Reaching under her skirt, I tear off her underwear, palming her supple ass. She gasps into my mouth, but that soon turns to a moan when I slip my fingers into her ripe heat. Her pussy clenches at the intrusion, sucking me into the warm cavern. I never want to leave, but I don't have a choice, because after tonight…who knows what the fuck is going to happen.

She only pries her lips off mine to tear the t-shirt from my body. When I'm topless, our lips re-collide, desperately clinging to the other as I lift her up and walk her toward the couch. We fall together, our kisses never ceasing as we desperately undress each other.

The moment her magnificent tits are exposed, I pull away and work her pink nipple into my mouth. She launches off the sofa, only offering me more of her milky flesh. I can't get enough of her, so with her right breast still in my mouth, I lower my hand and thrust two fingers into her. She cries as she spreads her legs wider.

"Greedy girl," I hum against her areola, flicking her fleshy nipple with my tongue.

She madly unfastens the button on my jeans before yanking down the fly. Her hand shoots into my pants, desperately fisting my shaft as I suckle her breast. Her pussy is wet and ready, and I so want to bury my head between her legs and eat her out for a week, but we both need the most primitive connection known to mankind, because this is what links us as one…for the last time.

Without further ado, I yank my jeans down and align our bodies, staring deeply into those mesmerizing eyes. I know I'm bareback, but the condoms are in my room, and if I don't get lost in her body this second, I just may fucking die.

She nods, giving me silent permission to bring this home.

It's all I need, and I sink into her, unable to mute my cries because she feels so… fucking… good. I still the moment I'm buried all the way to the hilt. My cock demands I move, but I need to absorb this memory, get lost in perfection, because I'm going to do something I've never done before.

With the slowest of movements, I rock my hips, lower my lips, and then, we make love.

I've fucked plenty, but making love, before now, I couldn't even say the word without wanting to throw up, but as I savor every slow stroke and get lost in the sweet cadence of her lips, I'm a complete convert. Every emotion is heightened, and the feel of her small body writhing under mine is more than words can express.

Our bodies are slick, coated in perspiration as we lock eyes and get lost in one another. I don't know what the future holds, but this right now is enough. "I'm sorry," she whispers, a tear slipping down her cheek.

Bending forward, I lick it away, the salty sadness a reminder of everything we've faced. "Ssh, don't cry. It's okay."

"I just wish things could be different."

I understand what she means, because when we're coupled this way, everything falls into place around us. But sex isn't the Band-Aid I thought it once was. Mary and I are dynamite in the bedroom, but the sex stuff…I get it now, it will eventually fade.

The only thing that matters is growing old with someone who completes you, and until we uncover that…we will always have this— the memories. No one can take them away.

"I wouldn't give up one second spent with you, Mary Mitts. Once in a lifetime, you meet someone who changes everything…thank you for being that person."

More tears fall, but I don't know whose they are. It doesn't matter however, because I'll never forget this feeling for as long as I live.

We move in sync, our bodies entwined, our hearts beating as one. I know she's close, so I reach down and circle over her swollen clit. She rockets off the sofa, her hips swaying into me, pleading I give her what she wants.

I seal my lips over hers, fucking her mouth as I fuck her pussy. I'm imbedded so deep, I can feel the vibration pulsate along my cock. I suddenly pull all the way out, before slamming back into her. "Oh fuck! I can't…I love…" she cries, before her body shudders and she comes with an earth-shattering scream. The sight of her thrashing underneath me, of what she almost said, has me pumping my hips, and I follow her lead seconds after, pulling out.

I've never come this hard before, and I decide to finish this once and for all. "I love you!" I roar. It's a jumble of words, but they're said nonetheless. Do I regret them?

When she sobs, kissing over my neck, my chin, my lips, I know the answer is hell to the fuck no. If this is what living is… then I think I just took my first breath.

Eighteen

Many weeks have passed since I did something I thought I was not capable of doing—I sacrificed my happiness for the happiness of someone else. I suppose I now know that true love is indeed selfless, and you'd happily sacrifice your life for the person you love.

Dixon and Finch would be damn proud.

I've laid low, needing some downtime, because this concept of being a responsible adult is fucking exhausting. I'm seeing Dixon and Finch tonight because it's Dixon's bachelor party. As far as bachelor parties go, I'd have more fun knitting booties, but he made me promise to keep it low key. He wanted to get back to our roots and just have a few drinks like the good ol' days, gossiping like old hens.

I wanted to do something spontaneous, but since Mary left, the only spontaneity in my life is to have gin instead of scotch.

I'm doing okay. Yes, I miss Mary more than words could

ever explain, but when Maddy called me and thanked me for whatever I did, I knew that the saying rings true: if you love something, set it free. I can only hope the counterpart is also true: if it comes back, then it was meant to be.

I've been tempted to call her, break down her door and demand she give me a second chance, but I too have needed the time apart to figure out how I feel in all of this. Yes, we jumped into the deep end with both eyes closed, but now that she's gone, nothing has been clearer. I want her back, and this time, no holding back. But I know it doesn't work that way for everyone, especially women, who are a lot more in tune to their emotions than us guys.

So, I guess, now I wait. It all seems like a cop out, but what other choice do I have?

I've not spoken or seen Mary after the final time we made love, which might prove problematic, seeing as the wedding is a couple weeks away. But you can't force nature, you especially can't force a redheaded, demon woman. God, I miss her.

With all this time on my hands, I've decided to focus my energies elsewhere, because idle hands and all that. Just because I've turned over a new leaf with Mary does not mean I'm in line for sainthood anytime soon.

There are two sneaky little fuckers who are in my sights—they just don't know it. But today is the day, because payback, as they say, is a bitch.

I'm sitting in my newly furnished office, because after the shit that went down in here—literally, I needed to destroy anything that may have been contaminated with Gail's splooge. I gag at the memory, but when there is a knock on my door, I put my game face on, because things are about to get serious.

"Come in," I singsong, pretending to busy myself when Keira enters the room.

She's laid low, not knowing what's going on, as I'm sure she and Gail believed I would be rocking in a corner somewhere, emotionally and financially ruined. But it'll take a lot more than two amateurs to beat me.

"Hi, Hunter," she says, turning on the charm. But her sweet, innocent act won't fly with me anymore.

But I pretend to be the bumbling idiot she believes me to be. "Hey, sweetheart. How you been? Haven't seen you in a while. I've missed you."

She closes the door behind her, obviously buying into my bullshit. "I've been really busy. Mr. Gail has been working me hard." The bile rises as I try not to take her comment too literal.

I clench my thighs under the desk, but rein it in because I can't blow my cover. "Is that a new dress?"

She runs a hand down the stripy dress, which hurts my eyes. "Yes, actually, it is."

Leaning back in my seat, I cross an ankle over my knee. I take my time in examining her from head to toe, because someone who's a narcissistic bitch like she is, loves the attention. "You look fucking hot in it. I bet you look even better out of it." Her chest begins to rise and fall. "Come here."

She saunters over, ensuring that everything important bounces and wiggles, but I'd rather watch a giraffe striptease than touch this woman ever again. "Come on, I won't bite." I pat my lap. "Unless you want me to, that is."

She takes the bait and smirks.

When she's a few feet away, I stop her, raising my pointer. "Actually, on second thought…strip."

"W-what?" she stutters, her surprise clear.

"Strip," I blankly reply. This is getting old fast and I'm running out of time.

"Here?" she questions, looking around the room coyly. She had no issues bumping uglies on my desk, so I know this is once again all for show.

I nod, my gaze never wavering from her. "Yes, here. How can I fuck you if you're dressed? Do you want me to fuck you? Fuck that pussy? Motorboat those tits? Maybe fuck that tight little ass?" I go for the trifecta 'cause why the hell not?

The aggression turns her on, because I can see her rubbing her thighs together. "Yes. I've wanted your cock from the first moment you ate me out." I shiver at the memory.

Without a second thought, she lowers the straps of her dress and shimmies out of it, drawing out the reveal, attempting to be sexual and seductive. It has the complete opposite effect however, because her slow pace grates on my nerves.

"Those too." I point to her lacy thong and bra. They soon pool by her feet as well.

In nothing but her heels, my plan is finally set in motion. "Come here, sweetness." The fact that she's naked does absolutely zip for my sex-drive. She's the antidote for raging erections.

She ambles over, her small breasts perky and ready for the picking, but she is about five seconds from picking herself off the floor. "I think it's only fair..." I say, leaning further back in my seat, enjoying what I'm about to do. "That seeing as you fucked me, it's time I fucked you."

She pauses, almost tripping over her black heels, shattering her dream of walking her imaginary runway. "What do you mean?"

"What I mean is…why did you do it?"

"Do what?" she asks, but the tremble to her lips reveals she knows exactly what I'm talking about.

"My, my, watch your nose grow."

"I have no idea what you're talking about," she says with bite, finally showing me her true colors.

"Don't fuck with me, Keira. I'm giving you an opportunity to explain yourself." Her baby blues are widened, her red lips parted. She's so sprung. When she attempts to pick up her underwear, I uncross my legs, lean forward, and steeple my fingers under my chin. "You have ten seconds to explain, otherwise I call HR and inform them that you're not only naked in my office, but you're also fucking your boss. They don't take too lightly to office romances around here, especially when you're fucking half the office."

She pauses from slipping one leg into her thong. It appears she's sick of pretences too. "You wouldn't dare." I don't bother answering, but instead pick up the phone.

She reads my seriousness and quickly kicks away her underwear. "See, that wasn't so hard. Now, I'll make you a deal. You tell me everything, and I'll let you leave, unscathed. I'll forget the fact that you're a backstabbing, lying she-devil, and you get to leave, scot-free."

She ponders over my offer, no doubt counting how many steps there are to the door, but in the end, she surrenders. "Okay, fine. Can I at least get dressed?" I laugh in response.

When she trembles, I feel a smidge sorry for her, but then I remember she tried to ruin my life. "Aaron told me to seduce you to find out all I could about Mr. Yeong. It was supposed to be easy. With your reputation, this should have been done weeks ago, but what Aaron didn't take into consideration was that redheaded bitch. She's your Achilles' heel."

I look up at the ceiling, counting to three before I lose my temper. "You speak about her like that again…and our deal is off. Understand?"

She seals her lips, as she knows my threats are not empty. "Aaron told me to keep trying and I did, but I never meant to fall for you, Hunter."

And the Oscar goes to… "Oh, please, do you take me for a fool?"

"It's true!" she cries, advancing forward. Looks like Dixon was right after all—I have my own Juliet Harte in training.

I thrust out my palm. "That's close enough. Stick to the basics. What was in it for you?"

She sniffs, wiping her nose with the back of her hand. "He said he would split half with me, and you know how much he's worth. I don't come from money like you. I've had to work hard to get where I am."

It all came down to money. She had no qualms ruining my life so she could afford the latest threads. I'm beyond disgusted. If she was that desperate for cash, I would have hired her and paid her double.

I can't help but laugh at her little sob story. "Oh yes, I can see how hard you've had to work. Fucking your way up the corporate ladder must require some skill. You sure as shit fooled me."

"Aaron hates you, and I can see why," she sneers, her innocent, doe eye act gone. "He figured why not destroy everything you love, because not once did you show him the respect he deserved." If I didn't know any better, I'd say this heartless witch had feelings for the asshole.

"Fuck me," I say, shaking my head in disbelief. "Gail is angry 'cause I didn't invite him out to lunch? Tell him to grow some balls and stop being a whiny little bitch. I worked my way to the top fair and square, and the only way Gail could beat me was by cheating. Too bad I've always been two steps ahead."

Keira cocks her head to the side. "What does that mean?"

We're now in the final innings. "What it means is, call your boss."

"What?" she gasps, shaking her head violently. "You said you'd let me go. If I told you, you'd let me leave."

"Well, you're shit out of luck," I reply, holding out the receiver.

"You lied." Tears fall down her cheeks,

"Boo hoo, cry me a river. So did you." I wave the phone because this isn't over, not even by half.

In times of crisis, it's all about self-preservation, and Keira displays just how highly she thinks of herself and the need to survive when she lunges over the table, her lips like tentacles as they attempt to latch onto my face.

I spring up, almost falling onto my ass. I knew this would happen, which is why, you always must have a Plan B—fucking amateurs.

Looking at my watch, the internal countdown commences. Five. Four. Three. Two. One.

Right on time, the door bursts open and in rages Gail. "You fucking rat…" But his words perish in a flat death when he sees Keira naked in my office.

In his hand, he holds the envelope I asked Frankie the intern to deliver right on 11:53 a.m. It's now 11:59 a.m. My talent is clearly wasted here, because move over Rick Grimes, there's a new sheriff in town.

"What the fuck is going on here?" Wow, I can't believe she's fucking this dickhole voluntarily.

"Close the door," I coolly command, while Keira dives for her clothes.

"He knows everything!" she cries, getting dressed.

"Yes, that's true. Might I add, it didn't take much to get her to talk."

Gail looks on the verge of stabbing me with my shiny new letter opener, while I grin, pointing to the two chairs in front of me. "So, this can go one of two ways. You can either do what I say, or…" I tap my finger, pretending to think over option two. There is no other option however. "Or, you can do what I say. Sit."

"We don't have to listen to him, Aaron! He's got nothing. I'll say he sexually assaulted me if he does!"

I yawn, so not amused by her theatrics.

"Shut up, Keira, and just sit down."

Gail eyeballs the living hell out of me. I wish I could take a picture to remember this moment forever. He slumps into the seat; visually commanding Keira to do the same. I actually feel sorry for her because this is what happens when you have daddy issues.

Once they're both seated, I reach for my glass of scotch and savor the burn. "I see you received my present."

"Present?" Gail shouts, holding up the envelope. "This is blackmail, you son of a whore!"

I tsk him. "Now, let's not resort to name-calling. All I require is for you to leave this office for good. I don't want you anywhere here. Actually, make that Manhattan and all of the surrounding boroughs. This is my kingdom, and if I so much as hear you sniffing around me or my clients, I will expose you for the extortionist that you are."

"What is he talking about?" Keira asks, turning to look at Gail, who pales.

"You wouldn't dare."

"On the contrary, I would dare. I double dare." Keira looks lost in translation, which gives me another idea. Plan C—Jesus, this shouldn't be so easy. "I spy with my little eye someone's boyfriend, who is blackmailing half of his clients. Not to mention, dabbling in a little money laundering on the side. Sorry, Keira, but you're dating a fraud."

"You put a fucking camera in my office!" Gail bellows, throwing the envelope at my head. Too bad his aim is as shit as his luck. "That's got to be some invasion of my privacy." Gail clearly doesn't appreciate the tape I sent him where he was the star actor.

"Please," I scoff coolly. "Don't flatter yourself. Everyone has one. There are creeps out there. This is solid evidence in a court of law." I repeat Mary's words with a smile.

This genius plan is in part, thanks to her. It only seemed fitting I bring down these two cheats with her idea. I needed solid evidence that Gail was dirty, but what I never expected to find was what exactly went on behind closed doors.

I have hours of footage of Gail blackmailing his clients, extorting them out of hundreds and thousands of dollars through threats. Instead of working for his clients, he was working against them, scavenging for any small shred of damning evidence he could hold above their heads. His portfolio is a sham.

They only stayed with him because they were afraid he'd reveal their secrets, some of which no multi-billionaire would want the media to know. This is bad, bad press for us if it ever got out. The board would not appreciate one of their senior brokers being involved in a scandal such as this. So, what this means is…Gail is so screwed.

"Is it true?" Keira asks, dreams of living life on the Riviera dwindling to none.

"Yes, it's true. If you don't believe me, I'm sure your boss can show you the evidence. There's hours of footage on there, so you might want to get comfy." I wave the envelope in case she missed the memo. "Otherwise, I can email you the link," I reply for him. "The money laundering"—I whistle—"hikes up into the millions. Maybe if you weren't so greedy, you'd have gotten away with the perfect crime. But you had to fuck me over, didn't you?"

"Excuse me?" Keira snarls, ready to pluck out Gail's eyeballs. DING! DING! DING! We have a winner. "You said there was no money. That you were waiting on Mr. Yeong."

"He has money. A lot of it. None of which was earned honestly," I add as a sidenote.

I knew this would be her Achilles' heel. The moment she mentioned money, it really was like stealing a dollar bill from this pathetic baby. Gail's silence cements his guilt. God, I really shouldn't be enjoying this so much, but the karma train is coming. Choo fucking choo.

"You son of a bitch!" Whack! I felt that smack from over here. "You said you'd take care of me!"

It appears all Keira is, is a status climber. She would clearly latch onto whatever man she could if she thought he would set her up financially. She uses her looks to get what she wants, standing on whomever for self-gain. There is no love, no loyalty. Just greed and lies.

I have no doubt if I showed interest and showered her with gold, she'd be calling me daddy.

Keira stands, crossing her arms over her chest, and glaring something wicked. "Fuck you both! I'm out of here."

"Keira, baby, wait, I can explain!" Baby? Gail stands, attempting to chase her out the door. Seriously, my devious mind needs its own zip code.

"Not so fast," I state, because I'm not done with her. She must also pay for what she did to Mary. "The same rule applies to you, Keira."

"What rule?" she screams, fisting her hair, which hangs from a lopsided bun.

"I'm giving you one chance to leave and never be found. One." I hold up my finger in case she missed the memo.

"I don't have to do anything you say. Unlike this asshole, you've got nothing on me."

I wish she'd stop making it so easy for me "Well, that's where you're wrong."

Both their interests are piqued when I tap away on my keyboard and flip around my screen. The image on there is one I have zero need to see ever again, but it proves my point. It also highlights the fact I'm not full of shit.

As Keira is getting rutted into by Gail, I spread my hands out in front of me. "The chairman of the board is a good friend of mine. He has zero tolerance against this sort of horseplay. He also won't appreciate the fact you broke into my office, Keira, and took something that didn't belong to you."

There, she now knows I know everything. I was playing her, just how she played me.

"So, if you aren't on the first plane back to bumblefuck, then I will be forced to send him a copy if you decide to stay."

"Fuck you, O'Shea!" Gail rounds my desk, towering over me in an attempt to intimidate me. He's lucky he's not copping a swift kick to the balls. "Go on, then, show him. I will explain that we're in love and that we made a mistake. I'll take the blame. You've got nothing on her. Nothing!"

"My, my." I press my hand over my heart. "What big teeth you have," I mock because this jackass makes stupid look like fucking Einstein.

His attempts to backpedal come too little, too late, because if he really cared about Keira, he wouldn't have dangled her like a carrot off a stick. He walks over to her, rubbing her arm like the big hero that he is. Too bad he's about to go from hero to zero in seconds.

Not bothering to turn the screen around, I press a few buttons and pull up the footage from earlier—the footage of Keira undressing at my command. Gail pales, while Keira flushes. "He told me to do it!" she pleads, turning to him, begging he see reason.

But the only thing he sees is Keira confessing her need to be fucked six ways to Sunday by yours truly—public enemy number one.

"You were supposed to flirt with him, not fuck him!" he screams, jabbing his pointer toward the screen.

"Oh, shit, really? Well, that just sucks for you."

"What's that supposed to mean?" he snarls, his eyes darting

between me and the screen.

So done with this conversation, I stand and brush an invisible piece of fluff from my white shirt. "It means…" I level the playing field, using Keira's words against her. "I fucked her good." It's what she told Mary in the bathroom, so I'm just repeating what she claims to be true.

"How could you?" Gail looks like he's about to tear up. I pass him a Kleenex.

"He's lying!" Keira begs as she latches onto his arm. We're all caught in a web of lies.

"I have no idea what kind of arrangement you have, but whoring out the one you love for your gain is fucking messed up. You should both be ashamed of yourselves," I say, plotting them against one another. I don't have to try hard, however.

Keira bursts into tears, while the world comes crashing down for Gail. "Game over, cuntwaffle. You lose. Now get the fuck out my office before I call security. You're trespassing."

Gail stands his ground, all huffy and puffy. His arms are out to the side, his chest rising and falling as he decides whether to flee or fight. If he knows what's good for him, he will pack up his office, change his name, and move far, far away.

"You've ruined me," he states, nostrils flared.

But that's where he's wrong. "That shit's not on me. We all make decisions, good and bad. Let this be a lesson learned." I can relate to this comment. We all can.

Keira is the first to take the plea deal, knowing this is the best it's going to get for her. She can now move away to some exotic country and find herself a sugar daddy who won't know the sins of her past. As she makes a run for the door, I decide to deliver some words of wisdom.

"Keira…" She stops, but doesn't turn to face me. "Don't settle. I don't claim to know or understand what toxic relationships you've been in, but if I were you…I'd get a dog." She yanks open the door and slams it shut, not at all touched by my speech.

Slipping into my suit jacket, I have no idea why Gail is still staring at me. This conversation was done like two minutes ago. "This isn't over." If that's his parting words, then boo hoo for him.

A few more seconds pass with him eyeballing me before he finally leaves my life for good. The moment he's gone, I take a deep breath, proud of all I've managed to achieve. I meant it when I said we're the master of our own choices, and I could have gone to the board with everything I have and ruined both Keira and Gail for good, but I didn't. I gave them a choice, and I can only hope they learn and move on.

Everyone deserves a second chance…and that's called tomorrow. I'm hoping when tomorrow comes, things may look brighter. And that right there, kids, is what adulting is all about. So why do I still feel like dying? Looking at the shelf where the book which is really a camera sits, I thank Mary for once again saving my ass. Wherever she is, I hope she's happy, and that when tomorrow comes…she'll put me out of my misery and fucking call.

"Holy shit. Is that really our best friend, Hunter O'Shea?"
In response, I flip Dix and Finch off. "Eat me."
I've missed these jackasses, but they understood I needed

time to get over whatever the fuck this is. How long does it take? I feel like I'm mourning, like someone has fucking died. I have no idea what the timeframe is for this sort of thing, so to dull the pain, I raise my hand, indicating I need scotch and I need it now.

"Have you been working out?" Dix teases as I pull up the barstool beside him. I know I look like shit.

"Have you changed hair product? Wow, there's so much volume." I attempt to run my fingers through it, but he dodges my advances. The guy has style, but I still like to give him shit for looking like an Italian playboy.

Before either start with the inevitable "talk," I reach into my back pocket, producing a bright pink sash. "What's a bachelor party without shaming the groom?" He doesn't have time to protest as I slip the novelty over his chest.

Biting my knuckle and sniffing away fake tears, I blubber, "My little boy is all grown up."

Dix peers down at his sash and bursts into laughter when he sees a picture of a bride and groom. "Game over. Nice," he says, reading what is written in white letters.

So far, things have gone exceptionally well. Typical of Finch to start the waterworks early. "I'm just going to say it…do you need a hug?" He outstretches his arms, while I throw a coaster at his head.

"Stop with the hugging and the pity party. I'm fine. A-fucking-okay." Both my friends can go to hell when they sip their drinks, not at all convinced by my below par acting. "Let's par-tay! Scotch. And two beers, thanks." The bartender looks at my haggard appearance and nods. We've all been there.

I can sense what's coming even before Dixon opens his

mouth. "How you been?"

"Fabulous. Now stop talking and let's get drunk already."

I know he wants me to talk about it because all he's managed to get out of me have been a few apathetic grunts and many fuck offs. But what do I say? I don't even know how to describe what I'm feeling, because everything hurts and I want to die. A tad overdramatic? Maybe, but life has lost its flavor since Mary left me.

"Cut the bullshit. If this were me, you'd slap me up the side of the head and tell me to snap the fuck out of it." On cue, he slaps the back of my head.

"Motherfucker! Well, lucky for me, I'm not you then," I reply, rubbing my scalp.

Once my drinks are set down in front of me, I dive for them like the desperate man that I am. I feel a touch better, but I know once the buzz wears off, I'll feel like roadkill again.

"Dix is right."

"Dix is never right," I counter, while Dixon flips me off.

Finch ignores our banter. "It's hard to believe that so many nights ago, we sat here, at this exact bar, attempting to get Dixon's head out of his ass. You can't blame us for wanting to do the same for you." When Finch realizes what he just said, he quickly leans forward and apologizes. "No offense."

"None taken." Dixon waves him off.

"The difference is I'm fine. I no longer have some she-devil trying to ruin my life, and I shipped Gail off to who gives a fuck. All in all, a good day."

"Have you spoken to Mary?" And just like that, my speech swan dives into epic fail territory.

"Why would you ask me that?"

"Just making conversation," Dixon replies with a smirk. "Besides, this is payback for being a major pain in my ass. But in saying that, if it wasn't for you, and you, big fella"—he nudges Finch in the ribs—"I wouldn't be marrying the love of my life in two weeks. You can choose to clam up, that's fine, but take it from experience, it won't get you anywhere. You'll end up even more miserable than you already are."

"That's not possible," I mumble into my glass. So far, this bachelor party blows ass.

"Hunt, dude, talk to us. No judgment. You can even cry a little if it makes you feel better."

"Fuck you." I smirk, hating how well Dixon knows me. I had a weak moment, and now, they're not going to let it slide.

Tossing back my drink, I reach for my beer, because I need alcohol to deal with these demons. "I fucked up. She fucked up. Bottom line is, we both need to find ourselves or something." I take a swig, making a pained face. "I don't even know what that means."

"See, that wasn't so bad, right?" Finch attempts to fist bump me, but I shoot him down.

"It's horrible," I state, the word vomit slowly rising. I try and cram it down, but it's useless. "The other day, I cried…at a fucking infomercial." Dixon almost gives himself whiplash as he turns to look at me, entertained. "Some chick said no one liked her 'cause she had yellow teeth. Her teeth were perfect, but she claimed after she used some charcoal teeth whitener, all the boys asked her out. So it had me thinking, maybe I need this shit. She looks content enough with her glowing smile, surrounded by doting men, maybe I needed some magical potion to make Mary like me again. But now I'm stuck with twelve boxes of this crap which tastes like Satan's asshole, my teeth aren't any whiter, and Mary still wants nothing to do with me!"

Finch nods considerately, while Dixon is about to fall off his seat in hysterics. Screw him.

"Oh my god," he pants, breathing steadily through his mouth as he grips the edge of the bar. "That is the funniest thing I've heard all day."

"Don't listen to him, Hunter. The whitener obviously is a metaphor for the void in your heart."

"And wallet," Dix counters, still laughing like the asshole that he is.

"Forget it." I go to stand, feeling like a complete chump.

"Oh, sit your ass down." Dixon yanks down on my arm, planting me back in my seat. Once he's semi-composed, he exhales. "Welcome to the real world, my friend. This is what self-sacrifice feels like. True love is selfless and what you did was pretty damn noble. From the small snippets of information you've given us, it seems Mary needs to find herself before she can find herself with you."

"Yes, that's exactly right!" I almost launch off my chair in excitement. "How long does that normally take?"

"There's no handbook, Hunt. It may take weeks, months, years, maybe never."

"Never? But she said she needs time to think, and I've given her that. I just…" I pause, pensively rubbing over my chest. "When does it stop hurting?"

Dixon sighs, wrapping an arm around my shoulder. "In the end, some of your greatest pain become your greatest strengths. You've already proven that."

"But I miss her. A lot." I peel the label from my bottle,

knowing I'm two sips away from breaking down and sobbing on Dix's shoulder.

"I know, man, but you can't rush these things. I know you want to call her, croon to Sinatra under her bedroom window, I get it. I've been there. We both have." Finch nods. "But you can't force this. Give whatever this is—love, friendship, co-existence, time to grow. That's the only thing you can do to be sure that she's the one for you."

"I already know she's the one for me. But what if I'm not the one for her?" The question tastes like acid, but I needed to ask it.

"Then you move on, buddy. You take this experience and you turn it into something amazing with someone else."

"I don't want anybody else. I just want her. The thought of touching another woman has me wanting to cut off my own dick. And you know how attached I am to it." The flirty bartender places another Budweiser in front of me with a wink. Do I give off a desperate, dateless vibe?

"On the house," she whispers. It appears so. I barely look at her because the red label reminds me of Mary's hair.

Dixon chuckles, ignoring the overhelpful barmaid. "This isn't your average scenario. Most couples break up because the guy does something stupid, but in this case, Mary is just as scared as you are of being happy. Guys are the ones who usually run away, but in your story, it's Mary."

"If this is supposed to cheer me up…it's not working."

"I know you feel like shit, but I promise, things will get better." Dixon's reassurance has me feeling less suicidal.

"You promise? 'Cause if you're fucking lying, you'll pay dearly at your real bachelor party. This is just a teaser." When he opens his mouth, I cut him off. "Just 'cause I'm incredibly moody, possibly going through puberty, and most likely will sob uncontrollably at the drop of a hat, does not mean I've forgotten about this rite of passage. It's going to be epic, and I need epic after…" And cue the tears.

"Okay, dude. I can't wait." Fuck, I love this big hunk of man. "But this right here"—he hooks his thumb between Finch and me—"it's all I want."

"We've come full circle," Finch says nostalgically. "I can't believe how far we've come. I'm honored to call you guys my best friends." Finch is trying to kill me. With my emotions running haywire, he can't say shit like that and expect me not to cry into my beer.

We raise our glasses, toasting to our good fortune of being alive. And the fact Dixon will be a married man in two weeks' time. "I wish I'd spoken to you sooner about this," I confess, while Dixon shrugs.

"Don't sweat it. You live and you learn. I'm only here today because of you two. You both carried me on your shoulders when I didn't want to get back up. I'll never forget that. I've got your back, brother. Always."

Finch sniffs, but it's useless. "Oh, man, I promised myself I wouldn't cry." Dixon draws him into his side.

I once believed that Dixon was the glue that held this threesome together, but I now know we've all been the adhesive at one time or another. What we have is an unbreakable bond.

As Dix flags down the bartender, I nudge him with my shoulder. "FYI, you were right."

"Can I get that in writing?" He smirks, paying for this scotch.

"Keira was a gigantic bitch in the making. Wonder if she consulted McCunty for pointers?"

Dixon's mouth parts in horror. "Holy shit. Tell me everything." He orders another round, hinting this is going to be a late night. Maybe this bachelor party won't suck after all.

The table is littered with empty glasses, and it's a sight I've sorely missed. I've told the boys everything and just like always, they've made me feel like me again.

I'm going to once in my life listen to them and give Mary the time she needs. Dixon suggested I take up a hobby to occupy my time. I informed him that annoying him is a pastime which suits me just fine. The liquor is running freely and we're all in good spirits, reminiscing about the good ol' days.

We've gone through a lot of shit together, and honestly, I'm surprised we're not in jail or dead. My mind has been Mary-free and it's been a nice reprieve.

"I need to take a piss," I very ungracefully state.

Finch nurses his second beer, while Dixon and I have lost count. As I go to stand, I almost fall onto my ass, no surprise there as I passed coordination about five shots ago. Finch and Dix shoot upright, offering me their shoulders, which I happily accept.

Dixon isn't any help because he's drunker than I am, but we sway toward the bathroom, laughing at how ridiculous we look. Finch is the navigator, no surprise there, but when he shrieks and suddenly dances in front of me like he's Patrick Swayze himself, I wonder if maybe someone slipped a mickey into his drink.

"Whatever you're on, I want some, and now." Finch ignores me and continues to rhumba in front of me, arms raised and waving frantically in the air. "What in the ever-living hell are you doing? I'm way too drunk to deal with this shit. And I need to piss."

I attempt to shove past him, but he dives forward and hugs me. "I love you, man." I look at Dixon, who shrugs.

Finch is holding on tight, veering me back toward the bar and away from the front window. "C'mon, let's get another drink. I want to get hammered and see some boobies!"

Tonight has just gone from fun to fucking funny. "Okay, dude, I just need to take a…" But the words die in my throat when a flash of red flickers before my eyes. I may be blind drunk, but I'd recognize those copper curls anywhere.

Finch exhales, letting me go. It takes me a second, but I realize what he was doing. He saw Mary walk by first, but why would he think I wouldn't want to see her? Yes, I'm hurting, but after talking to the boys, I'm in a good headspace.

This is what spurs me to say, "I'm going to say hello."

"No, Hunt, don't!" he all but screams, latching onto my arm. It's too late as I push through the crowd to find her.

It's a warm night and the sidewalk is bustling, but my six-foot-four frame allows me the height gain I need. I use her trademark red waves as my beacon and push my way through the crowd. Dixon and Finch are hollering behind me to stop, but now that she's within grasp, the devil is at my heels and I sprint forward, desperate to see her.

It feels like years since I last saw her. My heart beats like crazy, and I suddenly wish I wasn't so fucking drunk, because my brain and mouth are so not attached right now. "Mary!" I bellow, cupping my mouth with both palms, but she doesn't turn.

With sheer determination, I excuse myself as I charge through the throngs of people, most of which move off to the side when they see me coming. When she's a few feet away, I call out to her again. "Shortcake!"

Bingo.

She stops and turns her ear, as if questioning whether she really heard me or not. I clear up any confusion when I race toward her, tapping her on the shoulder. The moment she turns, fucking angels sing and a ray of light shines down from above. It may be a streetlight, but I don't care because she's here, standing before me, taking my breath away.

I want to say so many things, but I can't. I need a moment, because after so many weeks, I feel like my heart has kickstarted back to life. Those killer curves have me salivating, remembering how I traced my tongue over each one. Her long waves are flowing freely, framing her beautiful heart-shaped face. Fuck, I've missed her.

"Hunter?" I've caught her off guard, as she shakes her head, appearing to only just realize it's me. A flash of pink darts out to wet her upper lip, and it takes all my willpower not to drop to my knees and worship her like the goddess that she is.

Nothing else matters but telling her how I feel. I know I've said it once before, but now, I plan on screaming it at the top of my lungs. I'm not ashamed, because I love this woman with everything that I am and I want everyone to know. Dixon's advice of giving her time can blow me.

"Mar…" Sadly, my confession gets shot down in flames when someone juts their hand out, drawing attention to the fact that we're not alone.

"Hunter? I can't believe it. I've heard so much about you. It's so nice to finally meet you." I get doused with an icy cold bucket of 'what in the ever-living, fucking hell is going on.'

Standing in front of me is a Kung-Fu god. He could easily be related to Bruce Lee, because he has the movie star looks and a body made of pure granite. I've never seen this dude before, but Mary's reddening cheeks reveal that she has.

There must be some mistake. In my alcoholic state, I must be hallucinating. I rub my eyes to make sure. But when he's still here, palm still extended, waiting to shake the loser's hand, I know this is real.

They're both dressed nicely, probably because they just finished up with dinner, maybe a movie, and now they're going back to someone's apartment to do unspeakable nasties with the other while I go home to cry into my pillow.

Ripples of anger roll over me and I get ready to throw down. "Who the fuck are you?" I slap his hand away, as I have no intention shaking it. Now or ever.

"Hunter!" Mary snaps, quickly apologizing for my behavior, but this is only the tip of the iceberg. I lunge for him, ready to tear off his head and play lacrosse with it.

"C'mon, man, walk it off." Dix is at my back, dragging me away, but I shrug him off.

"You've heard so much about me? Funny that, because I've never heard of you. I should feel honored Mary mentioned me at all, I mean, it's been radio silence on her end for weeks…now I know why."

She glares at me, but fuck this. She was supposed to be clearing her head, finding herself, all of that Oprah shit, but now I see she was only finding some other sucker to play head games with.

"Dixon, take him home. He's drunk," she spits, gently tugging on her admirer's arm. The simple touch ignites a wrath so manic, I act before I can think this through. My heart is broken—what do I care if my arm is too?

With a warrior cry, I charge forward, fists swinging, and hook the motherfucker right in the jaw. Mary screams at me to stop, which only incites me to hit him again. The impact doesn't alleviate my pain or anger, so I attempt to strike him once more. My lucky streak is over with however, because my initial thought of him being a martial arts god wasn't too far off the mark. He bends low and fucking karate chops my neck, which drops me to the ground, winded and clutching my throat.

Finch drops to his knees, asking if I'm okay, but when I hear Dixon cry, "You motherfucker!" I know in about three seconds, he'll be tending to both our wounds. I underestimated Bruce Lee Junior, because it only takes him two. Dixon drops to the ground beside me, clutching his bleeding nose.

"Oh my god! He broke your nose!" Finch exclaims, paling.

"No shit, Sherlock," Dixon mutters from around his cupped hand. "I'm fine."

Finch however, is anything but fine because he goes from white to green to gray before my eyes. "Wow, it's so red. Blood is red. Blood..."

"Shit!" both Dixon and I shout, lunging forward to catch Finch, because he just fainted. I totally forgot he's squeamish.

"Finch!" I hoarsely say in barely a whisper, because I'm still attempting to retrieve my windpipe from the pavement. I slap his cheeks. "Fuck, he's out cold." Dixon rips off his sash and uses it as a makeshift pillow to place under Finch's head.

This would be fucking hilarious if it was happening to anyone other than me, but thanks to my recklessness, my two best friends look like roadkill. Some best man I am.

"I'll get a cab." As Mary attempts to hail a taxi, I thrust out my palm.

"No, you've done enough. Just go." Lifting my eyes to meet hers, I squash down the need to console her because I know I've just hurt her feelings. This isn't tit for tat, but she fucking destroyed me the moment she gave me a taste of something that was always going to be out of my reach.

"Hunter…"

"I said go, Mary." A crowd has formed, and I know the NYPD aren't too far away. Her poignant eyes glisten with tears, but she's made her choice, and I've made mine.

"Looks like some things never change."

"Looks that way, although the same can't be said for the men you welcome into your bed." Her mouth parts, as I've just offended her, but she's not just offended me, she's ruined me.

I know when she leaves because that emptiness returns.

In the cab ride back to my apartment, with Dixon and Finch by my side, I can't help but wonder if this is what closure feels like, because if it is…it can blow me.

"I'm sorry for being the world's suckiest friend," I say to Dixon. Finch is slouched in a comatose ball, probably regretting the day he met me.

"Don't be so hard on yourself." The fact Dix looks like he just massacred an entire village only cements my point. "You did just see…"

But I wave him off, not wanting to talk about this ever again. "I needed to see what I saw, man. I need to move on and accept this for what it was."

"And what was that?"

"Something that was bound to end in tears," I conclude.

Dixon sighs, moving his mouth from side to side. "At least you know."

I nod, wishing like hell that throat punch knocked me out cold. "I know I wasn't wired for this relationship shit, and I was stupid ever believing that I was. I thought this was amicable, that we were on the same page. What a fucking idiot I am."

"Hunt…"

But I'm done talking. "From now on, I forget about Mary. I thought our break-up"—I can't help but air quote our sham—"was anti-climatic, but now I know the reason is because we weren't ever really together. If we were, she wouldn't be so quick to replace me. The thought of touching another woman makes me sick, but it seems you're right, Dix."

He waits for me to continue.

"Mary did run away and I guess now…it's time I do the same."

Now is the time Dixon would reprimand me for giving up, but when he remains tight-lipped and gives me a manly hug, I know it's time I stopped moping and take a page out of Mary's book and move the fuck on.

Nineteen

"On a scale of one to ten…how angry is Cherry Pie?"

Dixon pauses from looping his tie, looking at my reflection in the full-length mirror. "Eleven." Groaning, I tip my head toward the ceiling, wishing I had some scotch.

Today is the big day—the day my best friend gets married to the love of his life. Readers at home, I know what you're thinking—about fucking time. But this story is about me, and my uncanny ability to create a shitstorm wherever I go.

Thanks to Dix being the chivalrous brute that he is, his nose resembles a potato. The swelling has gone down, but the bruising is every color of the rainbow. If you look over the rainbow, you just may see Dixon's nose. The doctors said it should straighten, but I think from now on he'll be known as Mr. Potato Head.

"Dude, I'm so fucking sorry. I can't believe he fly kicked you

349

in the nose. That takes some skill." Dixon chuckles.

It goes without saying I am DONE with women. After the bachelor party from hell where us three amigos ended up in the ER and a cucumber wasn't even involved, I promised myself that this was the last time.

This is for the best. I was crazy to think Mary and I would work. I mean, all we do is fight. She obviously thinks the same way, seeing as she's now shacking up with the karate kid. I made Dixon promise to mind his own business and not go snooping. Sometimes, the truth can be so much worse than what you could ever imagine, and I have a feeling this is one of those times.

"Don't worry about it. What's done is done. Besides, it adds character." I know he's only trying to make me feel better, but when Maddy and him are old and gray, they will look back on their wedding photos remembering what a jackass their best man is.

Ugh, I need a drink.

"Have you got the rings?"

Patting down my pockets, I open my mouth, faking horror. When Dixon looks about ready to cry, I smirk. "Of course, I have the rings." I grip my crotch, while Dixon blanches.

"Please tell me your cock is not minding the ring I'm about to slip onto my beloved's finger."

"It's the safest place to be. He hardly sees the light of day anymore, thanks to my newfound no pussy rule. Besides, your jewels next to my jewels. How fucking romantic is that?" Dixon shakes his head, not swayed. Fucking party pooper.

He reaches for his suit jacket, hinting it's time to get this show on the road. "Let me take a look at you."

Dixon grins, turning in a showy circle, but jokes aside, I think I'm about to fucking tear up. He looks like a groom from the gods, showcasing a rocking navy three-piece suit. A matching tie complements the crispness of his white shirt. A white rose is pinned to the lapel of his jacket. All in all, this entire ensemble represents just how far my best friend has come. He's jumped many hurdles and he's swam through tough tides, but in the end, he's here, about to marry his soulmate, and I couldn't be prouder to be standing by his side when he does.

"Are you fucking crying?" And just like that, I'm reminded why I love this man more than life itself.

"I'm not crying," I claim, discreetly wiping my eye. "I have something in my eye."

Dixon laughs, slapping me on the back.

"Come on. We're about to break tradition and be the ones who are late."

Swallowing down my drama queen episode, I slip into my matching suit jacket, and if I do say so myself, we're two fine looking cats. Dixon's father comes into the room, making that equation three cool dudes.

"Ciao, Papa. Pronto?" Mr. Di Matteo nods, and I've never seen him happier.

We make our way into the living room, Dixon doing a last look around his home to ensure he has everything. When he's set, he exhales. "Holy shit. I'm fucking nervous."

"Don't be. You've got this."

Dixon nods, rubbing his hands together, appearing to take in the fact that when he returns here tonight, he will be a married man. "Thank you, Hunt. I couldn't have done this without you."

But what he doesn't realize is that he's been my rock as well.

"You can make out in the car. Let's go already." The front door opens and in strolls my other half—Finch.

There was no way Dixon was only having one of us up there with him. In his eyes, we're both his best men, so it only seems fitting that is reflected on the big day.

"Sorry, Mr. Di Matteo." Finch quickly excuses his quip, while Mr. Di Matteo waves him off with a laugh. I can see where Dixon gets his sense of humor from.

With nothing but the road ahead, we make our way toward the car. When Dixon sees the beast in front of him, he stops and turns to me with a grin. "Your doing, I assume?"

The sexy ass, stretched, Hummer limo, is begging I take her for a spin around the block. "Damn straight. I'm getting hard just looking at it."

"I'm going to have to get those rings sanitized."

The driver arranges the ramp so we're able to wheel Mr. Di Matteo into the limo. We follow once he's settled in. Move over, Kitt, the inside of this thing is a disco on wheels. The moment the engine roars to life, I holler and crack open the good stuff.

"Champagne is the more traditional drink," Finch says as I pour a decent helping of scotch into three glasses. Dixon reaches for a bottle of water for his dad.

"Champagne can suck a dick. My best friend is getting married and he's hitting the hard stuff before he officially surrenders his balls."

As I pass around our drinks, I decide to call a toast—one of many, I presume. "Here's to you, Dix. I'd say good luck, but you don't need it."

"Cheers!" Finch says as we smash our glasses and throw

back our drinks. The venue is about thirty minutes away, so we have a lot of drinking time to spare.

I'm onto my third scotch when Finch says, "You going to be okay, Hunt?" I don't need a roadmap. I know exactly what he's asking. I could brush it off, but sitting here in my Sunday best has me feeling like a fraud if I don't confess that I'm fucking nervous.

Considering the last time I saw Mary, I pretty much hinted she can fuck off and never be found, I don't know how she'll react to being my partner for the day. I've missed all the rehearsals, but how hard can it be? Stand by the big man, produce the rings, sign some shit, then we're done. This is going to be a breeze.

"I'll be okay. I promise to be on my best behavior." Dixon's dad is the first one to snort in laughter, while the other two chumps follow suit.

When we pull up to The Ivy, Dixon rubs his palms onto his legs. "Fuck me, this is really happening." It's almost unheard of to see him nervous, but one can't blame him for wanting to shit a brick.

"It's okay. Just breathe. Think of Maddy," Finch wisely says. My words of wisdom are to pass Dixon the bottle of scotch, which he happily accepts.

Once he takes a decent gulp, he nods. "Let's do this."

The moment the driver opens the door, we're assaulted by flashes from the wedding photographer, who is photo happy. He has us posing in every position possible, and after a while, we go a little stir crazy and the last photo he takes is of me carrying Dixon over an imaginary threshold.

We walk into the grand foyer, where we're greeted by a man

in a bright orange suit. "You look absolutely ravishing," he says to Dixon, kissing both his cheeks. When he sets eyes on me, he winks. "You too, handsome."

"Thanks, Thomas. Thomas, this is my other best man, Hunter."

Thomas puts a hand to his hip. "You're the one I've heard so much about."

"Trust me, it's all lies," I reply with a grin.

"That's a shame then," he counters with a sly grin of his own. "Come on then, I'll show you where to stand."

Taking a look around at all the white, I realize this is really happening. Just beyond those double doors is where Dixon will be saying I do. Without further ado, I clap my hands together and smile. "Let's get this show on the road."

Thomas nods happily, pushing open the doors to reveal a fucking Garden of Eden. The ceremony is to be held outdoors, so the backdrop is green and lush. A white curtained arch is yards away, and on top sits an array of roses. A white, makeshift aisle has rose petals scattered on and alongside it, where white chairs, filled to the brim with people, are lined up either side. Bouquets of colorful flowers are attached to the end chairs, a white curtain sash draped between each. The final touch is the lake behind the archway. It doesn't get any more romantic than this.

"Like it?" Thomas asks when we're standing around, dicks in hand.

"You've outdone yourself," Dixon says in awe.

We walk down the aisle, Dixon shaking hands with family and friends, while Finch, Mr. Di Matteo, and I follow behind. It's a full house and the excitement is palpable. I forget my Mary woes and concentrate on what's important, and that's standing by my brother.

Thomas arranges us, changing the angle of our bodies until we're perfect. When he dallies a little too long, hands around my waist, I know he's sweet on me. "Save me a dance?" he says light-heartedly.

I nod. "You better have packed your dancing shoes."

When we're arranged with military precision, Thomas runs off, gesturing for something to commence. I find out what that is soon enough when a soft piece of music sounds over the speakers. Dixon stands tall, all nerves long gone, because in mere minutes, his soulmate will walk down this aisle and be his forever.

Finch beats me to the punch and blows his nose. "I always cry at weddings."

As we're waiting for the girls to arrive, Mr. Di Matteo wheels his chair over to Dixon and gestures he's to come close. Dixon does, and when I hear why, the waterworks threaten to start early. "Sono fiero di te, mio figlio."

Tears prick Dixon's eyes as he kisses his dad's forehead. "I'm proud of you too, Papa."

Oh my god. I need to pull it together because one blubbering best man is enough.

Dixon stands back in line and the doors open to reveal Heidi. Finch snuffles when he sees his wife looking more beautiful than I ever remember seeing her. She's wearing a soft lavender dress, which makes her look angelic. She smiles at Finch, shaking her head at his inability to hold back the tears.

She stands to the side, opposite Finch and mouths, "I love you." I'm pretty sure he can fill the lake behind us with his tears.

I know what's going to happen next, but even though I know, it does not make it any easier to accept. In seconds, Mary will be following in Heidi's footsteps, and I will be following in Finch's. I know I convinced myself that she's toxic, no good for my health, but tell that to my racing heart and sweaty palms, because I'm moments away from imploding. The music picks up and then, the doors open.

My heart stops beating.

Mary stands at the end of the aisle, her eyes ahead and focused on…me. I thought I'd see hate, anger, but instead, I see relief and a glimmer of a smile. I'm too far gone to even dissect what that means, but Dixon turns over his shoulder and smiles. "You've got this," he mouths, and his faith in me has me standing tall.

Mary commences her graceful walk down the aisle, and if this was a perfect world, she would be walking toward me, ready to say I do. But that dream is long gone.

Her dress matches Heidi's, and the color brings out the fiery red in her hair. She doesn't just look beautiful, she is a vision, one I will never forget. I want to pretend she isn't looking straight at me every step of the way, but she is, and I don't understand why. Only when she takes her place near Heidi does she lower her eyes, and my heart commences beating once more.

The guests stand and the music suddenly changes, the traditional wedding march announcing what's about to happen. Dixon inhales, and the doors open and an angel is delivered.

Madison stands in the doorway, her arm looped through her father's as she locks eyes with Dixon. This moment is one you see in the movies, or read about in books because it's absolutely perfect. There is no doubting their story ends in a happily ever after, and after all the turmoil they've been through, they deserve nothing less.

Maddy begins her walk, owning every step as the crowd coos and the photographer captures every moment. Dixon shuffles, running a hand over the back of his neck. He's nervous, not that I can blame him. So just how he has done time and time again, I step forward, placing my hand on his upper shoulder. No words are spoken, because none are needed. I'm here for him and I never plan on leaving his side.

Finch does the same, and we support our friend as he watches the love of his life seal their futures forever. Maddy stops when she's a couple feet away. Her father lifts the veil from her face, kissing her cheek. He shakes Dixon's hand, nodding his approval.

Finch and I retake our places, but Dixon seems transfixed, unable to tear his gaze from Maddy. Not that I can blame him. She looks beautiful.

The priest behind us shuffles from the sidelines to stand under the arch, hinting Maddy and Dixon are to follow, but Dixon has other plans as he swoops forward and kisses Maddy. The crowd laughs and claps.

"I'm pretty sure that happens after you're pronounced man and wife," I state with a chuckle. In response, Dixon, still lip-locked with Maddy, flips me off.

Once they're done, Dixon looks like a new man and smiles broadly. "Hello, Angelo."

"Hi, Dixon," she replies, her cheeks a bright pink as she touches up her lipstick.

"Whenever you're ready," the priest says with a smile.

Dixon and Maddy make their way to where he stands,

while Finch and I wait eagerly to see our boy bring this home.

"Today is a celebration. A celebration of love and commitment. It's evident that these two are the perfect examples of what that represents." The crowd laughs as their PDA also represented their wedding night is going to be a celebration of something else.

He goes on with his heartfelt speech and I listen, too afraid to do anything else. I can sense Mary, and I know that's fucking creepy. I was expecting a wave of hostility, maybe even a flying bouquet at my head, but for once in my life, I can't read her.

She's conflicted, that much is true, but why? I thought we were a done deal—last week's news. But I don't get that from her. I rub over my chest, the heartburn returning.

"Hunt…the rings." Finch's whisper wakes me the fuck up.

When I come to, I realize everyone is staring at me, Dixon included, who looks at my groin, shaking his head. I reach into my inner breast pocket and produce the rings. Surprise, fucker.

"I thought they were in your pants," he whispers when I hand the rings over to the priest.

"What kind of pervert do you think I am?" I admonish with a smirk. I give Maddy's cheek a kiss. "You look beautiful, Cherry Pie."

She smiles, giving me a tender hug. "You're still not off the hook." Fair call.

The priest blesses the rings and then the vows are to take place. "Dixon…"

Dix reaches for Maddy's hands and interlaces them tightly. In true Dix fashion, he wrote his own vows. "Angelo…saying I love you isn't enough, because what I feel for you…it extends past anything I've ever known. From the moment I met you, I knew you'd change my life, I just didn't realize how much so. You're the strongest person I know. We've overcome leaps and bounds and the fact you're standing here, willing to marry me, makes me the luckiest son of a bitch in the world. Sorry, Father," he adds, excusing his blasphemy.

"I choose you because there is no other choice…you're not the missing piece of my heart…you're the entire thing. My heart beats for you. Always. I love you because you are simply you. My Angelo."

Finch bursts into tears, and I pass him a handkerchief. The entire audience has teared up, me included, because those words are everything I feel for Mary. I may not be able to express them as eloquently as Dix, but I feel every single thing he feels.

I risk a look at her because my convictions are thrown to the wind, sinking to the bottom of the lake. I want to forget her, but how can I forget someone who gave me so much to remember? I know she's moved on, and here's hoping one day, I will too. But for now, I lower my guard and let go of my anger and allow her to see that I fucking miss her, and I probably will for the rest of my life.

Tears roll down her cheeks, but she quickly brushes them away. I openly look at her, knowing that in seconds she will mouth what a disgusting creep I am. But holy fuck, it's a miracle when something called a smile plays at her lips. The sun beams down, a sign from the heavens, and in response, I smile in return.

"Dixon and Madison have formalized the existence of the bond between them with those beautiful vows and the exchanging of rings. Therefore, it's my great pleasure to now pronounce them husband and wife. Now you may kiss your bride."

The air erupts with catcalls and cheers as my best friend takes his now wife and kisses the living shit out of her. Dixon's wedding band catches the sunlight, and fuck me, my heart swells. He did it. New York's former manwhore is officially off the table. But the way he's kissing Maddy, there definitely will be some on table action tonight.

Once the kisses and cheers are done with, the music plays and we're to sign the marriage certificate. Thomas runs over subtly and nudges me when I stand, rooted to the spot. Mary walks to the table, taking the pen to sign her name. I, on the other hand, have forgotten my name, because all I can center on is her.

Finally, after Thomas shoves me with all his might, I move, almost falling on my ass as I attempt to play it cool. Once Mary is done, she glances up and passes me the pen. I forget why I'm here. "Hi."

She blinks once. "Hi." I'm waiting for a string of expletives to follow, but none do. "I like your suit."

"I like you." It's out before I can stop myself. The mother of all slip-ups.

But I'm surprised once again when Mary laughs. Has she always been this beautiful? I know the answer is hell to the fuck yes.

Finch clears his throat behind me, snapping me into the now. I smile and she smiles back, before taking her place next to Heidi. Too much is happening and my brain is short-circuiting. I'm supposed to be done with her, but I feel like things haven't even begun.

Dixon looks at me, his arm wrapped tightly around Maddy

as he nods. A simple look can convey a million words they say, but this only suggests one—fight…for the one you…love.

"I'm proud of you," Dixon whispers into my ear as I guzzle my beer. I'm glad someone is, because after Dixon's heartfelt speech, all I can think about is forgetting everything I thought I knew and telling Mary this is not over for me, it never was.

But every time I get within three feet of her, I choke up and then run and hide. I know this isn't the time nor the place, but each drink gives me balls I've lacked this entire time. Verbal diarrhea is lapping at the surface, so when the emcee says it's time for speeches, I know this will only end one way.

I slam my lips shut and shake my head, staring wide-eyed at Dixon. If he gives me that microphone, I'm going to declare to the world that I love Mary and I want her back. But Dixon doesn't seem to care. "Since when have you held back? Don't disappoint me now."

Why is he goading me?

"Dix…" I protest, waving my hand. "I'm fucking…scared."

Dixon smiles, wrapping an arm around my shoulder. "It's okay to be scared. Being scared means you're about to do something brave." My giblets are on the cusp of sobbing like a baby, but Dixon puts us back on track. "So stop being a pussy and go get your girl." This speech is reminiscent of the one I gave him.

Right on!

Standing, I accept the microphone, which elicits a roar

from the guests. I roll up my sleeves. Game on. I take a moment to look into the sea of faces. The fact they're here, happy to celebrate the union of two people, spurs me on.

"Hi, I'm Hunter. The best man. As you can see"—I point to Finch—"there are two of us, but we all know I'm the better man." The crowd laughs, while Finch slow claps with a smile. "So, we're all here to celebrate the marriage of Madison and Dixon. I won't lie, there was a time when I wanted to marry Dix. I mean, look at him." I turn over my shoulder to blow him a kiss. "But if anyone else was going to marry my best friend, then I couldn't think of a more suitable partner than Maddy, aka Cherry Pie." The crowd coos, while I reach for my beer, needing the Dutch courage. "I won't go into detail because it could be used against me in a court of law, but Dixon has been there for me through thick and thin. Not once did he give up on me… even when most people did." I clear my throat, the air thick with anticipation. "Truth is, I look up to Dix, I always have. He's been able to turn his life around and find his forever…"

Oh, sweet Jesus, give me the strength.

Turning around, I look at Mary, who is sitting quietly, eyes lowered. Just the sight of her provokes me to spill my heart and soul. "I found my forever too…" She slowly lifts her eyes, her mouth parted. "But I fucked up. I'm sorry for the profanity, folks, but there is no other way to explain it. That amazing woman right there…" I point to Mary, who shakes her head, begging I stop. "She drove me crazy from the first moment I laid eyes on her. But I wouldn't have it any other way. I miss you, Mary. Truth is, I miss you all the time. Every second, every minute, every hour, every day. I know you don't feel the same way, but that's okay. I just need you to know that I'll be here waiting for you, because honestly, I don't want anyone else. You're it for me, Shortcake. You've ruined me, but I embrace the chaos because…" here goes nothing… "love is chaos, and I…"

I never get to finish my speech however, because Mary shoots upward and almost topples over her chair as she runs from the table and out the back door. I don't even think twice as I drop the microphone and follow in hot pursuit.

She's fast, running past the chairs which still stand from earlier and ducking under the arch. She continues sprinting toward the lake. The full moon provides the light I need to follow, and although she's quick, I'm quicker. I catch up to her in moments.

"Mary! Please, stop!" My pleas only motivate her to dash left. There is no indication she's going to stop, so with no other choice, I use my football skills and tackle her from behind. She falls with a thud, but I break her fall as best I can.

"Get off of me!" she screams, but I only hold on tighter.

"Not until you calm down!"

"I am calm. I was fine until you had to embarrass me like that. How could you?"

My arms are locked around her heaving chest as I press my trunk to her back. I can feel her heart is as frantic as mine, and I can only hope it's not only the chase which has left her breathless. "I'm sorry, but I had to tell you."

"And you thought a good time would be at our best friend's wedding, in front of hundreds of people?"

"I don't see a better time. Please, just let me talk to you." Her breaths slow down, but the anger never leaves her, not that it ever does whenever I'm involved. Once I think it's safe to let go, I loosen my hold, pushing off of her and sitting.

She launches off the grass and slaps my cheek. This woman has some right arm.

"I deserved that," I say, rubbing my stinging cheek.

"Yes, you did." The act of violence seems to have calmed her somewhat.

We both catch our breaths, waiting for the other to speak. Seeing as I started this, I suppose it only seems fitting I end it. "Mary, I'm sorry for embarrassing you. I'm sorry for a lot of things. But I'm not sorry for the way I feel."

A gasp escapes her.

"I know you've moved on, and as much as it pains me to say this, if you're happy, then I will have to just accept it and hope I can be happy one day too." I swallow down the taste of defeat. "I'm sorry for implying you were some bedhopping…"

However, when Mary laughs madly, tears leaking from her eyes, I think I've missed a chapter somewhere.

"What's so funny?" I ask, watching on confused as she clutches her side, wheezing.

"You…" she manages to choke out. "Sometimes…you just need to shut up." I open my mouth, offended, but she raises her finger, hinting this is one of those times. I comply.

Once she's done cackling like a mad woman, she reaches into her clutch, producing her phone. I watch with interest as she begins to FaceTime. When I see who it is, I'm tempted to smash her phone to smithereens.

"You couldn't wait to talk to your boyfriend until after I left? Here, I'll do you a solid…" As I attempt to stand, she latches onto my bicep and sits me back down.

"Hello, Jim." So, karate kid has a name.

"Hello, Mary." When she turns the screen so he can see

I'm sitting near her, he has the gall to smile. "And if it isn't the infamous Hunter O'Shea. How's the throat?"

"Fuck you, man. You got in a lucky shot."

Jim laughs, rubbing my nose in the fact he's a Kung-Fu ninja Jedi who is fucking the love of my life. "Whatever makes you sleep better at night. I have someone here who wants to speak to you."

Screw you, smart ass.

"I'm pretty sure whoever it is, I have no interest in talking to them." However, I actually choke on air when Jim passes the phone to the man who sits beside him. "Mr. Yeong?" I wish I didn't sound like a little girl, but I do.

"Hello, Mr. O'Shea. You're a hard man to track down." I open my mouth, but nothing except a strangled wheeze comes out. "I'm sorry about my son breaking your friend's nose."

"Your son?" Okay, now I just sound like I'm singing soprano.

Mr. Yeong nods. "Jim is my son."

So, Mary is dating Mr. Yeong's son. This day just gets better and better. "Well, you'll be pleased to know your son has chosen wisely. Mary is a great catch." Mr. Yeong's face twists into a confused frown, while Mary sighs, slapping her forehead.

"We're not dating, you idiot." Jim's face is back on my screen. "Don't get me wrong, she's…"

"What in the holy fuck is going on?" I exclaim, feeling like the stinky kid in class. Everyone is in on this secret, except me.

"You remember the fortune cookie, Mr. O'Shea?" He really wants to talk about this now? All I'm capable of doing is nodding. "It was empty because life is what we make it. There is no one fortune because of the many decisions we're faced with.

You were given a choice to honor my request, or you could have told me to stop being a stupid old man and moved on to someone else. But you never did. I respect that. A man with convictions, determination, and strength is someone I want to give my business to."

"What now?" My mouth hangs open very unattractively.

"I have a confession to make…there is no watch."

"Get the fuck out of here!" I very ungracefully shout.

"Well, there is, but the reason you couldn't find the buyer was because the buyer was me."

Now…don't I feel foolish.

"This was about honor—who was the better man. But more importantly, an honest man."

Words are coming from Mr. Yeong's mouth, but there is no way they can be true.

"Hang on…" I raise my finger, needing a minute. "Are you saying I went on a wild goose chase for nothing?" Mr. Yeong nods with a smile. "Fuck me sideways," I gasp, running a hand over my beard.

"If I'm going to give you my business, you have to have honor. You had to prove yourself to me, and you did. You made no excuses for your behavior because there are no ulterior motives to your game, and I respect that. I wanted a man to show intuition, but most of all…heart. And yours is that of a true champion. Trust is something I don't take lightly, Mr. O'Shea. I'm sorry for testing you, but I had to be sure."

"Why was Jim in New York?"

The screen shifts to Jim. "Because I'm presuming you screened your calls because every time we called, we got a silent fuck you in response. I came to New York to find you, but I remember my father mentioning a redhead who worked in your office. That asshole, Gail, claimed she was his informant, but it took me a few seconds to realize her loyalties always lay with you."

Looks like I got egg on my face.

"I tracked her down and we went out for drinks so I could explain everything. If it wasn't for Mary, and the faith my father has in you, we would be giving our business to someone else. But it seems you grow on people like a benign tumor."

"Thank you, I think."

Mr. Yeong smiles. The first time I've ever seen him happy. That sneaky motherfucker. "I've just made you a very rich man. Don't let me down."

"I won't. You're stuck with me now."

My head is reeling and I can't keep up. But Mr. Yeong is a busy man and I know my two minutes are up. "There is an old Chinese proverb I want to share with you, Mr. O'Shea. He who asks is a fool for five minutes, but he who does not ask remains a fool forever. You've got one shot at life…so make it great." The screen goes blank before I get a chance to thank him and apologize to Jim for being a dick.

My brain plays catch up because there is a lot to catch up on.

So, this entire time I was chasing this watch which actually belonged to Mr. Yeong. It was a test of strength, determination, and loyalty because he's right—his empire is worth billions and he needs to trust the person he puts his faith in.

This whole thing came down to one little word—trust. Something which was once foreign to me, now seems the ruler of my world. And that leads me to asking the one question on everyone's lips.

"Why would you help me, Mary? After everything I did and said, after the way I acted…why?" She is silent, lowering her eyes as she plucks at blades of grass. "You could have told Jim what a fucking asshole I am. That his business is better suited with someone else, but instead, you saved me…again."

Under the moonlight, I can see her lower lip tremble. She's weighing up what to say. "Because…because I love you."

I thought I knew what loving her entailed, but this…this is something else. A miracle. "You love me?" I ask, in case my imagination has slipped into fantasyland once again.

"Yes," she replies, finally meeting my eyes.

I don't know what to say or do. I'm alive, electric, my heart backflipping in utter delight. "Are you sure?"

She bursts into laughter. "Yes, I'm sure. I love and hate you all in the same breath at times. I've tried not to, believe me, how I've tried, but I just can't stop… I think I loved you from the moment I met you. I mean, it's perfect, like you said… the hunter and the lamb."

No more talking. I'm done for. Gone. Forever lost in this woman and I never want to be found.

I lunge for her once again, but this time, there are no more reservations, no more what if's. This is real. And she…is… mine.

We kiss like starved animals, and in a way, I have been. She is my moon, my stars, my sun, and without her, life is not complete. I drag her onto my lap, owning that mouth and expressing just how much I've missed her.

She threads her fingers through my hair, pulling at the strands, tiny mewls slipping past her lips as I hold onto her and never intend on letting go. "I love you," I mumble against her lips, over and over again. Now that I've started, I don't think I can stop.

"I'm still scared you'll break my heart…" she whispers, stoking my need to protect this woman with everything that I am.

Pulling away, I nuzzle her nose with mine. I do the only thing I can. I kneel before her, surrendering. "I'm scared of my heart breaking too. But as someone wise once told me… it's okay to be scared. Being scared means you're about to do something brave. I have no fucking idea what I'm doing, but I'm willing to try."

Tears spill down Mary's cheeks and she nods. "Me too."

I can't believe this woman is willing to take me as hers. After everything, she wants to try. What a fierce warrior I've come to love. "Are you sure?" I ask again, because once she says yes, this is really it this time. "I'll probably fuck up time and time again. And we will no doubt fight, and you'll question why the fuck you gave me another chance. I'm also a stubborn pain in the ass, who will make stupid decisions now and again. Are you willing to accept all that? Because, Shortcake, I'm a virgin when it comes to love. Be gentle with me," I say in a rushed breath.

She smirks, shaking her head at my idiocy. Settling on my lap, she places both hands against my cheeks. "Yes. It's hard to resist a bad boy…who's a good man, and you, Hunter O'Shea, are a Prince Charming in disguise."

Be still my heart and loins.

"Then it's settled…I love you, and you love me."

"Looks like it."

"I don't think I can stop smiling," I confess, sounding more like Finch as each second passes.

"I don't think I can stop kissing you," she counters, sealing her mouth over mine.

My dick throws confetti as the drought is finally over, and it's over for good. Just as I'm about to throw Mary onto her back, a voice douses my raging need to seal the deal in every possible way there is.

"Excuse me, but if you two could please come up for air for a minute, we have a cake to cut."

Mary chuckles against my lips, untangling her body from mine. "Sorry, Maddy. We got back together."

God, that sounded good.

"I can see that," she replies. "I can also see Hunter is quite happy with that fact."

For the first time ever, I redden. Holy shit. What is this woman doing to me?

We arrange our clothes and I stand, offering Mary my hand, which she accepts with a smile. When she doesn't let go, I want to beat my chest in pride. Walking to where Dixon and Maddy stand, I can't help but think how perfect this picture is. We don't need a photographer to capture this moment, because it's one I will never forget.

"C'mon, let's go to the bathroom before everyone knows you were rolling around in the grass with the best man." Maddy loops her arm through Mary's. She looks at me, biting her lip before pouncing forward for one last kiss.

I give what my woman wants, because who am I to deny her?

"Oh, god, you're not going to be one of those annoying couples, are you?"

"Yes," both Mary and I say from around each other's lips.

When we've made our friends wait long enough, payback for all the times we've been subjected to their touchy-feely crap, Mary pulls away, blowing me a kiss.

"I love you," I state proudly, while Dixon almost falls over his feet. "Get used to it, 'cause you'll be hearing it a lot."

"I love you, too." Mary giggles, before she and Maddy saunter off, heads together as they no doubt gossip about the best day of our lives.

Once she's no longer in sight, I take a deep breath, unbelieving how fresh the air is. I feel like a newborn.

"So…"

"So…" I counter, unable to wipe my grin clean.

"This is really it? No more fucking around?"

I can't help but laugh. "This is really it. This right here is a death of two bachelors."

"About fucking time," Dixon says with an exaggerated sigh.

"I thought I'd be mourning the day, but I'm not. I feel…"

"Like you've just learned how to breathe again?"

"Yeah."

"It only gets better, man," he confirms, reaching into his pocket to pull out a cigarette. When he offers me one, I accept, seeing as I feel like I'm celebrating a birth—the birth of me.

We're both silent, no doubt cataloguing over events which got us here. At the forefront is the reason why I'm here. "Whatever happens…" I say, blowing a ring of smoke. "Remember, you're always my soulmate, Dix. I love you, man."

"I love you, too."

The waterworks are bound to happen any time soon, but this time, I won't hide because I'm full of love and rainbows and shit. Dixon butts out his smoke. Just as I'm about to get in touch with my inner Finch, he does something which just reiterates why I love this man.

"What are you doing?" I ask, watching as he begins to unzip his pants.

"Are you going to suck my cock now? I mean, that was some sentimental shit back there. I thought you were giving off a 'I wanna suck your dick,' vibe."

"Fuck you, you asshole. How about you come up with your own jokes and stop using mine? I know I'm funny, but please, it's all about the delivery…" I say, as his words were the exact ones I used when we were off to save Maddy…another harebrained adventure.

As he opens his mouth, I lunge forward and press my lips to his. It lasts for about two seconds, but when I pull away, he looks like I just deflowered him. "Delivery, Dixon, learn…"

I never get to finish however, because he flicks me in the nuts. "How's that for delivery, jackass?" With balls in hand, we walk, well, I stagger back toward our women, changed men.

Who knows what's next for us. Anything is possible. But what I do know is our women aren't princesses that needed saving…they're queens who saved us.

— Acknowledgements —

My author family: Elle and Vi—I love you both very much.

My ever-supporting parents. You guys are the best. I am who I am because of you. I love you. RIP Papa. Gone but never forgotten. You're in my heart. Always.

My agent, Kimberly Brower from Brower Literary & Management. Thank you for your patience and thank you for being an amazing human being.

Sommer Stein, you NAILED this cover! Thank you for being so patient and making the process so fun. I'm sorry for annoying you constantly.

My publicist—Sarah Ferguson from Social Butterfly PR. Thank you for all your help.

To the endless blogs that have supported me since day one—You guys rock my world.

My bookstagrammers—Your creativity astounds me. The effort you go to is just amazing. Thank you for the posts, the teasers, the support, the messages, the love, the EVERYTHING! I see what you do, and I am so, so thankful.

My ARC TEAM—You guys are THE BEST! Thanks for all the support.

My reader group—sending you all a big kiss.

Samantha and Amelia—I love you both so very much.

Michelle, you're my soul mate. I love you always. Thanks for saving me.

Mark, you SLAYED this cover!

My fur babies—mamma loves you so much! Dacca, I know you're hanging with Jaggy, Dina, Ninja, and Papa.

To anyone I have missed, I'm sorry. It wasn't intentional!

Last but certainly not least, I want to thank YOU! Thank you for welcoming me into your hearts and homes. My readers are the BEST readers in this entire universe! Love you all!

About the Author

Monica James spent her youth devouring the works of Anne Rice, William Shakespeare, and Emily Dickinson.

When she is not writing, Monica is busy running her own business, but she always finds a balance between the two. She enjoys writing honest, heartfelt, and turbulent stories, hoping to leave an imprint on her readers. She draws her inspiration from life.

She is a bestselling author in the U.S.A., Australia, Canada, France, Germany, Israel, and The U.K.

Monica James resides in Melbourne, Australia, with her wonderful family, and menagerie of animals. She is slightly obsessed with cats, chucks, and lip gloss, and secretly wishes she was a ninja on the weekends.

Connect with Monica James

Website: authormonicajames.com
Instagram: @authormonicajames
Facebook: facebook.com/authormonicajames
Twitter: twitter.com/monicajames81
Goodreads: goodreads.com/MonicaJames
TikTok: @authormonicajames
BookBub: bookbub.com/authors/monica-james
Amazon: https://amzn.to/2EWZSyS
Join my Reader Group: http://bit.ly/2nUaRyi